# BLADE OF HOPE

## A BOOK OF THE VIRAGO

# S.E. BABIN

OLIVERHEBERBOOKS

# LANDS OF LUNAMOOR

KINGDOM OF
ROSES

KINGDOM OF
THORNEWOOD

KINGDOM OF
LIGHT

KINGDOM OF
CRYSTAL

LAKE
OF
SORROW

KINGDOM OF
WOLVES

KINGDOM OF
BEASTS

KINGDOM OF
WITCHES

LAKE OF MYSTICS

KINGDOM OF
SHADOW

# PROLOGUE
## HOPE AND DESPAIR

F ire licked the ground around her, warming her feet and ankles. She lay on her side, bruised and bleeding, tear-filled eyes adjusting to the scene. Smoke poured from the stone and mud walls of the villagers' homes. Bundles of hay crackled with flame. The only noise was fire and the blood dripping from her body onto the ground.

Nova rose to her knees, cradling her stomach. Her fingers trembled as she looked down. Blood bloomed on her soaked and dirty dress. She was no healer, but there was an injury, something deep inside of her broken. Her eyes fluttered shut for a moment, blocking out the sights and smells, the memory of what had been done to her, to her family. Her lungs burned with the need for air, but the smoke pouring around her showed no signs of mercy.

To her left lay the body of the woman who'd raised her, the woman she'd come to know as her mother. Her skirts lay bunched around her waist, discarded like a piece of filth. A sob broke from Nova's throat at the sight, and she reached trembling fingers out to touch her, jerking them back as they met cold, dead flesh. The last memory of her flashed brightly in her mind.

She'd tucked Nova and her siblings behind her while their father raised a club to defend them, seconds before someone had struck Nova in the back of the head, and darkness had overtaken her.

Their last stand to defend their home had been futile. It didn't matter. Nothing mattered anymore. The bodies of her foster siblings lay beside her, cold and still. Her brother's large blue eyes stared upward at nothing, frozen in an expression of resigned fear. Her sister's normally dimpled cheeks lay smooth against her pale skin. Their father lay next to them on his side, mouth curled in a grimace of final effort, one hand reaching for them even in death. The memory of something vital missing floated and flitted away from her before her addled brain could grasp onto it.

A sob of rage, hopelessness, and of things broken with no hope of repair tore from her throat. Everything burned around her, homes and shops once lovingly built by their owners' hands, now decimated by a kingdom who cared only for power and coins for the coffers. She lifted her hands to her face, wiping away what she could of the soot, grime, and blood. Pain blossomed within her and she bowed her head, steadying her breathing. She couldn't pass out. There were soldiers still in the village sifting through the wreckage, looking for whatever was left to steal. They wouldn't hesitate to finish her off if they saw she still lived.

A few feet away, the old bakery run by Mrs. Dobbins and her portly husband crumbled as her unfocused gaze skimmed across the horizon. A hint of the yeast the woman used in everything she made haunted the air with a touch of the fragrance so common in the village square. On Sundays, the scent of cinnamon woke Nova up early, and she'd bound out of bed to beg her mother for a bit of coin. The memory shuddered within her as it struggled to the surface. Now those once-happy scents mingled with fire, smoke, and death. She wanted nothing more than to wipe her mind clean of those things because seeing its ruins now made her want to curl up beside her dead family and tumble into the sweet release death had given them.

Her gaze lingered on a discarded sword a few feet away from their corpses. Nova's mind dimmed to a single thought. It would take only a moment. If she hit the right spot, she'd feel a spike of pain, nothing worse than what she felt now. She wouldn't have to go on, wouldn't have to remember, wouldn't have to think on this day in her dreams. And even though everything felt muddied and like she breathed underwater, she knew the memory of this day would never fade. It would always rise to the surface, bloody and painful. Something almost supernatural drew her to the weapon. Her fingers itched to pick it up. To end it all.

Die and remember nothing. Rise and remember every evil deed.

The world was a cruel place for girls. Her mother always told her so. Tearing her gaze away from the sword, she stared at the lifeless bodies on the ground and realized what an ironic twist of fate it was for her mother's corpse to so eloquently demonstrate just how cruel it was.

The cry of a small child sounded from several feet away. Nova jerked and fear of a different kind crept down her spine. How like the world to leave two helpless things alive in the wreckage. She inhaled a shuddering breath and coughed as her lungs burned with the effort.

The cry rose even louder. It was the cry of a thing that didn't yet know the world was evil. A cry of pure innocence, of basic needs not met, a cry she remembered from her own brother and sister when their mother had left them too long without the breast.

It would starve if she didn't do something.

If she did something, she'd remember.

If she did something, she couldn't lie down and let the elements take them both.

There was nothing left for her here. Nothing left for anyone. Everything good and just about this town had either been skewered on the end of a sword held by an uncaring kingdom or been licked clean to the bone by the accelerated fire started by what had to be magic, even as most of the last vestiges of magic had trickled away from the world weeks ago. Rumors swirled the king was involved. Others said the disappearance was punishment for living an 'ungodly' life. Nova thought no one knew what really happened, only that magic had slowly trickled away, leaving those reliant on it devastated and shells of their former selves. It wasn't gone from everyone. Not yet. But the unnatural purge of power from the world seemed to make it a question of not if, but when all of it would be gone, unsettling the balance of power back from mages to humans.

Nova watched the fire curl and twist over the rotting bones of the village. Nothing natural burned this fast. Nova knew that much just in the little learning her foster mother had given her when her father had been out of earshot.

She tried to stand but found she could only hunch, an odd stance that made her look weary and beaten, the bottom of her dress falling in a wet thump back to the ground. A moan came from her throat at the pain in every inch of her body as she tried to straighten. Her bodice was ripped and torn, exposing her chest to the air. She fumbled with it for a second before finally giving up and tying it in a knot close to her shoulder. A hoarse and bitter laugh tore from her throat. She'd chosen to wear white today. Of all days. Everything done to her. Every rip, every tear, every stumble and fall showed in her dress and on her skin. She swallowed hard at the muddy handprints embla-zoned across her hips, pressing her down, down, down. Then blackness before she realized the horror about to be inflicted upon her. *Survive now. Mourn later.*

Nova tiptoed through the wreckage toward the sound of the cry, hissing as her bare feet hit sharp stone and wood. Her heart told her to find the child. Her head told her to run. Nova usually listened to her head. It had kept her out of trouble and kept her pure, something her mother insisted on in order to make a good match.

Now, staring down at her mother's cooling body, Nova wished she'd listened to her heart a little more. Purity no longer mattered when you lay broken on the ground. She inhaled a shuddering breath and looked away. Dwelling on this would only keep her slow and dull-witted. She couldn't see the soldiers, but they were close. There were still things to destroy, so they would be here for a while. After them, the bandits and scavengers would come, rummaging through the wreckage of people's lives, looking for tokens to sell at market. If she were still here wandering through the muck, purity would be the last thing on their minds.

The cry rose and soared, an indeterminate babble from a tiny, hoarse throat. Nova followed the sound, her own sniffles covered by the child's grief and shock. She stepped over the dead baker and her husband, looking away from the children. War spared no one, no matter how young and innocent. The smell of yeast and blood tingled her nose and a choked cry wrenched from Nova's throat as she stumbled over the bread the woman had made earlier for sale at her cart.

She stopped, took a few steadying breaths, and looked around. Nova didn't know where to go or what to do, but as her survival instincts clicked in, she knew she would need food. Clothing as well, some coins, maybe a knife, though she wondered if she'd do more damage to herself than anyone else with it.

She bent down and scooped up two loaves of seed covered bread, gagging as blood dripped from the bottoms. Nova wiped it as best she could with her dirty skirt and tucked them under her elbow. With her other hand, she rifled through the baker's pockets and pulled out two shiny gold marks.

"I'm sorry," she whispered as she rifled through the husband's, too.

The cries had dwindled down to sniffles and whines, and she thanked the gods who had forsaken them for it. Those cries would see them both dead if the soldiers ever stopped their laughing and heard the left-over little girl. Guilt flooded her at not going straight to the child, but if they were to survive, they had to have provisions, and she was closer to them than her. If they had no food, saving her would be moot because they would both die, starved and exposed to the elements.

Nova ducked inside the baker's home, crumbling but still partially standing, and tiptoed into the children's room, carefully stepping over burning wooden beams. Her two children, close in age to Nova's own, lay outside next to their parents. Nova swept away the guilt plaguing her. The baker and her family were shells now. They'd have no need for their things any longer.

She quickly picked through the clothing, selecting two pairs of trousers, two dresses, and some underthings. She found a pair of shoes and several dresses fit for a much smaller child. Nova tucked them all and the bread into a small pack tossed carelessly beside the smoking ruins of a bed and rushed outside.

She shoved her feet into the dead child's shoes and hurried toward the still living one.

A crunching noise stilled her in her tracks. She ducked behind one of the few structures still standing and peeked around the corner, her heart pounding wildly.

Nova's breath caught in her throat when she realized who

she looked at. That little baby...the sole reason she was in this village. The sole reason for any hope left in this forsaken land.

The little girl sat on her rump, sniffling. Fat tears rolled down her cheeks, but she was no longer crying out loud. Nova knew her as the orphan girl, the one who'd come in the middle of the night with a woman who said little and protected the child fiercely. The child rarely came to market or even played outside, but she was round and full and looked well cared for. But this child was no normal girl. An orphan, yes, but if her mother was to be believed, this tiny sobbing child was destined to save them all.

A soldier stepped into the clearing. Nova shut her eyes for a brief moment. She should have turned the other way and run into the forest, creeping back into the village at night when the soldiers had all cleared out. Was she really the only one who could save her?

The child was helpless. Alone. And from the way the soldier stared at her, in grave peril. What kind of person would harm a little girl? One who looked like she'd barely started walking?

"Hello, little girl," the soldier said.

Horror rolled down Nova's spine. The child looked up at him, her face thoughtful. When the soldier smiled at her, the little girl responded in kind, a wide gummy smile spreading over her face.

Nova's stomach lurched.

"You and I are going to have so much fun together."

She should save herself. She should turn away, creep into the night, and scrub this scene from her brain. But the little girl got up and began to toddle over to the soldier. His eyes flashed with something Nova never wanted to see again.

Run. She should run.

Nova stepped out from her hiding spot. "Take me," she said breathlessly, her voice hoarse with smoke and grief.

The soldier stilled. His eyes narrowed as his expression turned thoughtful. But when his eyes drifted from her face to her neck and settled on her hips, his lips thinned. "Looks like someone already has."

Terror roiled in her stomach. The memory tried to surface, but she shoved it back down, into the deep dark hold she'd made inside of her. "She's only a baby."

Cool wind flickered over her skin. Gooseflesh rose on her arms and neck. Time stood still. She still had time to run.

She didn't have to fight. It wasn't her fight. Maybe this wasn't the same girl after all.

"Come here, baby," the man cooed.

The little girl raised her arms up, her face full of trust.

"*Take me*," she implored the soldier again, her voice rough and hoarse from the fire and screaming.

He snorted in dismissal and bent down to scoop the girl up. Nova screamed in rage and the last vestiges of her secret tore out of her hands, black and twisting, a shadow in the dying light. This was the secret that she'd held onto for so long, the secret she'd allowed her family to be slaughtered for. The secret that couldn't protect her when the man had come up behind her, forcing her to her knees before striking her on the back of the head. She swam in and out of consciousness, unable to reach for the power lying deep inside of her, powerless to save the ones she loved or even herself. But as the power welled up, she knew she could save this girl. She could do *one* thing right in the ruins of this place.

Nova swallowed hard, brushing those memories away and focused on the only thing she could. Her shadows curled and twisted around the man. At first, he stood, confused, the little girl forgotten at his feet.

Nova let her magic curl around him, soft and teasing, allowing the darkness to dance around him, a joyous bounce of energy. But when his wonder fell, and he realized what held him, she curled the shadows around his neck and pulled.

With one eye on the soldier and her hand raised to control her magic, Nova rushed over and scooped the child up, tucking her head against her shoulder. "Don't look," she whispered.

The soldier choked, his fingers going up to his neck to try to loosen the shadowy bands around it. But mercy had long abandoned Nova's heart. She watched him struggle, her eyes cold and hard, and when he fell onto his knees, his skin tinged blue, she still watched.

She watched until he died, and then she watched until the last vestiges of his blackened soul crept away from his body and slithered away into the dark forest.

"You! What are you doing?" The sound of footsteps rushed into Nova's conscious. She jerked around, only to see three new soldiers running toward her, drawing their swords.

"Don't look," she whispered again to the girl. Nova tucked her tight against her chest and dashed into the forests of Thornewilde, leaving the only life she'd ever known behind her.


NOVA RAN until she couldn't run anymore. The men had long since given up, but she didn't trust that others wouldn't be scouting in the woods looking for survivors. The little girl shivered against her chest. They were both soaked to the skin, and the sun had long ago dipped behind the horizon, bringing with it a misty bone-deep chill in the air. A fire was a risk she couldn't take, but she had to stop and rest. Blood pooled down her stomach and her thighs, and she felt weak with the loss of it.

She walked for several more minutes until she came to an area next to a stream. Brush covered the area, pinecones and needles, and fallen rotted trees. If someone tried to surprise them here, she'd hear them long before they reached her. She sat the little girl down on one of the rotted trunks.

"Stay there," she commanded. The girl blinked up at her with startling blue eyes.

The child couldn't be more than two. Someone had dressed her in a pink flower-covered dress and a matching bonnet perched crookedly on her head with little white shoes, still covered in her mother's blood. Her eyes were cornflower blue, big, bright, and silvered with tears. Rosebud lips quivered as she stared at Nova. What would she do with a child? She could barely take care of herself. But seeing the child's vulnerability and knowing if she looked the other way the little one would die ... even Nova wasn't so coldhearted.

She stepped forward. There were a million things she had to do to ensure they survived the night, but she didn't want this child to be fearful of her. When she was only a few feet away, the child merely stared, no fear in her gaze, only a resignation such a young child shouldn't have. She held out her hand.

"Hello. I'm Nova." Nova's smile wobbled on her face.

The little girl blinked.

Nova crept a little closer. "I have some bread." She blew out a breath, tears slipping down her face. Cold stung her fingers and her nose. The wet material she still wore clung to her body. In the back of her mind, Nova knew she'd have to change them both, otherwise they'd freeze to death.

She crept even closer until she was less than a foot away. "Are you hungry?"

A single tear rolled down the girl's face. A moment later, she sat up and slowly toddled to Nova, her arms out in trust.

Nova's heart shattered as she scooped her up and held her tight, shivering as the girl's wet dress slapped her on the collarbone. There was something so familiar about this girl. A thought, immediately dismissed, tugged at the back of her mind, forming a profound and stunning revelation. If true...Nova shook her head and slowly breathed out, her brow furrowing before she again tucked the thought away. It could wait. For now. Survival must be her top priority.

She swallowed hard and looked behind her one last time—and even though the trees blocked her view, and they were miles away, the sight of the terror and destruction the kingdom of Thornewood had wrought in its desperate bid for power burned in her mind's eye.

"What's your name?" Nova whispered.

"Harlow," the girl said, though it sounded more like *Har whoa*.

"That's a beautiful name, Harlow. We're going to take a trip, okay? I'll do my best to keep you safe." Nova choked on the words. "But I can't promise anything because I don't know if I can even keep myself safe." She exhaled her doubts and straightened her shoulders. "But I'll do my best. We're going to be okay." She had to believe this. If not for her own sake, then for the child completely dependent upon her for survival.

Harlow stared at her, icy blue eyes unblinking. She plopped her thumb into her mouth and Nova winced, thinking of all the things on that thumb that should never go into someone's mouth.

A moment later, when Nova straightened and inhaled a shaky breath, she clutched the child tight to her breast. As she looked upon the unknown in front of her, the girl Nova had once been disappeared and an enemy of the kingdom took her place, one forged in blood and fire.

# CHAPTER ONE

## THIRTEEN YEARS LATER

Harlow had a stone in her pocket and fear in her heart. She'd taken the last steps away from her village and into the kingdom two hours ago, and yet it felt like she'd been gone for years. Everything felt different here, unlike the quiet happy warmth of her home.

She wore good boots but layered patched skirts with threadbare wool socks and two overdresses. Her hair wasn't coiffed in the latest style or even in a neat braid, but she'd done her best. No one had fingers as nimble as Nova's. Since she'd left, Harlow hadn't been able to make a single straight braid. This morning, as she'd looked behind her in the small mirror she used to wash her face, emotion had welled up at the thought of leaving the only life she'd known behind.

Regardless, Harlow was clean. She'd washed in the spring behind their small home this morning, though she wouldn't stay clean for long with the amount of dust the horses kicked up as they clomped along the road.

She'd packed only what she could carry and, on her way out, stopped by the old church to tell the priest her parents had died two nights before.

The priest's face had quickly masked the expression of horror. It was strange, staying in the same house as the dead. But only a few days before, they'd been alive. Sick, but alive, and trying to reassure her they'd be up the next day and things would return to normal.

She was young, but not naïve. As soon as she heard the rattle in their chest a few days prior, she'd known the gods would force another loss on her. First her mother and father and siblings, lost in the Thornehollow village raids, then Nova some years back, and finally the two people she'd come to think of as parents. Nova might not be dead, but Harlow had died inside the moment she'd seen the parchment paper note on their dented and scarred kitchen table with no sign of her sister.

Harlow let out a deep breath. *Keep going.* She'd told herself this for days now. One foot in front of the other. *Keep going.* She'd lasted at home until the sweet and sickly smell of carrion began to permeate the house. Even then she thought she'd be able to take them outside and bury them, only to find the ground too hard to penetrate. She couldn't bear to leave them out there, victim to the cold and to the animals that prowled along the village, so she'd spent over an hour pulling and tugging their bodies until she'd laid them both in the same bed and tucked a threadbare blanket around them.

She clutched her beat up leather satchel close to her body. Everything she had was in there except for several oat bars and a couple of beef strips in her pocket. If the bag were stolen, at least she wouldn't starve right away.

Thoughts of starvation would come later. The gaze she'd felt burning into her back finally fell away and her shoulders dropped a couple of inches. It wasn't safe to relax here, but the true danger wouldn't begin until the suns fell behind the horizon. She'd left with no plan and very little money. She wouldn't eat tomorrow if she spent it all on a room tonight. The oat bars would last a few days, maybe even a week if she rationed them. The beef strips would last a lot longer, but Harlow didn't want to think about what would happen if she were out here for more than a day or two.

Back in the village, everyone knew everyone, and they took care of each other. Or at least she thought they did. The test came when Nova had left and the fever took her foster parents. She'd knocked on the neighbor's door and the wife, who'd always graced Harlow and Nova with a sweet smile, took one look at her and shook her head. She closed the door right in Harlow's face. Stunned, she'd stood there for a moment before knocking again.

It took her way too long to realize what it meant when no one answered. She'd gone to the next house and the woman there had shoved a loaf of bread at her but shut the door again.

She was too old. Harlow could work and work hard, but she'd bloomed over the last year and the men in the village had taken to staring at her a hair too long. No woman wanted to bring another girl into their household. Not at her age.

With no other family and no way to farm her family's land alone, Harlow was forced to leave. Her fingers caressed the cool, smooth stone deep in her pocket. No matter how close she wore it to her body, it never warmed. At first it disturbed her, but soon enough the stone became a tether, a way for her to remember some of the good things from her life before.

It was the only thing she had left of her sister and the man and woman who'd taken them in after they'd fled the village. She was truly alone in this world now. Her and the stone and the ever-present ache in her heart.

The smell of fresh baked bread and cinnamon hinted at some long-gone memory in her mind, there and gone in a flash. Beef stew took over the first smell, followed by fresh apple pie. Her mouth watered, but she pressed herself to keep going.

Her other hand crinkled the note Nova had left before she'd gone, her last link to her sister.

*If anything happens, go to the castle. You have a friend there. Find work. We will find each other again, Harlow. I promise you.*
-Nova

Instead of any reason why she'd left, she'd instructed Harlow to find work in the castle. At first, Harlow had laughed. She was a poor girl from a barely functioning farm. Sure, she could cook and clean, but she wasn't poised enough to be around royalty or even royalty's servants. Nevertheless, after some time grieving, Harlow, with no other good choice presenting itself, decided to follow Nova's last words. She'd never been a quitter, but life had never thrown her quite so many storms, either.

The castle loomed above her, a monstrosity of white stone and colorful windows. She looked away lest her emotions get the best of her and turned her gaze back to straight ahead. An inn sign swung in the breeze, the clink and clunk of the metal chains and wooden sign contrasting with the heavy footfalls and squeaky carriages clipping up and down the cobblestones. People dressed in a wide variety of fashion and color flowed beside and around her as she plodded along. A few gave her looks of distaste, but no one spoke to her. She was both invisible and reviled— two things she never thought she'd be.

As much as she dreamed of falling into a soft, clean bed, Harlow was nothing if not frugal. Her foster mother had taught her the value of a dime, especially when bargaining for a fresh loaf of bread. A small smile appeared on her face at some of the ferocious bargaining wars she'd been present at and the many harried vendors who came to the market day.

Her stomach growled in protest at the thought of fresh bread. *Keep going.*

The loud clank of bells and shouts rang out around the town. People scrambled to get behind Harlow. Her head swung around, trying to follow what was happening, but all she could see was the entire town splitting down the middle to open a path back by the edge of the road. Her mouth dropped open, and she was about to ask what was going on when a hand clamped around her arm and pulled her out of the road.

"Foolish girl," the voice hissed. "Be still and stand up straight. The royal procession is coming through."

She took a breath and swung her head up to see her mysterious benefactor, but the hand around her arms squeezed tighter. "Silence." A dainty hand gently pushed her head back around.

Four massive purple carriages rounded the bend. Harlow sucked in a breath at the sheer majesty of it. Though she had no idea what was going on, she stood there for a moment to watch, even knowing this would be a perfect time to steal some fruit and find a place to lay her head for the night.

But she couldn't help herself. The men on the first two white horses sat proud and tall, their gleaming armor reflecting light even with the weakness of today's suns. Most of the soldier's faces were concealed by helmets, leaving only their eyes uncovered. She locked gazes with one of them and felt rooted to the spot at the burning intensity of it. Eyes the color of jade studied her for a moment with unnerving intensity before flicking straight ahead, dismissing her like she was nothing more than an interesting bug.

Harlow's heartbeat skittered and slowed, but she watched his back for as long as she could before the stranger nudged her and hissed at her to look forward. She frowned but straightened, only to see a flash of dark hair and golden skin. The entire town went to one knee as the carriage passed and the only thing that saved her was the stranger's deft blow behind her knees that had Harlow falling to the ground only a hair of a second later.

"Stupid girl," the voice hissed again. "Kneel."

Harlow bristled at the insult but didn't dare say a word until the carriages had passed. When everyone rose, Harlow spun only to find no one behind her. She scanned the area to see the edges of a bright scarlet cloak and a lock of red hair under a hood disappearing into the crowd.

Intrigued, but with no time to chase the rude stranger down, Harlow straightened her shoulders and kept walking.


THE SUNS DIPPED behind the mountains, bringing with it a teeth-chattering drop in temperature. Harlow pulled the cloak closer around her and shifted in an effort to warm the freezing stone of the rooftop she'd chosen to sleep on. It had finally stopped raining, but the roof was as even as you could get and had pools of standing water all over. She'd found a dry spot away from the light, but the stone was damp with all the humidity and the rain, making it seem like Harlow was about to try to sleep in a swamp.

The building she chose was a few streets away from the main road, with low lighting and mostly hidden from the elements. The way the roof was shaped provided Harlow a small alcove to tuck into, protecting her from anything but the dampness and additional drizzle.

She settled in, tucking her leather satchel close, and waited for sleep to claim her.

# CHAPTER TWO

## UNEXPECTED ASSISTANCE

Hushed whispers and the slide of shoes over stone woke Harlow. She froze in place and slowed her panicked breathing. Flurries of snow had dampened her hair and her hands were stiff with cold. Flexing her fingers to get the feeling back in them, she strained to listen.

"She's asleep. I saw her earlier. She's got a bag full of something and brand-new boots." The voice was rough but young, the accent from the lower classes.

Her father had given her a small knife before he died, one he used to butcher the chickens on their farm. She hadn't sharpened it since he'd given it to her, but it could make someone think twice about harming her. An object didn't have to be sharp to hurt someone. Harlow slowly pulled it out of her pocket, double-checking that the stone and letter were still there.

She quietly put the strap of the bag over her shoulder and waited. They knew she was here. She could run, but she was on a roof. A fall would put her down faster than any lack of food would, and who knew what they would do to her once she could no longer fight. She could scream. But Harlow had fallen asleep to the sound of the occasional cry for help, wondering if anyone ever responded to the sound.

She had to fight.

"Come out, girl," the voice said.

Harlow's nostrils flared. She picked up the blanket and straightened to her full height. Even then, she barely cast a shadow on the ground. She might not be tall, but she was quick and sometimes speed mattered more than strength.

Two young boys came around the corner. One, the one with the rough voice she suspected, was tall and broad, large in the way many of the young farm boys were back home. The other, leaner and slight, about Harlow's height. His eyes held an apology.

"I'm not giving you my bag," she said, her voice stronger than she expected.

The taller boy grinned, a dark and damaged thing, two missing teeth giving a macabre edge to the cruel twist of his lips. "We didn't plan to ask you."

Her gaze flicked to the shorter boy. They locked eyes, but the smaller one looked down.

She'd find no help from him.

Her fingers trembled, but she held on tight to the blade still concealed within her skirts.

He took a step forward. One, two, and on the third, Harlow took a step back, her shoulders hitting the stone of the chimney.

"Hand it over," he demanded.

"No." Her voice wobbled this time. Fear coursed through her veins. The things in her bag weren't of much value, but they were hers and she wouldn't let some faceless boy take the last vestiges of her life from her.

The light cast dark shadows over his face from the trees. His eyes were dark, that much she could see, and his face was covered in old bruises. She straightened. "If you come one step closer, you won't like what happens to you."

The boy laughed then, the sound like crunching glass. "Maybe I would." His gaze skimmed down her neck and all the way down her feet, leaving a searing line of filth down Harlow's skin. He took a step closer to her, so close he could reach out and touch her if he wanted to.

Her gaze flicked left, then right. She had a few feet either way, but if she jumped, she'd break an ankle at a minimum. The shorter boy, noticing where her eyes went, took a step to the left. Behind him, there was a smaller house with a flat stone roof. If she had to jump, she could make it. His eyes flashed as if to say, "Do it."

The more immediate problem clamped a hand down on Harlow's shoulder. His face leered over her. "We don't find too many girls out here," he said, his hot, fetid breath rancid in her pale face. "You know what we do to girls we find in the night?" he asked.

It was a rhetorical question, Harlow knew, but she screwed up all of her bravado and flung an insult in his face. "Perhaps dissect them as you try to find out why they all think you're abhorrent?" she snapped. If Nova were here, she'd swagger and insult and then beat them handily with whatever she found lying around. But she wasn't Nova. All she had was her bravado and a knife she'd never used on anyone else.

The younger boy gasped in surprise at her words. His eyes widened, and he took a step back, his face stricken.

The hand moved from her shoulder to her throat. Seconds later, he dragged her up the chimney by her throat, her airway cut off. She struggled against him, but it was no use. Harlow had no chance of beating him with strength. She had to beat him with intellect.

The brute's other hand traveled down the front of her blouse. Harlow whimpered.

"Dex," the other boy said. "Just take her satchel. There's no need for that."

The boy snorted. "Said by someone who's never had it."

"Dex," he warned. "Don't be stupid. We aren't animals."

But Harlow's mind had gone numb. Her throat clicked with fear a second before her mouth opened and a screech of pure primal rage erupted. She raised her hand and drove the knife down to where his upper shoulder met his neck. A roar escaped the boy, and he stumbled back, blood spraying Harlow's face and eyes. She slumped down the chimney and rolled, harsh coughing racking her body.

Something skidded to her. She clutched it tight in her fingers as she stared up at him. "Run," the younger boy whispered urgently. "While he's still down. He will not soon forget this."

He helped Harlow to her feet and pressed the satchel into her hands. "Do not stay on the warmer roofs, girl. You'll always find trouble there. You're safest in the miserable areas. Even wretches like us don't like the cold much." A sad smile graced his lips and Harlow gave herself a moment to study the youth. He was her age, with lighter hair and what looked like hazel eyes. Hard to tell in the moonlit darkness. His teeth were white and straight, which told her he must not have been out here for long.

"Go," he hissed, the other boy's pained moans covering up the sounds they made. He pressed something made of soft wool into her hand and turned away from her. Harlow stared at the boy's back before she wrapped her cloak around her, shoved the blanket in her pack, and rushed away, careful to avoid the blood still pumping out of the boy's neck.

# CHAPTER THREE

## WITH FRIENDS LIKE HER...

If they wouldn't accept her here in the castle, she had nowhere else to go.

Her stomach growled as she crept closer to the servants' entrance. The smell of freshly baked bread made her salivate. When was the last time she ate? Or bathed? Or had any sort of comfort? A touch. A smile. Harlow shoved those thoughts down deep and forced the tears threatening her eyes to dry. They would not serve her well here.

She glanced down at the shoes that had seen better days and shifted to where the patched dress she wore would cover the holes in them. Her prized new boots had disappeared from the rooftop she'd left them on after the encounter with those two boys. She'd gone back only to find a dark bloodstain and a scrap of fabric from the dress he'd torn during his dying throes. The morning had started out with rain but had settled into a fine, drenching mist that covered everything. Her curls lay plastered against her face, and her teeth chattered as she waited. She had no idea what she'd say, but this was her only chance and she had to make sure she was quick and clever.

The door opened. A pretty woman with blonde hair and

cold blue eyes spotted her. Her eyes flashed with something, but she shook her head at Harlow.

"Get out of here, girl. If Melda sees you, she'll take the broom to your hide."

Harlow swallowed, clutching the stone even tighter in her hand. Perhaps it would give her strength and maybe a touch of luck. "I'm not begging. I'm looking for work."

The woman's mouth turned down. "That's what they all say. Then they steal our bread and pilfer our coffers." She shook her head. "I can't let you in. The missus would have my hide. Best you leave while you still can walk." The woman's face was hard. "We're all trying to get by. Ain't no room for someone coming in to fight for more of our share. I won't tell you again. Leave while you still can."

Harlow opened her mouth, but the woman didn't wait for her to speak. She merely shook the old rug she held out, flinging dust and the gods knew what else into Harlow's face before she slammed the old wooden door.

Painful tears sprang to Harlow's eyes as she bent over, damp fingers smearing dust and dirt over her face as she tried to dig the grit out of her eyes.

Hopelessness speared through her, overruling the hunger coursing through her body. She had to get in. It was Nova's last request to her. Never lose the stone and find work in the castle. Harlow had never let Nova down.

But Nova had let her down.

When it mattered, Nova wasn't there.

Harlow sat on the stoop and rested her chin on her hands. Her gaze caught on the people walking past her, few looking her way. Those who did sneered at her as if she wasn't worth the air she breathed. She took a deep breath and looked down at her feet. Judgment wasn't something she was used to. Not like this.

After a while, when no one else came out, Harlow gave up.

She took her bag and wrapped her cloak tightly around her, shivering against the wet chill in the air as she took off down the cobblestone road.

PATIENCE IS the difference between death and survival, Nova once told her. Harlow had whined about it because patience was the antithesis of getting what she wanted right then. She felt it all over again as she debated on how best to achieve her goal of not only getting to the castle, but being allowed entrance.

A group of girls passed by Harlow as her thoughts wandered in the past. Snippets of their conversation drifted by her. A tall redheaded girl with an imperious look on her face led them. She was tall and willowy, her skin a pale porcelain. Her dress was in fashion, though Harlow could tell it had been repaired more than once. The other girls wore similar dresses– long layered skirts with leather boots. All had their hair done in a braided updo–the look of girls used to hard work. Nova used to do her hair the same way before they went out to help with the chores on the farm.

"Mother said being a maid in the castle is not so bad. Plus, there's that handsome commander everyone is talking about," said a smaller girl with mouse brown hair and a too large nose.

"He won't be looking at you now will he, Shanda?" the redhead said. Twitters of laughter rang out. Harlow's stomach ached for the girl, but she craned her head and crossed the street to trail them, close enough to hear most of it but far enough away to avoid suspicion.

"You shut your mouth, Ella," said the smaller girl. "If you run it like you do in the village, you're going to wind up with worse than a black eye next time!"

Harlow blinked at the ferocity in the girl's voice. Ella turned crimson and a hateful gleam sparked in her eyes. The other girls gave the smaller one a wider berth and hurried ahead of them.

"You might have gotten this position based upon your mother's relationship to Cressida, but you should watch your back." Ella's mouth curved into a cruel smile. She loomed over Shanda, but to her credit, Shanda did not cower.

"And you might have gotten this position by raising your skirt to every randy soldier who passed by the village, but you better watch it too. I might not be pretty on the outside, but I don't have an ugly heart." Shanda took a step closer, her face tipped up to Ella's sneering one. "No one will wed a serving girl who bends over and wiggles anytime an eligible man passes them by. If you don't change your ways, you'll end up with a whelp and a fat greasy husband who slaps you around on days that end in Y."

Harlow choked on a laugh and slipped into the shadows of an alley.

The sound of a fist cracking against bone sent her back pressing into the stone. A startled shout rang out and the sound of a body hitting the ground made Harlow shut her eyes. She waited a moment before she peeked her head out around the corner.

Shanda lay in a heap on the ground, her hand pressed against her cheek. Harlow rushed over, making sure Ella didn't see her, but the taller girl never bothered to look back.

Harlow reached down and helped Shanda up. The girl frowned at her but let her help. When she was standing, Harlow gently pulled her hand away. "Let me see."

The girl dropped her hand and Harlow winced. The wound was already beginning to swell. "I think you'll have a black eye."

To her surprise, Shanda grinned. "At least I'm not an opportunistic whore."

A laugh bubbled from Harlow and a plan began to form in her mind. "Tell me, are you new to the castle?"

Shanda nodded. "The queen goes through servants like candy. We're the next round chosen from the local villages."

Harlow eyed Ella's slim back. "What's your history with her?"

The girl dusted off her skirts. "She's from my village. From the second she got breasts, she's flaunted them to everyone that will look."

"That's not so bad," Harlow said weakly.

Shanda laughed. "It is when it's the husbands looking. The wives couldn't get her out of the village fast enough and practically begged the castle to take her. It might have been okay if that's all she did, but Ella is a real nasty piece of work. She hates everyone, it seems, and takes her anger out on anyone unfortunate enough to be around her."

"It sounds like working with her would be a nightmare." When Shanda nodded, Harlow saw her opportunity. "It just so happens I'm looking for a position in the castle," Harlow began. When Shanda's eyes lit with interest, Harlow elaborated, telling the girl just enough of her story to sound sympathetic.

They walked together, keeping a safe distance from the other girls. When Ella trailed a little behind, Shanda nodded and motioned for Harlow to slip into the shadows and wait.

"Ella!" she called. "I might have a black eye, but you're still a loose-skirted, blackhearted tyrant!"

Harlow pressed her lips together to keep from laughing and wondered what it might be like to have a friend like Shanda.

AS SHANDA PREDICTED, Ella turned right around, pounding down the cobblestones toward her. Shanda slipped into the alley next to Harlow. "She's almost here," she hissed. "You ready? We won't have long."

Harlow nodded, her fingers clenched tight around a large piece of discarded wood she'd found. She didn't want to hurt Ella, just put her out of commission for a little while. The thought of it made her heart hurt. She was no better than that boy Dex from the roof. "Hide," she urged Shanda.

The girl frowned at her, but Harlow pushed her. "Hide! You shouldn't let them see you."

Hurt flickered in Shanda's eyes, but she did as Harlow bade her, tucking herself into a cranny between a fruit bin and the stone wall of a small shop. Harlow pressed herself against the other wall, her cloak concealing her light hair as she waited.

Ella came skidding around the corner. "I'm going to make you pay for that, you little witch!"

Harlow knew she wasn't a hero, but she never planned to be a villain. Sheer desperation drove her next actions. She didn't taunt the girl or do anything other than wait for her to step past. As soon as she did, Harlow stepped out and hit Ella in the back of the head, right in the vulnerable place Nova had shown her so long ago. If she thought too hard about it, she might be disturbed by all the things her sister had taught her, but right now, all she felt was thankful.

Ella dropped like a stone and Harlow let the wood clatter to the ground as she lurched forward to catch her before she injured herself too seriously. Shanda stepped out from her hiding place, her eyes wide. "Is she okay?"

Harlow grunted with effort as she dragged Ella behind the fruit bin. "She'll be fine. A pounding headache and a lump should be the extent of her wounds." Harlow made quick work of the girl's outfit, trading her clothes for Ella's larger ones. She had to roll the skirt down several times to account for her lack of height, and she let the girl keep her boots. The only unfortunate thing was Ella had red hair, but if she stayed far enough away maybe they wouldn't notice until it was too late to change. Harlow shrugged back into her cloak and tied it around her neck before she tucked the girl's feet underneath her so no one walking past would see them and come to investigate too early. When that was done, Harlow peered inside the fruit bin, looking for twine. The only thing inside was a heftier rope. Sighing, Harlow took it and tied the girl's legs together using the knot her foster father had showed her two summers ago when he'd taken her hunting in the woods. It wouldn't keep her forever, but it would slow her down some. Even Harlow had to take some time trying to figure out how to unknot it, but she'd only made it a lot worse before her father had taken pity on her.

Harlow stepped back to examine her handiwork, Shanda peering over her shoulder. "Who are you, girl?"

Harlow looked back. "Just a village girl with a strange sister," she said without thinking.

Shanda laughed and grabbed her hand. "Come on. We don't want to be late." With a critical eye, she looked Harlow up and down, making her want to shrink within herself. "But first, you need to wash. You smell like a dirty horse trough." Shanda took her hand and led her deeper into town.

SEVEN OTHER GIRLS stood with her. Harlow stood at the end of the second row next to Shanda, careful to keep her head down. "Don't worry," Shanda had whispered on the way over. "It's every woman for herself when we get into that line. They won't keep all of us. Maybe half if we're lucky."

Harlow nodded and slipped into the row next to her new acquaintance and waited for the servant entrance to open once again.

A younger girl came out a few minutes later. She stepped in

front of them, examining them with an intense stare. One of the seven tilted her chin up at her perusal and the girl's eyebrows went up. "Step out of line, then," she said and pointed to a place beside her. Two more girls were pulled until there were four left.

Harlow clenched her fists at her sides and steadied her breathing. Everything depended on this. Shanda brushed her fingers across Harlow's hand in sympathy. She hadn't asked why Harlow wanted inside so badly, but she'd trusted her all the same. The girl passed by them again, giving them all a thorough look. Harlow felt laid bare by the look and held her breath until she nodded once.

"You four follow me inside the castle." She flicked a glance at the girls who stood beside her. "You three will be escorted back to your villages. Wait for the guards to come out and tell them where you're from. They'll see you safely back."

Harlow let a soft exhale escape. *Step one complete.*

She followed the other girls in, careful to keep her hood up. Shanda walked beside her, mouth gaping as she looked around at everything. "This place is so grand!" she whispered as they followed the leader to a massive wooden door with black iron handles.

The girl stopped and looked them over once more, chewing on her lips in thought. "Heard we were supposed to have a redhead here, but it wouldn't be the first time Mary told me something wrong. She's been here for years, and sometimes I think the poor chick is blind as a newborn. Come in and mind your mouths."

She held the door open, and Harlow slipped through with the rest, sighing as the warmth of the kitchen hearth seeped through her bones.

The other girls, including Shanda, were taken away by other maids, leaving Harlow alone with the one who'd chosen them. She tried not to overthink that, to squash the trill of dread flowing her veins, wondering if she'd already been found out. The woman chattered as she led them in, speaking of Mary and her odd, sometimes random selections of new kitchen and maid staff. The redhead, Harlow found out, was selected due to a well-timed bribe and a sob story from her mother about the girl's ruinous actions when it came to her own virtue and the well-being of the village. She held in a grimace as the woman talked, hoping her actions wouldn't come back to bite her in the end. Bribes weren't uncommon, but then again, neither was future blackmail, and Harlow didn't have a penny to her name to keep the ruse going. When the girl mentioned how the future queen approves all the selections, Harlow felt a little light-headed and wondered if her impulsive actions might be the end of her.

Several women stood at the large wooden table kneading bread. Another stood scrubbing pots and pans at a large sink. The noise was loud enough to wake the dead, but Harlow hadn't heard such a wonderful cacophony since before her parents died.

The girl gave her an odd look. "Come on then. You look like you're freezing. We'll get you a uniform and a pair of new shoes." She frowned. "That's all you have?"

Harlow nodded. She'd never had a lot in the first place, but she'd been living on the street for the past few weeks and anything valuable she'd had to spend quickly. The smaller boy's advice and the coins he'd slipped into her hand had kept her safe but freezing. She'd barely slept a wink since that night.

She'd left her new boots and a silver ring her mother had given her behind that first night in her haste to leave, her escape aided by that same boy she thought about every day. The wool scarf he'd pressed into her hands still lay around her neck. He didn't seem like the kind of boy who'd listen to the brute who'd attacked her. Shaking her head, she tried to put those thoughts away. She still wasn't safe from the streets yet.

Harlow followed the girl's slim back through the kitchen and down a long, stone hallway. The temperature dropped several degrees as they left the cheery warmth of the kitchen, but Harlow had finally escaped the bone chilling wet dampness of the outdoors, so this felt positively balmy.

"My name is Cressida," the girl said as she moved swiftly down the hall. "I'll be in charge of you for the first two weeks, then you'll be mostly on your own." Cressida took a sharp left and opened a small room. Harlow followed her inside, nearly choking at the dust getting stirred up.

"If you get caught stealing, we'll toss you out on your ear. If you get caught stealing by the queen or any of the nobility, you'll lose a hand before you're tossed. Never speak to the queen or the princess unless they speak directly to you. If they do, answer only the question you're asked. Never elaborate. They don't care." Cressida tossed a cloak and several other items to Harlow, making her feel like she was juggling.

"Do you understand?"

Harlow nodded.

"Good." Cressida's blue-grey eyes narrowed. "When's the last time you've had a bath?" The woman's nostrils flared. Heat crept up Harlow's cheeks. She'd gotten the worst of the grime off after Shanda led her to a clean trough, but bathing outside on a cold winter's day wasn't ideal or even comparable to a real bath.

"A few days," she murmured.

Lies and they both knew it.

Cressida snorted. "The maid quarters are this way. I'll show you to the bathing rooms. Wash quickly and meet me back in the kitchen."

Harlow bobbed her head and obediently followed the

woman down what felt like an endless hallway. They stopped at a massive wooden door, and Cressida fumbled at her skirts until she pulled out a round metal key ring. "Your room is through here. There's a linen towel and a bar of lye soap there."

Cressida didn't wait for her to respond. Her shoes made a clicking noise on the stone floor until she stood before a door with the number twelve burned in the heavy oak. She unlocked it and pulled the key from the ring. "Take this and make sure you don't lose it. We have extras in the head maid's office. We won't come into your room unless we absolutely have to, but," she looked both ways before her voice lowered, "I wouldn't keep anything too valuable in here. Some of the others have sticky fingers. Mind your possessions and keep what you can't bear to lose on your person, you hear?"

Harlow nodded. She didn't have much with her, and she never went anywhere without the stone in her pocket.

"Good." Cressida pointed to a small towel and a misshapen bar of soap. "Grab those and I'll show to you to the baths."

HARLOW HAD HEARD about the Thornewood baths before, but thought the rumors were just that. Cressida took her down two additional flights of stairs into a cold and damp part of the castle. Just as Harlow had gotten the nerve to speak up, it opened into a massive bathhouse. Candlelight flickered over the red stone walls, and the sound of water trickled throughout the area.

Harlow's breath caught as she stepped forward. Cressida put a cautioning hand on her arm. "Wait. There are three areas here and you don't want to get taken by surprise." She pointed to the left. "Over there, through that hall, is the men's area. Women are obviously banned."

Obviously. She couldn't see anything other than stone walls and a bend that took people around the corner.

"To the right are the women's baths."

Harlow nodded. "What's straight ahead?"

Cressida cleared her throat. "The royal baths. Never go in there if you know what's good for you." She took Harlow by the arm. "Come on."

They took the right path. As soon as the stone curved, humidity dampened the curls still clinging to Harlow's neck. The sound of roaring water grew closer. Soon enough, Harlow stood in a large bathing room with two large pools on either side. There were two women in the one on the right engaged in conversation. The pool on the left was empty.

Harlow glanced at Cressida. "So..."

The maid grinned at her. "The first time is weird for everyone, but you get used to it. The pools are heated and regularly cleaned." She gave Harlow a gentle push. "Meet me back in the kitchen in half an hour."

"Um."

Cressida pointed. "There's a dressing room a little farther up if you need it."

Harlow nodded. "Okay." This almost felt worse than being on the street. Nova had never been all that modest, a fact that had bothered their parents to no end. Harlow was young enough to have been influenced by her foster mother. Bathing in front of people felt like the epitome of vulnerability to her.

Cressida left, not bothering to say goodbye. Harlow stood there for a moment, listening to the whispers of the two girls in the pool, feeling their heated stares on her. She squared her shoulders and wandered off to find the dressing room.

Ten minutes later, Harlow wanted to scream in frustration. The baths were labyrinthine, twisting, turning, and confusing. Twice she'd ended up right back where she started, but this time, she stood in an unfamiliar, circular area where several areas were partitioned off with curtains.

"Thank the gods," she muttered. She started for one of the rooms when a shorter, golden skinned teenager wearing a large, blue robe walked out from one of them. The girl stopped and gave Harlow a curious look.

"Hello," she said, her voice a low timbre echoing in the stone room. Her hair was dark as a starless night and curled down her shoulders in an ebony sheet. Torchlight flickered in the room, casting shadows everywhere, but it made the gold in the girl's eyes shine like treasure.

"Hello," Harlow greeted, even as she struggled to tear her eyes from the stunning girl in front of her. "I'm sorry to disturb you. Cressida said there was a dressing room down the way, but I'm afraid I got lost."

"You aren't disturbing me." The girl studied Harlow, her gaze skimming over the freckles on her face she was always so self-conscious of, down to her blonde curls, and the tops of her shoulders. "Come," she said after a moment. "I'll lead you to one of the better rooms."

"Thank you," Harlow breathed, relief spilling through her.

"My pleasure." The girl led Harlow down a small stone hall until she arrived at a single dressing room, hidden from all the others.

"Oh," Harlow breathed. "This is perfect!"

The girl chuckled. "The baths can be intimidating for a first timer." She pulled a small golden key from her robe. "Please keep this and feel free to use it whenever you need."

Harlow frowned down at it, something about it making her glance up at the girl in curiosity. "Cressida didn't say anything about a key."

The girl shrugged, her eyes glinting with amusement. "She must have forgotten."

Harlow took it. "Can you tell me how to find my way back to the baths?"

The girl pointed. "To the left. Don't make any turns until you come to a fork. Then take the left one." She tilted her head. "What's your name?"

"Harlow. I'm one of the new maids." The lie slipped off her tongue too comfortably.

"Hmm," the girl said. "I thought the new maid assigned to Cressida was supposed to be a redhead."

Harlow schooled her face into blankness. "I can assure you I am not a redhead."

The girl's eyebrows lifted before she burst into a merry laugh. As if she caught the careful wording and understood the insinuation behind it. "I can see that." The girl sketched a bow. "I must be off, Harlow. Please enjoy the use of the dressing room. Do not lose the key. I'm afraid I only have one more. Cressida does not have a copy of it."

Harlow looked down at the key clutched in her fingers. Why didn't Cressida have a copy? Interesting. "I won't," she promised.

The beautiful girl turned to go, but Harlow wanted a second more with her. "What was your name?" she blurted.

Dimples appeared in the girl's cheeks. "Just think of me as a friendly benefactor. Welcome to the castle, Harlow. I'm sure I will see you around soon."

With that, she turned and walked away. Harlow watched her until the long tail of her blue robe disappeared around one of the stone corners.

Something had happened here today, and she didn't know what. Shaking her head, she unlocked the dressing room and gasped as she walked inside it. From the outside, it barely looked like it would hold one person. On the inside, the room stretched at least six feet back. Three shelves on the left were filled with perfumed oils and different kinds of soap. Harlow eyed the soap in her hand, comparing it to the ones on the shelf and more misgivings filled her stomach. Fear clenched her belly tighter, as she felt an invisible noose of her own making slowly closing around her. If she made it through this without getting thrown out on her ear or worse, it would be a miracle.

To her right were two hooks. A blue, silken robe patterned with white flowers hung on one. The other was empty. A small wooden bench sat at the back and beside it was a shelf full of towels. Not linen like Harlow held. She ventured forward and touched the one on top. It was made of something softer, fluffier, and felt like running her fingers through a cloud.

Harlow frowned as she looked around, feeling like she'd wandered into a trap. She quickly shucked her shoes and under-things, pulling the soggy gown away from her skin before peeling it off with great relief. It landed with a damp splat beside her. As much as she wanted to snag one of the soft towels, they felt forbidden, so she refrained. Harlow wrapped the thin linen towel around her, gathered up her wet clothes and rushed from the dressing room, remembering to lock it behind her.

# CHAPTER FOUR

## A GENTLEMAN WITH LYING EYES

There was little time to scrub the way she wanted to, so the bath was quick, dirt from her travels swirling away as she washed. The linen towel barely soaked up any of the bathwater remaining in her thick hair, but she did the best she could with the unruly mess. After a hasty braid, a quick glance in the foggy mirror made her grimace at the state of it. She hurriedly dressed and shoved her feet into her boots before she made her way down the hall and back toward her quarters. Looking up, she gaped at the dozens of doors in front of her and had a moment of blind panic. Where were the maid quarters? She spun around, trying to get her bearings. Everything looked the same in this place.

A sharp breath of annoyance burst from her before she turned around and headed down the hall, her gaze swinging to and fro, searching for something familiar. She felt almost naked in the hallway and had no confidence in her new position here. In time she knew it would come, but today her nerves were scraped raw, as if she were in a cage with no doors. She came upon a heavy, wooden door that looked like every other heavy wooden door, but this one was slightly ajar. Maybe Cressida had left it open for her to find her way back through this labyrinth. She pushed the door open, shutting it hastily behind her, and expelled a breath of relief.

Harlow clutched her satchel close and was about to step forward when she saw a man sitting a few feet away. He had one ankle resting on his other knee and held a floral teacup. One of his perfectly manicured brows rose at the sight of her. Light streamed in through the window behind him, casting beams of sunlight across his scarlet hair and dark tunic.

Her mouth fell open. "Um. My apologies." She spun to find the door handle, but the man cleared his throat.

"A moment if you will?"

Harlow's shoulders slumped and she slowly turned around, aware of how she looked and knowing she'd be kicked out on her ear in the next few moments.

She slowly turned. "I am new here and do not know my way around. My sincerest apologies for disturbing you."

He had the reddest hair and brightest green eyes she'd ever seen. There were a few redheads in her village, but all of them had a smattering of freckles across the bridge of their noses and belonged to the same man. This man looked *nothing* like the unfortunate Mr. Watters or his whelps.

His face seemed carved of marble, both handsome and touched with callousness. She swallowed hard when she realized she'd trapped herself in a room with what had to be a nobleman. If he were the type, he could do whatever he wanted to her, and she'd have to endure it. That was the way the castle worked. Or so she'd heard. It was the same everywhere.

Harlow's fingers trembled as she reached behind her and fumbled for the doorknob.

"You aren't disturbing me," he said. "Would you like a cup of tea?"

Harlow shook her head. She was rooted to the floor, unable to move, fear keeping her paralyzed.

"What position did you take?" He didn't seem disturbed by her presence. Merely curious.

"Maid, sir."

One red eyebrow rose. "Did you now? And do you like it?"

"It's my first day, sir."

"Ah." He poured himself another cup of tea and studied her as he sipped. "You do not have to be afraid. I mean you no harm. Please sit for a moment and indulge me."

HARLOW SWALLOWED hard but still didn't relax. She shook her head to decline his offer to sit, only realizing after it was too late she should have said yes. Her fingers were close to being numb from her grip on her satchel and all she wanted to do was run.

"My name is Lucien." He sipped his tea. "I hail from the Kingdom of Roses. Where are you from?" There was something... knowing in his gaze. It made her uncomfortable but curious too. Her history knowledge came from Nova's odd, eclectic mix of random facts given to Harlow a little at a time when she least expected it. It led to her remembering those tidbits and using them at the oddest times. Like now. Harlow racked her memory to come up with a memory from a conversation where Nova mentioned the kingdom's long history of knowledgeable botanists and stunning floral exports, leading to a wealthy monarchy. Lucien himself somewhat resembled an odd, brightly colored flower.

"Originally Thornewilde, sir."

His head tilted at that. "Thornewilde?" Lucien's voice sharpened.

Harlow nodded.

"How old are you?"

"Fifteen, sir."

His nostrils flared. "You were in the raids."

"Yes." All these probing questions were disturbing, and anger was beginning to scratch at her skin. "Why?" she asked before she could bite the impertinent question back.

Lucien's brows rose before a smile quirked over his lips. "Why indeed. What is your name, girl from Thornewilde?"

"Harlow."

Something sparked in his bright eyes. "Harlow," he repeated. "Interesting name."

"Thank you." There was a lilt on the last word as if it were a question. Maybe it was. This man acted too familiar. Like he knew her.

"How did you come here to the castle?"

She broke into a cold sweat. "I was told to be here at the castle today. I'm Cressida's new maid."

He set his teacup down and stood. Harlow took a step back, her shoulders bumping against the door. Lucien stopped and held his hands up. "I promise you, Harlow. I mean you no harm. I'm merely curious. You look familiar to me."

"I don't know how that could be. I am no one, sir."

Lucien stopped a few feet away, his gaze perusing her face. His brow furrowed before a small smile broke over his face. Silence fell between them before he shook his head once, as if he were reminding himself of something. "I can assure you that is not true." He gestured at the door. "The maid quarters are three doors down on the left. The door is a different color. I'm afraid I must be off too. I have an engagement I am almost late for."

Harlow nodded. "Thank you, sir."

"My pleasure."

She turned to go, but Lucien spoke once again. "I wish you the best for whatever you're looking for, Harlow."

Her skin went clammy, and she turned back to look at him once more. Harlow had never seen him before; she was sure of it.

So why did it seem like he knew her?

# CHAPTER FIVE

## DUPED

Harlow rushed into the kitchen with barely a minute to spare, her wet braid slapping the back of her neck as she skidded to a stop in front of an amused Cressida.

"You smell much better," she observed as she skimmed Harlow from head to toe.

The boots she wore pinched her toes, but she hoped once she stretched them a bit, they would be okay. The skirts were a size too big, forcing Harlow to knot them at the back. The weeks she'd scraped by in the village hadn't fared well for her waist-line. She hadn't realized how thin she'd become until she'd scraped every inch of dirt off her skin in the pool. By then, she hadn't cared if anyone else saw her. The realization of how close she'd come to starving to death had dissolved any modesty left in her rail thin body. She'd have to figure something out when the new maid came looking for her rightful place, but for now she was safe and warm and clean. It was all she could ask for.

"Thank you," Harlow said and fell still. The other women around her paid her no heed, but she felt eyes on her back. When she turned, the woman who'd shooed her away the first time stared at her, daggers in her cold blue eyes. Harlow averted her gaze and focused on Cressida, but the maid was nobody's fool.

"Flora hates everyone," Cressida confided in a whisper. "Be careful not to be alone with her."

Harlow's nod was shallow, and she did not look at Flora again.

"Come. I'll show you the rooms you and I will be responsible for. After the two weeks are up, they will be turned over to you. Perhaps we shall see some of the royals about today. There's a new prince in town," she said as she turned, and Harlow hurried to catch up to her. "They say he is the future queen's betrothed. I have not seen him yet, but the rumor is he's quite handsome."

Harlow cared nothing for men or women or anyone, really. Maybe before everything happened, this would have roused her curiosity, but now all she wanted was to survive. She'd heard of the royal family and the events of the last decade when Thornewood had become landlocked with no way out of the court. It had happened after the queen had usurped her king's authority, relegating him to the background and forcing the lands from a kingdom to a queendom. In some regards, citizens, especially women, welcomed the change. In others, a simmering resentment brewed from the males angry about all the power they'd lost to hands they never deemed worthy.

Women, however, stepped up and learned trades, becoming soldiers and craftsmen, and flourished in their newfound power, but the long overdue changes had yet to trickle all the way into the surrounding villages, leaving the women there still acting as wives and homemakers, most beholden to their husband's will. Time might slowly change things, but Harlow had yet to see those young fruits ripen.

The shift resulted in a short-lived rebellion where two other kingdoms gained control of some of Thornewood's surrounding lands, resulting in their current landlocked status. The queen had yet to retaliate, leading to quickly stifled questions and rumors. Why she hadn't sent her soldiers out to reclaim the territory became the subject of riotous debate, but at the same time, magic slowly drifted away. Those brave enough to try to connect those dots met strange ends until eventually, most questions only formed in the minds of Thornewood's subjects, never on their lips.

Trade had all but trickled to a halt and the worried whispers around town were about imports drying up and what happened when their food supply started to wane.

Farms were plenty around Thornewood, Thornehollow, and the surrounding villages, but Harlow's family had always been quick to ease their mind saying they were not bound to their lands. The queen had gone on only one trip since then, escorted by a dozen of her finest Kingsguard. Only two of the guard had returned and the queen had never left again. No whisper ever made it around about what happened during that trip or where those men had gone.

The entire castle felt very much like a held breath. What would happen when it finally exhaled? Harlow shivered. "Will her betrothed bring trade to our villages? Salt and sugar and cloth?" These were the things her mother coveted over the last few years before the illness wiped only the need to survive from her mind. The Kingdom of Roses was mostly known for exporting exotic plants and flowers, but their trade status with other kingdoms remained strong and healthy. Unlike their own.

Cressida shrugged. "He came with twelve large caravans filled to the brim with goods. No one has yet seen what he brought with him. He arrived in the dead of night and spent the next couple of days recovering from the grueling trip. Today is the first time he's been out and about within the castle walls."

"And this is the first time he's met the queen?" Harlow

asked as her gaze drank in all the sights. She'd always loved color, bright jewel tones— greens, and purples, burgundy and brilliant blues. The castle was filled with an abundance of color, though Harlow had only seen the maid's quarters and some of the halls. The artwork hung high above them was filled with scenes of riotous color, flowers bursting with blooms and landscape scenes with stunning gardens. Her thoughts drifted back to the lovely girl she'd run into at the baths, and as she opened her mouth to ask Cressida about her, the woman held up a hand to stop her just as the sound of bells drifted down the hall.

Cressida stiffened. "Move to the walls and stand straight, Harlow. Head up, shoulders back. Do not meet their gaze."

Harlow turned and stepped back until her shoulders hit the cool stone. She didn't say anything, and neither did Cressida as they stood beside each other. The sound of bells grew louder, a cheery rhythmic sound, matching the color splashed all over the walls.

The guard came first, a tall handsome man with steely dark eyes. His gaze missed nothing and crawled over every inch of the floors and walls until it landed upon them. Harlow stiffened at his intense gaze, and when his eyes widened just a fraction when his eyes met hers, Harlow's brow furrowed.

He wore midnight black leather armor, covering him from the neck down. It flashed under the lamplight, so dark it looked blue. A wicked curved sword was fastened to his side, held in an ornate scabbard. He stared at her, his eyes searching for something. She felt exposed under his gaze, confused about why she was being scrutinized.

"Stay still," Cressida hissed.

Harlow locked herself into place, not realizing she'd shifted under the man's perusal. Behind him followed two other men, not nearly as impressive as he was. They were at least two inches shorter and of a smaller build, though they both were armed with two wicked looking swords. Behind them walked a small, frail man, so at odds with the three men in front. He must be someone of importance to be surrounded by such a flagrant display of military power.

The smaller man wore a crown and robes of the deepest purple. Harlow stiffened. The king. Should she bow? She shot a panicked look at Cressida, but the woman didn't move an inch.

Harlow snapped her head forward and didn't look again until she could see them all out of her peripheral vision.

She'd never seen any of the royal family before, but the king looked ancient, far older than she expected. He'd long ago lost his hair, and what was left rose in wisps as he moved. The crown sat at a slight angle on his head, as if his neck was almost too weak to bear the weight. His lips were fleshy and pink, but his brown eyes were ordinary and sank deep into his face. Harlow had never heard good things about the man, but the kingdom had been at peace for a while now, so how bad could he be?

The woman who walked beside him looked like a jewel escaped from its containment next to the paleness of the king. Her hair was dark as night and coiled into a perfect braid around her head. A crown of purple amethyst and deep red garnet sat straight on her head. A large white stone that flashed with a bright blue fire in the light rested on top of it, the other stones descending all the way to the back.

The queen.

Her eyes were dark and bright and the dress she wore was so dark blue it almost looked black. She moved with a liquid grace, unlike that of the king who shuffled his steps and swayed back and forth like a boat on rocky seas.

But as impressive as she was, it was the girl who walked behind them who took Harlow's breath away.

Hair of the darkest ink swept up from her neck and coiled

into an extravagant braid around the simple amethyst and diamond crown she wore, those same white stones sprinkled all over it. Her eyes were a stunning gold in the bright light of the hall and her skin had been touched by the sun, glowing golden against the deep, rich purple of the gown she wore. She moved like liquid silk and Harlow's stomach sank as their eyes met.

The key she'd tucked into her pocket burned her hip like a brand.

The future queen's lips curled into a tiny smile. Crimson heat crept up Harlow's neck as she looked away, only to meet the gaze of the fierce looking man in the front. His eyes narrowed at her, and she looked away, straight at the man who walked beside the future queen.

His hair glinted with crimson fire as he moved. The light glittered against it, making it look like melted jewels. His eyes were a bright, intelligent green and his lips were full and curved in an amused smile as he took her in. Shock rooted her to the spot, and Harlow held his gaze for a long moment until something flickered in his eyes. Seconds later, she dropped her gaze, staring at her feet until the party passed them by. Her stomach churned with apprehension and something that felt strangely like betrayal. Could this day get any stranger? First the future queen in the baths and then her betrothed when she mistakenly stumbled into the wrong room?

She didn't know if she was cut out for this. This *life*. This bowing and scraping and dusting and minding her tongue and feet and expressions. There was a freedom in village life. She could run and jump and sing and dance, and when she got home, she had a simple meal and a loving smile waiting for her. Soft fingers to braid her hair, blankets that smelled like her foster mother's flowers. Not this. This tense, stiff atmosphere. The need to find her sister burned in her, the urge to leave and search no matter how long it took imprinted on her soul. A niggling doubt in her soul whispered she could never go back. Things would never be the same, but Harlow held out hope that this new stage in her life was merely a mark on the soil– temporary and easily remedied.

"WHAT ON THE god's green pastures was that?" Cressida hissed a couple of minutes later. "No one ever looks at the royal family the way you did. You'll be lucky to keep your head, you stupid girl!"

Harlow debated whether to tell her she'd already met the future queen. "Sorry," she muttered instead, choosing to keep her secret for a little while longer. For now, trusting anyone was a luxury. One she didn't have.

Cressida blew out a breath and jerked her head to the door closest to her. "You better hope they forget about you," she warned as she stepped inside.

Doubtful. Cressida shoved a duster and rag in Harlow's face and rattled through the list of chores so fast it made her head spin. "When you finish here, I'll check and clear you for the next room."

"Are the chores written down somewhere?" Harlow asked.

Cressida's brows crept up to her hairline. "You expect all the servants here went to a fancy school for letters, do you?"

A blush heated Harlow's cheeks.

"Use your brain, girl. That's why the gods gave it to you." Her stern look softened. "You'll get the hang of it soon enough." She gestured at the large fireplace. "And don't forget to clean the ash out of that. The bin is over there." Cressida pointed in the corner of the large and ornate room. "You have half an hour."

She walked out, quietly shutting the door behind her. Harlow stared at the door for a moment before she sighed. Nova had better know what she's doing by ordering her to the castle. Harlow had a feeling she was cut out of sterner cloth than living her life as a maid. Nova always spun tales of wonder and adventure and told Harlow she could be whatever she wanted. Harlow didn't think scooping ashes out of a fireplace or cleaning up a royal's teacup is what she had in mind. When Nova spoke of magic, a spark lit inside of Harlow, like a flint striking steel. It stirred something slumbering deep, never fully awakening, a tiny flame hinting at familiarity or kinship. As time passed and life hardened her to certain things, Harlow waved those feelings away, dismissing them as childhood whimsy. Then she stepped into this place and wondered if Nova's words might have hinted at something greater awaiting her. Shaking her head at herself, Harlow bent down to the fireplace with her brush and pan. For now, she had to be content with a warm bed and food to eat. Wallowing in her fantasies could wait until her duties were finished.

# CHAPTER SIX

## DESMINDA

S hade stared at the princess, a familiar, disapproving glower on his face. "Who is she? The angry girl you seem so amused by," he demanded.

Desminda didn't really know. "A new maid," she told him, studying her fingernails as she watched the flames from the fire-place flicker light against the terrible wallpaper her mother had chosen. They sat in the greeting room, a place Desminda had always hated. Why they called it the greeting room, she didn't know. This was the place where people came to gawk at their wealth and ask them favors. Never just to say hello and check in on things.

"A maid, you say?" Shade asked, his eyebrows rising.

"That's what she said." Desminda kept her tone deliberately bored. She'd bet her left boot that girl was no maid. Giving her the key was an impulsive, borderline stupid thing to do, but something about Harlow made the back of her neck tingle. As if she were meant to keep the girl close to her. She trusted those niggles of intuition. So far, they'd never steered her wrong.

"The new maid assigned to Cressida is supposed to be a redhead," Shade observed in a bland tone.

"Oh relax. She isn't here to kill us all." The strange girl looked like a scared rabbit. But what *was* she here for? She wasn't a maid. Desminda knew within a week the girl would fail at all the tasks Cressida set in front of her. Not that the act of cleaning was difficult. At least from what she'd seen. It was working within the confines of all the rules her mother had set. Only the strongest of maids survived the nitpicking. Harlow seemed like the type to scoff and find work elsewhere.

Shade's gaze narrowed. "What about the Virago?"

Desminda sat a little straighter. The thought had crossed her mind, but it required girls of a certain...temperament. She'd only seen a little of Harlow's. "You think she would do well?"

He snorted. "I've never even spoken to the girl, but even watching from afar, I can tell she's no maid. We first need to find out why she's here. Then we can see about moving her over. If she wants to go."

"She'll want to." Why she felt so strongly about it, she couldn't say.

"Mary chose the kitchen staff, and you signed off. And yet, we're missing a redhead." He gave Desminda a long look. "We may need to ask where she came from." Shade poured himself another glass of tea and her a cup of coffee as they waited for two representatives of the Kingdom of Roses to enter. Supposedly Lucien's uncle and one of his cousins. Desminda thought they were more than likely either spies or sycophants. Either way, she didn't like them and couldn't wait to see them on their way.

"Her name is Harlow," she said with a shrug. "That's all I know."

Shade flinched. "Harlow?"

Desminda nodded. "Are you alright?" Shade had gone a shade paler, the hand holding his teacup shaking almost imperceptibly.

Shade put his cup down so hard, an audible crack rang through the room. "What village did she come from?"

What in the world? "I do not know. I ran into her in the baths. Other than that, I know nothing about the girl." She watched as Shade paced up and down the room, his expression like he'd seen a ghost. Desminda stood. "Shade?"

He scrubbed a hand over his face. "I need to see her."

She'd never seen Shade act this way over anyone. "Of course. She's probably in the kitchens."

Shade didn't say another word before he walked out.

*Strange.* Desminda tugged her skirt up into her hands and rushed out after him, quickly whispering to one of the guards to delay their visitors until they returned.

FLORA FOUND her before Cressida did. Harlow stiffened as the woman entered the room, her eyes narrowing as she took Harlow in.

"Found your way into the castle, did you?" she asked, still approaching her. Her index finger trailed over the tables she'd just dusted. Harlow took a deep breath. She'd have to go back over it with a cloth to get Flora's fingerprints out.

"I don't know what you're talking about," Harlow said.

Flora grinned, her crooked teeth fighting for space in her small mouth. "I won't say anything," she said quickly. Too quickly.

The duster in Harlow's hand stilled. "Oh?"

"Sure. We all need friends, don't we?"

Harlow didn't like the sound of that. "Sure," she agreed, only because Flora looked at her expectantly.

"Good." Flora stood too close to her now. "Cressida is weak. Obviously. She'd let an assassin walk right through the front doors if their sob story was good enough."

A chill went down Harlow's spine. "I'm no assassin." If she were, she hoped she'd be much more sophisticated than whacking a girl over the head and stealing her clothes. Guilt roared through her at her actions, and she hoped her ruse stayed intact. If it fell apart, Nova wouldn't have to worry about finding her. The queen would display her on the gallows as a deterrent to future thieves.

"Don't care if you are," Flora said. "What I care about is the silver I have tucked into my bedroom, saving to get out of this place."

Harlow slowly began to realize where this was going. "I have no money," she protested.

Flora smiled again. "Not now you don't. We work for generous benefactors. You'll get a fair wage should your... previous indiscretions remain secret."

The room grew too hot. Harlow had just stoked the fireplace before Flora came in, and she still stood too close to the heat source. Sweat beaded at her hairline as she thought about Flora's proposal. She had to stay here. Nova would come for her.

She had to.

"How much?" she asked after a moment.

The door flung open a second later. Flora straightened, her chilling smile dropping from her lips. She bowed deeply and Harlow followed a second later.

"Excuse me, Your Grace," Flora said humbly.

The future queen nodded, and Flora rushed out, not bothering to look back at Harlow.

The conversation was curtailed for now, but she knew Flora would find her at the first sound of clinking coins. Harlow watched Flora's back for a moment too long before the woman disappeared out the door.

# CHAPTER SEVEN

## THE INVITATION

Harlow wasn't in the kitchen, so Cressida led Desminda and Shade to the room where she'd left the poor girl. Guilt speared Desminda at the look of betrayal on Harlow's face when she spied her walking with her family. She hadn't meant to blindside her, but Desminda had no friends in the palace and when she realized Harlow had no idea who she was in the baths, she couldn't help herself. Loneliness followed the crown, and seeing Harlow shining like a beacon in the dim lights of the bath made her yearn for companionship—friendship, something she'd never had before. Sure, she'd had acquaintances, those in similar positions thrust into the same prominence as she, but those relationships always skimmed the surface, never diving below to a deeper understanding of each other.

Shade entered the room first with Desminda close on his heels. She watched as Harlow looked up, paled, then straightened, the duster in her hand stiff at her side. The other girl, some kind of flower name, Desminda remembered, hurriedly assured them she was just leaving. An odd tension in the room had her studying the older woman. Her gaze flicked over to

Harlow, whose own gaze rested on the other woman's back. An expression of fear lingered in her eyes before she blinked, and it washed away. Harlow turned her attention back to them.

"I'm just finishing up," she said by way of greeting. "Would you like me to leave now?"

Desminda barely clamped her lips together in time, silencing the smile threatening to form. The first rule, made up by her mother, was for the servants never to speak to them. Only the head maid and the chef were allowed to directly engage in conversation. She felt it was a stupid rule. What if there was an emergency? Would someone have to mime there was a fire in the kitchen so they wouldn't run afoul of the rule?

Shade stopped in front of Harlow, his eyes everywhere at once. "Who are you?" he said, his voice a touch hoarse.

Harlow's blue eyes flared. "I–um–I..."

"Spit it out, girl," Desminda said.

Harlow's eyes flared with irritation before she hid it. There was a fire inside of this girl. One Desminda looked forward to exploring.

"You aren't the maid," Shade said. His posture was rigid and his jaw tight.

Desminda wasn't sure what was going on, but something about this girl had triggered all of his instincts.

Harlow bowed her head. "I can be," she said after a long moment. "I came to the castle looking for work and came in with the maids."

"Do you want to be a maid?" Shade asked.

Her head snapped up at that. "Does *anyone* want to be a maid?"

Desminda covered her laugh with a cough. She studied Harlow, the small build but straight spine, the long, curly hair tangled in a still damp braid, the cold blue fire of her eyes. Why had she come here and where would she go when Shade tossed her out on her ear?

"Shade," she murmured.

He held up a hand, quieting her. Something he rarely, if ever, did. Whatever this moment was, it was important to him. Desminda, stung a little at his dismissal, held her tongue. She'd allow this lapse in propriety for this moment.

"Answer the question. Do you want to be a maid?" Shade took no step closer, but he loomed over the poor girl. Harlow trembled under his perusal, but she tilted her pert chin up and met his gaze.

"No," she said simply. "I do not."

"Then what do you wish to be?" he asked and waited.

Harlow's brow furrowed. "That is a leading question, sir. I come from no money and no means. We don't merely get to say what we wish to do and have it done. We do what we have to in order to survive."

Shade's intense look turned thoughtful and maybe even a little sad. "We have a new program," he began. "For girls your age." He turned to Desminda. "Perhaps the future queen can explain a little more."

Desminda gave him a curious glance. "We're training an elite guard. For the future queen."

Harlow's look was withering. "For you, you mean."

The impertinence. Desminda held in her laugh. "Yes. For me."

Shade's gaze bounced back and forth between them. "The training will not be easy," he interjected. "Most girls will fail within the first week."

"I'll be issued a sword?" Harlow asked.

Shade blinked. "Yes."

"A real one?" she pressed.

"Not at first," he admitted. "A wooden one while we train,

then a practice sword once the basics are covered and we're sure no one will impale themselves on it."

Harlow tilted her head, a small frown forming on her brow. "And the bathhouse. Will I have to use it again?"

Desminda turned away from them to hide the grin.

Shade's voice turned wary. "No," he said slowly. "We have separate quarters for the Virago."

"The Virago?" Harlow questioned. "What does that mean?"

Desminda turned back around. "In literal terms, it means an ill-tempered woman."

She didn't miss the way Harlow's blue eyes flared with delight. "Others define it as a warrior woman," Desminda continued.

"How long does the training take?" Harlow asked, her blue eyes sparking with interest.

"One year," Shade answered.

"And when it's over?"

Shade's nostrils flared. "When it's over, the Virago will be stationed at different points within the castle or in surrounding villages. One will be chosen to guard the future queen."

Harlow's gaze flitted to Desminda, and the future queen felt like shrinking. The girl was *really* not happy about their meeting in the bath house.

"And will the future queen be sworn to honesty when it comes to the Virago who tie their life to hers?" she asked.

Desminda sucked in a shocked breath. Shade coughed and covered his mouth in what Desminda thought couldn't possibly be genuine amusement. The sheer gall of this young girl questioning *her*!

"As a Virago, you will be taught to hold your tongue," Shade said, no amusement in his voice now. "There will be times when your words will be used against you."

Harlow set the duster on top of the fine credenza. "And if

holding my tongue could result in the queen being endangered?"

*The Heavens help me*, Desminda thought. Would all the Virago be like this?

If so, Shade would have his hands full over the next year. Her mother's popularity had fallen over the last few years, the uprising resulting in their landlocked status, lower food rations, and the lack of magic leading to a quietly simmering citizenry, and with it an uptake in threats to the crown. Desminda, safe in the confines of the castle, felt no danger, but Shade's quiet, yet urgent insistence of her safety behind the scenes led her to suggest the creation of the Virago. Once their training finished, she would step up and lead with Shade's experienced guidance.

"We'll discuss such matters further in your training if you decide to join us." He took a step closer to the door. "Pray tell, what is your surname?"

Harlow blinked. "Fischer, sir."

Shade stilled, his eyes narrowing in thought, though he said nothing for a long moment. "And where were you born?"

"Thornehollow before we moved to Thornefall. Though I originally came from Thornewilde. My parents died during the uprising."

Shade nodded, seeming not at all surprised. "And your mother's name?"

Harlow tilted her head, studying him. "My mother's name was Therina."

"Your real mother or your foster mother?" Shade pressed.

Harlow's lips thinned. "My real mother's name was Isabella."

Desminda's knees almost went out from under her. Shade *knew*. His odd line of questioning made more sense now. He knew who she was from the second she told him her name. The realization of who stood before them shook the foundation of her entire being. Harlow, the slight thing standing before her was the baby taken from the castle in the middle of the night, weeks before magic was outlawed by the crown. She'd been young when it happened. Very young, but she'd heard the story all the same. Desminda might have remained clueless had Shade not put the pieces together for her.

The heir of magic. The girl who'd disappeared. The daughter of the fearsome Stonehand mage and the crown's potential downfall. This tiny girl could be the ruin of them all.

She schooled her ragged inhale of breath, her thoughts running wild as she realized what they'd let into her home. The only thing stopping her from calling the guards was the fact that Harlow appeared utterly clueless about her astounding history and the true story of her birth.

Not to mention if Shade thought Desminda was in danger, he'd strike the girl down where she stood. Her breath slowed and evened, but a fine tremor took residence in her hands, and she clenched them in fists against her voluminous skirts.

Desminda slid her gaze over to Shade, but the man's face was practically stone.

"Would you like to become a member of the Virago?" Shade asked.

Desminda's mouth fell open in astonishment. What was the game he played? Shade knew the danger she represented to them all. Why would he offer such a coveted spot to her? If she knew who she really was, Harlow might be an enemy to them all.

Harlow studied him, her gaze flicking back and forth from him to Desminda. "It's better than scooping ash out of a fireplace, and I'm quite handy with an axe." Her expression darkened at that. "Though mine was stolen after the fever raged through Thornefall. I'm keen to get another."

Shade didn't acknowledge her axe comment but nodded.

"Come down to the stables in six days and I'll see you properly outfitted."

Relief and perhaps something else flickered in the girl's expression. "I will," she assured them.

"Good," Shade said. He held the door open for Desminda and they sailed out, leaving Harlow alone. Questions burned in Desminda's throat, but she'd always trusted Shade, and he'd protected her with a stalwart heart and a strong sword arm. She swallowed her doubts down, trepidation beating in time with her heart.

Only time would tell if she'd regret this day and her trust in Thornewilde's most faithful and loyal warrior.

# CHAPTER EIGHT

## THE CULPRIT

A voiding Flora for the next six days proved to be an impossible task. Everywhere Harlow went, the horrible girl followed. She pretended to cozy up to Harlow every time Cressida or any of the other girls walked by. Harlow caught a couple of sympathetic glances, but no one interceded on her behalf. Perhaps they'd all fallen victim to Flora's scheming.

The last day before she was supposed to meet Shade at the stables proved to be the most challenging. She'd gotten up early, ready to get a head start on her chores. Harlow had grabbed her satchel and all her belongings and cleaned up the room before she slipped out and locked the door, tucking the metal key into her pocket.

She headed to the bathhouse first, though she'd never gone back to the princesses' dressing room once she figured out who it belonged to. Now she choked down her modesty and bathed quickly, always ensuring she tucked her bag into a hidden alcove. It was the only time she let the stone go, and she always felt empty without it.

Harlow quickly washed, scrubbing her hair with the sliver of ash soap provided to all of them. Within two minutes, she was out of the pool and drying with the thin towel given to her when she first arrived. She tucked it around her, nodded to the two other girls in another pool, and disappeared around the corner.

Her bag lay in the middle of the stone hall, its contents upended and scattered all over. Harlow gasped and went to her knees, hands scooping up her meager belongings— the blanket she'd brought from home, the pins she kept in her hair, and the clothing she'd painstakingly washed two days before in anticipation of her move.

She sighed in relief as she tucked everything back in, but her heart stopped as she realized the stone was missing. Harlow moaned in agony and frantically ran her hands over the floor, crawling and peering in tiny places around the corner of walls where the stone could have skittered. Why the bag was out of the alcove was something she'd figure out later, but maybe she hadn't tucked it in correctly and it fallen.

That excuse burned in her belly. It wasn't possible. Harlow always took the utmost care with her belongings because she had so little, and what she did have was more precious than gold. The last vestiges of her life lay in that bag, the only piece she still had of Nova, the final memory that told her once upon a time she'd been loved and cherished. Losing it felt like the last piece of herself ripping away, erasing the person she used to be before her life had fallen apart.

Rage warred with sorrow at the loss, churning into acid inside of Harlow's gut. Only one person could have done this. Fingers trembling with fury, Harlow fell to her knees, gathering all the spilled items and hurriedly shoving them back inside. When she rose, the anger lifted with her, blooming like a sunset inside her heart. A moment later, she hurried down the corridor, on the way to confront the person responsible.

.  .  .

THE CULPRIT SAT on her bed, eyes full of malice. She tossed the stone up and down like a coin and grinned when Harlow burst into the room.

Harlow's fingers burned for the comfort of her ax, but she knew it probably was a good thing she didn't have it. The urge to bury it deep in Flora's skull might overrule her common sense.

"Give it back," she hissed before Flora could say a word.

Flora's eyes widened, a tiny hint of fear flickering through them, before they narrowed, dismissing Harlow's rage. "Someone hasn't learned her place yet, has she?"

Harlow vibrated with the urge for violence. "Give it back, Flora. I won't ask you again."

In answer, Flora tossed the rock up and caught it again, her grin widening.

Harlow took a step forward.

"Uh uh," Flora tsked. She waggled her index finger at Harlow. "You owe me. And I want to be paid."

Flora hadn't told anyone her secret, but Harlow bristled at being extorted. She'd just received a few coins from Cressida, but she asked the woman to hold on to them for her until she purchased a lock box.

"That's why you went through my satchel," Harlow blurted.

"And much to my surprise, the only thing you had worth having is this pretty little rock." Flora held it up to the light, the white stone flashing with brilliant and vivid blues and purples. "I've never seen one like this. I think I'll keep it."

Harlow was due to the stables within the next five minutes. Being late was the absolute last thing she wanted to happen today. She didn't have time to argue with Flora. "I don't have any money. Cressida is holding my pay."

"Is she now?" Flora asked. "I suggest you get it back and give me what we agreed on."

Thoughts of the ax flashed through Harlow's mind, but she

took a deep breath. "That rock is the only thing I own. It's worthless."

Flora tossed it again. "It isn't worthless if it means something to you, now is it?"

She'd *kill* her. Harlow wasn't materialistic. She didn't care much about what she wore or what shoes she had. The important things lay in her heart. But the stone was deliberately given to her by Nova. It seemed stupid when she sat and thought about it. It was just a stone after all, but some things were unexplainable, and Nova never did anything without a reason. Her sister told her to keep it safe, so she did. That's how their relationship worked. Nova led. Harlow trusted. Even when it was hard. *Really* hard. Even if it were only a pretty bauble, it was *hers*. Losing it to Flora wasn't an option.

"This is the last time I ask, Flora. If you don't give it back, you'll find me...unpleasant." She would be late for the stables. The big man in charge of the new Virago didn't look like he entertained excuses.

A choked laugh escaped Flora. She stood, tucking the stone in her pocket. "Unpleasant?" she snorted. "You're a trampled flower, girl. Faded, bruised, and good for nothing anymore. You'll work your fingers to the bone with no appreciation from anyone and fend off advances from noblemen every time." Flora studied Harlow, her eyes lit with vicious glee. "And if you're unlucky or not quick enough, there won't be any fending to be done. You think you can best me?" Flora laughed. "I've seen more in a week than you've seen in your entire life, girl."

Nova's words sprang to Harlow's mind as she watched Flora moving closer, slow like a snake. "*If you're in the right, strike first, strike hard, and strike silently. If you have to explain yourself later, you aren't the hero.*"

When Flora took one step too close, Harlow met her eyes. "I tried to warn you."

Flora's lip curled in a snarl, but just as she opened her mouth to further gloat, Harlow's fist slammed into her face.

"No one likes bullies," Harlow hissed, wincing at the pain in her hand. She'd punched Nova before, but her sister had allowed it and she'd pulled back so as not to hurt her. A punch when she'd meant it felt completely different. "Come near me again, and a fist in the face will seem like a gift."

# CHAPTER NINE

## SHADE

F lora lay on the floor screaming, blood spurting from the nose the new recruit had undoubtedly just broken. The wild urge to laugh coursed through him as his eyebrows rose in surprise. He'd thought Harlow was bluffing when she told Flora the results would be "unpleasant." A strange sense of pride filled him at Harlow's grim promise and her follow-through.

A broken nose landed far on the wrong side of pleasant, he'd say. Shade pushed off the wall and walked over to Harlow, who still hadn't seen him. "Next time, hold your elbow higher and drive from your lower body. You'll get more power behind it."

Harlow jerked her attention from Flora who'd finally stopped screaming, resorting to low, tortured moans as blood continued to stream from the injury.

"May I?" Shade asked, gesturing to her elbow.

Harlow nodded, her bright blue eyes wide with apprehension. He stifled a smile. The girl acted like a scared rabbit and punched like a battering ram. If she thought striking Flora would prevent her from joining the Virago, she'd be sorely mistaken. In fact, his timing was serendipitous for he'd stayed up most of the night wondering about this girl, the Stonehand mage, and whether his decision would fulfill the promise he'd made to her father so long ago. A memory from long ago rose within him, bringing with it a fresh wave of grief. No matter how much time passed, the memory of Harlow's bloodstained blanket trailing from his arms and the frantic ride through the kingdom to get her to safety would never leave him.

Shade lifted Harlow's arm. Her frame felt so thin he could feel most of the bones as he raised her elbow just slightly. Then he leaned down and patted her calf. "Push up from the ground, through your calf, femur, then your hips. Rotate," he gently shifted her hips while also moving her arm, "then strike."

Harlow nodded and stepped away. "Like this?" She perfectly replicated what he'd shown her.

Shade nodded. "Exactly." He eyed her even as he bent down to help Flora up. Flora glared at him as she staggered up from the ground, her face a macabre mix of dirt and blood. "Who taught you how to throw a punch?" he asked Harlow.

"My sister, sir," she replied.

He eyes darkened at the revelation. "Sister?" Shade kept his face carefully blank. He played a dangerous game. Each step he took danced on the edge of disaster.

Harlow nodded. "She taught me a lot of self-defense." She dropped her eyes. "When I got older and had to go to the village."

Shade's lips thinned. It wasn't easy for any girls in any of the villages, but most of the time, wives kept their men in line. Being a maid in the castle would be especially full of pitfalls for this girl. The Stonehand Mage's daughter would bloom into a great beauty one day not too far away, and the maids and serving women were seldom safe anywhere the nobility went. He studied her for a moment— thick blonde hair in a damp, messy braid, bright blue eyes, a complexion of peaches and cream and the same small smattering of freckles her mother had. Her back was rigid, and her nostrils flared. The fist of her right hand clenched and unclenched as she stared at Flora.

Protectiveness roared through him. She was a vivid mix of her mother and father, and it hurt his heart as he looked at her.

He held Flora steady as she regained her footing. Her posture slumped over as she held the apron of her dress up to her face to staunch the blood.

"You will learn more techniques for self-defense and battle," he told Harlow. And you will learn how to use the law to enforce the queen's will."

Flora tried to pull away from him, but his grip firmed. He turned his attention to her. "Now, pray tell, what did you do to Harlow in order for her to bloody your nose?"

Flora sucked in an outraged breath. "Che stold mah mon ay!"

Harlow snorted and stepped toward her again. Flora cringed and took a step back. Shade still held on to the woman's outstretched arm and she bumped into his chest as Harlow approached. Without missing a beat, Harlow bent and started fishing through Flora's skirt pockets.

Flora struggled and screeched in protest, but Harlow merely kept digging until she pulled out a small, shiny stone. Shade sucked in a breath as he realized what she held. He remained silent as he didn't think the girl realized its significance. Harlow straightened and put her face close to Flora's. "If you touch my things again, I'll break more than your nose." Her words were clipped and tight, vibrating with seething anger.

Shade released Flora's arm and leaned closer to her. The woman flinched and he relished her reaction. He couldn't stand those who abused others and had recommended Flora's removal more than once. Perhaps this would be the piece that collapsed her fragile house. "If I hear a peep of this gossiped about, I will personally see you replaced. There is a harsh penalty for thieving in Thornewood." He punctuated his words with a cold smile. "To your great fortune, Harlow's fist is enough punishment. Go see the healer. If she asks you how you came by the injury, you will blame your own stupidity."

Flora gave Harlow a death glare but quickly left the room leaving a trail of blood droplets all the way out the door.

Shade examined Harlow. "Are your bags packed?"

"I have no bags. Just my satchel."

"You brought no clothes?"

Harlow glanced down at herself. "Just this. And it was given to me. All my other belongings were stolen besides the dress I came in. It was beyond repair."

A long silence stretched between them. Things would change beginning now. He always expected to see Harlow again. In fact, he'd planned on it. Not like this, but life never worked the way one wanted it to. There was so much he needed to teach her, so many things she needed to know. And yet, he still had too many secrets to keep from her. At least for now. It seemed dramatic to believe everything rested on her shoulders, but it was close to being true. Guilt and grief warred in his heart —guilt at what he had to put her through and grief for everything she'd lost.

"Very well," Shade said after a moment. "Then follow me."

# CHAPTER TEN

## ENCOUNTERS OF THE STRANGE KIND

She'd heard of him before. Everyone with a beating heart had. Shade Montello acted in several capacities within the royal court, specifically as Commander of the royal Kingsguard, and now as leader of the Virago. His battle exploits were legendary and spoken of over dinner tables in every village. Thornewilde had no recent wars or skirmishes, but in the past when things hinted at conflict, Shade led the charge to ensure their borders remained secure.

Walking beside him now, watching as he moved, his sharp gaze taking in everything, Harlow finally understood his reputation. He held his frame straight and tall, though not stiff. Shade moved with a fluid grace, each step sharp and even. The man was dreadfully handsome in the way that made him almost painful to look at. It seemed unfair to bestow such dark angelic beauty on someone who held barely restrained violence in his very being.

Shade said little as he led her through the grounds and into the stables. His footfalls were twice the length of Harlow's, so keeping up with him was a flurry of brisk walking with a few skips tossed in so she didn't lag behind. He towered over her, his height casting a shadow over her small form as she scurried after him.

Maybe she should be afraid, but it was hard for her to feel fear anymore. Not after everything life had thrown at her. He didn't seem cruel, though everyone had the ability living deep within them. Harlow felt it within her sometimes—the capacity to take a life if she had to. She'd done it once, all those weeks ago when it had come down to him or her. There had been days when life had given her more than she thought she could bear, but through it all, Harlow pressed through, for one simple reason. Within her existed a deep, burning desire to *live*.

It was only at night when she wondered what kind of human it made her because well-meaning people probably didn't think about things like taking another's life. But perhaps most well-meaning people weren't turned out onto the streets starving. Maybe if they were, they'd get more comfortable with their capacity to do terrible things.

Shade pulled open the stable doors with a soft grunt and jerked his head. Harlow lowered her eyes and hurried inside. Her boots hit soft hay immediately and the sharp tang of leather and horse hit her nose. She stepped far enough inside for Shade to walk around her.

"Follow me," he said. Without waiting, Shade headed to the back. Harlow took a moment to look around. Most of the stalls were empty, but there were three at the back occupied. One held a large gray beast, another a pale palomino. The last one looked like a nightmare on four legs. Massive and the color of a starless night, the beast stared at her. Harlow took an involuntary step back.

"Don't get too close to her," Shade warned from a few feet away. "You'll lose a finger."

The horse snuffed. If Harlow hadn't known better, she

would have said it sounded like derision. She studied the horse for another moment before she turned away.

A soft whicker of noise made her look back again. The horse stared at her and the intelligence in its eyes took her breath away. She frowned and ventured a glance at Shade, but he'd already turned to go.

"I'll come back," Harlow whispered before shaking her head and following Shade. She felt foolish, but there was something about the horse that felt savage and untamed but called to her lonely heart.

SHADE STOOD in front of a large open chest waiting for her. His gaze skimmed her up and down, but it was perfunctory and not like the men in her town used to look at her. A frown lit his face. "You might be too small for the clothing in here." He bent down and rummaged through it, occasionally pulling a piece of clothing out, frowning at it, then putting it away again. Eventually, he held up a pair of leather breeches, a shirt that had seen better days, and a long overcoat.

"These might work," he said, handing over the clothing. "At least until we can get the tailor summoned."

Harlow took the bundle, unsure whether she should thank him or not.

"The Virago quarters are scheduled to be finished tomorrow morning. There's a small room upstairs. It has shelter from the elements and a lantern. If you're careful not to burn the place down, you can sleep there tonight." He studied her. "Unless you'd rather sleep in the maid quarters?"

"No," Harlow blurted, holding the bundle tight against her chest. "Here is fine."

Shade nodded. "Very well." He pointed to a ladder. "The room is up there. You'll see it once you get up to the second

floor. Turn right. There's a small mattress and several blankets."
He opened his mouth to say something else but shut it.

She stood there awkwardly and was about to head upstairs
when he sighed. "I'll have dinner sent to you in a few hours. If
you need something, light the lantern on the front of the stables.
Someone will see it and retrieve me."

Harlow nodded. After a moment, Shade gave her a thin
smile and turned to go.

Tension slid from her shoulders as she watched him walk
away. The soft sounds of the horses, the smell of the hay and the
leather, all of it sent a melancholy sadness crashing through her.
Her sister always said she'd have a horse one day, and not like
the dumb beast her foster parents had. A smile flickered over
her lips at the memory. Their horse had been a dutiful sort, but
Nova always said it had the personality of a rock. It stood like a
statue if you pet it, told it to go, told it to stop, or really told it
anything. Her father had taken to fastening a stick to the top of
the bridle and tying a carrot to a thread at the stick's end. Only
by dangling it right in front of its face could he get the stubborn
horse to go anywhere. Once it started walking, he could lead it,
but getting it to that point proved difficult.

Nova, in her dubious youth, had tried to take the horse to
meet a boy in another town only to get caught when the beast
wouldn't move from the front yard no matter how many false
promises she made it. Her mother came out to turn the lantern
down and caught Nova in one of her best dresses whispering to
the horse about all the sugar she planned to give it if it would
just go.

If she'd only known all she needed was a stick, some thread,
and a carrot, Nova could have wandered the countryside all she
wanted, their parents none the wiser. A smile wobbled over
Harlow's lips at the memory, quickly falling away as grief
threatened to overwhelm her.

The sound of one of the horses whickering drew Harlow over to the enclosures. She couldn't tear her eyes away from the black mare. They stared at each other until Harlow came a little closer. She didn't dare stick her hand in the stall for fear she wouldn't get it back.

Up close, the beast was even more fearsome. It stomped one great hoof and threw its head up before it stilled, its dark gaze upon her. Harlow's breath shook as she took a step toward the stall.

"Hello."

The horse huffed.

"My name is Harlow. I'm new." She grimaced. "Though I don't know how long I'll be here." Harlow slowly walked up to the stall. The horse was close enough to nip her if it wanted, but it did nothing, merely stared at her. A sigh escaped her as she leaned against the locked door. The other stall doors were merely latched closed. "You're a troublemaker then?" she questioned as she toyed with the lock.

The horse huffed again and moved a bit closer. Harlow stilled. "You can bite me if you want. It wouldn't be the worst thing to happen to me." She snorted. "But I'd rather you didn't."

A noise from outside startled her. The footfalls sounded heavy, unlike Shade's almost silent steps. Unsure what to do, Harlow looked around and braced herself against the wall of the horse's stable, pulled herself up and over, landing on silent feet. She crouched low, shivering in fear as the horse skittered a few steps away.

Stupid. *Stupid*, she thought. She belonged here, didn't she? Shade gave her permission to be here. So why was she hiding like a thief?

The doors opened and someone shuffled in, slamming the doors behind them.

Harlow crept to the edge of the stable doors, crouching low

against a pile of fresh hay. The horse stared down at her, nostrils flaring. All she needed was her stupid decision to get her trampled to death. Harlow slowed her breathing and squeezed her eyes shut, whispering a silent prayer to a god she didn't think would answer.

"Bloody princesses," the person muttered. Harlow peered under the crack in the stable door. The man, whoever it was, stumbled toward her on unsteady feet. "Thinks she can do what she likes." He sighed and burped.

Harlow grimaced in distaste. Whoever this was had been in his cups for quite a while. She sat still as a stone and waited for the man to leave. If she'd had a hair more brains, she would have run up to bed. But no. She was stuck in a stall with a horse of a dubious nature. Granted, it had made no move to harm her, but Harlow didn't feel comfortable it wouldn't. The beast had stamped her foot down a few times, perilously close to Harlow's and flared its nostrils at her a few times.

She wanted to run a hand down her broad, silky flank, but due to her current predicament, the horse had all the control. Harlow was in its world right now so she wouldn't dare do anything to jeopardize their temporary peace. The man came closer, still muttering to himself about princesses and duty. She could see his feet, kicking up dust as he dragged them. He wore a pair of frivolous purple slippers with jeweled buckles.

She'd never understood the wardrobe choices of the nobility, but she'd never seen shoes quite like this on the feet of any dukes or duchesses. Or anyone for that matter.

Her heartbeat picked up as the realization of who this might be came to her addled brain. The king was too old to be as spry as the person wearing these shoes. Desminda had no other siblings. There were a few other royals from other courts in right now, but all of them were female.

Lucien. This had to be Lucien. Harlow swallowed hard and

sent a glance up to the ceiling, begging for this man to pass her on by. It was bad enough she'd met him like she had earlier. Being discovered in the stall of one of the royal beasts wouldn't end well for her, she realized. Even if she had permission to be in the stables, she doubted she had permission to be buried in the hay of a beast the quartermaster had yet to break.

The feet stopped right underneath the stall she crouched in. Harlow's back broke into a cold sweat. She squeezed herself as close to the front wall as she could, but when she heard the shocked intake of breath, Harlow realized the game was up.

Her shoulders slumped as she tilted her face up right into Lucien's openmouthed gape.

"Girl!" he gasped. "Do you wish to die, you poor, dumb thing?"

A quick blast of anger roared through her at his patronizing tone. "I assure you; I am perfectly fine."

The heir to the throne of the Kingdom of Roses frowned. Even though his eyes were glassy with drink, she could still see the thoughts whirling through his head. Lucien glanced at the horse, getting more nervous by the second, and then back down at Harlow. "I'd get out of there if I could," he said slowly. "Looks like the mare is getting ready to act." Lucien's red hair glinted with gold in the lamp light above them. A lock of it fell into his eyes and he shoved it out of the way with an addled frown.

"The mare was fine until you got here," she snapped. Silence fell between them. Harlow wanted to groan with horror at her words. "Sorry, Your Grace," she said and ducked her head.

Lucien snorted. "Perhaps you're right then. Though I find it hard to believe she'd let you in here without trying to kick off your face." His gaze went thoughtful. "Or perhaps it's not so hard considering you're cowering in the poor lass's hay and trembling like a leaf."

She *was* trembling, but it was very poor manners of him to remark on it.

He placed a hand over the stall door to help Harlow out, but the beast screeched out a whinny and reared back. Lucien gave a shout of alarm before he jerked his hand away and stumbled back a few steps.

Harlow could do nothing but stare in horror as the beast reared above her. A whimper escaped her, and she gathered her arms over head and tucked her knees in as close as she could, waiting for the inevitable blow to strike.

But no blow came and ever so slowly, Harlow lifted her gaze only to see the horses' muzzle an inch away from her face. A shrill squeak came from her throat as she threw her hands out in front of her in fear.

The horse snuffled at her and took a step back.

"Harlow!" Lucien hissed. "Are you...alive?"

Harlow rolled her eyes. "No." Future king or not, Lucien wasn't too smart tonight. For a moment, a vicious sort of glee infected her as she imagined Desminda forced to listen to Lucien prattle on.

"Oh, oh dear. That's terrible," Lucien said.

A laugh bubbled from Harlow's lips.

Silence fell for a moment before Harlow heard the disgusted snort.

"Idiot," Lucien hissed. Seconds later, he sighed, and a self-deprecating chuckle rang through the air. "Clever girl. I suppose you aren't dead. You've experienced a miracle today, friend. I know of at least two people this horse has trampled in apparent glee."

Harlow finally reached up to the mare and held her hand out, close to its chest, but not quite touching. Asking for permission.

The horse clomped one foot and shifted so that Harlow's fingers connected with its skin.

"Oh," Harlow breathed. The horse's fur felt like the sable they used to sell in the fancy markets that came once a year in her village. Even in the low light it glimmered. Sleek and silky and the color of night, the horse was the most beautiful thing she'd ever seen.

"Come out then," Lucien's voice intruded. "Allow me the pleasure of personally meeting one of the future Virago. I'll reintroduce myself officially this time. I knew you wouldn't be a maid for long, though I admit I'm surprised by the speed in which you've found yourself another position."

She looked up, not knowing why she asked for permission, but doing it all the same. The mare snorted and shifted just slightly so Harlow could stand. When she straightened, she groaned with relief. All the stalls were large, but none of them had a horse the size of a small carriage living in it. Harlow's muscles had seized with fear and were cramped from the small space she'd curled into after Lucien had appeared.

"Thank you," she whispered to the horse. Harlow stepped up to the wall and with a few quick jumps landed outside of the stall and in front of Lucien, the future king of Thornewood.

She wobbled for a moment before hastily dropping to her knees. "Your Grace."

Lucien snorted. "We're in the stables and your future monarch is quite inebriated. If anything, I should prostrate myself before you and beg you not to tell anyone what you've seen or heard tonight."

Harlow dared a glance up. One of his reddish eyebrows rose.

"Do get up then and tell me why you have a wish for an untimely death?"

Harlow stood and glanced over at the horse. The beast was

truly massive, almost supernaturally so. "I panicked." It was the best and worst explanation she had.

"Perhaps you should start at the beginning," Lucien said.

He didn't seem so inebriated anymore so Harlow stared at him longer than she should, her mind working to try to figure him out. People used others for their own gain. Nova always warned her, though her sister protected Harlow from most of it. Now that she was alone, Harlow had to figure things out on her own. In Lucien, she sensed someone who wouldn't hesitate to do the same if it furthered his own ambitions. Was this an angle he worked? Befriend the poor, lonely girl and worm his way into further influence over the Virago? Or even worse, with Desminda? But she had no influence, so why would Lucien be interested in knowing her?

A memory surfaced, touching Harlow's mind like a gentle breeze. She and Nova sat on the edge of a pond, their swinging feet flicking sprays of glittering, cool water in the air. The day had been warm, and Nova particularly intense. She went through phases where one day she'd be normal and full of life, then others where a furrow had prickled her brow, and her eyes seemed unusually haunted. That day was the latter. "Harlow, I want you to remember this. It might come in handy in the future." Harlow groaned, making Nova laugh. She'd been full of these lessons over the years. Nova reached over and clasped Harlow's fingers in her own. "When someone of a higher station looks upon you like a friend, you should be wary for you can give them nothing, and they can give you everything."

She still wasn't quite sure about the meaning of it, but a tingle started in her hands as she remembered her sister's words, and Harlow realized the dirt she now stood on might be flat, but the long road in front of her was no longer so balanced. With a bob of her head, Harlow told Lucien enough but not so much it would give herself away.

Although, she truly had nothing. No name, no money, no horse, no true hope until a stable, a horse, and a chance at doing something bigger than herself arrived in the unlikely form of a handsome older man and a princess she'd do well to be wary of.

"When I heard you, all I could think to do was hide," she said, ending her story and hoping Lucien was one too many drinks in to question her.

"There are no brigands in Thornewood, Harlow."

There were brigands everywhere, she knew. Some just wore nicer clothes and covered their ill deeds under the guise of the law.

His eyes widened when he saw her expression. "Treason lurks on your face," he said. Though his voice was light, it held a warning.

She stiffened and looked down. "My apologies, Your Grace."

He laughed then, a cheerful, bright sound. "No need to apologize. Questioning things is how change occurs, is it not?"

Not in her eyes. With her status, questioning got you a sword in the belly or double the taxes. At her silence, Lucien's laughter died. "Right," he said after a long pause. "Perhaps not." He sighed and gestured for her to walk with him. "Come. We'll take one of the back paths, if you're so inclined."

The horse neighed and reared, the sound a crack of noise in the quiet stables. Lucien took a step back and held out a hand as if to shield her from the beast.

Harlow looked up at the mare and again noticed a glint of keen intelligence in its eyes. If she said it out loud, it would sound preposterous, but tonight there was a kinship with the animal. Perhaps tomorrow she would come downstairs and this would have all been a strange and wonderful fluke in the universe.

But tonight? Tonight, she knew the mare warned her not to go.

And tonight, since it had spared her life once, she would listen.

"I'm afraid Shade wishes me to wake up at an ungodly hour, Your Grace." Turning down a prince would have never been on her list of things to do, and though it felt foolhardy, something told her to stay firm.

His eyes flashed as if he wished to argue, but he inclined his head. "Of course. Perhaps another time then."

A soft whicker of sound came from the stall.

Harlow smiled, though she knew it didn't reach her eyes. "At your request, sir."

Lucien left her then, but Harlow didn't move for several minutes. When she did, she reached over the stall door and let her hand trail down the silken muzzle of the mare.

"Thank you," Harlow whispered, feeling slightly foolish.

The horse nudged her once and stepped away, leaving Harlow bereft of its warmth. A long, cold night would greet her, though Shade had assured her she would have the amenities she would need.

# CHAPTER ELEVEN

### BEAST

The smell of hay tickled Harlow's nose as the first rays of light seeped into the stables. She sighed and shifted, her back meeting warm resistance as she moved. Harlow stiffened until she remembered where she was, then sighed and relaxed.

She'd lasted only an hour upstairs last night. There had been a wash basin filled with spring water, a small bed, and a fresh change of clothes, but the place was too quiet, and loneliness had seeped into her bones as soon as she'd undressed for the night. After she'd tossed and turned for what felt like forever, she'd gathered her threadbare blanket and headed downstairs, feeling her way through the darkened stables and over to the mare's stall door.

It was still awake when Harlow climbed over the door once more, the mare making no move to stop her. Harlow spread her blanket out on the fresh hay, marveling at how clean the stall was, and laid down, staring up at the animal. She spoke a little, her whispers quiet and hesitant in the still night. At first, she spoke of Nova, then her foster mother and father, and finally about the circumstances of how Nova found her, though those were more Nova's words than hers. All she remembered was smoke and fire and grief until finally the warmth of Nova's arms.

She spoke of happier times when she and Nova faced the world together arm in arm. One long ago memory rose within her, and she laughed as she recounted it in hesitant, lilting whispers. The mare nuzzled her hair, and Harlow reached with hesitant fingers to stroke its silky face. It came during yet another lesson on patience, a virtue she always struggled with, but this time, her foster mother outsmarted Nova, much to her consternation.

Their mother walked past carrying a basket of fresh bread, a treat Harlow and Nova coveted. Nova nudged her sister.

"Watch and listen," she said. Her sister rose and hurried over. Nova reached over to snatch a piece of bread from the bag she carried, but she received a smack on the hand for her effort.

"Nova! You know better. The bread is for dinner."

Her sister pouted. "Harlow and I are hungry."

"You two are always hungry." Their foster mother wasn't a pretty woman, but she was smart, and she was kind, and that was more than either one of them would have if they'd chosen the wrong village all those years ago.

"What if Harlow and I swept the porch?" Nova swung her arms and skipped beside her, Harlow watching them intently.

Their mother's eyes narrowed. "Did you not eat lunch then?"

Nova shrugged. "We did, but fresh bread from the market is the best kind of treat."

Their mother laughed and turned, her eyes searching for Harlow. As they always did, her face softened when she saw her, and Harlow's heart flipped over. The woman had not given birth to her, Nova had been adamant for her to know, but she loved her all the same.

"Sweep the porch," she began.

Nova celebrated too early.

"And peel the potatoes for supper and you can each have a hunk before dinner."

Nova's shoulders slumped, and she sighed. Their mother smiled at the both of them as she headed up the stairs and into the kitchen to work on dinner. Nova flopped back down beside Harlow who stared up at her with curiosity.

"Is that what patience means?"

Her sister snorted. "It doesn't always work when you've been outsmarted. But a little. If we're patient and do some work beforehand, we can have bread before dinner and maybe some extra with it."

"Hmm," Harlow murmured unsure what she was supposed to learn but excited about bread, nonetheless.

An equine snort brought her back to the present, the memory fading away as the great beast shifted and lay its massive bulk beside her. Harlow's heart pounded with fear, but she moved herself over to the horse and adjusted her blanket to cover them both.

She could have sworn the horse sighed. And for a brief moment, Harlow had once again felt safe.

The mare stood in the middle of the night, jostling her awake, but stayed close, keeping Harlow wrapped in safe warmth.

Her fingertips brushed against the mare's silky mane once she stood up, careful to adjust the blanket once more. "I have to go."

She was supposed to meet Shade over at the new training area half an hour after sunrise. From the way the light hit inside the stable, she had maybe fifteen minutes to dress and get over there. With a few nimble jumps, she was outside the stall and rushing upstairs to get ready.

.  .  .

HARLOW VENTURED around the corner of the training ring toward several girls standing in three separate lines. Shade stood in front, ramrod straight, his arms clasped behind his back. When he saw her, he jerked his head at the extra space in the last line.

She ducked her head and rushed around to the back, settling herself next to a tall, dark-haired girl who didn't even deign to nod at her. Stung at the chilly reception, Harlow turned to face straight ahead.

"Today, fifty young women will embark on training designed to hone your physical prowess and shape you into the first generation of new Virago, protectors of Thornewood's royal family. Your future queen created this new guard, building it from the ground up, and molding it to meet the future needs of the crown. Each of you should feel pride knowing you are hand-picked to ensure the monarchy's continued reign."

He walked in front of each girl, stopping before them, and meeting their eyes as he spoke. "The future queen's new Virago must be tough. They must be smart." Shade moved to the next girl. "Each one of you will be called to make difficult decisions one day." He moved to the next girl, a tall, lean blonde. Harlow couldn't see her face, but the back of her head was done in an elaborate braid she never could have done herself. "Some of you will be assigned to the castle. And some of you, one day, may be forced to make the ultimate sacrifice."

He turned and stepped back to the front of them. "If any of you want to back out, now is the time. No one will judge you. You'll be returned to your families and resume your life as normal."

No one moved.

Shade waited a moment longer before he nodded. "Good. My name is Shade Montello. I am the current Commander of the Kingsguard and new Commander of the Virago. The future queen has designated no rank within her guard and so you will address me as Shade. There will be no commanders, no leaders, no one is better. You are all equal and you will treat each other as such." Shade drew his sword. "No one is above any other. You will live and die as a team."

The girl in front of her shifted. A few others let out breaths of surprise.

"Ginger has kindly brought your issued gear over. She's waiting inside to measure you for your leathers. Training starts tomorrow. You'll spend today setting up your dormitory areas and ensuring everything is ready for tomorrow. Any questions?"

One girl, a small redhead, timidly rose her hand. "Will there be meals served, sir?"

"Lunch will be served in the dining facility next door at noon. Dinner promptly at sundown. No ale is allowed."

Harlow stifled her smile at the groans of dismay. Her mother had never allowed her to drink ale and when she sneaked some out of the house and Nova caught her, she'd gotten her ears boxed for her troubles. She'd never tried it again. Apparently, she was the only one who didn't enjoy a tipple before dinner. Harlow squashed building sadness within her. It wasn't the time.

Shade held a hand up to quiet them. "You will treat your body like a temple. Fresh air, fresh water, exercise, and mental stimulation. Spirits pollute the temple and will not be allowed."

Two girls stepped out of line. Shade's eyebrows went up just a hair, but he swept his arm out to the rest of us. "Please see Ginger," he said, gesturing for them to head into the dormitories. Both girls lowered their eyes and rushed past him, never once looking back at them.

"Anyone else?" he asked.

No one moved, though several of the girls shifted uncomfortably.

"Very well. Follow the other girls and settle yourselves in."

Shade gave them a shallow bow and left them in the courtyard.

THERE WERE FIFTY GIRLS, Harlow with the dubious honor of replacing the thirteenth. A few of the girls gave her the side eye when she finally found her cot, the last one on the row. The cot was small, but she was smaller still and had slept on worse over the last few weeks. Someone had left threadbare blankets and small pillows for everyone. On top of the bed lay a scarred practice sword, an old leather scabbard, and a small belt with multiple compartments.

Harlow picked up the belt and dug through the empty pockets, wondering why there were so many. What would happen during practice to make her use all of them? At the foot of the bed lay an old wooden trunk, presumably storage for things she might have brought with her. The cots looked like they'd been originally six per row. The last bed, Harlow's, looked like it had been squeezed in at the last minute.

Every girl had the same items lying on top of their cots, but most of the girls had brought at least one satchel with them. Ignoring the pain in her heart at the turn her once calm life had taken, Harlow reached down and opened the trunk. At the bottom lay a slip of paper and a small lock. She glanced over to the other girls going through their issued items but didn't see anyone else pull anything out of theirs.

Harlow lifted the items, tucking the lock into her pocket. She unfolded the paper and a whiff of scent puffed up, a tantalizing combination of vanilla and cardamom. The scent was a memory she couldn't place right away. Something recent, the smell an exotic combination of expensive spices she used to smell when the traveling market had come to her village. It wasn't until she opened the note that she realized where it had come from.

*Harlow*, the letter began. *Please accept this small token of apology for my earlier subterfuge. It isn't easy to make new friends in my position and I regret I hid my identity. If Shade asks you where the lock came from, please tell him it was a gift from an anonymous benefactor. He will not believe you, but he is a gentleman and will not press further unless it becomes an issue in the future. Best of luck in your training. I know you will do well. Desminda.*

*How did she know I could read*, she wondered. Most villagers could not, and Harlow did her best to hide that fact from others because of earlier jealousy from peers her age. Nova taught her away from the eyes of their parents and cautioned her to reveal the knowledge only when she had to.

The letter had been written in purple ink, a color so rich that Harlow had never seen it used on paper outside of the palace. In her village, the dyes came from their harvests. Pink and red being the most common from the beets her mother grew. Blue was a rarity and depended on whether they could afford cuttings of the woad plants when the traveling merchants came. She only remembered having that dye once. Nova had been beside herself, dancing with a blanket of the softest pale blue wool their mother had given them during the winter solstice.

The plants didn't grow naturally in their area, but their father had set up an ingenious sunroom inside the house, protecting it from the elements but also giving it the light it needed to thrive. He was only successful in growing one single, small crop, making the solstice gift even more precious. After that, he'd tried repeatedly with little success, even with the sunroom's help. Harlow was convinced the room had saved their lives over a few particularly hard winters when they'd brought out of season vegetables to the market for sale. Several of the villagers had questioned them, but Father had cleverly covered up the room to hide it from prying eyes until he was able to build a large partition preventing anyone from seeing what it was.

Harlow tucked the note in her pocket, intent to destroy it the first chance she got. While she appreciated the lock, she wasn't too keen on being singled out by the queen. She planned to be here as an equal member of the team and if anyone saw this, it would undermine her.

And yet... Her fingers brushed the lock in her pocket. She would use it. The stone Flora had stolen still wasn't safe but being able to secure the trunk would give her some peace of mind if she ever had to part with it.

Harlow tucked her meager belongings inside and secured it, rising only to meet the eyes of the dark-haired girl who'd stood beside her this morning.

# CHAPTER TWELVE

## MELARA

The girl had beauty with a dangerous edge. She was tall and limber, like most of the girls there, with dark hair entwined in a neat, complicated braid. Her eyes were dark as well, the color of the black sand river a few miles away. Harlow used to tuck her toes into the dark sand and marvel at the deep ebony color of it against the paleness of her skin. It made the river dark as night, a twisting force of water that slithered along the edges of her old village.

Her skin was darker than Harlow's by several shades, touched by both the sun and genetics. Next to each other, they looked like day and night, but where Harlow was quick to smile, this girl had an expression of stone, making her wonder if anything had ever caused her lips to curl with amusement.

Harlow said nothing, waiting for the girl to tell her why she loomed above her like a dark goddess.

"Thirteen is an unholy number," the stranger said.

Harlow blinked. It wasn't actually, but people in the surrounding villages lived and died by their superstition sometimes. She knew the superstition regarding number thirteen was based in myth, but it ended up being unlucky for people anyway because of the false beliefs that followed it.

"Actually," Harlow said, "the myth of the number thirteen is based on a legend about the earlier twelve gods and the thirteenth who wasn't invited. In his anger, he murdered one of the other gods and plunged the world into darkness." Harlow stared up at her, cursing her diminutive height for the millionth time. "It's a legend and has no basis in fact." She pointed to the window, the light spilling through the room, highlighting everything with a soft afternoon glow. "If it did, the two suns wouldn't exist."

The girl sneered at her. "You think you're smart, girl?"

Harlow didn't think much about herself, but Nova had forced her to read everything she got her hands on. Her head was stuffed full of facts about history and other things she'd never found a use for. "I don't see what it matters. I'm a person. I'm here. I'm in no way unlucky."

"I heard the commander took a liking to you after you broke a girl's nose." The hard-eyed girl plopped down on her bed, lifting her muddy boots onto Harlow's new, neatly placed bedspread. Anger filled her at the audacity of it and the girl's profound disrespect. She clenched her fist, her fingernails digging deep into her palms.

"Get off my bed," Harlow said through clenched teeth.

The girl grinned at her, strong, straight, bright white teeth gleaming in the soft light. She was beautiful on the outside, but Harlow began to suspect that perhaps her core was a deep, rotted hole. "Make me."

The other girls around them began to pay attention, some of them moving closer to encircle them. There wasn't a lot of room in the dormitory, especially with Harlow's extra bed shoved against the only other walkway.

She held her hands up. "I don't want to fight with you. To

be honest, I don't know why you want to fight with me. Shade will be back soon, and it's better for all of us if we try to get along." If she cared about anyone's opinion, it was his. Harlow wasn't sure why, but there was something about the man that made her search for his approval, like an unfurling flower bud seeking the sun's first light.

"Melara," the girl said. "My name is Melara. And you're unwelcome here."

Harlow stifled a sigh. "And why is that?"

Melara shifted, rubbing her muddy boots further into the thin blanket. Rage uncurled in Harlow's veins. She itched to punch the smug girl right in the face, but she wouldn't give into it. Being a maid wasn't in her veins. Whether this was remained to be seen. But if she couldn't be a maid and she couldn't be a Virago, then she'd be tossed out on her ear and her chances of finding Nova would plummet. She'd probably starve too.

One thing at a time.

"They skipped the number until you arrived. Strange don't you think? You don't belong here."

Harlow glanced around at the other girls. Most of them had already given up any pretense of not being curious about them. "Do you all think this?" she asked, loud enough that her voice ricocheted.

Several of them looked away, giving her the answer.

She crossed her arms over her chest. "I'm here and you can't make me leave."

Melara stood and stepped toward her, towering over Harlow. She had to tilt her head up to see her, which made Harlow even angrier. The injustice of it burned through her veins. She had just as much right to be here as any of them did.

But then Melara did the one thing guaranteed to set her off.

She shoved her one handed, knocking Harlow off balance. The back of her knees hit the side of the cot next to her, forcing her into a sitting position. She sprang up and faced Melara, her face burning with anger.

Nova always told her anger was useful in some situations, but that Harlow's burned too brightly to be productive. She'd worked hard to control it over the years, but there were a few times where Harlow couldn't help how she reacted.

Bullies were at the top of the list. She drew in three deep breaths and counted to ten before she stood back up, a trick Nova had taught her when Harlow felt that anger burning bright like a flame inside of her.

*"People use anger to get you to react and make a mistake. Making a mistake could mean your death, Harlow. The mark of a true, disciplined warrior is to shove it down, deep down, and lock it up tight. Keep that anger burning bright. Treat it like a coal and keep it lit, but don't let it out until you must. People will pick at you and poke you. They'll tell you that you aren't good enough."* She'd tilted Harlow's chin up at those words and she remembered how she never got angry when she had to look up at Nova because she loved her so much. *"But the only one who can judge is you. Use your anger, Harlow, but don't let it control you."* Those words came back to her, and the simmering flame inside of her died down and turned back into an ember, burning deep in the recesses of her heart.

"Leave her alone," a voice said. Harlow turned to see the tall blonde girl walking up to Melara. "And get your filthy boots off her bed, you disrespectful bitch." The girl smacked Melara's boots off Harlow's blanket.

Harlow tensed for the inevitable confrontation, but to her surprise, Melara did as she asked and stood up in one fluid motion. She stood too close to the girl, her eyes like burning coals against her dark skin.

"We're all here for better or worse, and working together is the only way we'll all make it. We don't have to be friends," she said, her eyes full of cool amusement at Melara's expense. "But we do have to get through training. If we fracture the first day, then none of us are good enough to protect the queen." Her lips curved into a smile. "Stuff your outdated prejudices back into your box of perceived slights, Melara, and work on your footwork. We both know you're terrible at it."

Melara glared at the girl's back when she turned on her heel and walked away. The blonde girl didn't even glance down at Harlow before she drifted back to her own area.

"I'd watch my back if I were you," Melara hissed at Harlow as she went.

She resisted the urge to roll her eyes at Melara's idle threat. Standing up, she murmured an apology to the girl whose bed she landed on.

"Leslie," the girl whispered, her pale cheeks coloring slightly as she finished unpacking. She said nothing else, and Harlow felt like that was all the friendliness she would get tonight.

But she glanced over at the blonde girl who'd stepped up to stop their inevitable fight, and wondered what her ulterior motive was. Kindness was in short supply she'd come to find, and the feeling of a favor owed hung heavy over her head.

Nova had once told her a favor held for ransom was no favor at all. She now knew what her sister had meant by it.

# CHAPTER THIRTEEN

### DAY ONE

The first day of training began when the moon still hung heavy in the sky and Harlow's limbs were weak with exhaustion. She woke with a jerk at the scream of a bird of prey right outside her window, her heart pounding with fear at the unfamiliar surroundings.

She longed for the mare's warmth at her back and the simplicity of waking up in the stable with only the smell of hay and animals surrounding her. The sound of steady and heavy breaths deep in sleep fell around her. Harlow stared up at the ceiling, willing herself to calm down. Nova had told Harlow to go to the castle, so this was what her sister wanted, wasn't it?

Somewhat. She'd never mentioned the Virago, and Harlow wasn't sure if this was what Nova would want for her at all, though she knew Nova would know Harlow wasn't exactly cut out to be a maid.

She'd hide out every time her mother tried to force her to do her chores and nine times out of ten, Nova would find her down at the black river trying her hand at fishing with an old stick and some string she'd pilfered from her father's workshop. She'd fashioned a hook out of an old earring she'd bought from the market during a particularly good winter harvest. Her mother couldn't be angry at her if she returned home with a basket full of fresh fish.

The memory of one particular day came back to her, flooding her mind with a memory so powerful tears sprang to her eyes. She even remembered the color of dress she wore that day. Pale yellow, one of her mother's old dresses tailored to fit her by her mother's skilled fingers with a needle.

Nova had found Harlow even though she'd moved at least half a mile down the river from the last time she'd caught her. Harlow had sighed at the sight of Nova's lithe body sliding down the dirt and rocks of the hill, down by the river's edge.

"You plod through the woods like a randy bull searching after a cow," she greeted Harlow. Nova wore no smile today. Unusual, and it made Harlow's fingers clench tight against the stick she held steady in the water. She'd heard the waters here were stocked with pink, fleshy fish that might fetch a pretty price at the market.

Nova had never been great at fishing, but Harlow had always had a little more patience than her sister. Nova was good at other things, things involving people. Words and stories and manipulating people to do what she wanted. Never her family, only others outside that circle. When things got lean, they could count on Nova convincing someone to part with food or drink or fabric or a number of odds and ends. It had always fascinated Harlow, but she never had the knack for it.

Harlow stumbled over her words more often than not, saying the wrong thing at the wrong time or saying something true when a clever lie was called for.

"One day I won't be here," Nova said.

Harlow jerked, her stare a brand against Nova's face. "What?"

Her sister smiled then, but Harlow always knew when

Nova didn't want to. It was a false smile full of teeth but no heart. "One day I'll grow up, marry, and move far away from you."

Harlow laughed then. "You won't marry," she said with all the confidence her youth and security could offer here. "You said yourself that men are brash and full of bluster and prone to violence."

Nova slung an arm over her shoulders. "You're right. Perhaps I won't marry, but one day I'll leave this place to find my future and I want you to be able to take care of yourself."

Harlow jerked the pole when she felt a nibble from under the surface of the dark water. A fish launched itself from the river, an elegant arc of silver and glittering beads of water in the high afternoon light. She grinned at Nova. "Well, I know I can feed myself," she said as she slowly maneuvered the fish to the shore.

Nova grinned back. "Perhaps I should take you with me, then. I'll fight marauders with my trusty sword arm and you'll keep us both fed with your odd fishing device and savvy way with nature."

Harlow leaned against her, content in that moment, breathing in her sister's soft, comforting scent. "You'll starve if you leave without me," she said, only partially joking. They both fell silent for a few moments, Harlow only shifting to toss the hook, wriggling with a tiny guppy, back into the water. "I go wherever you go. Sisters don't leave each other."

But they had, and they did and here Harlow lay, alone in the dark, on an uncomfortable cot, her heart aching with the memories of the family she once had.

A loud clanging had Harlow shooting out of bed, glancing frantically around, searching for a weapon to defend herself with. The doors opened and with it, a shadowed figure strode in, moonlight gleaming against his dark hair.

She relaxed as she recognized Shade.

"Wake up!" he barked as he walked by each of their beds, kicking out at the legs of the cots when the girls inside them groaned and rolled over. "Day one of training. Get your gear on and line up outside!" He stopped at Harlow's cot and nodded once at her. She was the only one awake and standing. Without a word, he turned around and walked back outside.

Harlow blinked at his back and stood there in silence for a moment before she reached for the key tucked into her pocket and unlocked her trunk.

*Day one*, she thought. Day one of the rest of her life.

She shivered. Something lay ahead of her, something no one could see, but she sensed it. Even though she didn't know what it was, she hoped it at least led her back to Nova, to family, to someone who cared about her.

It was the only thing she wanted.

# CHAPTER FOURTEEN

## THE DARK KNIGHT

S hade loomed like a dark knight. He stood still and quiet and waited for them to line up, his rapt gaze not missing a thing. All the girls were sleep deprived, some of them more than Harlow. She'd dozed off last night to the sounds of muffled tears and sniffles. While she felt empathy, she wasn't sympathetic as she might have been had things been different for her. She'd lost everything, and it had hardened her heart more than she thought might be normal.

They were here. They were fed. They had an opportunity to make a difference in the world. For those reasons, Harlow felt they were luckier than most everyone else.

Shade hadn't allowed them to break their fast this morning. Instead, he stood in front of them holding a wicked looking sword that glinted when the light struck it, a shimmer of silver in the soft light of the moon. Every one of them held a wooden practice sword— a sorry looking piece of equipment, scarred and battered, its better days long behind it.

Several of the girls had quickly oiled their swords before they'd rushed outside in an effort to impress Shade, she assumed, but Harlow had not. Why would you oil wood when you're probably going to use it for practice? It would look better but slip right out of your hand when you tried to use it.

With a fluid movement, Shade bent and swayed, the sword held high above his head. "Sword work is an art," he began. "A brutal art ending in blood and pain. To know the sword is to know violence. And to know violence in this kingdom is to know freedom." He straightened. "The first rule of the sword is never to raise it in anger. The second is to never unsheathe your sword unless you plan to use it. The only exception is to maintain it."

Melara shifted uncomfortably beside her. She was one of the girls Harlow heard sniffling in the night, her cot only three away from her. Harlow knew what it was to miss your family, so she said nothing, and she wouldn't use it against her if Melara approached her. It was no folly to pine for loved ones, but Harlow's tears had dried the night she'd left her foster parents dead in their beds and set out to find a better life.

"Easton, Fischer, Stuart, and Belgrave. Step up."

Harlow sucked in a surprised breath and stepped out of line, directly behind Melara. The other two girls were familiar, but she hadn't spoken to them yet.

"Fischer with Belgrave," Shade said, moving her to one side. Melara he moved directly in front of her. Harlow swallowed down a groan of frustration. Melara's lips curled into a cruel smile as they faced each other.

He did the same with the other two girls until they stood a few feet away from each other, all holding their practice swords awkwardly.

"How many of you have ever used a sword before, outside of practice?" Shade asked, walking around them in a circle.

Only Melara raised her hand. *Of course she has*, Harlow thought. She probably stabbed anyone who looked at her wrong right in the heart. Harlow had only picked up a sword a couple of times. Nova preferred to teach her hand to hand. Nine times out of ten, she ended up covered in bruises after one of those sessions, but Nova made her practice at least a few times a week so she wouldn't forget. Her sister used a dagger more than anything, though neither of them had ever killed anyone.

That she knew of.

She'd kept the dagger sharp, clean, and lethal and used it on everything from skinning rabbits to peeling fruit. Harlow never quite got the hang of it and most of the time, she'd cut off a huge chunk of fruit when trying to skin off the peel.

Her sister tried to teach her how to use a sword. Harlow had whacked her too hard with it in all of her clumsy strikes, so after a week Nova finally gave up and limped away. Then it was the bow and arrow, which was even more disastrous and resulted in one of their neighbors getting a nasty surprise during their breakfast. It wasn't until Nova introduced her to the axe that Nova felt like she'd found home.

But there were no axes here, only cheap wooden swords, so she had to do her best with what she was given.

"What experience do you have?" he asked Melara. The girl grinned and swirled the sword in her hand in an elaborate arc.

But instead of impressing Shade, he knocked the sword out of her hand in a move so swift none of them, especially Melara, saw it coming. The girl jumped back with a hiss, holding on to her sword hand with her other.

"Do you think that will save you when a better swordsman sticks the pointy end of his blade in your throat because you're too busy trying to impress him?"

Melara swallowed, her face red with humiliation.

"We don't twirl our swords, girl. Do you see a parade around here?"

Her eyebrows furrowed in confusion.

"Do you?" Shade pressed. "Are there men and woman twirling swords and weapons for the enjoyment of dewy-eyed children? Jesters and bards? Elephants and horses dressed in holiday finery prancing up the main square?"

"No, Shade," Melara said, a touch of belligerence in her tone.

He stepped in front of her, his sword held loosely at his side. His expression wasn't angry, more disappointed. Harlow squirmed at his perusal, glad it wasn't on her. Though if she tried to twirl a sword, there was a distinct possibility of the pointy end winding up in someone's throat due to her sheer ineptitude.

"We are not duelists," he continued. "We are soldiers, warriors sworn into the service of the queen. Knowing how to twirl a sword is a party trick, Belgrave. Knowing how to find an opening to stick the pointy end of your sword into an enemy threatening your way of life during the heat of a bloody battle is the lesson. Save your tricks for someone else. They do not belong with the Virago."

Melara swallowed and bobbed her head in acknowledgment, seeming chastised by his words. It wasn't until he walked away that she met Harlow's gaze, a vicious fire burning within her eyes. Harlow knew at that moment whatever anger she held toward Shade would be coming for her soon.

She'd never missed her axe or her sister more than she had in this moment.

# CHAPTER FIFTEEN

## IMPALEMENT

U nder Shade's direction, they practiced by themselves, with him gently adjusting their feet or their positions as he supervised.

"Chin up," he told one girl. "Looking at your feet means not seeing the stab come your way." Then, "No. Hold it like this. Firmly, but not with a death grip." Harlow saw him grimace as he picked up the weapon. She was one of the girls who'd oiled her sword.

"What in the world?" he muttered, holding the wooden weapon dangling from two fingers. Shade held up a hand. "Stop. Who else oiled their swords before practice?"

Over half the girls raised their hands. Shade blinked for a long moment, then nodded once, a sharp expression that looked like it told him everything he needed to know. "Drop your swords," he barked.

Harlow didn't hesitate. When the swords were at their feet, Shade spoke again. "Rub them in the dirt thoroughly, then pick them up again."

He waited for all the girls to finish. "Now run your fingers over the wood. No slip and a possibly firmer grip?"

The girls murmured their agreement. "Oil at night and wipe in the morning. Never come onto the field with a freshly oiled sword. You could drop it on a moment's notice. And then what happens?" he asked, a dark brow arching.

"You'll impale yourself on the pointy end or end up on someone else's pointy end?" Several titters of laughter erupted in the line. It was the tall girl, the one who interceded with Melara, who had spoken.

Shade didn't crack a smile. His face still looked calm and cold. "Exactly. Impalement is serious business in the infirmary. The nurses get all a-twitter when they see a recruit coming in with an extra steel appendage."

Harlow's brows went up. Had Shade just made a...joke? She narrowed her eyes as she watched him, but the man didn't even crack a smile. A shudder went down her spine at the thought of nurses eager to see the clumsy Virago impalement injuries. The other girls eyed him warily.

They would all be much more careful to avoid the possibility of impaling themselves in the future.

But Shade wasn't finished. "Each day, you will wake up before dawn and practice your sword work. Tomorrow you'll meet Thornewood's Sword Master, Gillano Medevechi. He will walk you each through a series of practice bouts. There is no other person stronger with the sword, so you will listen and heed his instruction. Each day will also consist of lessons in history, weaponry, warfare, and day-to-day household management. After that, you'll be led in physical conditioning for one hour per day."

All the girls looked around at each other, confused by the last couple of words.

"He means exercises," Harlow whispered. No one in her village knew what it was either until Nova came back from one of her many trips touting the health benefits of it. People didn't exercise. They worked on their farms and in their houses and they tried to survive. When Nova had taught her such things as push-ups and pull ups, weird things that made her stomach ache for days and long, deep stretches that made her want to curl up like a cat, she found herself keeping up with it. Soon enough, she was stronger and more limber than she'd ever been. Nova refused to disclose where she'd learned it, but some of the women in the village didn't care. They flocked to Nova and asked her to teach them. It was hard not to notice how Nova had gone from reed thin to lithe and muscular in only a few short months.

It almost caused an uprising with the men in the village though, and half the women who wanted to learn stopped coming. The other half kept up with lessons in secret, though it would be hard for their husband's not to notice the changes in their wives. Gaining strength of your own changed the dynamic in a relationship. Even in their own house, it happened. As Nova sought more and more independence, their mother clung tighter and tighter to them both.

"Who said that?" Shade demanded. He turned to her and Melara, his eyes narrowing. "Fischer?"

"Yes, Shade."

"You're familiar with physical conditioning?"

Harlow nodded, the lump in her throat tightening. She wiped her sweaty hands on her breeches and stepped forward. A bead of sweat rolled down her neck.

"Show me," he said.

Confused, Harlow blinked. "Show you?"

He nodded. "Show us all what you do for physical conditioning. It's not a common concept with girls or women in the kingdom or in the surrounding villages. Girls are raised with the knowledge they will learn how to run a home and eventually become a wife and mother." He turned to face everyone.

"Conditioning will make you stronger. You'll run faster and longer. You'll breathe deeper and feel better. You'll turn your skinny limbs into muscle, which will help you lift things easier, including your swords. Conditioning isn't a commoner's concept. They work from sundown to sunup, but their work is of a different nature. Conditioning works on particular muscle groups and involves the entire body. Fischer here will show us what she does to keep herself in peak physical condition."

Harlow mentally grimaced at that. Peak physical condition might be an overstatement. She'd been sporadically practicing since her parent's death and had felt the lack of strength in her bones since she'd fallen behind on it. With a hard swallow, Harlow stepped into the open space and bent herself in half. She touched her head to her shins and held the position for about twenty seconds. A few of the girls gasped. "The lack of proper stretching locks up your muscles and prevents you from moving. It also invites injury." She recited Nova's words back to the Virago.

"Witchcraft," was whispered from the back. Harlow stilled, fear making her heart rattle in her chest.

Shade whipped his head in the direction of the voice. "Not witchcraft," he boomed out, "and I would urge discretion and caution when using that word. Harlow speaks of anatomy, the way the muscles and ligaments connect to the bone and the way they control the body. If you don't use your muscles, they contract and eventually atrophy." He swept his gaze around all of them. "We've all had a bedridden relative at one time. What happens when they have to get up and walk?"

A redhead girl from the back spoke up. "They can't. My grandfather can't walk anymore unless we help him. It's like he has to re-learn again."

"Yes," Shade said. "We keep our minds and our bodies

sharp and strong." He motioned at Harlow with his fingers. "Keep going."

She shifted into a squat, holding her hands out in front of herself, and stayed in the position for almost thirty seconds, then repeated the motion. Shade motioned for her to go on, so Harlow went through the entire series of exercises Nova had shown her including the on the floor exercises. She contorted her body into several different positions until she finally lay flat on her back and out of breath.

Shade reached his hand out to her and pulled her up in one liquid motion. "Good," he said close to her ear, his voice pitched low for only her ears. "Keep an eye out for Melara. She will come after you soon."

He let Harlow go and turned like nothing had happened. "Break your fast," he boomed out. "Return in forty-five minutes without your swords."

Harlow didn't have to be told twice. Scooping up her sword, she rushed through the other girls and hurried to the Great Hall, keeping at least two steps ahead of the other girls.

# CHAPTER SIXTEEN

## FRUIT AND FIGHTS

The Great Hall fed all the soldiers, the Virago, and anyone who worked with the horses or other animals. Even this early in the morning, it was hustling and bustling with people.

Harlow was the first person in line. She'd scooped up a wooden tray and scooped orange colored soup from a tureen, adding a healthy portion of crusty white bread on top. With her tray in her hand, she headed over to an empty table and sat down, popping up one more time to get a cup of tepid water and a tiny cup of juice. The juice in Thornewood was precious and only in season once a year. Most of it went to the royalty, but some, usually the pulpiest parts, went to the Great Hall for the soldiers. The cup was barely larger than a thimble, so Harlow tossed it back, allowing the fragrant orange liquid to slide down her throat. It had been a while since she'd had any form of juice. Her mother had grown oranges on the property but sold the best ones at the marketplace. They got the bruised, scarred fruit that tasted just as good. Some of her favorite memories were waking up to the sound of her mother smashing oranges and gathering the juice into a glass. Harlow remembered racing Nova to see who could grab it first.

This fruit wasn't an orange. The unfamiliar taste slid down her throat, surprising Harlow. She stiffened and waited, but it tasted of a mix between a lemon and orange, a combination she'd never experienced. She'd try to find out what it was later, but her stomach rumbled in protest at the smell of the soup in front of her.

A few minutes later, the tall blonde girl sat down at her table followed by the darker girl, Melara, and another girl with long brown hair messily tied up in a tail.

Harlow's gaze flicked over Melara, even as she itched to move down to another seat. Melara grinned at her. "So, you condition, do you?"

Harlow didn't even bother to answer the question. People like Melara answered it for themselves. "It won't help you. You can condition all you want to, but when my sword slices through the soft skin of your belly, it won't matter."

"What did I ever do to you?" she asked quietly.

The brunette girl looked away. Bloom's gaze rested steadily on the both of them. Walking away was always a problem with their kingdom. People couldn't afford to step into someone else's battle. When they did, they died. What was left was a kingdom of apathy and distrust. Her eyes lingered on Bloom, but the girl seemed perfectly content to stay out of it.

Melara snorted. "You're the number thirteen. You're unlucky." She leaned forward and sneered. "And you took the slot that should have been offered to my sister."

Harlow sat up straighter at that. "So, you don't care about the number thirteen. You care about your sister not being the one who took the number and my bed." It wasn't a question, though Harlow didn't know the details. "I was offered a spot in the Virago, and I accepted. I can't say what happened with your sister, but I'm here because my place was earned and given."

Melara leaned forward, so close to Harlow their noses

almost touched. "You didn't earn this. Someone saw your pretty face and your golden hair and they offered it to you." She snorted. "Back in my village, a girl like you would be flat on her back at her first bleeding. Pretty and innocent, you'd be fatted up like a lamb to slaughter and offered up to any single man who hadn't lost his fertility in the mine accident."

Harlow stared at Melara, her anger beginning to rise. Everyone knew about the accident, but the state of the villagers' fertility had been a well-kept secret. "Do we define someone's heart by the state of their loins, then? Is this what we've become? We are people, Melara. People driven by love. By purpose."

Melara snorted and drank her juice in one quick swallow. "Listen to you, the little idealist. Everything is so wonderful and perfect, and one person can make so much of a difference." She waved her hand in dismissal. "You don't have what it takes to be here. Everyone knows it."

Harlow sat up straight, breathed deeply through her nose, and counted to ten in her head. She didn't want to be here. At her old home, she had a room of her own, a comfortable bed, food in the stocks, chickens, and land. Here she had a cot and a small trunk filled with few meager possessions. Everyone she loved was gone. Everything she knew was destroyed. Harlow wasn't a warrior. She never wanted to be one. But she was here where she had a purpose. She'd done what her sister wanted. She was in the castle, training to be one of the queen's elite guards. Whether she would make it through the training remained to be seen, but sitting here now, across from a girl wearing a sneer and judging her for everything she stood for, she knew she would rather die than relent.

Harlow stood, fingering the wooden sword in her belt and wishing it was her favored axe. It was stolen from her the first night she'd left her parent's home, and if she found the person who swiped it, she would kill them.

"Stand, Melara," Harlow said. The sounds of conversation died down. She felt like she was in a tunnel– she and this girl who hated her for no real reason. "Stand and fight me. If you want to secure your sister's place, then fight me for it. If you win, I'll stand aside and let her take my place. But if I win, you will never speak of this again and you will find your place in the Virago and work with us, with your teammates to secure Thornewood."

Melara's brows lifted. She stood, her fingers gripping the wooden sword. Holding that sword made them all look like little children rushing through the streets of the village playing pretend soldiers. If the situation wasn't so serious, she might have laughed.

Maybe that's what they were doing. Pretending they had any control over this, over what they were or were forced to become. Women had little choice over their life in this kingdom. It was grow up, learn the ways to manage a house, find a husband, then bear children. Stepping onto the castle grounds made her feel out of control for the first time in her life. She had the opportunity to learn something, to learn how to not only defend herself but the future queen. This was how she'd find her sister. And if people like Melara tried to get in her way, she would plow right through them. She didn't care what it took. Harlow would find her way back to her family.

Her fingers gripped her practice sword tight, but she let her fingers uncurl. It dropped to the ground and Harlow kicked it away. She lifted her right hand and motioned Melara forward with her fingers. Sword fighting wasn't natural for her. If she tried to battle Melara like this, she would lose.

The girl stepped forward, keeping her sword close. Melara struck, her speed breathtaking, the weapon a blur as she tried to knock Harlow aside. With a quick back step, Harlow dodged Melara's strike. She took a deep breath and let her sister's words whisper into her memory. "*Swords are a tool, one of many weapons meant to silence you. All you need is your body. Know when to strike and when to walk away.*"

Melara moved like a snake, sinuous and graceful. At first glance, Harlow couldn't see an opening, but as she watched closer, she realized Melara favored her right side by just a hair. She was left-handed which put her at a disadvantage any way, but she stepped heavier on the right. Harlow had no weapon, only her wits.

Bouncing on her heels, she waited until Melara got close enough to strike her with the sword. When her muscles tensed and she edged toward her, Harlow ducked and spun out of the way, punching upwards right through Melara's guard. The blow hit home, landing square in the middle of Melara's stomach.

Melara sucked in a gasp of air at the blow and slowly sank to her knees. The sword slipped from her hand as she reached up to protect the area Harlow had struck and seeing her weakness, she struck twice more— one sharp blow to the face and another to her chest.

Blood streamed from her nose and Melara dropped like a stone, her mouth gaping open like a fish gasping for water as she curled onto her side. One hand curved over her stomach and the other covered her nose as angry tears flowed from her eyes. Tense silence fell in the dining hall. The other Virago's eyes were on Harlow, hot and accusing. The injustice angered Harlow. Hadn't they seen that Melara provoked the fight?

Abandoning her breakfast, Harlow ducked her head, the weight of everyone's judgment prickling against her spine, and rushed out of the dining hall.

# CHAPTER SEVENTEEN

## THE SCENT OF ROSES

Harlow burst through the doors, hot and angry tears filling her eyes, blurring her vision. Fighting never used to be a part of her life, aside from Nova teaching her how to spar and defend herself. Ever since she'd left, all Harlow did was fight.

She pulled in a choked breath of air and blindly made her way down the hall trying to find an area she could slip into and pull herself together. Crying wasn't an option for her. She would not show weakness.

A hand reached out and plucked her from the hall. Harlow squeaked in surprise. Strong, warm hands steadied her. She looked up into the Prince of Roses strange green eyes. A gasp pulled from her throat as she tried to step away.

"Stop," he said quietly, both of his hands on her shoulders. "Calm down, Harlow. Stay here for a moment."

She blinked up at him, her heart fluttering like a trapped animal.

Lucien's mouth was turned down, his eyes focused on something behind her. They stood in a dark alcove, his body too close to hers, but it didn't feel uncomfortable, just...odd. "Be still," he whispered in the quiet. "Shade is out there looking for you, along with that tall, strange girl."

"The one with the braid?" Harlow asked stupidly.

A soft snort escaped him. "Yes. That's a perfect description. Bloom is her name, I think."

She stood with him for a few moments and ever so slowly, she felt the tension slip away.

"What happened?" he demanded.

Harlow shook her head. This wasn't a future king's problem. It was a stupid squabble with stupid girls. Perhaps handling it like she had was a mistake. Maybe she should have used her words. A smile curved over her lips at the thought. Nova always told her words were for bards and fists were for girls because men never listened to them anyway. Might as well be strong and fierce rather than weak and subjugated.

She sobered. Maybe Nova hadn't been the best influence on her after all. The path her life had taken was an utter surprise, and while Harlow had taken the lessons Nova had imparted to heart, she never once thought they would be applicable to her.

But by the same token, Nova was right. No one listened to girls. And wasn't that strange in a kingdom like this where woman ruled? Seemed like they only listened to people with power.

"It's nothing," Harlow whispered.

Lucien's lips curved in an odd smile. "You single handedly took down a girl with at least four inches of height over yours in front of hundreds of witnesses. She'll be in the clinic for a while and more than likely live with a handy bump on her formerly perfect nose. You've a target on your back if you hadn't one before."

Harlow sighed, a frustrated puff of air. "I don't know what it is. Stupid superstitions about the number thirteen. I took her sister's place, I guess."

Lucien's eyes cleared. "Ah. Well, that's because you broke another girl's nose in the housekeeping quarters." His eyes filled with amusement. "Perhaps you can see the pattern here?"

A soft laugh burst from her lips even as embarrassment crept up her cheeks. "She stole from me." The shame she should have felt never came. Harlow despised people who stole from others.

"I didn't say she didn't deserve it. Shade does like his blood-thirsty females. Desminda will need people like you around her as she matures into Thornewood's queen. The commander of the guard would know which was the better choice for her personal guard. Melara is a fool blinded by loyalty to her family."

Harlow said nothing, slightly turning to see where Shade and the other girl were.

"They're gone," Lucien said. "Do you feel better?"

"I do. Thank you."

He nodded once and released her, stepping further away. "I owed you for my disastrous showing in the stables the other day."

"What day?" Harlow asked with an impish smile, already poised to step out from the alcove.

A grin bloomed on his face. "Right. I have no idea what I'm talking about." With a short bow to her, Lucien slipped out of the alcove and into the hallway, adjusting his deep purple vest and looking for all intents and purposes like he was out for a lazy day's stroll.

Shaking her head, Harlow leaned her head against the cold stone of the wall and took in a few deep breaths. She would answer for what she did to Melara. Whether to Shade or her fellow Virago, she wasn't quite sure.

With a deep inhale, Harlow stepped out of the alcove and headed back to the dormitories.

. . .

SHADE ASKED them to be back within forty-five minutes, but the incident in the hall hadn't taken long. Her stomach was a growling reminder of her lack of food. Feeling miserable, Harlow detoured on her way back and stepped into the stables. It was still early by castle standards, but a few people milled around inside, getting ready for the day. They gave her a curious glance when she walked over to the stall holding the great mare. When she stepped too close, a boy about her own age spoke up.

"Miss! I wouldn't. She's a mean one and the master won't be inclined to sympathy when she takes a piece out of you." A lock of blond hair fell over his face. He looked familiar somehow, like she'd seen him somewhere. His hazel eyes widened when he saw her and he looked away, abruptly turning his back to her. "She'll bite you," he said gruffly. "It's the only warning I'll give."

Harlow's brow furrowed. "Have we met?"

His shoulders tensed. He was on the shorter side, though not as small as Harlow. "I'd imagine not. I'm new here."

"I'm from Thornehollow. Though I grew up in a village closer to the castle called Thornewilde. My name is Harlow."

"Lant," the boy said. He still faced away from her.

"Perhaps you know my sister?" She wasn't sure why she was pressing this boy to speak with her, but there was something about him she couldn't put her finger on. "Nova?"

"No." He bent down and grabbed a bucket, filling it with feed. "If you know what's good for you, you'll be gone before Quartermaster James returns. He doesn't take too well to strangers around his horses." Without waiting for her to respond, Lant left her alone in the stables. The others had already gone to do their own chores. She stared after his back for a long moment trying to place where she'd seen him before, finally shaking her head at his strange behavior when she failed to place him.

The mare was just as large as she remembered, her coat shimmering a coal black in the low light. The two suns were high in the sky, but the stables made their own shade to keep the animals cool. She reached her fingers over the stall and the beast bumped its head against them.

"I can't stay long," she said, stroking its silky head. "I'd much rather sleep here with you than stay in the dorm with those beastly girls." A sigh escaped her and with a look in both directions, Harlow hopped into the stall and stood next to the beast, leaning her head against its chest. She no longer feared the mare when she knew she should, but there was a kinship with it she'd never felt before. "I don't belong here," she whispered. "I don't think you do either."

The horse whickered, its breath warm against her face.

"I'm angry." The confession fell from her lips. "At everything. Nova, my parents, myself. Melara." Tears fell from her eyes. "I can't stop being angry. It's consuming me and I don't know what to do." The warmth of the beast comforted her, its presence an intimidating but solid weight against her body. "I want my family back," she whispered.

"Harlow?"

She stiffened, a cold sweat breaking out against her skin.

*Shade.*

Harlow squeezed her eyes shut, wanting to meld into the wood and disappear.

But when she looked up, Shade loomed over the top of the stall, his eyes wide with horror and surprise. "Are you *mad*?" he blurted, his gaze tracking between me and the mare behind me.

The horse reared its head and neighed.

"Get out of there," he said, his voice calm, but there was a tremor to the words. He held his hand over the stall. The beast regarded him for a moment before jerking forward to nip at him. A curse ripped from his lips.

Harlow lay a hand against the mare's body. "Calm," she whispered. "He is a friend."

Whether she was lying remained to be seen, but she didn't want to see Shade hurt. Ignoring his hand, Harlow gripped one of the wooden beams and scampered up and over the stall, landing on the other side.

Shade gripped her by the upper arms and looked her over. "That was the stupidest thing I've ever seen!" he hissed, his grip tightening until it was almost painful.

"She won't hurt me," Harlow insisted.

"She is a wild beast!" Shade inhaled, his nostrils flaring. She watched as he got himself under control. Releasing her, he stepped away. "Follow me. You and I have much to discuss."

Harlow glanced back at the mare before she rushed after Shade, her stomach lurching in anticipation of what the next few moments might bring.

## CHAPTER EIGHTEEN

### EVERYTHING HURTS & WE'RE DYING

O nly Melara sat in the dormitory when they returned. Her nose had been bandaged and two black eyes were beginning to form on her face. Harlow stepped out behind Shade and met her gaze. A promise of retribution glowed within those dark depths.

Shade motioned for Harlow to take the cot opposite Melara, probably a good idea since the other girl looked positively murderous. He stood between them but slightly off to the side so they could see each other, his hands clasped behind his back. His face was blank, his eyes glowing with ire. She still couldn't place his age, though this close to him in the daylight, he couldn't have been more than thirty-five. A young age to be in the position he was, but if the stories were true, he'd more than earned his place in the Kingsguard and now with the Virago.

"What is the issue here?" he asked. The question wasn't directed to either of them and Harlow hesitated to answer because she felt like it would sound like she was complaining. She would not do that or anything to jeopardize her place here. Whether she belonged here would be revealed soon enough, but she'd rather die than go back to working with Flora.

Melara glared, her face a storm of anger. Shade waited, the seconds ticking by in one of the most awkward silences Harlow had ever experienced. When neither answered, Shade snorted and pinched the skin between his brows. "We cannot be successful if we do not work together. Whatever this conflict is, you will have to work it out." He turned away from them, looking outside, his shoulders broad and strong. Harlow took a moment to really look at him as she contemplated whether to be the first one to speak. She hadn't done anything wrong. Well, maybe breaking someone's nose wasn't exactly right, but defending herself was not a crime.

Shade wore his usual black, the color an apparent staple of his wardrobe since she'd never seen him wear another. He was armed to the teeth— his sword strapped on his left and a wicked blade on his right. His dark hair curled past his collar, and he moved with a lethal grace, silent like a cat, years of sword work and conditioning evident with every step. His shoulders lifted and fell with a sigh.

Harlow felt Melara's gaze on her. She turned and looked at her. Whatever Melara saw in her eyes made her blink and look away.

"Melara doesn't think I belong here," Harlow said when the silence dragged on too long.

Melara gasped in surprise. One of Harlow's brows rose as Melara's eyes narrowed, daring her to deny it. The girl's jaw clenched.

Shade sat on someone's cot, his posture loose and graceful. "Oh?" he asked, not looking at either one of them. He studied his fingernails for a moment then folded his hands neatly in his lap. "Melara, is this true?"

Melara swallowed hard. She quivered with rage. Harlow would pay for this dearly, but in this moment, she thoroughly enjoyed Melara's discomfort. "My sister should be here," she rasped, her voice thick and sludgy from the blow to her nose.

Shade tilted his head in acknowledgment. "And you think you know who should protect our queen better than me?"

Harlow blinked, every cell in her body screaming *danger, danger!* She cast a look at Melara and even though she hated the girl, she wanted to scream at her to back down and step away. Whatever this was wouldn't end well. But Melara, the stupid, stupid girl, spoke again.

"She deserved a place here."

"The Virago originally had fifty spots available. The thirteenth was given to someone who showed great promise when your sister failed to. I could have allowed your sister into the Virago, but I can guarantee she would have failed out in the first two months."

Melara gasped and stood, her palms clenched into fists. "Lies!"

Shade stood in one powerful movement. "Question me again, Belgrave, and you will find yourself tossed back into the backwater village you came from. Harlow is here to stay. You two will make up your differences and learn to work as a team." His gaze slid over to Harlow. "And you will refrain from solving everything with violence." Shade's eyes hardened as he spoke. "Becoming a Virago takes strength— both physical and mental. "Fists are the last resort in diplomacy. The future queen will not have a bunch of thugs as guards. We learn to use our body second only to our mind." He looked away. "Are we clear, Trainees?"

Harlow stood. "Yes, Shade." She bowed her head. Melara wouldn't back down. She'd just have to figure out how to work around it. Though not being able to punch her nemisis disappointed Harlow more than she thought it would. And she wasn't sure what that said about her.

Shade nodded to them both. "Everyone else is waiting outside. Gather yourself and be outside in two minutes."

Melara and Harlow stood mere feet apart. The girl's glare hadn't softened. If anything, it became a brand on her skin, a furious inferno Harlow struggled against.

"You'll pay for this," Melara hissed as she swept past her and out to the training grounds.

A sigh escaped Harlow as she watched her go. She continued to pay every single day she was here and without finding her sister. What was one more thing?

HARLOW FOUND a place in line next to the tall girl with the elegant braid, Bloom, if she remembered correctly. She couldn't see a thing over any of the other Virago's shoulders and had to strain to hear Shade as he spoke. There was tension in the air, all of them unsure how to act or what to say given what had transpired earlier.

Guilt filled Harlow even though she knew it wasn't all of her fault. Only part of it was.

"Go!" Shade said. Realizing she'd missed the majority of Shade's words, Harlow stood there like an imbecile until she saw everyone else take off running. Not knowing where they were going, she broke into a short jog, following behind the other Virago.

Running was up there with sewing for her. Necessary for certain things, but a massive pain in the neck. If only she could get the benefits of running with the physical expenditure sewing took. Her mother could knit a massive blanket without breaking a sweat. But running felt like Harlow had waded in quicksand and drowned in humidity. She followed close behind two other girls, the redhead and someone with dark skin and short cropped hair. Neither spoke to her, but their shoulders tensed when she came closer.

Tears pricked in the back of her eyes. It was only the first day. This too would pass.

THIRTY MINUTES LATER, she lay a few feet away from another girl as they both hurled up their guts. Shade loomed over them, a disapproving glare on his face. Several other girls lay flat on their backs, heaving great gasps of air into their lungs. Bloom and another girl seemed fine, the first looking upon them with no judgment but cool amusement in her eyes.

When the meager contents of Harlow's stomach were gone, she sat up with a groan, holding her aching head with both hands. Her hands and feet pulsed with the beat of her wildly pumping heart. Not waking up tomorrow seemed a distinct possibility if she felt this bad right now.

"All of you are in piss poor shape," Shade murmured more to himself than them. "Tomorrow we will work on upper body strength. Everyone get up and walk back to the dormitories. We're done for today. Spend the rest of the day organizing your areas. Ginger will come find you and assign you chores based on today's observations."

A few brave girls groaned, but Harlow stayed silent. Misery leached into her bones, but she'd press through this. She had to. There was nothing else for her.

He motioned for them to get up. Harlow tried but her body didn't want to cooperate. She moaned in pain, rocked to her knees, and sat there for a moment waiting for the dizziness to pass.

"Dehydration is real and dangerous," Shade remarked. "Water skins are on your cots. Keep them filled at all times and drink more water than you think you'll need." He paused as they finally all got to their feet, Harlow and a couple of others swaying with fatigue. "You'll visit the privy more often than you like, but once your body acclimates, you'll notice you feel much better."

He nodded to them. "Released, Virago." Shade jogged away.

Harlow glared at his back. "Show off," she muttered.

Bloom snorted in amusement. "Come on, Fischer," she said, holding out her elbow. "You look like you're about to collapse and it'd be a shame to have a third broken nose around here."

She blinked in surprise, wondering how she'd heard about Flora, but took her arm all the same. Her body shivered with weakness even as she forced herself to stay in step with the girl's long strides. As soon as they stepped inside the dormitory, Harlow weaved and lurched toward her bed before collapsing face first onto the scratchy blanket.

# CHAPTER NINETEEN

## BOOKS!

Night had fallen by the time Harlow awoke, her eyes gritty with tears and dirt. A soft puff of breath escaped her which turned into a quiet sob as every ache and pain, bruise and scratch made itself known. The sounds of quiet, steady breathing reached her ears. She twisted her face to the high window. Stars twinkled outside, the night dark and cloudless.

Her stomach growled in protest. Harlow slowly sat up and swung her legs onto the ground. She steadied her head in her hands and waited for the room to stop spinning. If she didn't find something to eat, she wouldn't be good for anything tomorrow. The way it felt now not even food would help, but nourishment was both needed and wanted, and food always made things better at least for a little while.

She still wore her uniform and when she stood, a sour puff of air wafted from her. Harlow grimaced and gagged. The only baths she knew of were in the castle, and she was too afraid to ask any of the others. As far as returning to the castle, she doubt she'd be welcomed there. With a sigh of frustration, Harlow quietly shuffled to the exit. She'd spotted a few blackberry bushes on the trudge back here earlier. They'd have to do for now until she could get breakfast in the morning.

Quiet as a mouse, Harlow unlatched the door and crept out into the quiet night, careful to re-latch it before she tiptoed away. Cool night air brushed against her skin. Her shoulders fell and she took a deep breath of the cool night air. Being alone and being lonely were two different things and tonight, the loneliness was a shroud hanging heavy over her shoulders. Even with forty something other girls a few feet away, she still felt like she was all by herself in a brand-new world she never prepared for.

She hurried over to the grassy area by the dorms, huffing in pain as her muscles protested. Crouching, she found the bushes she'd spotted earlier and plucked handfuls of berries, holding them in the palm of her hand and eating as fast as she could. If Nova could see her now filthy, bruised, and hunched in the dirt like a feral, rabid creature she would laugh her head off. She ate until she couldn't eat anymore, then sat in the cool grass, her thoughts wandering.

The stars flickered above her, the wind carefully blowing strands of hair loosened from her sloppy braid against her face. Harlow scooted back until she rested against a tall oak tree, settling into watch the clouds drift lazily in the sky. Physical exhaustion wracked her small frame but going back in and trying to sleep again wasn't an option.

She looked around and spotted the stables but waking the mare up for comfort seemed unfair. It wasn't the mare's fault she had no one and the horse deserved to rest as much as anyone else. A tall building loomed behind the stables, one she'd seen before but had never explored. Most of Thornewood remained a surprise to her and sneaking around would not endear her to anyone, but Harlow had always been more curious than what was good for her. She got to her knees, her breath coming out more like a groan. Harlow stayed that way for a few moments before she put a hand up, bracing herself against the trunk of the tree and helped herself stand.

Everything hurt and her mouth felt like the sawdust they lined the stable floors with. With a soft groan, Harlow limped her way over to the building.


SHE SPOTTED two guards on the way, both of them oblivious to her presence. Harlow frowned at the appalling lack of vigilance on both their parts but carefully crept around them. They might not be paying attention but lumbering through the streets like a pained bear would no doubt draw unwanted scrutiny.

She turned a corner, and the streets opened up, wide and empty, illuminated by the soft starlight and a few scattered lamps burning with weak, orange light. Her eyes missed nothing as she walked, her heart pumping with adrenaline as she quietly roamed the streets of Thornewood. The castle loomed in the backdrop, at least a mile away, its majestic turrets reaching for the stars. Harlow thought about Desminda for a moment, the future queen's dark hair and how it shimmered in the starlight. She batted that thought away with an annoyed huff.

She'd protect the queen if she had to, but her main goal was to find Nova. Whatever avenue opened itself up for her, she would take. Whether it was protecting the queen or someone else, she'd do the work to reach her ultimate goal. Her sister always said they would find each other. Harlow didn't understand it at the time, why they would need to, and how they would if it was ever time, but a path lay before her, wide and open, and Harlow would continue to walk it no matter what obstacles lay in front of her.

A crinkle of paper jerked her out of her thoughts. Directly in front of her, a piece of parchment rolled across the stone.

Ahead lay a series of wide marble steps. She craned her neck to read the words etched into stone above.

"A library?" she gasped. With one last look around and less care than she should have shown, Harlow bounded up the steps, ignoring the screaming in her muscles as she navigated the slippery steps. She peered inside the foggy glass but couldn't see much.

Harlow tried the door and to her surprise, it opened with a loud creak. She froze for a second, sure she'd be overrun with guards, but when no one came, Harlow tossed caution to the wind and entered.

BOOKS WERE a luxury few people could afford and even those who had the funds rarely invested in. Her mother and father never kept any on their numerous shelves, instead choosing to stock them with spices and herbs, dried fruit and other canned goods, ensuring they would never starve during the harsh winters. Not that they could afford many novels, but they'd had some good harvests where money had been almost plentiful.

Nova, with her quick fingers and pretty lies, had taught her to read using a copy of an old farming manual she'd filched from an elderly, cantankerous man who stared at her a little too closely. Her sister, though, was always more clever than her, so Nova had sidled up to the man in feigned interest. And even though the man was grumpy and smelled like unwashed animal, Nova smiled and preened, pretending to listen to his lecherous words while her slim and skilled fingers quietly slipped behind him and onto the slim booklet he'd left carelessly lying on the back of his cart. Harlow had watched Nova effortlessly maneuver him until she'd shoved the booklet into the back of her skirt and beneath her blouse. As soon as it was secure, she'd smiled prettily and left him gaping after her as she stepped into the crowd and disappeared like a wraith.

They'd run back to their home breathless with laughter. And even though the memory of learning how to read by sounding out letters about the birthing habits of cows made her gag every time she thought about it, those secret stolen moments with her sister always warmed her. After that, when Harlow's letters had improved, Nova had stolen more and more material until eventually she'd managed to get her hands on a novel that had introduced both her and her sister to the ways of a man and a woman. Nova was way more uncomfortable about it than Harlow was but finally justified it by announcing she needed to learn proper human anatomy because stabbing a man was an art.

A smile flittered over Harlow's face at the memory. Nova's sneaky fingers lifted more goods than Harlow would ever be comfortable with, but she'd learned many things from their ill-gotten goods and, in the process, gained stolen, quiet moments where she and Nova would sit together whispering quietly or sometimes not at all, content to sit in the silence with each other.

Harlow carefully closed the door behind her and ventured in, the sharp smell of ink and parchment surrounding her. If she never found a home again, she'd be content to live in a library for the rest of her days. The peaceful rhythm of words and songs and stories set her soul at rest and her mind at ease.

Before magic was purged from the land, Thornewood had outlawed citizens' use of the royal libraries upon the coronation of the new queen. This angered scholars and citizens alike who felt like the new rule would prevent their children from gaining a necessary education for their future. When the uprising became a little too vocal, the fall of magic occurred, distracting everyone except for those who knew how to connect the dots.

The dots Harlow slowly began to connect herself, though she still couldn't reconcile the princess with the mischievous smile with the family who might be responsible for the queendom's current predicament. Also, one who valued their head upon their necks knew not to whisper their heretical thoughts to anyone who might have reason to stab them in the back. Which, with a hefty reward offered for violators, was almost everyone.

She could only think the libraries were banned due to the prevalence of books on the theory and practical application of magic, though now all those books had been purged from the lands. Her sister tiptoed around the subject, though Harlow suspected from the way her mouth tightened every time she brought it up that there was a lot she wasn't saying about it.

Nova cared naught for rules, though she cautioned Harlow again to keep her intellect secret, for if Thornewood had reason to suppress education, perhaps there were other more sinister workings behind the scenes. This had been years ago, and those initial thoughts had died off as most uncomfortable thoughts did when prosperity and food and hope was brought back with the queen's new rule. That lack of concern had always bothered her sister, though she could never put her finger on the reason.

The rules were brought in with a wave of violence and death. First the rule on books and education, second the purge of power leaving families who practiced magic as their profession starving and destitute in the streets and crippling other mages who used magic for both offense and defense. Nova called it a cleansing, but the word always made Harlow's stomach hurt. After all, it was how they'd found each other, and she couldn't feel anything other than blessed that Nova had plucked her from her home's wreckage and brought her to a place where a husband and wife with no children of their own and food to share had welcomed them.

Even though hunger still pricked at her belly and unease

walked chilled fingers down her spine, Harlow ventured through the library like an explorer in a brand-new world. She wiped her juice stained fingers on her breeches, careful to ensure all the blackberry juice was gone before trailing her fingers over the leather spines over the first shelf of books.

She assumed it was after midnight, though there was no moon in the sky to tell her for sure. Shade had woken them up some time around four in the morning yesterday, so she had a little time to spend here provided she didn't get caught.

The library was quiet, her footsteps a whisper of sound against the hard stone floor. Shelves loomed above her, filled to the brim with parchment and books and guides and manuals. Here there was material to learn, explore, expand, to love or hate, to swoon or to blush. She plucked a book out and studied the title.

*The Royal Families of Thornewood: A History of Birth and Death*

She grimaced and put it back before plucking another from a few rows down.

*Gods, Goddess, and the Religious Monarchy: A Study of Control and Faith*

Intrigued, Harlow tucked the book under her arm and moved on.

SHE EXPLORED FOR OVER AN HOUR, finding one other book she planned to sneak back into her room. Placing them in her trunk seemed dangerous, especially with Melara's wrath a target on her back. She'd have to figure out where she could hide them before she made it back to the dorm. If someone found these... she shuddered at the thought and looked down at the small books she held. Was the written word worth the possible punishment?

Harlow exhaled a breath and clutched the books tighter as she walked out into the cool night, ensuring she'd left everything the way she'd found it. Minus the two books she'd taken.

As she walked, the question bounced around in her mind before she settled on the answer.

It was.

The pursuit of knowledge was always worth the pain.

# CHAPTER TWENTY

## TANGLED TRUTHS

Privacy in a room full of almost fifty women was laughable. Harlow carefully made her way back in, quiet as possible. The breathing wasn't quite as steady as it was before, telling her that some of the girls beginning to rouse, possibly from the squeak of the door as she'd reentered. It would make hiding the small books close to impossible, but she'd make it work. How she would find the time to read them, she didn't know, but having them with her made her feel like she had a piece of Nova with her.

She slipped off her boots and slid back onto her cot. If anyone told Shade she'd slipped out, she'd tell him some of the truth. It wouldn't be a lie. It just wouldn't be the entire truth. Her teeth would no doubt be stained purple from her foray into the blackberry bushes and would reveal the story of her adventure last night. No one who knew who she was saw her last night, and Harlow suspected not a single soul had witnessed her venture into the library.

If she woke the next morning surrounded by guards, she'd deal with it then. But for now, she carefully and quietly slid the books underneath the small mattress on her cot, knowing she'd have to move them at first light. Perhaps when everyone else was distracted getting ready and rushing out to line up for the day's duty.

MORNING LIGHT CAME TOO SOON, spilling weak, dappled light into the room. She sat up abruptly in a panic. Why had Shade not come to gather them? Harlow looked around the room, her heart slowing down as she realized she was not the only one still in the room. Every girl still lay in their cot, though Bloom was just beginning to sit up. They locked eyes, and she gave Harlow a brief nod before she turned away to make her bed.

She released a slow breath before moving to do the same. The air shifted and Harlow inhaled, smelling herself with the motion. She gagged and lifted an arm gingerly to smell underneath. Harlow's eyes watered at the stench.

"My god," she whispered to herself.

The girl next to her shifted and rolled to her side. "You smell like a pig sty," she muttered. "The baths are in the small building behind this one. If you want to make friends, you'll be late rather than try to form up with all of us smelling like you do." She had dark skin, darker than Harlow had ever seen, and close-cropped curly hair the color of an Ironbark tree. Her eyes were the color of mined amber, an expensive stone from the neighboring Kingdom of Light, a place she'd never been but heard stories of in the market.

"I'm Harlow."

The girl snorted. "After yesterday, everyone knows who you are. I'm Helena. Now please, stop offending my nose and take a bath."

Harlow bobbed her head and fished for the trunk key she'd hung around her neck. She unlocked it, Helena's bright eyes watching her curiously. Tucking a pair of undergarments under her arm, she also selected a new pair of breeches and the only other shirt she had. Conscious of the books lying under her mattress, she pondered over what to do, but the matter of it was taken away when the door unlatched and Shade thundered into the room. Every girl shot up from their cot, standing ramrod straight, including Harlow and Helena.

His hair was freshly washed, an unruly lock sliding down to his forehead and giving him a rakish air. He wore black again, his weapons strapped to his side. Shade's expression was grim as he stopped at the front of the room.

"Matters unrelated took me away this morning so we are beginning late. You have an hour and a half to attend to personal matters and eat before we convene back here to start for the day." His gaze traveled over every girl before it landed on her. "We shall all conduct ourselves with proper decorum today, are we clear?"

Harlow muttered an affirmative and with one last, long look at all of them, Shade turned on his heel and left.

A shaky breath escaped her, and she sank back onto her cot. Harlow waited for the girls to mill out to find their breakfast, growing antsy with anticipation as one girl lingered behind, setting Harlow's teeth on edge. As soon as the door clicked behind her, Harlow dropped to her knees and began to search around for somewhere to secure the books. She had little time to find somewhere and the pressure of it made the back of her neck ache. Her fingers combed over the rough, knotted floor beside the trunk of her bed, digging as she tried to find a loose board. There were always loose pieces in a floor like this, but whether there would be enough room to shove two books in remained to be seen.

A few minutes later, Harlow spotted a small alcove out of the corner of her eye, lodged in between the small supply lockers and the wall. She looked around to make sure she was alone, then crab walked over to the spot, wincing as her muscles screamed in protest. The only reason she saw it was because she was small and crouched down against the floor, but it would be perfect if the books fit because it was close to her and less noisy than trying to pry up a wooden board every time she wanted to read. She slipped one book in, then the other, gasping with relief as the spines almost matched the wood perfectly. It felt like the gods were approving the choice of a heretic. She stacked them on top of each other. One flopped against the wall and Harlow frowned trying to figure out how she could make it look better when the sound of the latch made her jerk away from the spot and rush back over to her bed.

She snatched up her towel and clothing and rushed past the other trainee without saying a word.

WHILE NOT AS fancy as the baths inside of the castle, the water was piping hot and the pool mostly empty. One of the other trainees eyed her as she walked in. Harlow didn't know her name, only that she was one of the many girls who'd lost her breakfast after Shade's forced run. Harlow looked away, setting her things down on a scarred wooden bench and quietly peeled her clothes off, wincing with disgust at the sight of them.

She took a step into the hot water, sinking into the steaming water, far away from the other trainee. A sigh of relief slipped from her lips as she sank to her shoulders. The water hit every bruise, scratch, and bump on her body, slowly soothing the aches away. There was little time to dally but still she sat there with her eyes closed for a few moments before she began the work of unknotting her hair.

Grimacing at the twigs and leaves falling from her braid, she attempted to finger comb the knots out, quickly realizing it was a lost cause. With a growl of frustration, she reached for the soap, hoping the lather would ease some of the tangles.

"Let me," a voice said.

Her shoulders stiffened, and she cursed herself when she realized the trainee had swum over to her with barely a sound. "I have it," Harlow said, her voice rough and ragged.

"It doesn't look like it," she said, her voice touched with amusement. "Look, if you go out there with ragged hair, Shade will get onto all of us for not working as a team. Let me help you."

"What do you want in return?" Harlow muttered.

The girl laughed softly. "You're as trusting as the rest of them, aren't you?"

"I learned the hard way."

"Well, not all of us earned an enemy on our first day of training, so maybe you have. Where are you from?" The girl was pretty, with a wide, pale freckled face. Her hair was plastered to her head, and it looked to be a mousy shade of brown. If friendliness was a person, the way the girl looked would be it.

"Thornehollow originally." She skimmed over all the details. "We moved when I was a baby."

"I'm from Thornehill. Lacey is the name." She gestured at Harlow's hair. With Harlow's nod, Lacey's nimble fingers worked through the mass of tangles, picking out leaves and twigs, dirt, and debris.

"You look like you've been tumbled something good, girl," Lacey murmured.

A surprised laugh bubbled from Harlow. "There was no tumbling I'm afraid. Part of it was the run. The other part was my frantic dig through the blackberry bush last night after I woke up too late to eat.'

"Ah," Lacey said. "I thought I heard someone leave."

"I didn't eat breakfast or lunch," Harlow said, trying not to sound grouchy.

"In your defense, you were very busy beating Melara to a pulp." Lacey didn't sound upset about it, merely curious.

"Well." She struggled to find something appropriate to say that wouldn't alienate Lacey. "Let's hope that's the end of it then."

Lacey laughed, a bright, infectious sound. "If you hope for that, then you don't know Melara."

Harlow's shoulders fell as she sighed. "I figured."


HARLOW'S BRAID was free of tangles and freshly washed when she walked into the Great Hall. Only the Virago paid attention to her. The burn of Melara's gaze was heavy against her skin as she accepted a bowl of porridge and a ripe apple. She made her way over to a partially empty table, far away from her, and dug into her food. The other girls didn't acknowledge her, instead keeping their heads down to eat. No one spoke. Maybe they were all afraid of Shade's wrath.

Maybe they were afraid of hers.

She blew out a breath and picked up her spoon to eat.

Day two had to be better than day one.

# CHAPTER TWENTY-ONE

## DIRTY, ROTTEN HEALER

Hope was for fools and twittering maidens. Shade was either the world's biggest optimist or the world's biggest masochist. He'd paired Harlow and Melara together. *Again.* When he'd rattled off the pairings, they'd both gaped at him like he'd suddenly grown horns. Even the other girls were surprised and gave them a wide berth as they all lined up for their upper body workouts.

Why they needed a partner for this, she had no idea. So far, all they done was push-ups and some weird thing where they laid on their side and lifted themselves up with one arm. By noon, all the trainees dripped with sweat and groaned every time Shade gave them a new exercise to practice.

By the time the workout was complete, at least three girls were crying and several more huddled by the tree line hurling up their breakfast. Shade had no sympathy. He merely waited for them to finish and motioned for them to get back in formation.

"Break for lunch. Ginger will meet you back in the dormitories to escort you over to the classrooms."

No one hesitated. The formation broke apart and the

trainees scattered in all directions, most heading straight to the dining hall.

HARLOW WAS JUST ABOUT to step into line when something hard slammed into her side. A scream tore from her throat as she stumbled back, pain shattering through her arm. She slammed into a wooden post on the front porch and slid down, landing on her rear end.

"So unlucky," Melara drawled, twirling the practice sword she'd struck Harlow with. A vicious grin creased her face. "You might want to be more careful. It's easy to trip around here."

Her hand crept up to her chest as she gasped for air, pain roaring through her veins. Tears of humiliation streamed down her face. Some of the girls twittered with amusement but most looked away, uncomfortable. Bloom was the only to step out of line, a brave move. With so many others waiting for food, there was a chance she wouldn't be able to eat.

She bent down beside Harlow, sympathy in her eyes. A brief touch of her hand and her gaze went back up to Melara. "Cruelty has no place in our ranks, Melara."

Melara rolled her eyes. "Neither does weakness," she snarled.

A smile curled over Bloom's lips. "How quickly you've forgotten about yesterday." She rose, looming over Melara, her gaze sweeping over all the trainees in line. "We are better than this." She paused. "Aren't we?"

Most of them shifted uncomfortably. "One bully will ruin this team if we allow it. Stand up and make your own decisions. Follow those leaders who show you a better way." Her gaze lingered on Melara. "Not an easier one."

She held her hand out. Harlow took it, easing up to a standing position. Her teeth gritted at the pain in her arm. It shot down from her shoulders and into her upper back. Moving it brought on excruciating pain, so she held it tight against her stomach.

"Her shoulder is dislocated," one of the girls in line said quietly. "She needs the infirmary." Harlow had never heard the girl speak before. She stepped out of line, a dark and quiet thing. Her hair was wrapped in a coronet braid around her head and her deep brown eyes were full of unease. "I'll take her."

She motioned for Harlow to follow.

Melara took a step forward, her eyes flashing with anger.

Three other trainees stepped out of line— Helena and two others she'd never spoken to.

"That's enough," Helena said. Melara towered over her, but Helena didn't cower. "Harlow hasn't done anything to you. Leave her alone."

"She's done everything," Melara snapped.

The dark-haired girl touched Harlow's arm. "Leave it," she murmured. "Your shoulder needs to be looked at."

Harlow sent a quiet look of thanks to Helena and followed the other trainee to the infirmary.


THE TRAINEE, Kalen, left her at the entrance and hurried away. She'd said little on the way over but muttered an apology for Melara's behavior. Harlow said nothing to that because Kalen had nothing to apologize for. If anyone needed to apologize, it should be Melara.

Nova always told her to remember for every action on the surface, there were hundreds more that happened before driving the one you saw. She didn't understand it at the time, but after everything that had happened and caused Harlow to use her fists one too many times, it suddenly made sense. Many things she never used to understand made sense now. Harlow wondered if Nova had taught her these things in order to prepare her for the sadness life could bring.

Something drove Melara to behave the way she did. Something more than her sister not being invited into the Virago.

With a sigh and a thought to examine it later, Harlow sent a whisper of thanks up that the infirmary doors were open. Any upper body movement made her want to collapse in a pile of tears. She stepped in and immediately stopped.

The future queen sat on a cot, blood dripping from her index finger. Pain marred her perfect brow, and she watched the poor, trembling healer attempting to thread a needle. She looked up at Harlow's entrance and a smile began to bloom on her face before she stifled it. Instead, she nodded.

"Looks like we've both had interesting days," she quipped.

The healer looked up, relief filling her eyes. "Your Majesty?"

The queen's eyebrows rose. "See to her first then. Hers looks more serious than this tiny cut." That tiny cut oozed blood onto the wooden floor.

The healer stood, but Harlow shook her head. "She needs a cloth before you see me. Put pressure on the wound." She kept her voice low, but the healer winced and ducked her head.

"Sorry," she whispered. The healer turned back to the queen and wrapped her finger in white cloth. "Put pressure on this," she told her.

Desminda snorted. "I heard her." Her dark gaze met Harlow's. "Perhaps you've missed your calling. Should I speak to Shade about moving you from training for the Virago to the healing arts instead?"

Harlow's heart pounded at Desminda's presence. She hadn't forgotten what she'd done, but it was hard to stay angry at her, especially with the impish look she bestowed on her now. "I lived on a farm, Your Majesty," Harlow explained. "We tended to wounds quite often."

Desminda jerked her chin at Harlow's shoulder. "What happened to you?"

Harlow thought about spilling her guts, telling the princess everything, all her pain and turmoil. She yearned for a kind and earnest ear. But the princess was not the one. She'd never be the one. To think she would be was playing a fool's game.

And fools never won.

"Training accident," she said when the princess tilted her head as the silence lingered.

"Mmm hmm," Desminda murmured.

The healer pulled Harlow over to a cot next to Desminda. Her fingers were frigid and trembled when she laid them on Harlow's shoulder. "You need to tell me what happened so I can properly correct it."

Harlow's gaze flicked to the princess. She'd rather not. "I–I fell."

A sharp laugh burst from Desminda. "Just like I did this sewing." She waved her finger at Harlow. "I cut it on a rock when I was outside digging in my gardens. Shade is positively furious." She lifted her gaze to the heavens. "He thinks I should leave gardening to the castle workers because we pay them." Desminda waved her finger. "They've ruined my tulip bulbs two years in a row because they don't plant them deep enough! And don't even get me started about the herb garden. Basil turns black if you expose it to water after it's harvested. They ruined the pesto I had planned to make, and I had to throw away an entire season's harvest." A huff of air escaped her.

Harlow stared in fascination at the two high spots of color on the future queen's cheeks even as her stomach churned. Desminda was beautiful. Inside and out. She'd met nobles before when they came to the village looking for secret things they didn't want to buy in Thornewood–bits and baubles of left-over magic, some real, most not. As if gossip didn't spread like wildfire back to the castle. If you wanted secrets kept, you had to bring a lot of coin to bribe someone. None of them behaved liked Desminda. They spoke down to everyone, sneered behind their backs, and sometimes right in front of their faces. Everyone assumed the villagers were simpletons and treated them as such.

But Desminda spoke to her like an equal, almost. Like a friend.

This was a dangerous game she played.

"I got into a fight," she admitted. "Sort of. Someone pushed me and I fell into a wooden post."

Desminda's eyes widened. "Who?" she demanded. The charming, impish girl was gone and in its place was the woman who would one day rule their people. Her eyes went hard as she waited for the answer. "The Virago are not bullies," she snapped. "And if there is one who is not treating their fellow trainees like they should, they will answer to me."

Harlow swallowed. "I'd rather not say." The healer gasped and pressed too hard on her shoulder. A strangled cry of pain tore from her throat.

The future queen's lips thinned. "And why not?"

Harlow thought about it. Her answer would determine whether she would be respected or reviled within the Virago. She met the queen's amber gaze. "We are only in our second day of training. It takes time to work as a team. Every one of us is from different areas, different cultures and none have a soldier's background. We're all under stress and we all miss our families." She dropped her eyes. "Allow me the chance to fix this problem myself, Your Majesty. I was the target. I should be the one to address it."

Desminda shifted, and Harlow lifted her eyes to her. The future queen studied her, her golden gaze unreadable. Finally, she nodded. "Very well. But if this persists, I will bring it up with Shade and whoever this is will be removed from training. Do I make myself clear?"

Harlow breathed a sigh of relief. "Yes, Your Majesty. I really appreciate—"

A loud crack sounded in the room as the healer popped her shoulder back into socket with zero warning. Harlow howled in pain.

The healer released her, backed away, watched Harlow for a second, then nodded. "The best way to do that is when someone's distracted." She gave her a bright smile. "Feeling better?"

The pain disappeared seconds later, but Harlow still dragged in gasps of shocked breath, her eyes wide with surprise at the clever betrayal.

"Well," Desminda said with a chuckle. "Perhaps the little healer has more of a spine than I gave her credit for." She waved her cloth covered finger around. "Can you do me next, please? I have some dirt to dig in."

# CHAPTER TWENTY-TWO

## MUSIC RETURNS

Dusk streaked the sky with purple and orange fingers and the first peek of the moon rested in the sky. People milled around the square, haggling over prices on fabric and fruit and other odds and ends. The spices of the meat carts sent a tantalizing scent into the air, and she inhaled deeply as she walked along, lost in thought.

She'd taken the long way back to the dormitory, not looking forward to the judgmental eyes of the other girls, but especially those of Melara. She examined the problem every way she could, but she couldn't figure out a solution to it. Melara was angry over her sister, but Harlow knew it couldn't be the only reason why she treated her so poorly. Harlow had become an unintentional target, and she had to figure out how to turn that around.

Bullies didn't become good people overnight. Sometimes they never became good people. But they didn't become bad overnight either usually. Harlow had to prove herself. Violence wasn't the answer. She'd already gained the upper hand on her in the physical sense, so she'd have to approach it in a different way.

Maybe they could be friends.

A bark of laughter escaped Harlow, turning a couple of heads her way. She smiled meekly at them, and one woman gave her a curious look before she went back to her perusal of the apples in the peddler's wooden box.

She turned the corner, the dormitory just up ahead, when a girl wearing a long, red cloak with intricate embroidery, a white shirt, and snug brown breeches hugging her slim frame stepped into her path. Her hair was the color of a summer sunset, orange and red and yellow, vivid even in the rapidly dimming light. Her eyes were the color of jade chips Harlow had once seen in a ring on a nobleman's finger, and the woman's gaze danced with amusement as it locked with Harlow's.

"Good evening," the stranger said, her voice light and mesmerizing. An instrument was strapped across her chest, and she had the quick, light step of a dancer.

Harlow's mouth fell open. "You're a bard," she blurted.

The girl grinned, a wide and happy smile on her stunning face. "Guilty as charged."

Harlow had never seen one before. Bards were rarely seen after magic had fallen, disappearing wherever they went to once their songs were sung. The word was the cleansing had taken the magic of the bard's voices, the nimbleness of their fingers on their lutes and lyres now stilted and curved. The notes had gone sour, and most music had left the Kingdom of Thorns.

Nova had scoffed at that. Though she rarely talked about magic, she'd called the rumors foolish. *"You can't take a voice, Harlow. Only in death does a voice stop. A bard's magic is inherent, born deep within their veins. Their powers aren't controlled by the same things controlling the kingdom."* And then she'd stopped talking, pressing her lips tight together as if she'd said too much.

But if that were true, where had they all gone? And why

was the music filtering in and out of the pubs and stew houses slightly off? It always sounded odd to Harlow's ears, a discordant note here and there, so minute it was almost unnoticeable.

"Careful, girl. Gaping like that, you'll catch flies in this weather." The bard stepped around her, quick and nimble, her hair streaming out of the jaunty, wide hat she had perched around her head.

Harlow spun around. "I've never seen one of you before."

The bard's eyes went dark and sad for a moment. "Bards tell the truth, no matter who listens. People are too afraid to listen anymore. Danger lurks around every corner for my people." She touched Harlow, a whisper against her skin, Harlow's skin tingling when she passed. The bard winked then and turned away, her darkness from a moment before gone with the bright twinkle in her eyes. But she looked back over her shoulder before she melded away into the crowd. "Magic is not gone. But it is lost. Find it Harlow. Before it's too late for all of us."

Harlow blinked, but the girl was gone. She shouldn't be. Even in the dusk falling around Thornewood, the bard's bright red cloak should have been visible in the sea of brown and grey clothing.

But there was no sign of her, as if she was only a figment of Harlow's imagination.


BOTHERED, Harlow hurried into the dorms, not stopping until she'd made it back to her bed. Her shoulder still ached, though the pain wasn't anything like it had been. She felt the eyes on her back but acknowledged no one. Dealing with Melara could wait.

The bard's presence had overwhelmed her. She knew she hadn't imagined it. Her bright green eyes burned within Harlow's memory, the red coat a sharp contrast against the dull colors of the Thornewood villagers. She stood out, like the bards in Nova's stories used to. But then she'd melted away like she'd never existed.

Harlow had to find her again.

Exhaustion crept into Harlow's bones, there before but forgotten when she'd spotted the bard. She sank onto her cot, a groan rising in her throat, and laid on her back, staring up at the wooden cross planks of the ceiling.

*Magic is not gone.* The bard's words repeated in her head over and over again. But it was. She was too young to remember in detail, but every once in a while, when the woman who'd taken them in dipped into her husband's spirits, she'd reminisce. Her voice grew softer, and her eyes grew wistful, and she'd whisper how the forests once lit up with golden light, the fairies who lived there blessing their foraging. She spoke once of the bards, of their power and voices, and how they spread the word of magic across the land. She told stories of fearsome power and women who could heal with a touch. Harlow had sat at her mother's feet, fascinated, her eyes and ears rapt with her lilting voice and tales of another time, a time Harlow desperately wished she'd seen.

*Magic is not gone.*

Then where was it?

*Find it Harlow. Before it's too late for all of us.*

SHE JERKED AWAKE SOMETIME LATER, a pull she couldn't explain tugging her from her sleep. Her clothes were askew, dusty from the day, and wrinkled from her exhausted collapse in bed. She sat up as quietly as she could and rolled off the cot, wincing at the creak of the wood cracking through the night.

Something called her. A feeling she couldn't explain

prickled at the back of her neck, a siren's call outside into the dark of the night. She followed it, the clasp on the door whisper quiet this time as if someone had oiled it especially for her.

The air was humid, her skin cooling with moisture almost as soon as she stepped outside. Summer was ending, ushering in fall with hesitant fingers, reluctant to let go of the warmer air and green landscape. Harlow's thoughts scattered to Desminda, imagining her stooped in her garden, fingers dark with Thornewood soil. The image made her swallow hard before she banished it. As soon as she did, green eyes and vibrant red hair followed, the red cloak disappearing in front of her eyes, a specter laughing at her in the night.

*Magic is not gone.*

An unexplainable force pulled her toward the center of the forest. She hesitated a moment, remembering Nova's stories about beasts prowling Thornewood's forests, but the feeling didn't go away. With a deep breath, she squared her shoulders, wincing slightly at the pain from her injury, and plunged into the darkness of the night.

She'd never gone this deep into the woods. Hunting was easy around the land by her former home, the soil fertile and rich for creatures foraging for food. Deer could never resist her mother's gardens, even though her father waited, carefully hidden with his bow and arrow for that one buck who'd proved too curious. They ate like kings for a time, and the deer shied away for only a little while until the family planted something else the animals couldn't resist.

But there were no deer tonight. No owls or snakes or foxes or any of the more dangerous creatures, the large tawny striped cats that used to stare at them from the edges of the forest when night had fallen. It was quiet. Too quiet. Goosebumps rose along Harlow's flesh as she walked, pulled toward something she couldn't understand. A fog rose around her feet, opening a curving path ahead. She stilled, her gaze everywhere at once, looking for any hint of danger.

But she didn't feel afraid. She felt like whatever waited for her at the end of this shimmering path was something she was meant to see or know. If this wasn't magic, she couldn't imagine what was.

The sound of music came, slowly at first, filling her senses, and tugging her forward. Soon, it consumed her. Her steps grew quicker and quicker until she was running along the path, searching for the sound of it. A voice rose, lilting and elegant, each note perfect in its simplicity, singing a song she'd never heard before.

> A girl of thorns was born this night,
> A girl of magic, so sweet, so light.
> Torn from hands that loved so well,
> Surrounded by fire, a child's fierce hell.
>
> A child of night, of stars, of dreams,
> A child of hope, of magic, drawn by screams.
> A struggle of conscience, a will so fierce,
> A bond forged from fire, no man can pierce.

She ran through the fog, her heart soaring with the music. Her legs pumped, flying through the woods as she sought its source. Blood thrummed through her veins as she ran, fierce joy soaring through her soul.

Harlow stumbled into an open clearing. A fire burned in the middle of it, but no one was there. She bent over, her hands on her knees, gasping for breath. Her gaze searched wildly for the voice. A groan of despair croaked from her as she realized she was alone.

Dejected, Harlow sank to her knees. Emptiness filled her

bones and sorrow soaked her heart. The voice had drawn her, carrying her here on winged feet. And then it left her here with nothing.

A sob tore from her throat, and she didn't know why. She'd never felt this way before, like she'd been so close to the discovery that would tell her who she was, something that would lead her back to Nova.

Harlow sat there for a little while, her head bowed. Firelight flickered over her skin, lighting the night with a deep orange glow. Finally, she sighed and stood, her gaze flickering over the area. She investigated the clearing, seeing nothing of interest. It wasn't until she stepped closer to the fire that she saw something, a white flash that seemed familiar to her. Harlow bent down, scooping her fingers through the dirt until she lifted a white stone.

It was almost identical to the one she had hidden in her trunk.

Her hand buzzed with something unidentifiable as she held it. The same feeling the one her sister had given her elicited. She frowned and rolled it around in her palm, the firelight bringing out flashes of blue light in the stone. The words of the song flitted away from her mind. Harlow grasped at them, desperate to remember, but they slowly disappeared.

They were about her and Nova. She was sure of it.

But that made no sense. They weren't anything special. Neither one of them had powers or might or anything other than stubborn tenacity, Nova more so than her.

A sigh escaped her as she tucked the stone in her pocket. She had no idea how long she'd run and no idea where she ended up. The trees were high around her, and the thought of going back through the dark woods sent a frisson of fear down her spine. Something had flooded her veins during her mad rush to this clearing, something she couldn't explain.

It wasn't magic. Was it?

Harlow walked around the fire, her gaze skimming the ground, looking for any clues she might have missed. Even if this *was* magic, leaving an open fire in the middle of a forest clearing seemed to be the height of irresponsibility. The woods bordered the village of Thornewood, and small houses built mostly of wood sat along the edge. A strong burst of wind could send burning embers into the trees and send the entire forest up into an inferno, spreading into the village.

When she finished investigating, she scooted a pile of dirt up with her boot, but just as she was about to start kicking it onto the fire, it extinguished abruptly. No smoke, no embers. She gasped in surprise, sure her eyes were playing tricks on her. Harlow bent, touching her fingers to the ground.

Cool to the touch.

Fear and awe combined curled her toes. If she hadn't been convinced before, this convinced her. She'd just had her first experience with magic.

And even though she knew she should be terrified, she couldn't shake the feeling that she'd finally come home.

# CHAPTER TWENTY-THREE

## A MARCH OF MISFITS

M elara's eyes glowed in the low light as Harlow crept back to her bed. She ignored her, too exhausted to fight. The problem between Harlow and the hostile girl wouldn't resolve itself right now and all she wanted to do was crawl back in the bed and sleep for however long she could before Shade came barging in.

Melara said nothing, only watched Harlow intently. Even when she shut her eyes, she still felt Melara's eyes on her, waiting for something Harlow was too tired to give her. The new stone sat in her pocket, cool even against the fabric.

Her eyes drifted closed even as her thoughts still spun with the wonder of the last couple of hours.

WHAT SEEMED like only minutes later, Shade's booming voice resounded through the dorm, threatening them with an hour's extra conditioning if they weren't dressed and outside in ten. Harlow bounded up, forgetting the abuses of her body over the last few days. She hunched and groaned once her feet hit the ground, doing her best to ignore the pain as she hurriedly dressed.

Day three. She no longer expected things to get better.

The moon had disappeared behind the trees and the first light of dawn began to scrape over the sky by the time Harlow made it outside. She was, of course, the last one out. Several of the girls gave her heated glares as she scurried to take her place. Shade's gaze lingered on her for a moment too long before he cleared his throat.

"Step out of formation," he began.

Everyone looked around, not sure what he meant. Shade stepped forward with his arms stretched out in front of him and separated his arms, moving the girls in the front of the formation apart. Soon, everyone scattered until they all milled around and waited for whatever Shade was doing.

He barked out names as he held his pointer finger to the ground. The first girl scrambled to where he pointed, followed by the second, then the third, and so on. By the time he got to Harlow, she'd released a long, relieved breath. He'd lined them up by height, so she now stood in the back, next to a girl with hair the color of a summer dandelion. Harlow nodded to her, but the girl merely stared at her for a long moment before turning back to face the front.

She blew out a frustrated breath. Making friends was so much harder than she thought it would be. There was always Nova in the village, so she'd never gone out of her way to make extra friends because her sister was always her favorite.

In hindsight, that might have been a mistake.

Shade stood to the side of them, walking around and adjusting some of the girls so their formation looked like several perfect lines. "This is the formation you will use from now until you graduate. Every day you will come out from the dorm and stand next to the person you stand next to today." Harlow wanted to breathe a sigh of relief. She was so short she couldn't even see the back of Melara's head.

"Today, we will learn to march in unison. It sounds easier than it is." A woman walked up next to Shade as he spoke. She held a wicker basket on one arm and adjusted her blue cloak with the other. Harlow had not glimpsed Ginger since the first day she'd come in and she wondered what her role was with the Virago. The girl wasn't much older than Harlow. She fell a little on the plump side, her cloak accenting her generous curves. When she smiled, a dimple peeked out from one cheek. Bright blue eyes and a pale cream complexion glowed in the morning light. But it was the way she looked at Shade that made her wonder the most.

Harlow tilted her head and studied them. No one could deny Shade's wickedly dark good looks. In fact, she'd overheard several of the trainees tittering about him in the dormitory. But Ginger looked like she belonged with someone friendlier, someone who lived more in the light.

Shade was a man who lived under a cloud of violence, someone who'd seen too much and wore it on his skin. And from the way Shade purposely ignored the woman's doting look, he knew how she felt.

Ginger turned her head and locked gazes with Harlow. From the way her eyes narrowed, Harlow suspected she knew where her thoughts lay. She blinked and dropped her eyes. It wasn't her business anyway.

She stopped listening to Shade a few minutes in, her thoughts wandering back to the night before. The stone felt heavy in her pocket. She'd had no time to secure it in her trunk and she could only hope her pants were snug enough to keep it locked tight against her skin so she wouldn't lose it.

"Harlow!" Shade barked.

She jerked in surprise, her heart racing like a rabbit. Harlow snapped her spine straight. "Yes, Shade!"

"Your birthday. It's in a couple of weeks, yes?"

Her gaze flew to his. "No?" She meant it to be a statement, but the sound came out as a question. Her birthday wasn't for months. What an odd question.

Shade's eyes were heavy on her face. One dark eyebrow went up. "Are you sure?"

She snorted, but at Shade's dark glare, she chewed on her lip. "I'm sure." She'd know her own birthday, wouldn't she?

"Are you fifteen then?"

Harlow looked around, but everyone studiously ignored her. "Err. Yes."

"Who else is turning sixteen?" he asked.

Two other girls raised their hands. He nodded. "Good." An uncomfortable expression crossed his face. "Sixteen is an important time in a young woman's life. It is the crossing from childhood into adulthood. A time to cast away those things we cling to in our youth and embrace the things that will take us into the prime of our life."

A few girls shifted awkwardly.

Harlow shook her head. "I don't understand," she blurted. "Why does this matter?"

Shade waved a hand. "Forget it," he said in dismissal. There was a tension in his frame that wasn't there before.

"If I didn't know better, I'd think he was about to ask about our menses," a girl whispered. Several snorts rang out.

Shade sighed. "Attention!"

Everyone snapped their posture straight, the awkwardness momentarily forgotten.

"Forward march!" Shade boomed.

The Virago lurched forward in an awkward attempt at a formation. Everyone's footwork was off, their steps off kilter and shoulders bumping. Growls of frustration rang out as Shade made them start and stop over and over again.

Even Harlow grunted with annoyance every time she stepped on the person's heel in front of her, whispering apologies to the poor girl's boots. But she couldn't concentrate on the task ahead of her.

Was there something special about her sixteenth birthday or was Shade just being strange?

# CHAPTER TWENTY-FOUR

## THE BEGINNING OF THE END

Almost two weeks passed with no more incidents between her and Melara. Harlow was almost to the point of beginning to relax, but every time she did, she'd feel a gaze burning against the back of her neck and tensed up all over again.

She felt a marked difference in her strength with every run or push up. Harlow moved faster, her muscles turning lean and flexible. Her strength had increased and she could even hold a sword and use it in a mostly passable manner. Her preference still leaned toward the axe, but so far Shade hadn't seemed too inclined to provide her with even a practice one. Somewhat understandable. It was hard to hang an axe on a uniform. They didn't exactly make scabbards for those.

The friend situation remained the same. Helena wasn't friendly, but she never treated Harlow poorly, even going so far as to nod to her and whisper a polite hello when they passed each other.

Bloom began the day with an even more elaborate hairstyle and seemed to have a knack for the sword Harlow knew she never would. Kalen, the girl who'd walked her to the infirmary, never spoke much. Every time their eyes met, Harlow saw the guilt still lingering there. She could approach Kalen if she wanted and talk about it, but earnest conversation wasn't her strong suit, and she'd probably make it worse if she tried.

Melara stayed away from her, but Harlow felt an odd sense of foreboding hanging over her shoulders every time they were in close proximity, which was most days of the week.

Tonight, they all sat around the small fireplace Ginger had stoked for them, shining their shoes. Harlow had a knack for getting the best shine, so she traded some of her chores in exchange for skills at boot shining. The trick, she'd learned, was a soft cloth, flame, a little water on top of the polish, and simple elbow grease.

Conversation ebbed and flowed, but Harlow sat quietly, her back up against the stone wall, concentrating on getting the glossy shine on the tip of the boot she worked on.

The room was warm and cozy, restful and relaxing. Her thoughts were lost in other things when a crash jerked her out of her reverie.

"Where are they?" Melara screeched.

Several eyes swung to Harlow, but she had no idea what was happening.

Bloom stood. Harlow really needed to ask the rest of the girls their names. It seemed too presumptive if she never spoke to them, though, so she quietly kept to herself and tried to ingratiate herself into the team by being quiet but productive.

"Where is what?" the tall girl asked.

"My letters," Melara hissed. "From my sister. They're gone."

"I'm sure they're here somewhere," the other girl soothed. "How about we look for them?" She reached out to touch Melara, but the trainee shrugged away, her boots booming against the wood of the floor as she approached where Harlow sat.

Harlow set the boot she held down, wanting her hands free if Melara attacked her. An ill-feeling had plagued her all day, a low-level headache pulsing against her temples. There had been an ache between her shoulders and nausea had turned her away from both lunch and dinner when they'd gone to the Great Hall. She had an empty stomach and little tolerance for Melara's bullying tonight.

But she wouldn't show her fear. Instead, Harlow stretched out her legs and tilted her head up to the girl. A vulnerable position, to be sure, but a powerful one if the curl to her lip and the subsequent rage flashing in Melara's eyes was any indication. The girls to either side of her discreetly moved away as Melara loomed over her.

"Where are they?" she hissed.

Harlow shook her head. "I have no idea what you're talking about."

"You took them. I know it." Melara crossed her arms over her chest. "You're going to give them to me and you're going to do it now."

Harlow merely crossed her legs at the ankles. "I have no need for any of your letters. They wouldn't serve me and I'm not like you." Even though her heart pounded, Harlow looked away and studied her nails. "I don't take from the weak just to ease the violence in my heart."

She saw the boot a second before it connected with her face. A loud crack signaled the breaking of her cheekbone. Blood spurted from her nose and pain roared through Harlow's face as she spun but was too slow to completely avoid the blow.

Gasps of shock rang out through the dorm as everyone scrambled to their feet. Bloom moved to step in.

"No!" Harlow barked, holding her hand up. Blood dripped down her face. "It's time we settled this for good, wouldn't you say?"

Melara's smile was vicious. "There's only one way to settle this."

Harlow snorted, even with the pain. Blood bubbled from her nose as she struggled to her feet. "You are weak, Melara. Only someone who was scared of losing would attack her opponent from a vulnerable position."

Melara's fist clenched against her side. Her face turned ruddy with rage. "It doesn't matter how you win as long as you do."

"I think Shade would disagree with that. As well as most of the girls in this room." Harlow shook her head. Her cheekbone burned with pain and the right side of her face felt like it was both numb and on fire. Harlow's words slurred slightly. "For the last time, I did not take your letters. If you continue to approach me, we will settle this, but I don't think you'll like how we do it."

Melara launched herself at Harlow.


SILENCE ROARED through Harlow's head. It was as if every sound in the room had been sucked out through a vacuum, leaving only her and Melara. Even though the fire still crackled, the other girls scrambled to get out of their way, and the wind howled against the windows, signaling a storm the likes of which they'd rarely seen in Thornewood, the only thing she could hear was her sister's words in her mind.

*"Don't pick a fight you can't win, and if you aren't sure you can win, then don't fight fair. Honor means nothing if you're dead."*

The way Melara was coming for her made her wonder. Death flickered behind the hostile girl's eyes and Harlow had no idea what she'd done to warrant it.

She dared a quick glance around, her gaze singling out a girl standing behind the rest of them that she didn't recognize. With ·

fifty of them, it wouldn't be unheard of to not immediately recognize someone, but they'd been together for weeks now, marching in formation together, practicing and eating together.

She'd never seen her before; she was sure of it. A cruel smile graced the stranger's lips as she raised a piece of parchment in the air and waved it around. Just as Harlow was about to cry foul, the girl disappeared through a window, sleek and silent.

A gust of air had Harlow jerk back, just in time to avoid a slash to her neck.

Her eyes went wide at the blade in Melara's hands.

Whatever this was had gone from bullying to pure violence.

Melara wanted her dead.

Most of the girls ran out, either to avoid any culpability of what was about to happen or to get Shade. With the way Harlow's luck ran these days, she didn't think they'd bring anyone back to help her.

She and Melara circled each other. The blade flashed in her opponent's hand, glinting in the firelight. Harlow swallowed hard as she carefully measured her footwork. She wouldn't put it past someone to trip her.

And wasn't that something, to work beside these girls for weeks now and wonder whether they had her best interests at heart. There was something off here, something rotten at the core of it. How had Shade not seen the heart of this girl when he'd seen Harlow's heart so clearly?

Nausea coiled in her stomach, even worse than it had been before. A cold sweat trickled down the back of her neck. She'd never had a fever in all the days she could remember, but she felt hot and cold all at the same time. Her teeth gritted as she watched Melara.

"Why?" she croaked.

Melara snorted. "Because you don't belong here."

"And you do?" Harlow asked, fighting the urge to vomit. Being sick had never come at a more inopportune time.

Melara stopped her pacing, the knife loosely held in her hand. "I was born to be here." Truth dripped from her words.

Exasperated, Harlow threw up her hands. "Then why are you trying so hard to jeopardize it?" she blurted.

Melara blinked and, for the first time, she hesitated.

Seeing her chance, Harlow struck. She held no weapon, nothing that could combat the wicked slice of the knife, other than the leather vest and pants she hadn't yet taken off. And lucky for her, as Melara's first swipe glanced across the vest, exposing the beige linen of Harlow's undershirt.

"Stop," Harlow begged, staggering under the weight of whatever was happening to her. "We don't have to do this."

"You say that because you know you're going to lose," Melara said, her mouth curving in a smirk.

No one stepped up to interfere. No one begged them to stop. No one did a thing, instead choosing to leave them to solve it. Harlow wondered if they would step over her corpse and ignore it when she died. Just like most of them had while she was here.

Anger, pure and alive, set her veins ablaze. She looked at each girl she could see, accusation hot and burning in her eyes. Most of them looked away, their cheeks flaming with humiliation.

"I am embarrassed to be part of this," Harlow bit out. "I am embarrassed to eat beside you each day and embarrassed you'd let this happen without stepping in to stop it."

No one said anything for a long moment. Melara hadn't made her next move, and Harlow calculated her rate of survival in her head. She moved slower today, every step she took setting dizziness off. At any moment, she felt like her stomach would empty.

"We were here before you," one of the girls finally said. "We worked for this opportunity."

Harlow scoffed. "And I haven't?"

The accusing glares told her all she needed to know.

"I've worked with you every day. I've tried to get to know some of you." Tears of frustration made her voice thick. "And I feel like I've been shut out since the day I got here. I am alone," she whispered.

Melara struck again.

Harlow didn't bother to move. She screamed, all her rage and hopelessness exposed for everyone to see, the broken parts of her laid bare. Something deep inside of her cracked, and a well opened, a deep, wide pit of flaming embers, a power she'd never known unspooling. The stone she'd kept in her pocket warmed and pulsed against her skin, but she barely noticed it. She gritted her teeth at the pure fire burning inside of her, searching for an outlet.

Harlow threw her arms out and chaos answered.


SHE NEVER TOUCHED MELARA, but the girl flew back, her spine and head cracking against the other side of the wall. Windows shattered outward and wind ravaged the inside the dorm, spinning debris in a circular storm. Screams of horror rang out as the other trainees scattered, ducking under beds and escaping outside, wherever they could go to get away from the mayhem Harlow had unleashed.

A light of pure white burst from her palms, destroying everything in its path. She threw her hands up and the ceiling burst open, raining wood and stone around their heads. Harlow could hear nothing and everything at once, a buzzing noise floating around her even as she struggled between horror and wonder.

And then, all at once, the light snapped off, the well inside of her sated and slumbering. She fell to her knees, her breath hoarse and gasping. Horror-filled gazes burned her skin. Melara's body slumped a few feet away, but she didn't care. All she could feel was the certainty that this was what she was. What she'd been born to be.

A monster.


THE SOUND of water roused her. Harlow blinked awake, then winced as bright light burned her eyes.

"She's awake," a low, familiar voice murmured.

Harlow swallowed, her dry throat clicking, and opened her eyes fully, only to peer up at angry dark eyes.

Shade loomed above her, dark and fierce. His hair was disheveled, a lock of it falling over his forehead.

Murmured whispers formed around her.

He snapped his gaze away. "What happened here?"

No one said anything for a long moment.

He straightened. "What. Happened. Here."

"A storm," another familiar voice said. "We've never seen the like of it."

"A storm?" Shade echoed incredulously.

"A storm," several of the girls said in unison.

Shade's nostrils flared out. "But the windows burst outward?"

Another long silence. "We tried to escape," the voice said again.

A hoarse barked laugh came from him. "This is your last chance to tell me the truth. Otherwise, tomorrow morning, you're going to work so hard you'll drop."

Harlow tried to speak, but it came out as a croak. Shade snapped his attention to her, but someone else spoke up. "It was a storm. We were sitting around the fire doing our chores and the wind picked up outside. The next thing we know, the ceiling broke open, and we were all trying to get out."

Melara.

Why would Melara defend her?

"And the front door wasn't an option?" Shade said dryly.

"Something blocked it," Melara said.

"Convenient," he drawled. "I walked in here just fine."

"The wind was awfully fierce," another voice said.

Tears sprang to her eyes.

Shade pinched the space between his brows. "Where are the other girls?"

No one said a word.

"Virago!" Shade boomed. "Where are the others?"

"We don't know," a voice from behind her said quietly.

Harlow couldn't yet move her limbs. Every piece of her felt like it was on fire. Her nausea had subsided, but exhaustion leached through her bones. She wanted to hug the floor and sleep through the week.

"There are thirty-seven of you missing." Shade's voice was dangerous and low.

"Perhaps they were afraid," one of the other girls said. The girl with the braids. *Bloom*. That was it..

"The Virago are not afraid," another girl said.

Helena.

Shade looked at all of them, his gaze heavy and lingering. Finally, he looked down at her, and there was something in his eyes Harlow couldn't guess at.

"Come," he said gently. "You need to see the healer."

Harlow couldn't stand. A whimper escaped her. Shade's lips thinned and seconds later she found herself scooped up into strong, warm arms.

"Tomorrow. Before dawn. Be outside in formation wearing your conditioning clothes."

Silence rang in the room as Shade's heavy footfalls fell.

Right before he stepped out into the cool, night air, he paused. "And Virago?"

No one said a word.

"Tonight you have proven yourself worthy of your title."

# CHAPTER TWENTY-SIX

## SHADE'S DILEMMA

An honorable man wouldn't keep secrets from his future queen. But a man sworn to protect his kingdom at all costs would if it meant he would uphold his oath.

Desminda stood next to him, her lips pursed in thought as they both stared down at the girl who was proving to be more of a handful than they'd bargained for. Harlow lay still and quiet, her hands crossed over her chest, rising and falling in time to her breathing. A promise of great beauty lay etched in the youth of her face. The princess shook her head in disbelief. "A storm they said?"

Shade nodded, unwilling to trust his voice right now. Every single girl left in that dormitory had lied to his face. And he couldn't be any prouder of them.

He'd chosen fifty knowing there would be several who wouldn't make it. Losing thirty-seven of them never occurred to him. Thirteen were left. Thirteen girls who would swear themselves to the kingdom in a few months' time.

His worst nightmare had come true just like Stonehand warned him it would. His friend had known his daughter's birthday down to the second. Shade meant to be in the dorm when it happened, but the queen had delayed him with some nonsense, and he'd gotten bogged down in politics and petty word slinging instead of being there when it mattered.

The dormitory would take weeks to repair, and he would have to find trusted agents who wouldn't ask questions to do it. The trainees would need another place to stay and most of their gear would need to be replaced. His mind spun with the million things he had to do but he burned with pride. He'd handpicked every single girl for the Virago, knowing some of them would never make it. He'd picked girls who prickled with too much pride. Others who preened with too much vanity. Even more who thought they were warriors but shivered with fear when they glimpsed a sword. But then he'd seen Melara, fiercely proud, savage with a blade, burning with anger and rage at the world who'd left her behind. He hadn't known which way she'd go until today. Then Bloom, a strange girl with nimble fingers and a clever tongue. And Harlow. Stumbling over her was a complete, fortuitous accident.

Thirteen years ago, the new queen, Raima, sent troops into all of her territories to force the common folk to bend to her will. Magic was ripped from the world, sending their kingdom to its knees. Stonehand was exempted, his magic something *other*, something no one had ever seen before. Thus, the reason Raima had conscripted him years before into her service, a premeditated act Shade hadn't seen the reasoning of beforehand. When the veil lifted from his eyes, he'd questioned everything, every choice he'd ever made in his godsforsaken life.

He'd urged her to reconsider, to find another way, but Raima refused. What transpired had brought Shade to his knees. Stonehand's daughter was lost, long thought dead until he'd ran into a girl with eyes of starlight in the local market and followed her home only to find her nurturing a girl with eyes like the summer sky and pale yellow hair. Marion's eyes.

"They claim the damage was done by a storm. Do you believe them?" Desminda asked, jolting him out of his memories.

His jaw clenched. Much like her mother, Desminda had always been more perceptive than most. A trait he'd usually appreciated. But not today. The future queen knew who Stonehand's get was, but she had no idea the kind of power unleashed tonight.

"A storm did rip through the town," he said, avoiding a direct answer.

"Mmm," she said, the tone noncommittal as she gazed down on Harlow. The girl had passed out in his arms a few steps into their short walk to the infirmary. A long, shallow cut marred the perfect skin of her collarbone. Bruises peppered her face and jaw, new and old. Her arms had shallow cuts all over, injuries that would scar if she'd been a normal human.

But she wasn't. She never had been.

When Stonehand told him the news of Marion, Shade staggered, his knees giving way. Marion was a witch, a powerful one. A memory of her quick smile and wit unfolded in his mind. She'd been gorgeous, pale blonde hair, eyes of cornflower blue, and nature power the likes of which he'd never seen. Shade was no stranger to magic. His mother had turned potions in the market square for years, his father a mere farmer. No hint of magic ever graced his veins, but he'd seen with his own eyes the way her concoctions would flash a bright white or some other color then fade into something normal, safe to travel to the square with. She'd sat there for hours, waiting for the perfect nobleman or woman to come by, searching for someone with power and the ability to keep a secret. She'd take them back into her caravan, show them what she'd made, and take their coin, leaving them with the promise of the continuation of their lineage nine months later. He suspected his mother had been responsible for fifty percent of the nobles born all those years ago.

He'd lost her, just like Harlow had lost her foster mother, in the village raids thirteen years ago. Her real mother died young. Too young. But her sacrifice ... well, her sacrifice was the girl he now held in his arms. Marion had sacrificed everything to save her daughter, and those who came after had done the same. The power swimming in Harlow's veins gave them all hope, a potential future countless people would stand up and die for. Something they *had* died for. He had to make this all mean something. They'd come so far, and they'd all suffered so much.

"Does she have power?" Desminda asked.

"I don't know," Shade lied. He loved his future queen. But she was royalty and like all royalty. She was prone to fits of pettiness. Desminda was different in many ways, and he loved her all the more for it, but royalty came with a cost. And Desminda had paid it. He knew her secret. She kept it close to her, wrapped tight under layers and layers of subterfuge and secrecy, but it had surfaced one evening when she thought she was alone.

She would deny it until the day she died, but his friend's daughter and Harlow weren't that different when it mattered.

"You know what has to happen if she has power." The statement fell like stones at Shade's feet. He glanced at Desminda, struggling to hide his disapproval. He'd draw his own sword if she thought to harm Harlow.

From the way she flinched, he knew she'd seen it in his eyes.

The ruling family of Thornewilde hadn't always been this way. Maintaining their power base and trying to secure more turned them against each other. Many years ago, he and Desminda's father shared a kinship, not easily broken. When Stonehand and Marion arrived, Shade realized their kingdom was akin to a damaged ship full of slow leaks, each decision taking them ever closer to peril.

When the king chose to march on the other kingdoms, Raima's love fractured. For a while, Shade saw the potential she had, until her ideals clashed with her religion, and she tied the two together, colliding into a disastrous queendom where magic was forced out with an iron hand and a new religion was trotted in and enforced with subtle threats and fear. The new religion proclaimed magic treasonous, and to dabble in it meant eternal damnation. But the people were slow to adapt, and most only did so on the surface, quietly practicing their traditional ways in the secrecy behind closed doors.

Not long after, the king began to show signs of illness, whatever ailing him a slow and insidious process. Now, Shade didn't recognize the man any longer, only flashes in his daughter, sometimes kind and bright and others like this, calmly discussing murder.

"Magic cannot exist," she echoed weakly, the same words her mother had said over and over again.

It *could* exist. And after tonight, he knew it was possible to bring it back.

"So they say," Shade mused.

They fell silent, watching the healer work on Harlow. The cut wasn't the serious issue. Although Harlow had been aware earlier, she'd fallen into a comatose state on the way over. Stonehand had warned him of this some time ago. Mages coming into their power went one of two ways, a slow burn off or a supernova. Harlow had gone the way of the latter. If she was half the mage her father was, she would come out of this coma.

He couldn't bear to think of the alternative.

"Would you cut her down yourself?" Shade asked. He shouldn't have said anything, shouldn't have let his feelings intrude on this.

Desminda turned her shocked gaze to him. "You care for her." Accusation dripped from her voice.

"I care for each of the girls under my tutelage."

Desminda snorted delicately. "Even the thirty-seven who are traipsing through our forests blindly as we speak?"

A grim smile curled onto Shade's lips. "Most of them will not last through the month. The forests of Thornewilde are not for the weak hearted." He might walk a fine line between loyalty and treason, but the missing Virago showed cowardice and weakness when it mattered. Their disappearance told Shade where they stood concerning magic and its potential return, standing at odds with his view and that of most of the kingdom's citizens. While losing that many potential Viragos to the woods wasn't ideal, Shade's viewpoint fell on the pragmatic side. He'd deal with whatever the beasts left behind, but even if they came crawling back to him, they'd never serve the queen. And if any tried to harm a hair on Desminda's or Harlow's head, they'd meet the pointed end of his sword.

"Perhaps," the princess agreed. But she lifted her chin in defiance. "And perhaps as we speak, they plot to take our kingdom down." Her heavy gaze landed on Shade even as her voice lowered to barely a whisper. "Magic has landed this night in Thornewood, whether you admit to it or not. Lie to me all you want, Shade. I can smell it in the air, feel it on my skin." Her gaze flickered to Harlow. "It drips from this girl, this mage you protect at all costs."

Shade met her dark gaze.

"Is it worth our kingdom collapsing?" Desminda asked. "This promise you made to your friend?"

Shade glanced down at his best friend's daughter, the bruises and cuts and wear and hopelessness, then back at his future queen, the one he'd sworn his life to.

"For hope, every loss is worth it."

# CHAPTER TWENTY-SEVEN

## THE HEALER

S he woke to candlelight and uncomfortable warmth at first. Then pain. Excruciating agony hammered through her veins. Her head felt like a blacksmith pounded inside of it, her mouth dry. But there was something else, something beautiful in the midst of all her darkness.

A pool lived in the depths of her soul. A cavern filled with a bottomless depth of power, an unfamiliar yet welcome sensation. Harlow squeezed her eyes shut, unwilling to go back to normal life, to pain and hopelessness. She wanted to stay here with this feeling of hope blooming deep inside of her. The real world was too much. Too loud and violent and devoid of hope or love.

If she could, she would stay here forever.

"I know you're awake."

Harlow wanted nothing more than to ignore the husk of that voice, to curl up inside of herself and touch the thing living deep within her, shutting out the rest of the world. But Harlow wasn't brave enough to ignore the authority of Desminda's voice.

She blinked her eyes, wincing even in the low light. Pain speared through her head.

"Your Majesty." Harlow's voice sounded like she'd eaten sawdust.

"Tell me what happened," her voice demanded.

Harlow wasn't brave enough to look at the future queen yet. Every time she had before, she felt like all her secrets would spill like honey from a hive.

"A storm," she croaked.

"A storm," Desminda echoed, her voice stark with disbelief. "I've never once been in the company of so many beautiful liars."

Harlow said nothing, and the quiet night ticked away in the silence.

Desminda exhaled a puff of air. A swish of fabric sounded, and Harlow felt someone next to her. Trickling water landed in a bowl behind her, and blessed coolness touched Harlow's forehead a moment later.

A sigh broke forth from her parched throat at the gentle touch.

"Why do you lie to me?" Desminda asked.

Harlow was no liar, but the magic that had torn from her soul was a source of tentative hope for her, a moment in time that made her feel like if she only stayed the course, the world would be restored.

"I've never seen a storm its like before," Harlow answered, the lie slipping cool and easy from her tongue. Maybe, when it truly mattered, she was the best of liars.

The cool cloth against her skin paused. Desminda exhaled a soft breath. "I would like to be your friend," the future queen whispered.

Harlow had never heard a more alluring lie, even though she wanted to curl those words around her and hold them close forever. She lied by necessity, but Desminda lied for power, for information, for control.

"Do you think friendship can begin with a lie?" Harlow asked, remembering how she'd met Desminda.

The future queen abruptly realized her mistake and the clever way Harlow had trapped her. A soft snort came from her throat. "Perhaps I should ask you that question," Desminda replied. "I dare say not divulging my identity is vastly different from treason.

"Can two lies cancel each other?" she continued. "Or do they pile on top of each other until the truth becomes indiscernible?"

The answer seemed clearer to Harlow than to the future queen. Nova had never lied to her, not until she told her she would never leave her. But she wondered if something had happened, something so grievous Nova had no choice other than to leave her in the dark of the night.

"I think some lies are necessary," Harlow said. "For to reveal the truth would be to bring pain to those you love."

"Is love not pain?" Desminda retorted. "Pain of the most exquisite kind?"

Harlow wouldn't know. Love did not equate to pain for her, even through all of it. Nova would have never left her if she didn't have to. Her sister searched for something, something even more important than Harlow. "Love is hope," she responded. "Love is a way forward even through the darkness."

The future queen paused in her ministrations. "You've the heart of a poet and the work ethic of a yeoman, Harlow." She plunged the cloth back into the water as Harlow rolled onto her side, her gaze meeting the liquid gold eyes of the queen. Her breath caught as Desminda's ebony hair flashed midnight blue in the candlelight. Her tawny skin glowed, the hollow of her throat exposed. Shade must have gathered her from her quarters because she'd never seen the queen so unkempt. She wore breeches, a tan brown color encasing her coltish legs. Desminda bent over Harlow, her shirt gaping to expose the golden skin of her collarbone, the long sleeves folded up exposing slender forearms, flexing with muscle as she wrung the linen cloth out.

Harlow reached out, stopping Desminda from touching her burning skin again with the moist cloth. "Do you think love is pain?"

Desminda's gaze met hers. Emotions flickered through her eyes, hope and pain, and joy and sorrow. She looked away. "Love doesn't work for me as it does for you," she admitted. "I don't have the luxury of love without conditions."

Harlow gazed up at the person above her, royalty who'd debased herself to ministering to a liar and a heretic. "Don't you?" she asked, holding her breath as her confession became clear to the future queen.

Harlow had known love, the tender arms of her foster mother, her foster father, and the firm arms of Nova, who'd loved her but also taught her hard lessons. But she'd never known the love of another who didn't see her as someone to be protected.

Desminda stood above her, vulnerable and stunning, her dark hair unbound, curling down her shoulders. They were alone, together during the darkest of nights, when magic had been loosed in their world again.

"Harlow," she whispered. Desminda leaned forward, a curl of dark hair brushing Harlow's cheek. Her breath whispered against her face as the princesses' eyes flickered shut...

The door flung open, a frigid breeze blowing in, brushing away the promise of something new blooming between them. Desminda jerked away, her fingers trembling. The washcloth slipped from her fingers, landing with a wet plop on the ground.

"Oh," the healer breathed. "I didn't expect to find you here, Your Majesty." The girl bobbed her head and dove into an awkward curtsy.

Harlow squeezed her eyes shut, thankful and angry all at once. *Softhearted fool.* She meant nothing to the future queen. She was someone disposable. Princess Desminda could have anyone. She didn't want someone like Harlow, battered and bruised, abandoned by everyone who'd ever loved her.

But the way Desminda's eyes flickered, heat making her amber eyes glow, Harlow wondered for a moment if there could be a different future in store for her.

"I'll take this over. Shade is behind me. He asked if you would await him outside. He's there to escort you back to the castle."

A cool smile flickered over Desminda's mouth even as her eyes glowed with heat. "Of course," she told the healer. "I'll grab my cloak and meet him outside."

Harlow waited until Desminda had left the room to blow out a slow breath.

The healer's lips thinned as she looked her over, checking her eyes and ears. She tutted and shook her head. "You're asking for trouble there, Miss."

Harlow turned her face away. "I didn't ask."

# CHAPTER TWENTY-EIGHT

## THE BOY IN THE NIGHT

The healer wanted her to stay the night, but Harlow refused. She didn't want to go back to the dorms, but she didn't want to stay in the infirmary either. Against her better judgment, Harlow eased herself off the wooden cot, wincing as she took her first few steps.

There wasn't a single part of her body that didn't hurt. Her outside finally matched her insides. She blew out a breath and nodded to the healer. Emily was her name, mentioned after Harlow had snapped at her about Desminda.

The healer had to be used to angry people. After all, her patients were all in pain or ill or at the end of their lives. They'd have a lot to be angry about.

Emily mentioned her mother had been a healer— one of the few blessed with true healing magic. After the magic had gone, her mother hadn't the heart to carry on and had abandoned her. Emily's eyes had turned sad as she told the story. When Harlow asked if she was angry, the healer had shaken her head. "How could I be angry? They ripped away the thing that made her who she was. My mother was never the same person after that." Emily had paused for a moment, her gaze far away. "I'm sad over it. I hope one day she gets it back."

Harlow's thoughts strayed to what happened in the dorm. Her mind had played hide and seek with it for hours, not wanting to investigate it for what it really was.

She had magic. Powerful magic if the damage to the dorm was any indication. She'd found it again, just like the bard asked her to. And now she had no idea what to do with it. Or where the mysterious bard had gone to.

"Farewell," Emily said.

Harlow lifted her hand in a wave. "I'm sure I'll be seeing you soon."

Emily giggled. "Let's hope not, but you're probably right."

Harlow stepped into the cool night air and headed straight for the one thing she knew would bring her comfort.

THE MARE SNORTED a greeting when Harlow crept into the stables, cautiously looking around for anyone else. The hour had grown late and most of the townspeople were safe in their homes. Shade would have her head if he knew she'd come here instead of going straight back to the dorms, but there was a lot on her mind she had to deal with and she couldn't bear going back and facing all the accusing eyes.

"Hi," she whispered as she hurried over to the mare's stall. The horse pushed its head above the door, eager for the stroke of Harlow's fingers. She obliged, gliding down its sleek nose. "Mind if I come in?"

The beast huffed. Taking that as permission, Harlow scampered up and over the stall door, landing nimbly on the balls of her feet. She looked up at the great horse, once again marveling at its enormous size. "Do they ever let you out?" she wondered mostly aloud.

"They can't," a voice from behind the door said.

Harlow squeaked and stumbled back, landing on her rear end in the hay. "Who's there?" she demanded.

Wood squeaked and groaned. Seconds later, a boy peered over the top of the stall, far enough away that the mare couldn't reach him.

"Lant?"

He grinned at her. "If I hadn't seen this with my own eyes, I wouldn't believe it. No one can take her outside. She won't allow it."

Harlow stroked a hand down the horse's side. "That can't be healthy. Animals need sunshine and exercise."

Lant gave her an incredulous look. "And men need to keep their fingers and toes, girl. She's a nightmare. Any time anyone comes close to her, other than to give her food and water, she goes wild." He tilted his head. "So, I'm very interested to know what you did for her to allow you the liberties you've taken."

She frowned up at him. "I didn't do anything."

His brow furrowed. "She just likes you?"

Harlow snorted. "Is that so hard to believe then?" She studied Lant as closely as she could without being strange about it. There was something about him she couldn't quite put her finger on. His blond hair was a touch too long and his hazel eyes were...

She gasped. "You're the boy!" Harlow pointed up at him. "The boy from the streets!"

Color touched his cheeks. "Hush, girl," he hissed. "I'm new to this position and don't want anyone knowing about—" he paused and ducked his head.

"About how you rob poor young girls in the dead of night?" Harlow said, her voice vibrating with anger.

He lowered his eyes. "I'm sorry. I didn't know he would—" Lant cut himself off. "It wasn't right."

She scoffed. "How did you even come across someone like him?"

Lant lifted his head. Their eyes met. "He's my cousin," he said quietly.

"Oh." Family was sometimes the biggest trap of all. They could get you into a heap of trouble and you'd go along with it before you knew what was happening.

Lant smiled, a sad and tired expression. Harlow swallowed and the urge to ask her next question died in her throat at the look.

"You got him pretty good." The boy leaned back against the post holding the stall door up, his small frame folded up. "We couldn't stop the bleeding."

Her stomach lurched. "Oh, Lant. I am so so—"

Lant cut her off. "Do not apologize for trying to live. He was doing the same." His gaze darkened. "Or he used to. The streets got to him. He used to be a kinder boy."

She felt no guilt. No remorse. Lant was right. All she was guilty of was surviving. Striking the first blow had allowed her to escape. "You gave me money. And your scarf."

Lant looked away. "Seemed like the least I could do for you." His lips quivered. "And once Dex was gone, I had enough to scrape by for a while."

Harlow blew out a breath, her anger evaporating with the realization of his loss. They were all imperfect, weren't they? And what would she do if faced with the same choice? He'd helped her when it mattered and wasn't that what mattered now? "I didn't starve because of you."

"I'm sure you would have found a way. Perhaps I just made the path a little easier." He lifted a thin shoulder in a shrug. "Or maybe since you're here and the entire castle is a twitter with rumors of what happened inside of that dorm room, perhaps I haven't." Lant eyed the horse and when he moved a hair closer, the great beast stomped her foot. He held up his hands and resumed his original position.

"Can I take her for a walk?" Harlow blurted impulsively. She couldn't conjure sunshine, but the horse deserved to stretch its legs. If someone left her inside of a cage for that long, she'd be angry too.

Lant's eyes widened almost comically. "What?" he blurted. "Are you mad, girl?"

Harlow didn't answer. She looked up at the horse. "How about it then? Want to go for a walk?"

The horse didn't move or make any indication it heard her. It was almost like it had stilled in anticipation of the carrot Harlow dangled in front of her.

"Give me a lead," Harlow said.

Lant shook his head. "No."

Harlow patted the beast on the side and scrambled up and over the stall, a cry of pain slipping from her lips with the movement. The healer had given her something to numb the worst of it, but she still felt like someone had taken a hammer to her very marrow. "Very well then. I'll get it myself." She had almost no experience with horses, but how hard could it be to walk one?

"This is a terrible idea," Lant said, scrambling down from his perch on top of the stall. "If you lose her, who do you think they'll blame?"

"You weren't here," Harlow said. "And I'll mention walking by and seeing the horse run away."

Lant rushed in front of her, holding his hands up. "You can't! She's a wild beast. If you try to walk her, she'll run."

Harlow snatched the lead down from a hook in the wall and took it over to the stall. She climbed up and snapped it onto the circular connection on the bottom of the horse's bridle. "You can't run away from me, you got it?"

The horse snorted impatiently.

"Don't do this," Lant warned.

She sent an impatient glare over her shoulder. "It's cruel to keep her locked up like this."

"I'm not arguing the point, but it's unwise to suddenly trust a horse who's never been unleashed."

Harlow eyed the beast. "Do you want to go out?"

The horse's eyes glittered with anticipation.

"Don't make me regret this," she warned.

Abruptly, the mare went completely still, staring at Harlow with an unnerving intelligence. With a huff of laughter, Harlow reached up and patted her nose.

After a deep, nervous breath, she unlatched the stall.

# CHAPTER TWENTY-NINE

## SWEET FREEDOM

L ant's sharp inhale of breath was the only sound in the stable. The horse stood still as a statue.

"Come on," Harlow said gently. She gave a light tug on the lead and, for the first time, realized that was the only protection she had between herself and the horse. If the mare wanted to, it could yank it out of her hand and trample right over her.

She glanced at Lant. The worry on his face matched the worry in her heart.

Being foolhardy was apparently Harlow's favorite thing to do today.

"Let's go see the moonlight," she said.

The horse took one step out of the stall.

HARLOW'S HEART hammered within her chest. The beast had given her no reason to fear it, but this was different. The pen had represented safety. Now that they were in the open, anything could happen. She walked beside the mare, matching her steps to the horse's tentative ones. Lant quietly opened the main stable doors, and she led her outside. Moonlight glimmered against her coat and mane making her look like a creature from a fairy tale.

"We have to be quiet," Harlow whispered. Lant walked beside them, his face pale and his eyes darting every which way looking for anyone who might come up to the stables this late at night.

"Relax," Harlow hissed. "Everyone is asleep. I'm taking her to the path in the woods. No one will see her."

"This is foolish," Lant whispered beside her. "You have a way of bringing disaster with you, don't you?"

Harlow blinked in surprise. His words were a stab wound against her already damaged heart. She could have said a million things to him, but instead, she hurried her steps, leaving Lant behind. She glanced back and he had stopped, his hands shoved in his pockets and his shoulders slumped. A lock of blond hair glimmered in the moonlight, but she was too far away to see his eyes.

The horse walked beside her, quiet and steady. She could only imagine how it would look to anyone seeing them. Her slight frame would make it look like a child leading it.

They ventured into the path of the woods behind the stables, the place where she'd seen horses going in and out for their daily walks. They had a pen they used when they were training horses, but the path into the woods was maintained daily so there was no debris or anything to damage the animal's hooves. With the activity, most of the wild animals stayed away, so the place remained a good option to exercise the horses and other plow animals.

Harlow touched the horse's neck. The high trees dappled the moonlight, casting a silvery glow against the stones lining the path. Fireflies danced in front of them, their glow a steady beacon forward. The horse sniffed at one of them, curious about the light the bugs gave off. Harlow grinned and patted the horse. "Lucciola," she whispered quietly. "That's what I'll call you."

The beast huffed.

"Luci for short?"

The horse gently bumped her with its head. "You like that?" she asked it. "It means Firefly."

Nova had taught her, or tried to, another language she'd picked up from a book. She said it was from a land far away and if they ever needed it, they could speak it to each other. Harlow had forgotten most of the words by now, but she remembered *firefly* because every evening during the spring, she and Nova would run outside catching the bugs in a glass jar and watch them for hours.

In a way, the horse reminded her of Nova. Her sister's hair was dark as night, her eyes a cool silvery color that always reminded Harlow of the moon. She always imagined Nova as a fey thing, wild and unfettered. Nothing could hold her back.

Not even Harlow.

They plunged on through the woods, a little quicker this time. Luci tossed her mane back and began to prance making Harlow laugh.

"I'll try to come back when I can. It may not be easy breaking away after everything that's happened." Not to mention the magic she held within her veins. She felt it there, a pool of untapped power. It was sated for now, but for how long?

Luci stopped. Harlow looked around, trying to sense something, but there was nothing. Luci lifted her head up, and Harlow imagined she was trying to see the moon in all its glory. "We have to go back," she said.

The horse shivered and tugged Harlow forward. "Luci," she warned. "We have to. I have to get back to the dorm. There's a lot I need to answer for."

Luci tugged her forward again. Harlow resisted, but she

knew if the horse was serious, she wouldn't be able to fight her. "Come with me."

Luci stopped moving. Her dark gaze locked with Harlow's as if she was trying to tell her something. Harlow reached out and touched the space between Luci's brow, stroking her shimmering coat. "If I had a horse, I'd want her to be just like you." She reached around and hugged Luci around the neck. Harlow breathed in the comforting scent of hay and animal, something different in Luci's smell than other horses, deep and mysterious. Luci's warmth soaked into Harlow's face and neck, and she rubbed her cheek against the side of the mare's silky coat.

Harlow never wanted much. A place to call home, a family, people who loved her. She never thought much about anything else until she lost everything. The world was a hard place when you were alone, but there was freedom in making your own decisions and choosing your own fate. Since Harlow arrived, Luci stayed locked in the pen most days, only the bravest venturing forth to try and exercise her. It had never worked out, Luci's temperament fickle and angry, forcing her continued confinement.

Why she'd chosen to trust Harlow, she'd never know. Sometimes in life there were moments where you had to trust back, even if it felt dangerous. Harlow had done the same in some regards, but maybe there was one more step she could take. Maybe Luci was trying to tell her something and maybe there was more to this moment than even Harlow could fathom.

She pulled back a few inches, lifting her eyes to Luci's. A kinship existed there, perhaps affection, maybe something even deeper. Was it fair to cage those you loved?

Her throat thick with tears, Harlow leaned in and squeezed Luci one more time.

When she stepped back, she unhooked the lead from the horse's halter. Luci and Harlow stood on the path, moonlight glowing against their skin, facing each other. Tears gathered in Harlow's eyes at the thought of not seeing Luci again, but the mare's freedom meant more than her feelings.

A moment later Luci ducked her great head low, bending one of her legs down. Harlow's breath caught. She leaned forward and planted a soft kiss on Luci's head, her fingers stroking her soft nose one final time.

Moments later, Luci turned and took off in a storm of thundering hooves and glimmering mane.

LANT'S GAZE filled with accusation when she came back with an empty halter, but she couldn't feel guilty. Harlow's heart still soared with wonder at the joy of Luci's freedom. A gift like her should never be caged. She wasn't sorry. She'd never be sorry for giving something so magnificent its freedom.

When Lant looked at her for an explanation, Harlow shrugged. "She took off like a shot."

"And managed to unhook her lead?"

"She's a smart horse."

Lant sighed and held his hand out. Harlow handed over the lead and followed him back to the stables.

"Where will you sleep now?"

Harlow's spine stiffened. "What do you mean?"

"I've seen you sneak in here."

"I have no idea what you're talking about."

Lant held the stable door open for her and followed her in, reaching over to hang the lead up. "If you don't want to take the cot upstairs, there's a silver bay a few stalls down. She's got a sweet disposition and loves humans."

Color crept up her cheeks. "I sleep in the dorm," she snapped.

Lant shrugged. "But if you didn't, the bay's name is Laurel."

Harlow huffed out a breath. "Good night, Lant."

"'Night, Harlow," he said. "Be careful out there. Rumor is some strange things are swirling out there in the dark."

A chill crept up her spine as she slipped out of the stable. She hugged the buildings as she hurried back to the dorm. And when she opened the doors to the dorm and saw the lamps dim and all the girls tucked into their beds, she heaved a soft sigh of relief that she'd have a reprieve of at least a few hours before she had to answer questions.

# CHAPTER THIRTY

## TOSS A COIN TO YOUR BULLY

S hade flipped the coin in her direction. Melara snatched it from the air and tucked it into her pocket. She watched Shade warily.

"This was what you wanted?" Melara leaned against the stone of the castle walls, away from the prying eyes of its inhabitants. Shade stayed in the shadows, his black clothing and hair making him seem like a ghost.

"We needed to know," he said.

"Perhaps there was a better way than cruelty," Melara mused.

He snorted. "But you are so very good at it, aren't you?"

Melara flinched and took a step back. "You saw the results. Those who know what magic looks like will know what happened."

"Many people in the castle are too young to remember. There is time."

"What will happen with Harlow?"

A breath escaped him. "Nothing for now. You do not need to concern yourself with it."

"She is young, Shade. Still innocent. Far more innocent than most of us."

Shade pushed off the wall and tossed her another coin. "Thank your sister for me. Breaking into the dorm was a touch of genius."

He nodded to her and disappeared into the shadows, a man of shadows and mystery.

A soft sigh escaped her as she watched the darkness for a sign of him. Why did she feel like he was a marionette and the rest of them his puppets?

# CHAPTER THIRTY-ONE

## LAUGHING TO KEEP FROM CRYING

S ilence was a shroud over the dormitory the next morning. Shade had strolled in before sunset, given them all a grim look, and announced they would have the next two days off while the damage to the dorm was addressed. They were all dressed in their conditioning clothes from the last instructions he'd given them, but none were going to complain about the reprieve.

They weren't allowed to leave the village, but they could do whatever they wished with their time. Before he left, he smirked and suggested they add some conditioning into their downtime and if they didn't, he would have no sympathy for the aches and pains they'd soon have.

Harlow watched his broad back as he strolled out. He hadn't said a word to her since yesterday. She'd woken up this morning, full of dread at the thought of being shown the door or worse. Instead, his eyes skimmed right over her as if it were a normal day.

Anyone who displayed a hint of magic went to the gallows or disappeared without a word, like they'd suddenly become a figment of your imagination. No one spoke of them again for fear they'd be brought low the same way. Others who'd fallen foul of someone powerful also disappeared sometimes, accused of magic or witchcraft, never to be seen again. Everyone in the kingdom walked a fine line between living and dying, but those who once possessed magic had to be twice as careful to avoid the same fate.

From the way her insides churned, today was anything but normal. She sat on her cot, her gaze roaming over the other girls. No one seemed eager to get out of bed or do much of anything really. The room was colder than normal thanks to the gaping hole in the roof. Fortunately, the good weather had held last night and looked to be holding this morning based on the twinkling stars above them.

The quiet began to chafe. The urge to say something about last night burned within her. Why the few girls who were left had protected her, she had no idea. But most of the trainees hadn't.

"Do you know where the other girls have gone?" Harlow finally croaked.

A loud, amused snort rang from the other side of the room.

Then someone else chuckled. Another girl giggled.

Soon, the entire room was bright with laughter.

Harlow's shoulders began to relax. Her lips twitched with the beginning of a smile and a few seconds later, her shoulders shook with amusement.

Bloom held both hands over her face and she rocked back and forth, her thin shoulders shaking.

"I can only imagine they're still running through the forest screaming," she finally said through gales of laughter.

"We have a hole— a massive hole in our roof," another girl shrieked with laughter.

"From a *storm*," crowed another girl.

They laughed for a little while longer and slowly began to sober.

Harlow sat on the bed, feeling lighter than she had since the first time she'd walked into this room. Melara stood, the lamp light casting deep shadows against her skin. Harlow felt the tension snap in the air as the girl walked over and steeled herself for what would inevitably turn into a fight, but to her surprise, Melara sat at the foot of her bed.

The flicker of firelight highlighted the deep shadows underneath her eyes. "Your last name isn't Fischer," Melara said.

Of all the things Harlow expected to come out of her mouth, those words weren't it. "Pardon?"

"Are you familiar with Magnus Stonehand?" Melara's dark gaze was calm and steady.

"Should I be?" Her brow furrowed as she tried to figure out what Melara was saying. The other girls were all sitting up on their beds, their attention rapt on them. A memory floated to her, hazy and indistinct— a conversation she had with Nova years ago where her sister brought up magic. It drifted away before she could grasp it.

Melara's look didn't change, as if she knew Harlow was clueless. It made her feel both better and worse.

"He was a great mage."

Bloom laughed and got out of bed, dragging her blanket with her. She settled herself at Harlow and Melara's feet. "He's a *legendary* mage," she corrected.

Melara gave her a long look. "Bloom." She sighed and rolled her eyes. "Let me tell it." Bloom gave Melara a cheeky smile and held her finger to her lips. Melara continued. "It's rumored his daughter would bring magic back to the world."

Harlow still didn't get it. She knew the parents who raised her weren't the ones who had given her life. When Nova found her in the wreckage of her village, she was with the bodies of her mother, father, and siblings. There was never any indication she was special or anything other than what she was.

But from the anticipatory silence in the dorm and the gleam in some of the other girl's eyes, it hit her.

They thought she was this Stonehand's daughter. Shock rooted her to her bed. Impossible. Wasn't it?

Harlow shook her head. "I—I'm sorry. I can't be his daughter. I don't know what happened. I just got so angry..." Her voice trailed off. Had her sister known this all along? More questions than answers spun in her mind.

"The heir of magic was lost sixteen years ago," Melara said. "She was born to Stonehand and a woman in the castle."

That memory floated in again, Nova's words about a woman in the castle flitting away on butterfly wings.

The girl at her feet jumped in. "It's rumored she was a servant, but my mother said she was so much more. She and Stonehand fell in love and for a while, she was able to keep her pregnancy a secret. But when she started to show, the queen demanded to know who the father was."

Melara sighed. "It's really quite romantic if you think about it. The woman, under the direction of Stonehand, lied to the queen and claimed the babe was the get of a visiting nobleman who'd long since returned to his kingdom."

All the other girls wandered over, most of them dragging their blankets. They sat, curling their feet under their legs and listened, rapt with attention.

"She and Stonehand kept the secret until the woman went into labor," Melara continued. "A storm came in that night, one so terrible it rocked the foundations of the castle, and with it rumors of a terrible omen."

Bloom sat forward. "With the birth of this girl, magic would soon fall."

Goosebumps broke over Harlow's skin. "But I didn't have

anything to do with it. I was a baby when magic fell. My sister..." Her words trailed away. "She found me next to my dead parents."

"Thornewood had something to do with it," Melara said quietly. "Every village knows it. There are other kingdoms, much further away that still have their power, though it is reduced." Her eyes met mine. "And then there are others who've never lost their magic, instead keeping it hidden, secret from even those who love them the most."

A girl from the back cleared her throat. "My mother was a healer."

Another girl behind Harlow spoke. "My father was a metal-smith. He could forge magical weapons from steel and iron and copper. Whatever someone brought, he could hone it with his power."

Melara bowed her head. "My sister was an empath. She could take anger away and feel whatever you were experiencing. My mother was a nature mage." A tentative smile graced her mouth. "I don't remember a lot from before magic fell, but I always felt like I was living in a fairy tale when I lived with them."

Bloom did not speak, but Harlow noticed something in her eyes. Something haunted and painful. Harlow blinked and looked away, but Bloom's next words stunned her. "The storm bought them time to smuggle the woman out of the castle with Stonehand's help. But the queen knew what he'd done, and she called for his execution."

"I don't understand," Harlow said. "Why was it a sin to fall in love?"

Melara smiled sadly. "Stonehand was conscripted into the queen's service when he was a young man. Power that extreme could never be allowed to walk free. With it, she secured her power base and the safety of her kingdom. When he fell in love, the queen took it personally. But when she figured out who the child was, she saw a powerful tool slipping away from her."

"You speak of the future queen's mother?" Harlow blew out a breath. It was hard to envision Desminda with a mother like that, but royalty played games. She'd seen it firsthand.

Several of the girls laughed. "Stonehand was already presumed dead by the time magic fell. No one saw him after the queen pronounced him an enemy of the kingdom. She wrested her control from the king with ruthless efficiency," Melara said. "It cannot be a coincidence that magic fell not too long after the child disappeared."

"Magic is a bargaining tool," Helena said. She'd curled up next to Bloom, her threadbare blanket barely covering her dark feet. "Kingdoms have fallen for less."

"We could all be killed for speaking of this," Harlow whispered.

"It's time someone spoke about it," Melara said.

Harlow gave her an odd look. "Why are you being so nice to me now?" she snapped.

A wicked grin touched Melara's lips. "Because I came here to find the Heir of Magic. Magic is activated by many things. Age, power level, and high stress or emotion. I suspected it was you from the moment I saw you."

Surprise burst within her. "But how? How would you have known?"

Melara's gaze touched Bloom's. "Because there are some people out there who still See things, Harlow. Some of the old folk knew the Heir would return. And some knew she would come to the castle."

The girl at her feet nudged Harlow's thigh with her elbow. "Plus, you're a carbon copy of your mother," she said, rolling her eyes at Melara's dramatics.

Harlow touched her cheek. "I am?"

Sympathy touched Melara's eyes. "She and my mother were good friends once. When magic was still strong, they had a portrait magician make a small painting of them. It still hangs in our house today. The future queen was too young to remember what she looked like, but I would urge you not to avail yourself of the queen too much."

She couldn't remember what her mother looked like when she lived in Thornewilde, but if what they said were true, she was not the woman who carried her.

"How am I going to keep this secret?" she wondered aloud.

"With us," Melara said.

Tears filled Harlow's eyes. "You were *so* cruel to me," she said, choking on tears.

Melara sighed and put her arm around Harlow's shoulders. "I'm sorry for that. But the world has suffered for a long time, Harlow. Don't you think a little pain is worth setting it right?"

She'd had all the pain one person should have to stand, but this didn't seem like the right time to point that out.

"I don't know what this means," Harlow said, her stomach clenched with apprehension. The burden of this seemed too much to bear. "I don't know what to do."

Bloom patted her knee. "You'll know when it's time."

And with those cryptic words, the last remaining future Virago began to make plans for their days off.

# CHAPTER THIRTY-TWO

### THORN OF TREASON

**B**loom and Melara invited her to go with them to explore the local village, but Harlow declined. She lay back on her uncomfortable cot, staring up at the ceiling. The dorm had quickly emptied after their conversation, leaving her in perfect quiet.

Her head spun with the implications of her birth. In some ways, it made perfect sense. In others, it made zero. She was just a girl. An orphan. Those were a dime a dozen all over the kingdom. There was nothing special about her. She was weak, emotional, and sometimes rebellious.

It seemed ludicrous to leave the entire fate of magic in her hands. Where were the adults to guide her? Someone to hold her hand and tell her exactly what to do? Could she fix the wrongs the kingdom had supposedly wrought? Was she even supposed to?

Harlow knew something was afoot. She never believed too much in fate, but coincidence was beginning to look less and less likely than someone or something slowly steering her in the direction of something much larger than herself.

Thoughts of the red-haired bard invaded her mind. She'd

never seen magic until she'd met her and thought perhaps the bard brought change with her. After all, few bards were ever seen once magic fell throughout the kingdom. Harlow's late-night sprint through the forest played through her head. Frowning, she rolled out of bed and unlocked the trunk by her bed. She still held the stone Nova had given her in her pocket, but the one she'd found by the fire that night was wrapped in cloth and tucked at the bottom.

Harlow rummaged through it and pulled the white stone out. The light in the dormitory was dim, so she took it over to a window and studied it. The only thing interesting about it was the blue flash when the light hit it. Other than that, it looked ordinary. She frowned and pulled the other stone out of her pocket, holding them up beside each other. A slight pull came from each of the stones, so subtle Harlow thought she imagined it. But as she moved them closer together, it happened again. She chewed on the edge of her lip as her mind worked to figure out what was happening, but when she edged the two stones even closer together, the left one she'd found at the campsite snapped out of her fingers.

Harlow gasped, fumbling to try to catch the stone, but she needn't have worried. It snapped against the one Nova had given her and stuck.

She peered closer but couldn't see a seam. It was like the stones had locked into perfect place. "Huh," she breathed. The stone pulsed once, twice, flashing a brilliant cerulean before it fell quiet in her hands. Melara's words came back to her, and she swallowed hard, wondering against all odds if her bones held unfathomable power. Who her parents were. What her purpose was. She blinked away the tears, basking in the knowledge that she had been so very loved.

The sound of the latch on the dormitory door squeaked. She

gasped in a surprised breath and shoved the stone deep into her pocket.

Lucien's face peered around the corner, his bright green eyes scanning for anyone else. When they fell onto Harlow, he pushed the door farther open and stepped inside.

They stared at each other for a moment. Lucien shoved his hands into his pockets and cleared his throat.

"I figured I might find you here."

"Friendless and alone?" Harlow offered. His eyes widened at her tone, and she ducked her head. "Sorry," she muttered.

But instead of reprimanding her, Lucien laughed. "Sometimes people with great stories still left to tell have trouble making friends." He stepped further inside and shut the door behind him.

Lucien, it seemed, had no trouble with impropriety. This wasn't even the third time she'd found herself alone with him. Had anyone walked in and seen them together, Harlow would bear the brunt of the gossip. She found she couldn't muster up much care.

"I don't have a story," Harlow said. "I'm merely trying to survive."

Lucien came closer and perched on the edge of one of the girl's cots. "I'm here to assure myself of your continued good health."

"You heard what happened." It wasn't a question.

Lucien's gaze lifted to the hole in the roof. "I think you should assume everyone heard what happened." He slid the look to her. "A storm, you said?"

Harlow peered at him, trying to see underneath the innocence of his words. "A storm."

"Hmm," he drawled. "I've never seen a storm leave this kind of damage."

Harlow said nothing, one of her sister's many warnings

coming back to her. *"Say little and then even less when you're unsure of the conversation's motive."* Had her sister known back then the challenges Harlow might face? It seemed uncanny how many times Nova had been right.

A smile flashed on his face at Harlow's silence. "You're a smart girl," he mused. "I heard a rumor of something more happening here than a mere storm. Would you care to elaborate?"

"I would not. This was a terrible freak storm. Nothing more."

Lucien studied his nails. "Do you remember magic, Harlow?"

She blinked at him stupidly. "Do you?" she countered.

Lucien chuckled. "I am not too much older than you, but I do remember the way my Nana's cakes tasted like heaven and I remember how everything she made tasted more delicious than anything I'd ever eaten. That is its own magic, don't you think?" He looked up. "I remember the roses surrounding the palace and my mother's fingers pricked and bleeding when she came in from caring for them. Those roses never stopped blooming, no matter if we had rain, sleet, or snow. And my father, well, my father had a way with weapons. His blade never missed its mark. Not once. So I suppose I saw magic in the way that some people *are* magic. There was never a light show or any indication they were anything than what they appeared to be on the surface. But isn't that what magic is? Not necessarily its own thing, but something that lives inside of some people and makes them who they are?"

Wariness filled her. "I wouldn't know. Magic has never availed itself to me." The lie curled within her, turning her stomach into knots.

"Ah," Lucien remarked. "Forgive me then. For a moment, I wondered if magic had appeared that night." He rose and sketched a shallow bow. "Perhaps your story was never the one meant to be told."

Fear speared through her veins. Did he know who she was? The cryptic words he spoke made her think so. "Magic is gone, Prince Lucien."

His eyes flashed with an unnamed emotion. "That is where you are wrong, dear girl. Magic was never gone. It's merely waiting to be resurrected."

He turned on his heel and exited the dormitory, carefully clicking the latch shut on his way out.

She sank onto the bed once he was gone, her pulse fluttering in her neck. His words were treasonous. But maybe they weren't untrue.

Harlow lay there for a moment before she got up and headed over to the spot with the library books. She dug them out of the crevice in the wall and settled herself on the floor.

Checking the door one more time, Harlow began to read.

# CHAPTER THIRTY-THREE

## THE RETURN OF THE BARD

Harlow's stomach growled. She hadn't eaten anything in a while, so she tucked the books back into their hiding place and headed out to get a bite to eat. Lunch had long since passed and the suns were slowly diving beneath the horizon. The light was beginning to dim, but she was still too early for dinner. Sometimes they'd leave bread and soup out for the latecomers.

With a hopeful heart and an empty belly, she pulled her cloak closer and moved through a sea of people, many of them laden with picnic baskets full of things bought from the market. This was the most freedom she'd been given since she'd been with the Viragos, so being out in broad daylight outside of formation felt strange.

Harlow took quick steps, dodging and weaving away from laughing children and families not watching where they were going. The Great Hall was not too far away, and she'd missed enough meals to hurry her steps before she missed any more. She hoped for the potato soup today. The bread they served with it had a hint of garlic and thyme and reminded her of her foster mother's herb garden right outside their kitchen window.

The remembered smell of thyme and basil passed by her, a phantom memory from better times.

"Care to visit a spell?" came a voice right by her ear. Harlow jerked and stumbled. Cool, quick fingers steadied her. "You do have a way of drawing attention to yourself, don't you?" remarked the voice. The fingers on her tightened when she tried to turn. "Don't look. Let me lead."

The voice sounded familiar. "I'm on my way to eat," Harlow said. "Can we do this at another time?"

The fingers clenched against her. "I'm afraid not, my friend. Time is in too short of a supply and the next few days will test you. I have some food in my pack. I'll share it with you while you listen to my story."

The bard. That's who she walked with. Harlow peeked down at her feet only to see the familiar scarlet cloak waving with the breeze.

"Clever girl," came the voice. "Now do not dally. Your friends will be back at the dorm soon."

Harlow let the bard lead her away from the village. "I'm not supposed to leave," Harlow insisted.

The bard snorted. "No one will notice your absence. It's imperative I speak with you away from the village's prying eyes."

"Everyone has already seen you luring me away."

The bard laughed quietly. "Have they now? I think you'll find no one noticed me or you if you ask later."

Discomfited, Harlow fell silent and let the bard guide her to an almost invisible path behind one of the bakeries in the village. The bard let go of her arm and motioned for her to go first. "After you."

Harlow frowned but gathered her cloak closer around her to avoid snags and stepped inside the forest.

"Magic still beats within this place," the bard said after they walked for a few minutes. "But there's an absence there too that sets my heart to aching."

"Where are you taking me?"

The bard had released her arm and gone ahead of her, the girl's vivid copper and strawberry curls contrasting with the deep red of her cloak. Harlow watched the sway of her slim back, the way the bard stepped and never looked in any direction other than forward. "Are you not scared?" she asked.

"The beasts who prowl this place know I am no danger to them," she responded after a moment. "This is their domain, and I am merely a wanderer. I take only what I need and leave the rest for them. In turn, I hunt the unnatural predators who wander this place, loosed from wild, stray magic leftover from the purge."

"The purge?" Harlow questioned.

The bard turned to her, a furrow in her perfect creamy skin. "You are so young," the bard marveled. "I forget you do not remember the day the magic fell."

"You aren't much older than me!" Harlow argued.

The bard turned away then, her shoulders slumping slightly. "I am older than many and younger than more," she said cryptically.

Harlow snorted. "Why must you always talk in riddles?"

The bard stopped outside of a small clearing. A structure built of mud and wood stood at the edge. In front of it was a small, doused campfire and three large boulders set perfectly around it as if they were chairs beckoning them to sit for a while.

Harlow followed the bard in, her memories flickering to the last time she'd been so deep in these woods.

"Please," the bard gestured as she slung off a small pack. "Make yourself at home. We have much to discuss."

Harlow sat on one of the smooth, cool stones, peering down at the fire and wondering how hard it would be to make one.

Her hands were frigid, even tucked into the pockets of her cloak. The bard glanced at her, her lips going thin. She stepped over to the fire pit and gathered up a flint and a piece of dry wood. "You're far too thin. Keeping up your strength will help you survive. Eat when you can and even when you can't."

Moments later, smoke filled the clearing and a tiny flame appeared within the bard's hands. She smiled, a grin that lit up her entire face. Harlow's heart thudded. The bard possessed an ethereal beauty, a rarity long gone from the world. Perhaps this was one of the reasons bards were so rare. She had an elfin face, with a slight upturn to her pert nose. Her lips were rosebud pink, the top slightly thinner than the bottom. A quick and ready smile, but eyes haunted with memories. Her hair bloomed around her head, wild and untamed. She was everything different from Desminda. Wild and free, tied down by nothing and no one. For a moment, Harlow envied her.

The flame sparked and soon there was a cheery, roaring fire. She put her hands out, relishing the warmth it provided. "What shall I call you?" Harlow asked after a moment.

"My name is Astrid," the bard replied. "Though I should tell you, it's in your best interest not to speak of me."

Harlow's glance slid over to her. Astrid sat on the opposite side of the fire, turning her hands to and fro over the fire. "Why?"

The bard grinned, a smile that lit her face up. "Because no one else knows I'm here."

Harlow gaped at her. "You mean...magic?"

Astrid laughed, a bright and merry sound. "I told you all magic is not lost. It's dangerous for people like me to be anywhere around this kingdom. If the queen heard a bard roamed her territory..." Astrid blew out a breath. "Well, I'd have to be nimbler and quicker than I'd like to be."

"Why risk it?" Harlow's fingers were finally beginning to thaw.

"Because Thornewood's people are oppressed. The suppression of magic is slowly seeping into other kingdoms." She shook her head. "I don't know what it is. Whether a spell suppresses the magic or if something more sinister is at play, but it's flowing from Thornewood to other places and the people are suffering." She shook her head, the copper and golden curls fluttering against her face. "It is against the natural order of things to strip away something that makes up a person. The absence of magic is like a phantom limb for those who've lost it."

"But you haven't," Harlow accused.

Astrid's eyes flashed with ire. "Be careful of what you assume. I've given up far more than those in Thornewood. My magic is a shadow of what it once was." She waved a hand. "I am not here to talk about me." Astrid slid that bright green gaze to Harlow. "I've heard you now know the story of your birth."

Harlow swallowed hard. "I don't know if it's true. It all seems so fantastical."

"Ah," the bard said softly. "And the damage to your dorm. Does that seem so fantastical in the light of day?"

"I couldn't control it," Harlow whispered.

"No one can control their magic when it manifests." Astrid tossed a branch onto the fire and watched as flames licked and popped against it. "It's the most dangerous time in a person's life. Did you harm anyone?"

She thought about it. "Mostly just myself," she muttered.

"Then you are already on the right track. I have been here for a while searching for you, Harlow. You're the heir to magic, but right now, your magic is dangerous. Suppressing it will only cause you harm."

Harlow snorted with ire. "I don't know anything about it. It's curled like a slumbering cat inside of me." She stared at

Astrid. "None of this seems real. I'm only a girl. I don't want any of this."

"No one wants to be a hero," Astrid snapped. "It's a heavy mantle to bear. And not everyone is cut out to be a hero. Most who fill their heads with visions of heroics and battles get cut down the first time they're exposed to a blade. This is why the best heroes are those who do not want it." She gave Harlow a bright smile. "And I can tell the mantle over your shoulders is heavy and burdensome. It will not lighten for some time."

Harlow sighed. "Can I at least eat something before you give me any more bad news?"

A dimple in Astrid's cheek formed, and she tossed Harlow over her pack. "There's fresh bread from the baker and some jerky left over from the last town I passed through. No soup, though." Her eyes glittered. "But don't get too downtrodden. The Great Hall ran out an hour before you left your dorm."

Harlow glared at her before rummaging through Astrid's pack. Out of spite, she didn't save the bard even the heel of the bread.

# CHAPTER THIRTY-FOUR

BREAD AND JERKY IS NOT A MEAL

"Why am I here?" Harlow asked after she finished chewing the last of the bread.

Astrid smirked at her as if she sensed her annoyance. "You and I must talk. Danger stalks you, Harlow Stonehand." Her eyes turned serious as she watched the flickering fire.

Harlow jerked at the name. It felt foreign and strange and yet so very right.

"You must stay on alert. The other bards feel something, too." Astrid rubbed a hand over her face. "But even we cannot sense what is about to happen."

"When?"

"We do not know. Your graduation comes soon enough. Then the Virago will be released to the castle. You must beware of the others who've left. Their fear of magic may lead them to do evil things in order to curry favor with Queen Raima."

Harlow's stomach plummeted. "They're still alive?"

Astrid's eyes went dark. "Some of them survive and plot."

Harlow let out a breath. "We did nothing to them."

"You did *everything* to them. You showed them a world where magic lives. You showed them true power."

"Then why did they run?"

Astrid poked the fire with a stick. "Because they fear you. Because they belong to the group who believes magic should be banished forever."

"I don't know how to use it," Harlow grumbled. "What good am I?"

The bard smiled. "You are as good as you will allow me to make you, Stonehand. I will train you to use your gifts, but you must commit to seeing me three times a week."

Harlow gaped. "Here? In the woods?" Her mind spun with all the implications. How would she have time to train with the Virago? To sleep? And how would she keep this all a secret?

"This is where I've staked my claim for a little while. It's safe here, protected by magic and concealed from the kingdom. I will show you what it means to be a magician, though I cannot help you with everything. I can show you how to control your magic, to conceal it from others until you are ready to show them. Until you are ready to finish the job your father couldn't."

At her words, tears filled Harlow's eyes. "My father. Was he a good man?"

Astrid's eyes burned. "He was the very best. Never forget that."

"But he is dead."

Astrid looked away. "So they say. The world shook when Stonehand's power faded."

"And left me behind to pick up the pieces." Harlow blew a strand of hair out of her eyes. "I don't know if I can do this."

"No one else can," Astrid said as she rose and brushed off the seat of her pants. "Come. I will walk you back to your dorm."

Harlow slowly stood. "You sure you don't have any soup?"

Astrid chuckled. "You've eaten all the bread, girl. What good is soup with no bread?"

Harlow sighed and allowed the bard to lead her back to the village.

BLOOM AND MELARA were already back in the dorm when she arrived. By then, the suns had dipped below the horizon, plunging Thornewood into darkness. Her stomach growled as she plodded to her cot and as she sat down, she noted the hollows in her legs that had never been there before and the way she could see every bone in her hands. *Too thin*, the bard had remarked.

It was her own fault, and she wondered if the magic now burning through her veins had something to do with it. She was far thinner now than when she had arrived, and she'd lived on the street for a while before then.

"We heard something interesting while we were out," Bloom said.

Harlow grunted, too hungry and tired to respond.

"Some books have come up missing from the library," Melara chimed in. "The last person seen there had curly blond hair and a cloak."

Harlow stilled, her heart pounding in the silence. "Huh," she said after a long, tense moment. "Are they looking for her?"

Bloom snorted. "They were until Melara here told them she was there that night and saw the girl running away in the direction of a neighboring kingdom."

"It was not my fault the head librarian assumed it was someone from the Kingdom of Roses," Melara said, laughing as Bloom swatted at her.

Her laughter felt foreign to Harlow. Just days ago, she would have sworn Melara could happily gut her. It wasn't easy for Harlow to act as if nothing had transpired between them.

Too much harm had passed, and though Melara had protected her secret, Harlow still felt the burn of her anger.

She couldn't return the books now. If the library was under more scrutiny and someone had witnessed her the last time, the odds of getting caught were much higher. She hadn't gotten very far in the old texts and some of it was so boring she felt like she needed wooden sticks to prop her eyelids open. She wouldn't mind returning them for something else, but it looked like her chance had passed.

A sigh escaped her, and she turned on her side. "Where do you wish to be assigned?" she asked the two girls.

Melara blinked. "I guess I hadn't thought of it," she admitted. "I don't think I care. To become a Virago is to be acknowledged as a warrior. I can be a warrior wherever I am sent." She tilted her neck up, eyeing the gaping wound in the roof. "Though I hope that soon, change will be wrought in this place and magic will be restored."

Bloom sighed and stretched her legs out in front of her. "Everyone I love is gone. I do not care where I go, but I hope I have friends there."

Harlow eyed the strange girl with the intricate braids. Something about Bloom sent her senses into overdrive. She was an odd one, yes, but there was more to her oddness than just Bloom's personality.

"You have friends here," Harlow blurted.

Bloom's eye widened with surprise and a sad smile formed on the girl's face. "Perhaps one of you will follow me then."

The dormitory doors opened then, and the other ten girls flooded into the room, their cheeks high with color and laughter spilling from their lips. Helena came first, her springy curls bouncing around her face. Kalen, the quiet girl who'd once walked her to the healers, followed, her dark hair flowing freely down her back. She carried a small basket overflowing with flowers. Their eyes met and the happiness in them dimmed slightly, but Kalen nodded and gave her a small smile.

Soon, all the girls were back in, their laughter dancing throughout the room. Bitterness and loneliness warred within Harlow, and she exhaled a deep breath. These were her sisters, for all intents and purposes, at least for the next few months. They had to work together. And, if they all agreed about bringing magic back, perhaps they'd become something more than sisters.

She shoved those feelings away, knowing the distance between herself and the others was self-inflicted. What had she done to be a better friend? Not much, she decided.

Harlow sat up and did her best to join into the conversation and if it felt a little awkward, the other girls did not draw her attention to it. Instead, they motioned her closer and brought her into their fold.

Harlow felt a little like a baby chicken being accepted into the flock, but as the girl's smiles grew brighter, Harlow's smile felt lighter.

Perhaps it was not so bad to be a chicken some days.

# CHAPTER THIRTY-FIVE

## SHADE'S ANGRY FACE

"Were every one of you born imbeciles or have you been practicing at it?" Shade roared as he whacked the back of Harlow's knees with the flat of his sword.

She hit the ground, gravel and hay crammed into her mouth as her face skidded along the dirt. She lay there for a moment, digesting the pain, until she slowly got back up, cradling her bruised ribs. She lifted her sword back up, wincing at the ache in her wrist.

"You move like Nana Kay's molasses!" Shade barked as he circled her. "Do you think an enemy will give you time to assess your wounds?"

"No Shade!" the girls called as one. Except for Harlow. She was too busy glaring at him to respond. Plus, she had no idea who Nana Kay was, though she could go for molasses. Whoever made the biscuits for breakfast really needed some additional training. Molasses might help them go down easier.

Shade smacked her again with his sword, moving so fast, she barely had time to move before pain bloomed in her shoulders. "Distraction is the enemy, Harlow," Shade warned. He shook his head, his dark hair tumbling around his face. He looked like some vengeful battlefield god ready to strike her down as soon as she looked away.

She was distracted and had been for at least the last week. Fatigue burned at the back of her eyes and made her limbs heavy. She'd met with Astrid twice this week, sneaking out of the dorm when the night was at its darkest and plundering blindly through the forest until she smelled the bard's fresh floral scent. Astrid would lead her each night to the same clearing and run her through the same exercise each time.

Clear her mind and focus on nothing.

What kind of advice was that? Could anyone ever focus on nothing? Wasn't focusing on nothing *something*? Astrid refused to answer that question, rolling her eyes every time she asked. "When you focus on nothing, you will not know it," she'd reply cryptically. Harlow would groan, adjusting her seat because stones would poke through her breeches into her painfully thin rear end, then she would try once again to clear her mind.

Astrid would lead her home in the wee hours of the morning after she was almost too tired to stand. She'd plod back to her room and collapse face first onto her cot until the suns peeked above the horizon, sending fingers of first light into her dorm.

Then, inevitably, Shade would roar into the area, whacking something with his blade, sending them all scattering out of their beds like insects under disturbed wood.

Not one single person had said a word to Harlow about her absences. Since no one knew the bard was in town, perhaps Astrid had covered her tracks, allowing Harlow to slip back in under the veil of magic. The entire thing disturbed her. This was the third week, and Harlow felt like she hadn't learned a thing.

Nothing was something. Or was something nothing?

She wanted to groan at the madness of it.

Instead, she faced Shade. His intense dark gaze took her in, seeing more than she ever wanted him to see.

Finally, he stopped, lowering his blade.

Harlow was covered in dirt and sweat, and more than a little blood.

"What is the matter with you?"

"Do you think thinking about nothing is something?" Harlow blurted.

Shade tilted his head, peering at her like she'd gone mad. "Anything is something," he responded, apparently deciding to humor the crazy woman.

"Exactly," Harlow groaned. "It *is* something if nothing is a task!"

Shade shook his head and pointed to the gate with his sword. "Perhaps a lack of water has addled your senses. Go drink."

Harlow's shoulders slumped as she turned to go.

"Harlow?"

She turned back to him.

"In the next two weeks, I would like to see some weight on you." His dark gaze was unreadable. "You cannot perform at peak physical condition if you are weak. Get double rations at the Great Hall for the foreseeable future."

Harlow bobbed her head in a nod and headed out of the ring, feeling dejected. She'd been eating as much as she could when she had the time and even Astrid was plying her with food, but she couldn't seem to gain an ounce. Her ribs were prominent against her skin, and the hollows of her cheeks were more pronounced than they'd ever been. Something was wrong, but she didn't know what it was.

She passed by Bloom, walking into the ring with her sword held down at her side. The tall girl leaned over to Bloom and whispered, "Speak to me this evening at the stables."

Harlow blinked but didn't acknowledge the whisper. Instead, she dragged herself over to the wooden bleachers and sat next to Helena. But not too close. Harlow might be exhausted, but she wasn't so out of it that she didn't notice her own smell.

A visit to the bath house was in order tonight.

SHE DIDN'T KNOW why she was here. Harlow clutched the key in her hand and tiptoed through the quiet castle on her way to the baths. She could have used the ones the Viragos frequented and now that she was here, she wished she had, but something lured her to the castle tonight and she couldn't make head nor tails of it.

There was no mysterious light or beacon she followed, just a sense of something being not quite right. Instead of turning toward the Virago baths, her feet had turned toward the castle.

She made her way into the baths, clutching her small towel and fresh clothing. The only sound was dripping water. No one occupied the baths this late, but Harlow's day had been filled with practice and chores. Tomorrow she had a visit with Astrid and she knew the bard cherished cleanliness. She had no desire to see Astrid's nose wrinkle when she stepped too close to her anymore.

Harlow blew out a breath of frustration. What was wrong with her these days? Nova would have wrung her hide if she'd failed to eat or bathe like she had lately.

She reached the princesses' private area and used the key to unlock it. Harlow stepped into the dressing room and sat down on the wooden seat, dropping her head and releasing a long sigh.

Privacy.

The first she'd had in weeks now. She sat there for a few moments, just soaking in the silence before she stood and stripped, grimacing as her sweat laced clothes thumped to the ground.

She wrapped the thin towel around her and stepped out.

Desminda stood there.

Harlow gasped and took a step back, clutching her towel to keep it from falling.

One of Desminda's dark eyebrows went up. "Hello, Harlow," she purred.

Harlow sank into an awkward curtsy, the towel creeping up to expose her backside.

Desminda choked on a laugh. "Rise, Harlow. I do not make half nude people bow to me in the baths."

Harlow rose, crimson heat flooding her face.

Desminda motioned a hand. "Please. I'll turn to conserve your modesty. I'd like to stay and speak with you a moment if you'll allow it."

Had anyone ever said no to the future queen?

"Of course, Your Majesty."

A smile quirked Desminda's lips, but she slowly turned. Harlow hurriedly dropped the towel and set it away from the water splash zone. She stepped into the water, almost groaning with relief at the heat of it. When she was covered as well as she could be, she cleared her throat.

There was no room for modesty while bathing with what used to be over forty other girls, but none of them were the queen. Desminda turned, her loose hair swinging against the stark purple of her gown.

Harlow swallowed hard. The warmth of the water soothed her aching and abused muscles, but she couldn't relax with Desminda's heavy gaze against her skin.

"Tell me, Harlow. Have you ever heard tales of the Stone-hand mage?"

# CHAPTER THIRTY-SIX

### LIAR, LIAR, HEARTS ON FIRE

The girl had grown wiser during her time with Shade, Desminda thought. There was no telltale motion of surprise other than a twitch of her lips. Harlow stared up at her, blue eyes guileless but also full of wariness.

Desminda had never seen someone with eyes that bright and every time Harlow turned them upon her, she felt laid bare.

"The Stonehand mage? I've heard of him," Harlow said, wariness coloring her tone.

"Do you know how destructive he was to our kingdom?" Desminda sat at the edge of the baths, not caring about the water soaking into the hem of her dress, turning the purple fabric so dark it looked like ink upon the floor.

Harlow's lips twitched, though not in amusement. Borderline rebellious. She'd have to talk to Shade about ensuring Harlow controlled herself better than this. A twist of those lips in her mother's presence would have been Harlow's downfall or at least worthy of the queen making an example out of her.

"I do not," Harlow said at last. "Though I also do not understand why we're speaking of this."

Desminda's brows went up at her words. "Every Virago

must eventually know the truth of the magic lost to our kingdoms."

Harlow's eyes narrowed. "Lost?"

Desminda stilled. "You think something else happened to the magic?"

"You don't?" Harlow dared to ask.

"You overstep," she warned, her heart picking up in speed. Harlow's already curly hair had coiled tighter with the steam, her face flushed with the heat of the bath. She looked like an angel, the light to Desminda's darkness, splayed there, innocent but scheming.

She had no doubt Harlow knew exactly what she spoke of.

"Can you tell me about the day magic was lost?" Harlow asked, those blue eyes pinning her in place. Desminda imagined what her life would have been like had she been born a lower noble. Could she marry someone else not chosen for her? Or at least have more of a say? Would sitting here in the baths with a beautiful girl bring shame upon her if they were caught? Her eyes flicked back over to the latch on the door, reassuring her that it was locked tight into place.

Harlow's eyes followed hers and Desminda watched as the hollow in her throat pulled and tightened. A pulse flickered in her throat.

Desminda let out a breath. This girl. Why was she so wrapped up in this girl? "The gods grew angry with us. Before my mother wrested control of the kingdom from the king, an angry wind blew through our kingdom and those surrounding it, and magic slipped away during the night, almost like a broom had come and swept it all away. Like it was angry at the thirst for power and tired of the corruption that had fallen upon our lands."

Pretty lies fell from her lips like rubies. Desminda didn't

know the exact truth of what happened to the magic, but she had long suspected her mother had something to do with it.

"A broom," Harlow echoed, her voice tinged with disbelief.

"A broom," Desminda said solemnly. "Though magic is much more complicated than that. But it disappeared that quickly and what didn't disappear leaked to a dribble."

"So some people still have magic?" Harlow asked.

Desminda shook her head. "No. Eventually those dribbles dried up and now the kingdoms are mundane."

"Do you miss magic?"

Desminda chuckled. "I am not so much older than you." By age, she was right. By responsibility, she felt like she was ancient. The weight of the crown was like a noose around her neck and it hadn't even sat upon her head yet.

These secrets were a poisonous mantle around her shoulders, everyday leeching into her skin until one day maybe all she would utter would be the lies everyone fed her.

Harlow tilted her head knowing Desminda had not answered her question. The girl saw everything and nothing and Desminda marveled at it.

"I miss the way it looked," she said after a moment. "I miss how good the cook's cakes tasted and how bright and fragrant the plants were." Desminda straightened and cleared her throat. She shouldn't have voiced those words. "But magic was responsible for many wrongs, and we should not miss it."

"Our thoughts are not our deeds," Harlow said and reached for the sliver of jasmine scented soap behind her. She dipped her head under the water and when she came up, water sluiced down her face, beading on her lashes and pale skin. Her lightly muscled arms reached up and rubbed the bar through her hair, and Desminda turned, tears pricking in her eyes at Harlow's beauty and the knowledge that nothing could ever come of this.

She knew who Harlow was and now she suspected Harlow knew who she was, too.

And if she knew that much, did she know where her fate lay and how it would wreck Desminda's world?

"Our thoughts have great power," Desminda said. "And we should take caution to rein them in lest they escape and cause great damage."

"You speak as if they live."

Desminda heard the amusement in Harlow's voice. The girl had no idea the damage a mage could do with focus and a few muttered words.

"They do," she snapped.

The trickling water stopped. Desminda turned. Harlow's hair was full of soap, her fingers stilled in her scalp.

Desminda sighed. "Before magic fell, many magicians used words to utter their spells."

"But magic is gone," Harlow said, her fingers again scrubbing through her scalp.

"Perhaps, but it has shown us that words have power, and that power has not gone away." Desminda leaned against the cool stone of the wall. "Haven't you ever been swayed by a pretty speech? Perhaps by a pretty boy?"

Harlow snorted. "I am not an easily swayable person. And certainly not by a pretty boy."

Desminda tilted her head, interest piquing. "Perhaps a pretty girl then?"

Their gazes locked and Desminda knew she was right when Harlow looked down, suddenly intent on studying the soap dripping from her hair.

"I am still not easily swayable," she muttered.

"I do not believe *swayable* is actually a word," Desminda mused, trying to break the tension. "Though appropriate in this case." She waved a hand. "But it's of no importance. We must get back to my story."

Harlow sighed and held up a finger just before she ducked her head under the water to wash the soap from her hair.

When she came up for air, Desminda continued.

"The mage was taken by my father because of his great power. During a visit to another kingdom, the king saw a demonstration of Stonehand's might and encouraged him to come to Thornewood."

Harlow's eyes darkened, but she did not interrupt. Desminda could almost read the thoughts running through her head. *Kings and queens and their games with words. If a king encouraged a commoner to go somewhere, they had little choice in the matter.* Of course, she'd be right, but her mother claimed the mage went willingly.

"Stonehand, under the king's direction, sought to conquer our surrounding kingdoms, but unbeknownst to the king, he was also working with my mother to wrest power from his hands to turn Thornewood into a queendom. The queen thought the king's actions would plunge Thornewilde into a continuous war. Stonehand agreed."

"I do not understand how he was destructive," Harlow said during the pause. "He was beholden to both of your parents."

Desminda paused before she spoke. Harlow's words seemed defensive, almost like she knew something she shouldn't. And if she did wouldn't that be curious? "He was sworn only to the king."

Harlow chewed her lip. "Being sworn to the king also means swearing to the queen. Anyone seeking to survive would not disobey an order from her." She wrung out her hair and tied it in a loose, wet knot against her nape.

"He was sworn only to my father," she said again, realizing what Harlow wasn't saying. She believed her father did not have a choice in his actions. Perhaps it was true in some ways. In others, Stonehand held a power neither of her parents fully comprehended until it was too late. "My mother had no say in any of the decisions being made around the kingdom."

"You're saying your mother did not have the power to make the mage pay if he did not do what she ordered him to do?"

How smart she was. Desminda tilted her head, studying Harlow through her lashes. "Do you know why I tell this story?"

Harlow snorted. "I truly do not, Your Majesty."

Now she used the honorific. Honestly, Harlow was exhausting. She doled out respect based upon whether she felt one deserved it from her. Desminda wanted to laugh at her spunk, but she was more worried it would one day get Harlow killed. She rose to her feet, picking up her wet skirts from the damp floor. "I tell this story so you will know when you are chosen as Virago, when you swear to me your allegiance, no matter where you are, you are sworn to me. Not my husband. Not the king or queen. Not to anyone else." Her eyes fell on Harlow, now sitting straight up in the tub, staring at her with an emotion Desminda couldn't quite place. It wasn't anger. Not exactly.

"You are sworn to *me*, Harlow Fischer." Though that wasn't her name and they both knew it. "No matter what happens in this kingdom, your allegiance falls to me."

Silence grew between them, thick and heavy.

Harlow's lips thinned with displeasure. Approaching the girl in the bath was the best way to put her at a disadvantage. Not that Harlow would dare have walked away from her. She was the future queen after all. Here she had a captive audience, and she could further gauge Harlow's thoughts.

"Of course, Your Majesty," Harlow said. "A Virago knows her place."

Desminda's lips twitched at that last rejoinder. "Good. I hope you enjoy the rest of your evening."

Harlow's eyebrows flicked up at that, but she bit back whatever she was about to say. "You as well."

Desminda turned and unlatched the door. "I would ensure you're out of the baths within the next ten minutes. Some of the maids like to come down here late at night for..." she paused. "Late night libations."

She already had the door almost closed when Harlow squawked, and the sound of splashing water trickled out.

Chuckling, Desminda swept out of the baths and down the hall.

# CHAPTER THIRTY-SEVEN

## THE FLAME HAIRED SUCCUBUS

Desminda had an eye for pretty things. Trinkets, fabrics, dresses, shoes, furniture, but most of all people. She liked to surround herself with quick minds, clever tongues, and pretty features. Perhaps it was her vanity peeking through or something more sinister, but she liked to surround herself with beauty. If that beauty talked, it was even better.

But one thing she couldn't stand was a pretty face paired with a vapid mind.

She sat across from Lucien's sister, a flame haired beauty named Celestine. Beautiful she might be, but the poor girl was blessed with the personality of a rock. Desminda had met her a few times before. Celestine had visited the Kingdom of Roses while Desminda's parents secured her and Lucien's match and they'd never taken to each other. The girl might be dumb, but she had a sharp tongue and every time they were around each other, Celestine always made her feel small at least once.

"This tea," Celestine said in her high, breathy voice. "Where is it sourced?"

"The wolf kingdom," Desminda responded. She wasn't sure

who she liked less, Celestine or Lucien. Either way, with their presence here, she found herself growing tired of the color red.

Celestine's auburn eyebrows went up. "Truly?" she sniffed. "It's surprising that such savages have such a delicate touch with tea."

Desminda wouldn't know. She hated tea. A strong, black cup of coffee would always be her first choice, though she dutifully sipped the black brew in front of her. It tasted bitter and dried her mouth out and she so hated the delicate cups she had to use. She always felt like she'd shatter one every time she picked them up.

There was a potter in the village who made clumsy, clunky ceramic cups. They always looked a little lopsided, but they were sturdy and vividly colored. She hid them from her mother who wouldn't approve of the rustic brightness, but Shade had secretly brought her quite a collection over the years, though her favorite was the purple and white one he'd brought back from his most recent trip. The potter must have suspected who her benefactor was because purple was a notoriously hard dye to find. She sent Shade with extra money the next time and had ever since even when she had no plans to buy another cup.

She longed for the comfort of it even as her fingers curled around the thin handle of the white, floral teacup balanced in her hands.

The princess of the Kingdom of Roses was a delicate thing, so thin that Desminda wondered if her bones would snap like twigs if she fell. Her lips were bright and pink, and her eyes were the same vivid green of Desminda's betrothed.

The betrothed who sat across from her now, his ankles crossed, and a small patient smile on his face at his sister's antics. Their eyes met and Lucien looked away first, as if he couldn't stand the lightness of her eyes. Perhaps the shadows inside them would drown out the jade of his own.

Or perhaps she would drown him in the baths if she ever had the opportunity. She imagined holding the future king of Thornewood down, using one of the many moves Shade had taught her to disable a man, Lucien's hair splayed in the clear water like blood.

"Your Majesty?"

Desminda blinked, jarred out of her violent fantasy. "So sorry. I'm afraid I didn't get much sleep last night. What were you saying?"

Lucien gave her a curious look. "Everything okay, my darling?"

Desminda gritted her teeth even as she plastered a polite smile on her face. "Quite. Just tired, that's all."

Lucien reached over and patted her knee. She loathed his touch. It wasn't that she loathed the touch of men. She didn't. It was just him. Something about the way he looked at her when he thought she wasn't watching. Cold and calculating. She felt the knife at her back always, but these days she thought it might come from Lucien's hand.

"What were you saying?" she asked Celestine.

"I wondered what I might wear to the upcoming dinner," she said. "I've brought a positively divine pink gown." She rolled her eyes to the heaven as she gushed. "We brought in a designer from the Kingdom of Crystal. He brought with him some of the most stunning crystals I'd ever seen!" She put a hand to her heart and fanned herself. "I chose the aurora crystals, and he's sewn them throughout the bodice of the gown. I'll sparkle like a goddess."

Desminda's mother always told her to never attract the attention of any of the gods, though Thornewood had squashed worship of anyone other than Helo, the one true god. She used to question how there could be many gods and all of a sudden only one, but her mother had quickly squashed any curiosity on her part with extra needlework lessons. She smiled politely at Celestine. "I'm sure it's stunning." Desminda set her teacup down and rose. "I'm afraid I must retire to my room. The heat gets to me these days for some reason. I think the queen might be adding additional cooling units in the castle soon."

"Wonderful!" Celestine said. "Ladies are not supposed to sweat."

Lucien gave his sister an odd look but rose with Desminda. "I'll walk you to your quarters."

Desminda lifted a hand to wave him off. "No need. I'm perfectly capable."

He gave her a closed lip smile. "I know you are. I would still like to escort my betrothed."

There was no way to escape this with grace. She bowed her head for a moment. "Then it would be an honor."

Lucien held his arm out. Desminda curled her fingers around his elbow and let him lead her out of the room.


THEY WERE out of earshot of the room before Lucien murmured. "You despise Celestine." Desminda blinked and slightly stumbled. Lucien steadied her and kept walking. "A queen should hide her emotions better."

She gaped like a fish. "Excuse me," she blustered.

Amusement twisted his lips. "Many people hate her, Desminda, but you are to be queen. She will be a powerful ally one day, not to mention she will sit on the throne in my kingdom due to my absence. It is unheard of for this to happen." His eyes focused straight ahead. "But due to Thornewood's...odd marital requirements and our respect of your queendom, our family has graciously agreed to my relocation to your castle."

Desminda snorted under her breath. "I'm sure our mineral

rich kingdom has nothing to do with your sudden willingness to accommodate us, either."

To his credit, Lucien chuckled. "We are royalty, Desminda. We rarely do anything for love, do we?"

They arrived at her quarters. She let go of him and studied her future husband. To many he would be devastating to look at, like some flaming god come to life. His hair sparked scarlet and gold and his eyes glowed under the natural light of the hall. But to her, he was merely a flower in a kingdom of thorns.

Flowers withered from their stems, but thorns were forever.

# CHAPTER THIRTY-EIGHT

## SNAKES IN THE GRASS

They'd lost twelve. To cold. To beasts. To cowardice. Three others twitched in the firelight, nervous and chilled, their gazes darting to every shadow in the night.

She didn't belong here, but someone had sent a message to her begging her to come. She'd stolen away after dinner, making her way carefully through the Thornewilde Forest. The moon was high tonight, allowing her to easily see ahead, but she could hear and sense things creeping and slithering in the woods around her.

They'd risked a fire tonight. Brave but perhaps more foolhardy than courageous.

She stopped at the edge of their camp, her gaze taking in the bedraggled girls, and one unfamiliar figure whose features were obscured by the dark cloak they wore. Something about the scene bothered her but she couldn't put her figure on what it was.

"Who is that?" she asked, not stepping out of the cover of the forest.

"A benefactor," the voice said. Female then. A higher lilt to her voice. "I'm here for information and for perhaps ... more if we mutually agree."

"What could you possibly have to give us?" she asked, stepping into the clearing. She kept her face carefully blank, not daring to allow the sympathy she felt for the former Virago to show on her face. They were essentially homeless, ostracized from the guard as soon as they'd fled into the night. Even if they all came back with their tails between their legs, Shade would never allow them to resume their places.

Something she had to keep in mind as she navigated the treacherous path ahead of her.

The Fischer girl had magic, stunning them all. Thirty-seven of them had fled once they'd seen the roof explode. Over half. She'd stayed behind and she wasn't sure why. But looking at the girls' lives now, she knew. Leaving meant forging your own way and their kingdom had never been kind. Even when it became a queendom, weakness was answered with a sharp kick to the rib or worse, not a hand up.

The stranger laughed then, soft and low, a beautiful sound at odds with the moonlit shadows streaking dark shapes against their skin. "I have the power to give you everything."

She snorted. "Everything?"

The woman raised a delicate hand tipped with manicured hands. Someone important then. "Everything. Serve me and you shall all have homes again. Places of importance. Money if you wish it. Husbands of noble birth. I have the power to bring all of it to you."

The girls all looked around at each other, the stark hope in them making her stomach lurch. They would do it. With or without her.

"And me?" she asked.

"For you, I will give much more. You're in a perfect position to advise me." She stood then, sprinkling a powder onto the fire which made it flare. Some of the girls jerked back. "Please," she said, holding out a beseeching hand. "It's just a powder designed to keep the fire going. The ground is wet, and I don't see any dry wood around."

She reached over and handed the pack to one of the smaller girls, a youth named Dell. Dell took it with hesitant fingers then stuffed it into the pocket of trousers that had seen better days.

"What is it you wish to know?"

The woman's lips curved then, and firelight flickered on the broad white smile. "Everything," she said again, delight edging her voice.

The Virago frowned. "And if I get caught?"

"If you get caught, you are not as good as I expected you to be." The woman sat back down, tucking the edges of her cloak around her. "Now tell me about the accident in your dormitory. The word is there was a freak storm?"

She looked around at her former friends and teammates. They'd already told this woman everything, she'd bet her last coin on it.

"There was a freak storm," she agreed.

"But the damage wasn't due to the storm." The woman's voice had gone flat as if displeased she was being toyed with. "Tell me about the magic."

The lone Virago shifted on her feet. Could she get away in time? Her mind finally caught up to what was bothering her. "Where is everyone else?"

Dell's gaze met hers. "Probably in the bellies of the beasts who caught them."

The Virago shut her eyes for a moment. "All of them?"

Dell shrugged. "Most probably. We've survived by sticking together."

Another girl tossed a stick at the fire. A girl named Lana if she remembered correctly. Small and dark and she had a fine tremor in her right hand, something that affected her enough that most of them knew she probably wouldn't make it to graduation. "We hear screams in the wood sometimes. And none of us relieve ourselves alone anymore. They like to pick us off when they think we're weak."

"Monsters do that," the woman said. "But the best kind of monster is one you can't predict." She eyed the Virago again. "Now tell me about the magic."

All those hopeful eyes landed on the girl. She swallowed hard and stepped forward.

# CHAPTER THIRTY-NINE

## THREATS AND SUNSHINE

Harlow's hair was still wet when she crept through the village toward the stables. She shivered with cold, glad she at least had brought warm clothing with her.

Bloom leaned against the side of the stables, one leg perched against the wood. She looked the picture of nonchalance, but Harlow knew better. Whatever Bloom wanted, she didn't want anyone else to know.

She nodded at Harlow and motioned for her to follow. Frowning, Harlow hurried to catch up with the girl's long-legged stride. Bloom lifted the latch on the stable doors and ushered her in.

"Come," Bloom said and led her upstairs to the room she'd first stayed in so long ago.

Harlow trudged up the stairs and watched as Bloom perched on the edge of the bed. "Sit in front of me."

She swallowed hard but plopped down on the floor right in front of the strange girl. Bloom peered at her, face inches away. Her strange colored eyes focused on Harlow's.

"How do you feel?" she asked after a moment.

Harlow shrugged. "Fine."

Bloom snorted and picked up her wrist. "You're burning through your reserves faster than you can keep food down. You should be weak and nauseous. Are you?"

Yes. She was. But to say so would be to show weakness.

Bloom laughed then, a too bright sound in the quiet stables. "After all this time, you don't trust me."

Harlow looked down, shame burning her face.

"It's okay," Bloom murmured. A dark wisp of hair had fallen from her immaculate braid. "You have a lot of secrets to bear, Harlow, but I'm not here to harm you." She dropped Harlow's wrist. "You're suffering from magic sickness. You need to expel the magic building in your veins."

Harlow blinked. "What."

"Exactly what I said. You have to expel it, or it will eat you alive."

"How do you know?" Harlow blurted.

Bloom studied her then. "You don't trust me. So why should I trust you?" She stood up, towering over Harlow, still on the floor. "If you don't listen to me, you will collapse and anyone in that castle who knows what magic is will know what's happening to you." She paused at the edge of the stairs. "And when they do, you'll think upon this day and wish you had listened to me."

Bloom headed down the stairs leaving Harlow in complete silence. She heard the click of the latch and the outside wind before the door snicked shut.

Harlow gaped after her. Bloom hadn't said a word about magic during the conversation they'd all had, but she knew exactly what was going on with her. Or said she did. She leaned against the hard wood of the stables and took a couple of deep, steadying breaths. Harlow walked her fingers up her ribs, counting each one easily. The ferocity of the Virago training would make anyone thinner, but even Shade had remarked on her weight loss. She felt like she was burning through all her reserves right now and maybe plowing through with sheer willpower.

Harlow swallowed hard and grimaced. Nausea roiled through her body and even tilting her head made her dizzy. She sat there for a few minutes having no clue what to do about Bloom's warning before she had pounded down the steps. The girl had never been wrong before. About anything. Bloom had stepped in to help her at great risk to herself. She'd be a fool not to listen to her.

With effort, Harlow stood and wandered over to Luci's stall, inhaling the fresh hay scent. Melancholy washed over her, but she smiled as she wondered what the great horse was doing now and slipped out of the stables to head back to the dorm.

She was supposed to see Astrid two days hence.

Perhaps the bard could help her.

# CHAPTER FORTY

## THE BARD WITH THE DRAGON TONGUE

Astrid took one look at her and gaped. "Are you not eating then?" She picked up Harlow's wrist and circled it, her fingers overlapping each other. "I'm a small thing, but you are wasting away, girl!" Astrid stepped closer, closer than she ever had before and inhaled. A second later, her eyes went wide.

"Hell's Gates," she spat. "You stink of magic!" Astrid circled her, her eyes everywhere all over Harlow.

She felt small and weak. Harlow swayed on her feet. Astrid steadied her with a strong but delicate hand. Her nostrils flared. "You've done nothing with your magic?"

Harlow shook her head.

Astrid squeezed her eyes shut. "I've never seen someone so simultaneously lucky and stupid at the same time. Why didn't you say anything?"

A weak shrug lifted her shoulders. "I just thought I was sick."

Astrid's gaze flicked behind her. "Well, I'm sorry to tell you, we're going to have to expel some of that magic and we can't do it here."

Harlow gaped. "This is already too far. I can't go much farther. I won't make it back to training in time."

The bard's lips thinned. She plunked her hands on her hips and studied Harlow. "I'll do what I can." Astrid led her over to a large stone with a flat top. "Sit there."

Harlow sank onto the stone grateful to not have to stand up anymore. "This is magic sickness?"

Astrid sighed. "Yes, and the worst case I've ever seen. You're lucky magic has been gone so long, girl. Twelve years ago, you'd be caught seconds after you walked out of your house looking like you do." She put a cool hand against Harlow's forehead.

Harlow sighed at the chill.

"You're burning with fever." Astrid put her hands on the side of Harlow's face. "If we can't get it all out, maybe we can expel some before you have to go back. Look at me."

Harlow met her gaze and marveled at her coppery hair. She and Lucien both shared red hair and green eyes, but the two could not be more different. Where Lucien was like freshly spilled blood, Astrid was the morning sun's streaks of colors across a blue sky. Lucien's eyes were calculating, and Astrid's were quick and clever and bright.

She was stunning to look at.

Astrid snorted. "Stop staring at me like some lovesick cow. I need you to concentrate on that pool inside of you. The magic lies coiled within you burning to be used. Close your eyes and I will try to guide you."

Harlow closed her eyes. Astrid's chilled fingers warmed against her skin. The bard's voice lowered and change and slid over her skin like satin.

"Look," Astrid commanded.

Harlow's eyes opened, but she was no longer in the forest. She was inside a starry endless sky. She gasped in shock and tried to pull away.

"No," Astrid commanded. "Stay."

Harlow stilled, her breathing fast and heavy. "Find your magic," the bard commanded.

She had no idea where to look, but the command in Astrid's voice made her bones ache. "Where?" she asked, hating how plaintive her voice sounded.

"Inside of you. Magic lies coiled in our souls. You know where it is, Harlow. Now find it. Astrid pushed her away, but Harlow still felt her fingers on her face.

She floated in oblivion, in a sea of stars. Everywhere she looked there was both darkness and light. There was no up or down or east or west, only stars and a night that went on forever.

"Think of how you felt when the magic burst from you. Remember its signature. Find it."

She thought about it, about the power she was helpless to control. She felt weak in that moment. Scared. Helpless.

A tug came from behind her. She turned, her body spinning in the night and pushed forward. Warmth spread over her skin as she floated toward the source of it.

"*Stonehand.*" This wasn't Astrid's voice anymore.

Harlow jerked and stopped abruptly.

"*Come, Stonehand.*"

She didn't want to move forward. The voice didn't sound evil, but did evil have a sound?

"*I have much to show you.*"

Harlow slowly drifted forward.

"*I've waited for so long to see you,*" the voice said.

"Who are you?" Male. Older from the sound of it. Power leeched from his voice.

"*A friend,*" the voice said after a hesitation. "*I mean you no harm.*"

"Where's Astrid?"

"*Still there,*" the voice assured her. "*I just intercepted the frequency for a moment.*"

Harlow drifted closer, and the stars gave way to a purple streaked sky. She looked below her and saw blessed ground. A sigh escaped her, and she let herself drift down.

As she got closer, she saw a figure below her. She stilled, but the voice spoke again.

"*Do not be afraid. No one can harm you here.*"

"Why?"

"*Because this is your soul.*"

Harlow frowned. "Then how are you here?"

"*I'm afraid that's a story for another day.*"

She landed a few feet away from the man and had to crane her neck up to see him. He was tall, even taller than Shade, massively built, and his hair was golden blonde. He looked younger than she expected, but his eyes were much older. They were kind but full of pain. He had a strong jaw and bright blue eyes. Harlow took a hesitant step forward.

"*Come,*" he said and held out his hand. "*We do not have much time.*"

Nova always told her to be wary of strangers, but she never said anything about strangers inside of her soul. And none of the books Nova had stolen for her covered anything quite this strange.

Harlow peered up at him and couldn't see anything in his face other than sincerity. She took a deep breath and allowed her fingers to touch his palm.

Magic exploded between them.


A SCREAM TORE from Harlow's throat. Her fingers were entwined in the stranger's. His back bowed from the magic, his lips twisted in a grimace.

Strands of dark shadows twisted from both of them but entwined with those were bright, sparkling strands of magic. Something about the shadows looked familiar, but she couldn't place them. A memory tugged deep at her.

"*Hold*," the man croaked. "*It will pass in a moment.*"

She stood with him, pain making her bones crunch against her skin. Her breath came out in harsh pants and the man standing beside her fared no better. "*Magic exacts a price*," he gritted out. "*You've contained far too much of it.*" His eyes scraped over her form though it was done in a perfunctory way. "*You should thank the bard for trying to help you, though she will be able to do little to ease your suffering. She'll be able to hold off the sickness for a while, but you're going to have to expel the magic someplace safe before you waste away.*"

"How do you know about the bard?" Harlow blurted. The shadows and light were slowly fading away and suddenly she could straighten again.

But they weren't in the same place they'd been before.

Harlow stood before a vast crystal blue lake. Her mouth opened in surprise.

"Where are we?"

The man stared down at her, an unreadable expression on his face. "*This*," he breathed, "*is your magic.*"

The lake was so large she couldn't see the other side. Harlow peered down at the water, but the color deepened to a blue so dark it was almost black. "How far does it go down?" she wondered more to herself than to him.

The man scrubbed a hand over his face, his eyes wide. "*I don't know.*" The answer was simple enough, but his tone made her think there was an extra meaning there.

"What?" She tugged her hand loose.

"*It's a miracle you haven't wasted away,*" he murmured.

"Harlow!" Astrid's voice sounded desperate and far away.

"*She is alright,*" the man said.

There was no answer for a moment. "How are you there? Harlow? Harlow!"

A lurch of magic tugged from her stomach.

The man grimaced. "*She's trying to take you back. I don't have time to explain. The fastest way to help you might not be the best, but it's the only thing I can think of.*" He knelt at the lake's surface. "*Touch your pool of magic and imagine it leeching back into the source.*"

Harlow frowned. "This will work?"

"*Nightmage?*" A voice said.

Harlow's brow knit together. She knew that voice...

Alarm rang in the man's face. "*It will work. Temporarily. You have to expel the magic periodically, Harlow. If you don't, magic sickness will creep up on you. This should last for a few weeks, but you're going to be in the same place you are now if you don't learn how to manage your power.*"

Her stomach tugged again, an invisible tug back toward Astrid.

"*Touch the lake,*" he said. "*Allow your power to flow back in.*"

Harlow knelt, the water lapping close to her fingers. She took a deep breath and touched the surface.

Memories flowed through her mind. Her sister with hair the color of ink and a wide, happy smile dancing with Harlow in the field behind their house, hair streaming like shadows behind her head. Her foster mother tucking a blonde curl behind her ear while she showed Harlow how to knead bread. A pup she'd found at the market who licked her face and showed her its belly.

A woman she'd never seen before. A blonde woman with eyes like crystal, holding hands and laughing with a big man...

Her eyes flew up to the big man standing above her. A sad

smile graced his lips.

"*Nightmage?*" the voice queried again.

Power leaked from her fingers as the memories flooded through her. A smoking cauldron, red smoke, fire, agony.

Thornewood castle. A desperate dash holding a small screaming bundle.

The man in front of her holding open a door that led to endless night. A tear-soaked goodbye kiss and a wail of sorrow from the woman as she fled into the dark.

Tears streamed down her face.

"*Magnus?*" the familiar voice screamed.

"*Hello, daughter,*" Magnus Stonehand said to her.

"*Is she okay?*" the voice said again.

Recognition roared through Harlow.

"Nova? Nova?!" she screamed. Harlow scrambled to her feet. "Nova?"

"*Hello, sister,*" the disembodied voice said. "*How I have missed you.*"

The tug of magic became more insistent. "No, no, no. Astrid, no!"

But Astrid couldn't hear her. "Harlow?"

"Astrid, no. Please no. Wait!"

Her father began to fade in front of her eyes. "*We shall meet again, daughter. Your journey will be long and hard, but we will aid you in any way we can.*"

"Nova?" Harlow cried, tears streaming down her face. "Where are you?"

"*Find me, sister,*" her sister said. "*Find me as soon as you can.*"

"Nova, I love you so much." There was so much she wanted, no needed to say, but all she could repeat was how much she loved her.

"*Beware, Harlow. Beware...*"

# CHAPTER FORTY-ONE

## A SLAP FOR GOOD LUCK

"Harlow?" Astrid's face swam above her. Harlow jerked and scrambled off the rock, then fell to her knees.

"You took me away," she sobbed. "You took me away from her!" From him. From her father. Gods. What was happening to her? Was she mad? Is this what madness felt like? She wanted to claw at her brain, sink deep into her magic, do anything to go back to that place where Nova's voice had swept over her skin, where she felt safe. Because she always felt safe when Nova was with her.

She could barely think about her father right now. Her supposedly dead father. Was he dead? Or was he in some dimension between?

But more importantly. Why were they together?

Astrid's face went bone white. "Who?"

Harlow covered her face with her hands. "Her. My sister."

Astrid's cool fingers touched her face. "Harlow."

The touch jerked her out of her panic. Harlow sucked in a ragged breath. "How is this possible?"

The bard sat down on the cool ground beside her and took hold of her hands. "Tell me what happened."

Harlow recounted what happened when her father's voice intruded on her thoughts.

"That's when I lost you," Astrid murmured. "It sounded like I was trying to communicate through cotton." Her face turned thoughtful. "Your father somehow stole the frequency we communicated on." Astrid shook her head in awe. "That takes some kind of power."

"My sister doesn't have magic," Harlow said. That was the strangest thing about it.

Astrid frowned. "Are you sure?"

Harlow laughed. "Of course, I'm sure. She practically raised me!" She scrubbed at her face with her hands. "To keep that secret from me..." Harlow trailed off. To keep the secret from her would be a betrayal of everything they had shared.

The bard scooted closer to her. "People keep secrets to keep people they love safe. It doesn't mean she didn't care."

Harlow grimaced. "We are sisters. We tell each other everything!"

Astrid sighed. "Everything?"

"Everything that matters," she muttered. "And magic matters."

"Magic is outlawed everywhere, Harlow. And not only is it outlawed, it's gone. Anyone who has even a hint of magic has to suppress their secret." Astrid held out her palm and a small flicker of blue flame appeared. "This is nothing more than a party trick." The flame disappeared. "And if anyone knew about it, it would get me killed."

Harlow pulled her legs up and tucked her chin against her knees, mulling over Astrid's words. Maybe she was right. Here she was hiding in the woods, trying to get a grasp on her magic. If anyone knew, she'd get taken to the gallows. Magic had already been outlawed by the time Nova found her, so revealing her secret could have been deadly to all of them.

"How did she find me?" Harlow whispered.

Astrid scooted back against a tree. "They probably couldn't risk contacting you with magic until your own had come in." She nodded. "It was smart what they did. No one but you could hear them."

"But how did they know what we were doing?"

"I can't answer that one. Each of us has the ability to see our well of magic, just like we did tonight. The only thing I can think is that your father was able to find you because you shared the same blood and he used that to disrupt the frequency between us."

"He's alive," she said with wonder. "My father is *alive*."

Astrid closed her eyes once and something akin to peace fluttered over her face. "No one ever believed he actually died. It's hard to kill a power like his."

Harlow stilled. "What?"

"He's Magnus Stonehand. The most powerful mage in existence. There was a funeral, but it was private, and the body was concealed. There have been rumors since the second that word broke of his death." Her eyes sparkled with glee. "If he's alive ..." her voice trailed off. Astrid's throat worked, and a sheen misted over her eyes. "If he's alive, there is hope for us all."

ASTRID ESCORTED her to the edge of the woods. On the way Harlow told her about what her father instructed her to do. Her skin was cool now, no sign of the fever or nausea that had plagued her, but the bard urged her to caution.

"We can try again if you start to feel ill, but we need to be far away from the castle when we do."

"Why?" Harlow asked picking through the brush and bushes in her way. Astrid never took the same path twice but today she must have been extra paranoid because burrs and thorns stuck to the damp leather of Harlow's breeches. Branches scratched her cheek and arms and tore at her hair.

"Magic can be destructive for those who are untrained."

The response didn't answer her question. Astrid motioned her forward. "I'll wait here. Hurry inside. The veil will drop the moment you're in bed."

So she *was* using magic to conceal Harlow's movements.

"I'll meet you here in three days."

With a nod, Harlow stepped into the clearing and hurried back to her dorm.

## CHAPTER FORTY-TWO

### BEFORE THE FALL - A MEMORY OF MAGIC

Marion peeked her head around the edge of Shade's door and smiled, her bright blue eyes crinkling at the edges. "Do you have a moment?" she asked.

He looked up from his papers, the taper candle beginning to burn down to a nub. He rubbed the back of his neck and smiled up at her, fatigue etched in his bones. "Marion. Of course." He motioned for her to enter.

Shade wouldn't do that for just anyone. The perception of impropriety was powerful in these lands and inviting a woman into his room was the height of uncouth. But this was Marion, and she had ways of shielding herself from the prying eyes of the castle's inhabitants. She was also his best friend's wife. Secretly. She and Magnus had hand fasted just a few days ago, and both he and Marion glowed with the blush of new love. Shade had been stunned when Stonehand had pulled him into a shadowy alcove of the castle and whispered the news. Shade immediately worried about how the queen would react when she heard the news, but that fear couldn't overshadow his happiness for them.

He suspected Marion glowed with the blush of something

else, too, but she'd yet to say anything about it. It would complicate things exponentially if what he thought was true. But he couldn't stop the warm happiness that seeped through him every time he thought about it.

She sat down at his table and made herself at home, pouring herself a cup of the bergamot tea he'd had the kitchen send up earlier. Marion inhaled deeply and sighed. "If I ever leave this place, I'll miss this brew. We have tisanes back home, not good, strong black tea." She rolled her eyes. "I'd kill to have this in my kingdom."

"Let's hope you never leave then. Although I don't think Stonehand would let you leave without him."

She chuckled, her fingers sneaking over her stomach with a quick touch. Shade's gut tightened.

Marion was with child. All his instincts screamed at him that it was so. His eyes flicked to her still-slim belly and back up to her face. She was stunning, Stonehand's wife, with blonde hair cascading down her shoulders and slim back, eyes of the brightest cornflower blue, and a quick and ready smile. He always felt lucky when she graced him with one of those smiles, so he couldn't imagine how Stonehand felt.

"What will you do?" he asked.

Marion stilled. A sigh escaped her. "I should have known something like this would not escape your notice." Her fingers curled protectively over her stomach. "I do not yet know. It is...a complication." Her smile wobbled. "Though a welcome one. I've always wanted a daughter. I have much to teach her."

Shade didn't have the heart to tell her about the goings on inside of the castle. An evil brewed under the surface, something secret and rotten that he couldn't quite decipher yet. She and Stonehand represented power that could not be ignored, and he worried for his friends, worried so much he'd taken to examining all the nooks and crannies and hidden passages of the castle, so if he needed to, he could quickly get them out.

It would mean his death, but if his death saved such love and hope, he thought it would be worth it.

Marion was the daughter of a powerful witch couple. She hailed from the Kingdom of Witches, a place most people thought was dark and wild. In some ways it was, but Marion had come to Thornewood, a tutor for one of the noble's young children whose magic had yet to be explained and brought with her light and laughter.

The first time Stonehand saw her, he'd stumbled over his own feet and stared at Marion, completely dumbstruck. And though Shade had thought Marion's beauty was beyond compare, he did not fumble or struggle to speak in her presence like Magnus had. For those reasons, Shade had stepped aside and with that, the two had found each other and grown a love even he was envious of.

His happy thoughts sobered. "You must not tell the king or queen, and you must be wary of little Desminda. She scampers through these halls with little worry or regard for anyone's privacy."

Marion smiled at that. Desminda was a welcome balm in the castle, a bright spot of happiness in an otherwise dour rule. The king was a grim-faced man, bent on securing power. His wife, the queen, was a beautiful woman, quiet and meek on the surface, but Shade saw something within her that gave him pause. She was not unintelligent, though many people thought quiet meant stupidity. Shade had been around enough to recognize those who preferred to listen, gathering nuggets of information like crows gathered shiny things, storing them away for the future. He was always careful in his speech around any nobility, but he was especially so when the queen was involved.

The king was a simple man, prone to plain speech and

words. He meant what he said, and he said what he meant. He took war as a man's job and a man's job must be finished, but the queen...well, she was the kind of woman who played the long game, he suspected.

"I plan to pack up before my secret is revealed. Magnus will follow me at a later time." Marion reached over and patted his hand. "Do not worry. We will protect our secret at all costs." She poured herself another cup of tea. "Now tell me, Shade, of the goings on. I'm afraid I am far behind on castle gossip." She blushed prettily. "Magnus has kept me quite busy, I'm afraid."

His laugh echoed through the room at her words, and for the first time in a long time, Shade's soul felt at peace.

HE STOOD at attention in the Great Hall, his soul aching and his heart miserable. Marion kneeled in front of the throne, her slightly swollen belly evident to those who knew her secret. The fashion of the day concealed her condition from most everyone else.

He'd helped her pack her bags the night before and they'd planned to see her off tomorrow morning before everyone else had awoken. The queen had blessed her return to her kingdom a week ago, but ever since then, something had been off. The queen smiled too prettily, but it was edged with a hint of malice. All Shade could think was either she had discovered Stonehand and Marion's secret, or she would punish them for Marion asking to leave before the queen wanted to. Either one would not surprise him. He'd served under more than one ruler, and most of them were fickle and capricious, content to change their minds on a whim.

Stonehand stood next to him, his posture stiff and tense.

"Do not let Queen Raima see you fret. It will not be good

for Marion," Shade said under his breath, so quiet only his friend's ears would pick it up.

There were at least a hundred people in the hall, all dressed in finery. This should be a normal day of answering the people's petitions, but the queen had summoned Marion in before she'd heard the first pleas of the villagers. This was something she'd never done before and as soon as Shade had heard, he'd pulled Stonehand from his studies to attend.

His friend was a massive man, and Shade often compared him to a golden bear. Stonehand towered over him by at least four inches. His arms were the size of a small tree, but his waist was lean and narrow. Shade wasn't an envious man, but he'd never seen Stonehand do any serious physical training, so how he'd gotten his enviable physique remained a mystery. When he'd asked, Stonehand had grinned and said he inherited it from his drunken father.

His friend was much like Marion in that he was quick to smile and slow to anger, but acrimony oozed from his pores at the queen's treatment of his wife. And yet, he couldn't say a word. If he did, their secret would be exposed, and Marion would be the one to suffer.

Stonehand was irreplaceable, responsible for the sovereign's iron rule over their lands. He'd thwarted multiple invasion attempts and had been a stoic and solid force of reason when the villagers had grown wary over the repeated attempts by warring mages to invade Thornewood.

Marion was merely a witch loaned to Thornewood from the Kingdom of Witches. But the queen did not know how powerful Marion was, only that she had the skills to teach their young children coming into magic. If she did know, Shade suspected Marion's position would become even more precarious in the kingdom.

Marion, though, had thought ahead and tried to leave before her pregnancy was discovered.

But the queen apparently had different ideas.

She sat atop her throne, her dark hair spilling around her pale face, crown glittering in the bright morning light streaming through the wide windows in the room. Her eyes shone with malice and Shade felt his blood run cold. The king was nowhere to be found. He found it odd that it was happening more and more and the last time he'd tried to have a conversation with the man, he'd seemed scattered, not the honed knife Shade had come to know.

"Be at ease," he whispered to Stonehand. "Whatever this is, we will overcome."

"She is with child," Stonehand said, his voice breaking.

"We will overcome," Shade repeated. "Do not make this worse."

The big man beside him trembled and straightened, his face slowly taking on the same blank expression Shade had perfected over many years in Thornewood's service.

"Good," Shade whispered. "Marion is smart and cunning. She will find a way to survive this."

Stonehand blew out a soft breath.

"Rise," the queen commanded.

Marion rose flawlessly, careful to keep her hands from brushing against the secret that would surely get them all killed.

"I have wonderful news this day," the queen said.

Marion stood still as a statue, her face frozen in an expression of mild curiosity and interest. "Oh?" she said. Her posture was straight, and her lips held the familiar smile of a vapid courtier. She was always better at playing the game than he was, and he couldn't help the spike of admiration he felt for her.

"Yes," the queen said, her voice carrying through the Great Hall, an effect of Stonehand's magic Shade had no doubt. He had yet to come across something his friend could not do, and that worried him even more than the careless power he expended during his tenure as the castle's chief magician.

"Several of the nobles have recently borne children of magical blood. We have no one in Thornewood to train those children, so I've created the position of Head Mage Tutor." The queen's lips curved in a cruel smile. "With this position comes great responsibility and the opportunity to mold our noble's children into powerful Thornewood mages."

Beside him, Stonehand stiffened. "She knows," he whispered, his voice an agonized growl.

"She does not," Shade said. "She suspects. Marion is too smart to reveal her secret."

"That secret will soon reveal itself," Stonehand muttered.

Marion's spine stiffened. There was no safe way out of this. "How wonderful," she said and inclined her head to the queen. "I'm sure the person who receives this great honor will make the kingdom of Thornewood proud."

The queen's eyes narrowed.

"Clever girl," Stonehand whispered.

*Clever girl indeed*, Shade thought.

"As I am on my way back to my kingdom, I wish you the very best in your search. I am sure the person you choose will have Thornewood's children's best interests at the forefront of their mind." Marion bowed deeply and held it longer than necessary before she straightened.

"I've spoken to your queen," his liege said. "I've expressed my interest in retaining your services...indefinitely."

Stonehand swayed.

"Easy," Shade murmured.

"The queen of witches was most gracious in her response and has extended your leave for as long as I require you."

Trapped. Marion was trapped and there was nothing he

could do other than watch his friend's world and the world of his wife and unborn daughter collide and splinter into pieces.

Silence held taut for far longer than was proper before Marian flashed a smile and bowed to the queen. "Of course, Your Majesty. It would be my great honor to continue in service to Thornewood for however long you have need of me."

The queen dipped her head in acknowledgement. "Thornewood thanks you for your service." She flipped a hand in dismissal and Marion bowed deeply before she straightened and hurried past them, not daring to meet either one of their gazes.

But Shade did not miss the fear shining bright in her eyes.

# CHAPTER FORTY-THREE

## ESCAPE

Shade stared at the bottom of his cup, slowly twirling the leftover liquid and debris in a circular motion. Every time he drank this tea, he thought of Marion.

He set the cup down and rose, striding over to the large window. With a precise yank, the curtains opened, sending light flooding into the room. Never had he been in a more precarious position than he was right now. Not even when he toed the line between friendship and treason had his loyalties been so firmly tested.

Against all odds, his best friend's daughter had survived long enough to make it here. He stared down below at the empty training ring, the place where he'd been taught as a boy how to defend himself and how to fight back.

The very place he now taught the handful of girls the same thing.

But how do you teach someone to survive when they were worth more dead than alive? Shade's fists clenched tightly against his sides.

This was their plan. It always had been. But neither of them knew how Harlow's magic would manifest itself or if it even would, and now he was barely holding on to his sanity.

Desminda knew who Harlow was. She suspected what had happened. But she'd always been his ally. Now he wasn't so sure. That little girl he used to toss in the air would one day be his queen, and her loyalties would be divided.

His thoughts drifted back to all those years ago, his head bowed with the weight of memories.

"SHE KNOWS WHO THE FATHER IS," Marion said through gritted teeth. Her hand poised over her massive stomach.

Shade rose from his seat at his writing table, alarm stamped over his features. He crossed to her in seconds, gently helping her inside. Each step sent agony over her features.

"My magic cannot hold, Shade." A low moan escaped her. "The babe comes, and I cannot be in this castle when it does."

Shade's heart pounded with alarm. It was a fool's game they'd played for months now, but the queen was no fool. It no longer mattered how she'd found out, only that she had.

He helped lower Marion to the bed, and she sat there, her head tucked in her hands. "I ask far too much of you."

Shade fell to his knees and took her hands in his. "And I gladly give it."

The door flew open seconds later and Magnus Stonehand strode in, concern and fear seeping from his every pore. His face fell with relief when he saw them, and he turned to shut the door. Shade rose and strode over to his friend.

"She must leave. Tonight."

Stonehand shook his head, but before he spoke, a low, deep moan rang from his wife. His eyes squeezed shut. "She cannot. It is too risky."

"It is riskier for her to stay!" Shade snapped. "The queen knows you are the father and the danger this poses for her rise to power. Magic has been...off for weeks now. If we don't get the both of you out of here, neither of you will live to see the sunrise." His eyes slid to Marion, panting and white with pain. "And neither will your babe."

Stonehand looked down at the ground, his jaw clenched tight. "What do we do?"

Shade nodded once and squared his shoulders. "Listen to me and do not deviate from what I tell you."

MARION HAD enough magic to cloak herself and Magnus from view, but she was unable to cloak her sound. They waited until she was between contractions and Magnus swept her up into his powerful arms before they headed out into the hallway. Shade walked at their back, keeping his eyes straight ahead. His two friends had disappeared beneath their veil, but he could hear Marion's pained exhales.

The sun had just set, plunging the castle into a silvery darkness. No one had come by to light the lamps yet, but it was only a matter of time. There was no access to the hidden paths within the castle from his bedroom, but the kitchen wasn't too far away. Inside the pantry concealed a dozen different pathways that Shade knew like the back of his hand. Fortunately, it was Monday and Sunday meant a massive meal. The queen gave most of the kitchen staff the night off, as they usually took leftovers in their own quarters.

It was the most luck they'd had in months.

They passed no one in the halls, but as they entered the kitchen, Shade went ahead of Marion and Magnus and stopped short.

"Nana Kay," Shade acknowledged. He kept his face carefully blank and moved farther in, holding the door open a hair longer than normal to allow time for the two behind him to slip in.

Nana Kay was an older woman with steel grey hair and an iron spine, but she was fair, and she made the best rabbit stew he'd ever tasted.

"Shade," she acknowledged, dipping her head. The woman gave him a curious glance. "Are you hungry then? I've some pumpkin soup I was just about to dish out and some leftover bread that I'll throw out later if it isn't eaten."

It was at that moment that Shade realized he hadn't thought of provisions, only getting his friends out. He looked around at the kitchen to see if there was anyone else there.

At his look, Nana Kay straightened, her brows knitting with concern. "Everything alright, young man?"

A low grating moan broke through the silence. Nana Kay gasped, her hand flying up to her heart. "What in the world?"

Shade held up a hand, but beside them, Marion dropped the veil.

"Nana Kay."

Nana's eyes went wide and when they dropped to Marion's stomach, her nostrils flared, and tears formed in her eyes. Then her gaze went to Magnus and a deep sigh escaped her. "I see." There was no disapproval in her voice, only a matter-of-factness that tied Shade up in knots. He would rather die than hurt her, but she might force his hand if she tried to warn the queen.

Nana Kay's gaze went back to him, and her eyes flashed with ire. "Don't you dare give me that look, boy. Did you think I would send a pregnant woman to her death?"

Shade looked down, shame burning through him.

Nana wiped her hands on a towel by the stove. "Well then, girl, I hope you like pumpkin, because it's about all I have. That, some bread, and a little chicken to spare."

Marion's smile wobbled, and she gently touched Stonehand's arm to put her down. She started to walk over to Nana, but the old woman rushed toward her, gathering her gently in her arms. She rubbed her back and gently pushed her away. "May the old gods bless you and your child." Nana looked up at Stonehand. "And may you find a way to escape the queen's wrath over this."

The old woman busied herself packing a small amount of food up for Marion and Magnus and when she finished, she pressed it into his friend's hands. "Go into the pantry, then. Shade knows his way around the underneath." Nana Kay pressed her hands on either side of Marion's face and dropped a soft kiss on the woman's forehead. "I hope you're blessed with a girl as beautiful as you are and as fierce as Stonehand's magic."

Then she turned her back to all of them and went back to stirring the pumpkin soup on the stove.

THE SCREAMS STARTED in earnest only a few minutes into their desperate plunge into the hidden paths underneath the castle.

Stonehand's face was like granite, his eyes pained as he held Marion tight. "Hold on, darling," he kept whispering. "We're almost there."

Marion sobbed and clutched at Stonehand, trying desperately to keep her pain quiet, but it was like trying to silence a panther screaming for prey. It was nature, and nature didn't obey man's rules.

They were almost at the iron gates by the sewers when bells rang out. Shade and Magnus stopped in their tracks. Shade's breath held as he listened.

Two bells for thieving. Three for church. Four for an assembly in the Great Hall.

And five for treason.

One bell rang, the booming sonorous sound loud even stories below the castle. The second. Then the third.

Stonehand's breath beside him was sharp but ragged.

When the fourth came, Shade's head bowed.

Then the fifth rang, loud and damning.

Shade held his hand up. "Let me see if we can get out this way. They're bound to have most of the entrances blocked."

"How many people know about these?" Stonehand asked. His friend knew about some of them, but Shade hadn't told him everything.

"Too many." Shade crept forward, his boots sloshing in the dank water toward the gates. But he'd only made it a few steps when they heard the sound of soldiers. He froze, then spun back to Marion and Magnus, waving frantically. "Go!" he whispered urgently.

They both took off in a run, Marion clasped tightly against his best friend's chest. Shade split to the left, his friend following close behind him. "There's another way," he huffed between breaths. "But it will take you into wolf territory."

The Kingdom of Wolves was no man's territory. No one who ventured in ever came out alive. Even guest rights in that kingdom were tenuous because wolves did not live by man's rules.

Marion moaned and quietly sobbed. "The babe is coming," she said between breaths. "I cannot hold out much longer."

"Shade," Stonehand begged.

He'd never heard such a tortured sound from his friend. The most powerful man in the kingdom, possibly the world, was almost to his knees. Magic wouldn't save his bride, nor would it save the babe she carried.

Shade stopped abruptly and put his arm on Stonehand's shoulders. "I will get you out of here. Do you understand me?"

Tears shone in Magnus' eyes. "Do not promise me, friend. Promise her. Get her out of here and you shall have my everlasting oath of fealty."

Shade reared back. "You do not pledge fealty to me. You pledge it to the queen."

Stonehand spat at that. "My fealty is with those I love. And I love you. You already have it, but if you get Marion away from this place, there will be nothing that could tear me from your side. Anything you need, I will be there."

Shade shook his head. "No. It was a blessing to have known you both and I will happily release you to the life you both deserve. Now follow me."

He took off running, praying he remembered the way through the twists and turns of the lower levels.

SHADE HAD ALWAYS BEEN a paranoid man. He had a backup plan for his backup plan, but he'd never once had to use them.

Until tonight.

Two horses he'd taken to planting outside at every hidden exit in the castle grazed quietly. Shade held the gate open for them both and Stonehand stopped, his voice choking with unshed tears. His cloak was pulled over his head, obscuring his features. Shade had done the same and gone one step further, pulling up a black silken mask over his nose and mouth.

His eyes met Shade's and there was enormous gratitude in them. But seconds later, Stonehand lifted Marion onto her horse.

"Can you hold on?" he asked her, his voice gentle.

"I must," she bit out. Marion sat up straight and took the reins.

Stonehand turned to his friend and clasped his forearm. "I will come back for you."

Shade stepped back. "No. You must never return here."

Stonehand smiled sadly. "I must. You know not what the queen plans, but I do. One day, I will return and make it right."

A twig snapped a few feet away. Stonehand's eyes went wide, and he swung up on his horse.

"Hold on," he barked roughly to Marion. "Do not let go." He slapped the rear end of her horse, and the mare took off like a shot.

"Straight through the forest. A few hours ride to the east. You'll arrive in the wolf kingdom," he said quickly.

With a solemn nod, his friend snapped the reins and took off through the forest after Marion. Shade quickly disappeared into the deep thicket of woods while he waited for the enemy to make itself known.

# CHAPTER FORTY-FOUR

## AN ARROW IN THE SHOULDER IS BETTER THAN ONE IN THE HEART

The next day, Shade sat with the queen, taking lunch in The Great Hall. His nerves were a ball of electricity, sparking with any sudden movement or curious look. It was not uncommon for him to dine with the queen, but something felt different this time. As if the queen knew something he didn't.

But it wasn't until the servants had brought out the lemon cookies and tea that it was revealed.

The doors boomed open, and two guards entered, holding between them a massive, unconscious man.

Shade's hand trembled as he set down his teacup with effort.

There was only one man that large with hair that golden in the castle.

The queen's lips curled up like a cat with a bowl full of cream. She stood and glided over to the two guards. With a nod, they released him.

Stonehand's head clunked against the stone floor. The queen snapped her fingers and one of the guards delivered a boot to his friend's stomach. Shade rose, keeping his expression uninterested, and walked over.

"You found him then?" he asked, impressed with how steady his voice was.

"He wasn't heading toward the Kingdom of Roses," the shorter of the guards said. "One of the other guards suggested we check some of the lesser used entrances and we found the two of them riding toward the wolf kingdom with stolen horses."

"The wolf kingdom?" the queen murmured. "Brave or stupid?" she wondered aloud.

Shade snorted with derision even as his heart plummeted. "Well, he's here now, isn't he?"

"He is, indeed," the queen murmured, giving him a curious look before turning to the guards. "And the woman?"

The taller one grinned, malice dripping from his words. "She won't be long for the world. One of my arrows took her in the shoulder."

Shade's world fell out from under him. It took all his discipline not to fall to his knees at his friend's side.

"Then where is she?" the queen asked.

"She managed to stay on her horse, but this one veered off." The guard snorted. "This one's too damn big for only one of us to take, so we decided we'd go back and collect the woman later."

Shade's eyes snapped up. "She isn't with you?"

The guard blanched and took a step back. Shade was the commander of the Kingsguard, but the queen was undermining his authority more and more. Maybe it was time he reasserted it.

"No, Shade," the guard said. "But we'll be able to find her easily. I can go back out right now and track her."

Shade snorted. "No need. I'll find her and bring her here." His eyes slid over to the queen. "With Your Majesty's permission."

The queen was too busy staring down at Stonehand. "Yes. Bring her back and make sure the babe is with her."

Shade nodded and was about to turn when she lifted her head. "And Shade?"

"Yes, Your Majesty?"

A wolfish smile curved her lips. "Dead or alive. Whatever is easier."

Bile rose in his throat. His fingers itched for his sword. After all these years, Shade realized maybe he wasn't a king's or a queen's man after all.

If his loyalty to the kingdom of Thornewood cost an innocent woman and babe their lives, then he'd cut his queen down and gladly pay the price for it on the gallows to save them.

He smiled, a tight, vicious thing. The queen's eyes lit up, thinking it was meant as agreement. "Of course. Dead or alive," Shade agreed, the words like knives in his throat.

"Then go, Commander. And bring Marion back here however you have to."

Shade spun on his heel and left them there, praying his friend would still be alive when he returned.

HIS HEART SQUEEZED every time he found a spot of blood on the ground. Shade meticulously followed her trail, cleaning up every single spot he could. When he found a tree with a bloody handprint on the pale bark, Shade's chest tightened, and it was all he could do not to roar his rage to the heavens.

The guard was right. Marion had left a trail even an idiot could follow. He couldn't imagine the pain and fear she experienced during that ride. Admiration for her burned within him and as he rode, slowly following and concealing her trail, he prayed fervently that he would find her alive.

And then he prayed her child survived the night.

He found her less than an hour later, her back curled

against a massive oak tree, her breast bared and a tiny babe suckling.

Shade's breath escaped in a shocked 'oh' of sound. Relief speared through him, and he squeezed his eyes shut against the tears threatening to form.

Marion's head snapped up and magic curled at the ends of her fingertips a second later. The ends of her hair lay against her skin covered in dark red blood, her porcelain skin pale white, her lips tinged blue.

"Hold," he said quietly to his friend.

A weak smile bloomed on her lips. "Shade," she breathed. The magic dropped from her fingertips, and she brushed bloody fingers against the babe's fluff of golden hair.

He took a few steps closer and, as he did, he saw the ragged edges of an arrow poking out from her right shoulder. His lips tightened as he bent down to examine the wound. Blood trickled steadily from around it. Pulling it out would only hasten what would happen. Her skirts were torn and bloody from her shoulder and the child's birth. He pressed his lips together against the howl threatening to break from his chest.

Marion shook her head. "Do not mourn for me, Shade. I am not dead yet."

But she was.

She just didn't know it yet.

Shade sat down beside her and when the babe finished suckling, Shade turned his head to allow Marion her modesty. Then she reached over and placed the child in his arms.

He swallowed hard against the lump in his throat as he took the tiny bundle wrapped inside of her mother's cloak. The babe smelled of blood and despair, but when he chanced a glance at Marion, her eyes were full of love.

"Harlow," she whispered to him. "Her name is Harlow, and she is a Stonehand." Marion leaned her head back against the trunk of the tree. "There is a prophecy about a child born to two magicians known only to my kingdom. The child will know great pain and heartache." Marion's mouth fell in a grimace of pain. "But she will bring great light to the world." She turned to look at Shade and he could see the brightest light he'd ever known slowly fading. Grief squeezed his soul, and he turned his head away so she would not see it.

"Shade." Her fingers lightly touched his arm. He drew in a shuddering breath. "Listen to me," she pleaded. "Listen to me and know my plan for my daughter."

So he did. They sat there together under the shade of that massive oak tree as the best woman he'd ever known laid out her plan to protect her heart and soul. Shade wanted to rage at her, to scream at her to fight, that he would get her help, that he would do anything to save her, and she knew it. Marion knew it and smiled at him and told him how much she loved him and how much Stonehand loved him, too. And then she asked him to protect her daughter because one day she would grow up to love him too. She asked him to watch from the shadows, and when it was time, she asked him to risk everything to save her.

His friend died next to him, the warmth of her blood growing cold against Shade's sleeve as the hours passed. And when her head slumped over onto his shoulder and Shade became brave enough, he stood, gathering the child and wrapping the cloak firmly around her tiny body.

Then he rode hard and fast into the night, right into enemy territory, with the child tucked close against his heart.

# CHAPTER FORTY-FIVE

## DARKNESS APPROACHES

The weeks passed and Harlow's sickness was held at bay. She still couldn't reach the pool deep inside her, though she tried and tried. Astrid was slowly losing patience with her, but Harlow couldn't find it in her heart to care that much.

Her mind stayed preoccupied with thoughts of her sister and her father, and she plotted to find them as soon as she could. Graduation loomed over them and so far, all thirteen looked primed to capture the best positions in the kingdom. Of course, all the girls wanted positions in the castle, but one was most coveted of all– Desminda's personal guard.

Harlow didn't want to assume anything. The warning Desminda had given her in the baths had stuck with her, so she'd given the future queen a wide berth and stayed on her side of the village. There was no reason for her to return to the castle anyway, so time slowly passed, and Harlow trained as hard as she could to make it pass faster. A few days a week she visited Astrid, so far to no avail.

As soon as she graduated, she would do whatever it took to find her sister. Her father would come next. She did not know him, but she knew Nova's heart and if they were together, perhaps he was a man worth knowing.

She was still poor at making friends, but it didn't worry her too much because the other Virago were all far better at it than her, and soon enough they'd included her in the folds of their friendship.

Melara was included in that, though Harlow still had trouble accepting her overtures of friendship. To her credit, Melara had acknowledged her hesitance and given Harlow her space.

Today, they studied the other kingdoms, though she couldn't help but feel this was only a cursory study. There were several kingdoms on either side of them. The Kingdom of Roses she was familiar with the most, though she had not seen the red-haired prince or his vapid sister around. She'd seen Princess Celestine once marveling over a tapestry during one of her training runs through the castle with Shade.

The girl was beautiful but had the intellect of slug slime, and Harlow knew that after seeing her for only a moment.

Below Lucien's kingdom lay the Kingdom of Crystal, then the Kingdom of Beasts, separated by the Lake of Sorrows. Directly to Thornewood's south was the Kingdom of Wolves and below it, the Kingdom of Witches. The Kingdom of Shadows lay to the far south, east of the Witch Kingdom. Above the shadow kingdom and connected by a small channel, lay the Kingdom of Light.

The wolf and witch kingdoms had the least information written about them, but there was a small note in the texts stating that any efforts to gather information had resulted in the death of multiple scholars.

A chill chased down her spine at that. Every kingdom had some form of resource to trade with the other. Lucien's export was flowers of all shapes and sizes, scents and colors, though their roses were famous in all the kingdoms. The Kingdom of Crystal was rich in ore and precious gemstones, and the Kingdom of Beasts, as macabre as it was, was rich in fur and skins, some which littered the floors of Thornewood castle.

The Kingdom of Wolves had no export listed, though there was a red x next to their name. The witch kingdom had the same. When she raised her hand, Shade had walked over and peered over her shoulder. His face had tightened for a moment so quick, Harlow wondered if she'd imagined it.

"What does this mean?" She pointed at the red marks.

"It means they are our enemies." Shade's jaw tightened.

"But what about the other kingdoms?" Harlow skimmed down the page with her finger and found no other marks.

"Politics are complicated," Shade said. "The kingdoms have history between them and certain...snubs are remembered."

One of the other Virago snorted. Shade whipped in the direction of the sound. "Bloom?"

The tall girl snapped straight in her seat.

"You have something to add?"

Bloom was the picture of frozen. One of Shade's eyebrows went up. "If you have intel to share with the other girls, this is the place to do it."

"It's not intel," Bloom said quietly.

"Ah. Then gossip?" Shade clasped his hands behind his back and walked over to her. Harlow cringed, thankful she wasn't in Bloom's shoes.

"Not gossip either." Bloom looked up and paled at Shade's expression. She ducked her head. "Other texts claim something was stolen from the Kingdom of Thorns. Something important. The wolves hid it for years."

Harlow was looking right at Shade as Bloom spoke. The man stiffened and his eyes darkened with an emotion she couldn't place.

"Stole?" His voice took on that dark, dangerous quality it often did when they were all about to suffer either with extra chores or physical conditioning so intense they would barely be able to walk straight the next morning.

Bloom cleared her throat. "Yes, Shade. Stole."

*Brave.* Bloom was both brave and profoundly stupid. Harlow squirmed in her chair.

She locked eyes with Helena. The girl pressed her lips together and squeezed her eyes shut. Over the months they'd been together, they'd all learned when to keep their mouths shut, but inevitably someone would forget, and they'd all suffer.

But this was the first time Bloom had done it and something deep within Harlow whispered that she should listen and listen well. Bloom rarely spoke without saying something profound, even if the words didn't seem like it at the moment.

"And what did the wolves steal?" Shade asked, still in his dangerous voice.

Bloom lifted her eyes up to the dark, wrathful man looming above her. There wasn't an ounce of fear in her voice when she said, "A child of magic."

A pin could have dropped in the room, and it would have sounded like thunder. Silence fell, thick and oppressive and, for the first time, Harlow felt real fear for one of the Virago.

Shade cocked his head like a predator studying his prey for weakness. Bloom met his stare and very slightly tilted her chin up in defiance.

Helena sucked in a breath.

They waited for Shade to order them into their conditioning clothes or to cut their rations in half for a week or...something.

But instead, a strange half smile formed on his lips, and he turned and walked up to the front of the classroom. "The first thing a Virago should do is listen. To everything. No matter how outrageous. There is a difference between hearing and listening and most people do not know what it is." He pointed to Melara. "Do you know the difference?"

Melara blinked. "Erm."

Shade pointed to Helena who merely shrugged.

His gaze fell on Bloom and one of his dark eyebrows rose. "Do you know?"

Bloom smiled. "Hearing is a physical act that none of us can help. Listening involves all parts of us and is both internal and external. When you listen, you strive for understanding. Hearing is merely the act of sound passing through our ears."

Shade blinked. "Class dismissed." He waved a hand at them.

No one moved for a second.

Shade's eyebrows went up, and he opened his mouth...

They all practically fell over themselves trying to run out the door before he got any words out.

# CHAPTER FORTY-SIX

## A SCARLET SECRET

Astrid sat in the middle of the clearing cross-legged and annoyed. "For the love of all the gods, it's been months. Your mind is like a plate of Nana Kay's rabbit stew, minus the delicious part! Jumbled and chunky and full of things no one is even sure about."

Harlow stared at her. She was cold, tired, borderline delirious, and every muscle in her body ached. Her lips twitched right before she burst into laughter.

"Harlow!" Astrid's nostrils flared, but laughter was contagious and soon enough she was giggling too.

Harlow flopped onto her back and put her hands behind her head. Above them, stars sparkled like jewels. They reminded her of the two stones still in her pocket. She sat up abruptly and dug through her breeches before pulling it out.

Astrid gasped and leaned over. "Is that..." She held out her hand. "Why is it bigger?"

Harlow looked up at her. "You tell me. Weren't you the one who gave it to me?"

"Only one," Astrid admitted. "This one is larger than the stone I left for you."

"So it was you who lured me to the clearing."

The bard snorted. "*Lured*," she drawled. "You make it sound so tawdry."

Harlow put the pieces together in her head. She held the stone up to the moonlight. "What is it?"

Astrid scooted over, shivering as she leaned against Harlow for warmth. "It's called a Luna stone."

Harlow dropped it into her hand and the bard flipped it over, studying the stone.

"There aren't any seams. My sister left me one and told me never to use it. When I put the two stones together, they merged."

Astrid's sharp eyes narrowed. "Your sister gave you one of these?"

Harlow nodded. "Why is that important?"

Astrid tossed the stone up. It winked blue in the moonlight. "Because this is one of the reasons why magic no longer works. These stones channel energy, and mages used them to store their powers."

Harlow caught the stone when Astrid tossed it up again. "I don't feel anything," she admitted.

"When magic fled the kingdom, all the stones were drained." She shrugged. "It was like something pulled all the energy out and moved it somewhere else." A darkness crossed over her eyes. "Plus, the villages were raided to retrieve any of the leftover stones, just in case."

"Is that even possible?" Harlow wondered aloud.

"With magic, most things are possible." Astrid scooted away and faced Harlow. "Give me your hands and let's try again. But this time hold the stone."

"But you just said they're all drained."

"Yes," Astrid agreed, "but *your* magic isn't gone or drained." She paused, chewing on her lip. "Have you ever sat at the edge of a river on a sunny day?"

Harlow tilted her head. "Everyone has."

"Probably not everyone," Astrid drawled. "But that isn't important. If the day was warm, were the rocks warm?"

She wasn't sure where the bard was going with this but nodded.

"And if it was a cold day, were the rocks still warm?"

Harlow shook her head. "They were cold."

"Exactly. On the warm days, the stone soaked up the heat from the sun. On chilly days, it soaked up the cold. The Luna Stones work in a similar way, but they don't respond to temperature, they respond to magical energy." She motioned with her hand.

Harlow grasped Astrid's fingers, the Luna stone tucked safe within her palm.

"Now try to empty your mind," Astrid said.

The stone was cool and inert in her palm. She wondered why it never felt warm before, but as she sat there desperately trying to empty her memory of thought, the stone flickered in her palm. Harlow gasped, but Astrid squeezed her fingers. "Keep still. Focus only on the stone and empty your mind of everything but it."

Harlow breathed in deeply and tried to follow Astrid's instructions, but the stone remained inert.

They waited for a few moments and when nothing happened, Astrid exhaled. "Let's try something else."

Harlow moved to tug her fingers, but Astrid tightened her grip. "Keep holding on."

Silence fell in the clearing, the only sound the chirps and clicks of insects and the occasional slithering of something Harlow didn't want to think about.

A lilting hum came from Astrid. Harlow stiffened, but Astrid gently squeezed her fingers.

In the mountains hums a song,
A song of yore and magic.
In the sky hums a bird,
A song of love so tragic.

In the grass hums a snake,
A song of wild earth love.
In the trees hums a panther,
A song of prey far above.

In the castle hums a lady,
A song of unfulfilled dreams,
In the village hums a widow,
A song of silent screams

The song made no sense, but Harlow listened for true music was rare and its own special kind of magic. Soon, her mind focused only on the words, on Astrid's lilting, stunning voice, and her shoulders relaxed. Her worries fell away, the threat of her secret shoved to the recesses of her mind. The pool deep within her stirred and shifted.

*Touch me*, it commanded her. *Use me*.

Harlow obliged, reaching out a tentative finger, her mind only on the power within her, curious about what she and that power could do together.

And when her finger touched that well of magic, the world roared its triumph.

# CHAPTER FORTY-SEVEN

## THE DARK RISES

The former Virago huddled around a fast-dying fire when a boom shook the entire forest. The cloaked woman with them stumbled, righting herself against a tree when the ground suddenly settled.

There were only ten of them left. Less than the Virago left with Shade now. Hunger and fear had turned their features gaunt, but they still held onto hope.

Hope in the form of a bitter woman who had so far refused to show her face.

But when the world stopped shaking, and the woman straightened, she let the cloak fall from her face. A cruel smile curled her red lips.

"There," she said with satisfaction. "There is the proof." She stalked up to the fire and slid her boot through the dirt, extinguishing the meek flames.

Several of the girls cried out with dismay. The others were too weak to do much of anything. "Rise," the woman said. "Rise and come with me. You will be kept in the forest no longer. We all have work to do."

The girls looked at each other, suspicion coloring every one of their gazes before one of them, the leader of their strange, malnourished crew rose.

"Come," she said after a moment. "It's either die here starving in the dark or die with her, hopefully with a full belly."

The woman smiled again and crooked her hand. "You'll have far more than a full belly if things go to plan. Magic is back and if we want to save this kingdom, we must right the original wrong. Thornewilde took it away from everyone." She tilted her head. "You can't punish all for the sins of a few." She clucked her tongue. "The world is far better without others holding too much power. If you want to make the world right again, you give magic back to those who deserve it. Everyone else will fall in line." She missed the concerned looks the girls exchanged as she pulled her cloak back over her head. "Follow me and be quiet. If you stumble, we will not stop for you."

The girls followed after her, the woman's long hair streaming in the night wind, and moonlight highlighting her porcelain skin. They were desperate and starving and they would do whatever she asked to better their own circumstances.

No matter what it was.

# CHAPTER FORTY-EIGHT

## A PROMISE FULFILLED

S hade woke with a jerk, his hands curling around the hilt his blade. He knew that sound. He'd heard it many times before. It was only a matter of time before the queen recognized it too.

With a murmured curse, he rolled out of bed and dressed quickly. He strapped his sword on and hurried down the corridors, swift as he could without drawing attention to himself. Not everyone would wake up, but that boom was loud enough to draw unwanted attention.

He slipped into the kitchen and into the pantry, opening the door to a familiar silent passage and hurrying through the shortcut to the Virago dormitory. The pantries held several passages, most leading to spyholes or outside the castle, but he'd discovered this one quite by accident a few years ago when visiting Desminda for tea.

Dim lamplight flickered through the windows, Shade strode into the Virago dorms, eyeing each and every girl and making sure everyone was in their beds. He knew before he saw the empty bed that Harlow would not be there.

He took a deep inhale. "Stay here. Keep the door latched.

The only person allowed to come in here is the queen or the princess."

"What happened?" Melara asked.

His eyes slid to Bloom. Her face had gone pale, her grey eyes large and wide in her face. "Ask Bloom," he snapped, then turned on his heel and left.


AN EXPLOSION like that could come from only one place. He saw no damage to the village, though some curious people ventured from their small homes to see what had happened. Shade strode past them, ignoring anyone foolish enough to ask questions. When he'd turned a corner into an alley between a small curio shop and bread bakery, he checked back to see if anyone dared to follow him. Satisfied he was alone, Shade took off at a jog and headed into the forest.

He remembered the first time he'd seen the girl. She was close to his age, younger by a few years, their circumstances so very different. She was short, lithe, and her hair was as dark as the ink from his well. Her eyes were like starlight, silvery and mysterious.

Shade stumbled when she turned her beauty on him, tripped and looked away, dumbstruck. She didn't notice him and thank the gods for that because he looked like a true idiot. He listened as she haggled over a loaf of bread as he passed by, unable to resist taking one more long and lingering look at her face.

His heart pounded, and his palms went clammy.

He was the commander of the Kingsguard, for all that was holy. What in the hell was wrong with him?

She wore an ill-fitting dress and her shoes had seen better days, but she argued with the passion of a rich merchant. There were few cheaper than the rich. He would know. His entire life had consisted of serving them.

She'd tied her hair back with a tattered ribbon as if she knew she had to keep up appearances and it angered her, so she'd done the bare minimum. She wore no jewelry and carried no purse, only a small market bag clutched tightly to her side. A suspicious bulge on her side had him curious, but she shifted before he could get a good look at what it might be.

Trying to edge closer to her without being suspicious, he picked up an apple and studied the shine and heft of the fruit while straining to hear what she was saying.

"Three clicks?" she said, outrage making her voice vibrate. "I could go down two stalls and get it for one!"

The merchant's mistake was looking where she pointed and seeing the rival bread maker hawking her wares. Shade bit down a smile.

When they finally made a deal and the girl tucked the bread in her bag, Shade watched her walk away, his thoughts a jumble.

THE SECOND TIME he saw her, he was better prepared, though his heart still sputtered to a stop when she came into the clearing. Shade leaned against a tree, tossing an apple up in the air, purposeful nonchalance etched into every line of his body.

She stopped abruptly, her fingers touching her side.

A knife. She had a knife tucked into her pocket.

Surprised filled him, followed by irrational and hot anger. What had happened to her for her to arm herself for a normal trip to the market? Women didn't often carry weapons. Their husbands wouldn't approve for sure, but also weapons were banned in the villages. Since Marion's death and Harlow's disappearance, the queen had become even more paranoid, if that were possible. Add to that the infirmity of the king, and things were much more tense than normal these days.

"Who are you?" she demanded. She clutched the bag tighter to her side. "I do not have any money. And if you try to take my bread, I promise you will not like what happens to you."

Shade bit down his smile. "I am not here to harm you."

She stared at him suspiciously before a bitter laugh tore from her throat. "A strange man accosts a girl in the forest when they are quite alone, and he promises he won't hurt her." She rolled her eyes heavenward. "Do you think I was born yesterday then? A fool with a skirt?" Her fingers slipped into her pocket.

Shame rolled through him. Of all the stupid things he could have done. He straightened. *Idiot*, he chastised himself. He cleared his throat. "I, ah, I realize I could have handled this better."

The girl snorted, but curiosity filled her eyes. "Who are you then?"

He sketched a slight bow. "My name is Shade Montello."

The girl took a step back, her eyes widening at the name.

He opened his mouth to speak, but she took one more step, then whirled in a motion almost too fast for him to see and took off running through the forest, the bag she was so protective of lying forgotten on the forest floor.

THE THIRD TIME he saw her, he'd brought a bag filled with bread, jams, and jellies from the market and sat on the ground, his back against a tree and his sword a few feet away.

She stilled at the sight, frowning down at him. "Why do you keep following me?"

He held out his hands. "You stumbled upon me. Is it fair to accuse me of following you?"

She took a few steps back.

"*Please*," he begged. "Please don't run."

The girl stilled. "What need have you of me? I am nothing."

She was wrong. She was everything. And she held something far more precious than gold to him.

"No one knows I'm here." He pushed the bag to her. "For my folly last time."

She took a few steps forward peering down at the bag. "I'll not be bought," she snapped.

Shade's sigh was bone deep and weary. "If I am caught here, it could mean my death. Please, sit a while and speak with me. I have a need only you can help me with."

She frowned but sat down, several feet away from him. Her posture was hunched and wary and she studied him like a hawk studies a worm as if she gauged where her knife could sink into his skin to cause him the most harm. But it was the look in her eyes that told him her story.

"Who hurt you?" he demanded.

The girl blinked, scrambled to her feet, and ran from him, swift and fleet footed as a deer.

Shade screamed his frustrations to the sky.


THE FOURTH TIME he had to follow her for she'd changed her path back home through the forest. He watched her for days feeling decidedly uncomfortable with his actions until she used the same way home several weeks in a row and he knew he could find her again.

This time he left his sword lying against a tree several feet away. He brought nothing with him but apologies.

She stopped short when she saw him again sitting against a tree, this time wearing nothing but breeches and a shirt. He'd even shucked his boots, his pale bare toes curling in the soft, loamy earth. The girl snorted with amusement but made no move to come closer.

He held his hands out. "I must offer apologies for my appalling behavior. I am not good with..."

She raised an eyebrow.

"Situations requiring a deft or careful hand. Or anything social really. I come to you and ask for you to sit awhile again. I promise I will ask nothing personal or probing. I am here for a reason which I will endeavor to make clear much sooner."

The girl sat once again, her tattered skirts pooling around her. She had another bag filled with bread and other things from the market.

"My name is Shade Montello," he began again. "I am the current commander of the Kingsguard."

"What need have you of an orphan girl?" she demanded.

Shade tilted his head. He'd bet his left boot she was no orphan girl. "I claim Marion and Magnus Stonehand as my close, personal friends."

The girl stiffened just slightly, her expression turning wary. Everyone was familiar with Stonehand's influence. "I do not know what that has to do with me."

"It has everything to do with you. They had a little girl three years ago."

The girl's silvery eyes narrowed. Her muscles shifted and tensed.

"Please don't run. *Please.* They had a little girl with golden hair and bright blue eyes. I was with her mother when she died." He licked his lips, frantic to ensure he explained to her what he wanted without scaring her off.

"I saw her mother," the girl said. "You were not there when she died. I was."

Shade tilted his head. "You were in Thornwilde during the raids."

He knew exactly what happened to her now. Rage pooled inside of his veins.

Her stiff nod confirmed it.

"Her *real* mother," he said. "The woman she was with belonged to the Kingdom of Wolves. She acted as Harlow's foster mother under the direction of her king."

The girl's brow furrowed. "The wolves? There were no wolves in the village."

"She was a nanny of one of the wolf families. As Harlow grew, they realized they couldn't properly raise the girl in their kingdom, so they sent the woman with her husband and Harlow to Thornewilde."

"Why?"

He inhaled and studied her, hoping he wasn't making a critical error in trusting her. Everything depended on what happened next. Her reaction could end with him swinging from the gallows. "Because the girl is the Heir to Magic. Her mother told me so."

"I don't know what that means," she said, though she looked away from him—the telltale sign of a lie. "Why should that matter to me?"

"Because I've watched you. I know what you are. And I know where you came from. Do not pretend to be a poor orphan girl with me." His fingers flexed and he forced himself to relax. He would be lost if she chose not to help him and forcing her was out of the question. For many reasons other than what happened to her. "Harlow's mother told me of a prophecy."

She watched him warily and stayed silent.

He held up a hand. "I'll not betray your secret. The girl's mother hailed from the Kingdom of Witches."

The girl's expression sobered. "It doesn't exist."

Many thought that. Not only was it real, their king and queen waited patiently in the shadows, watching Thornewilde, waiting for word of Harlow. If things went well, he'd have news for them soon. If not...then they might all be lost. "It does. Harlow is the confluence of two powerful bloodlines. Whether she inherits magic is still unknown, but it is likely. And when she comes into it, her power might shake the world."

"I still don't know what that has to do with me." Her fingers twisted around her market bag, the only sign of nerves she showed. She kept her face carefully blank, but her eyes gave away her fear. Not just at Shade, but for the Heir and what he might want for her. He saw her love and thought maybe...maybe this would go his way.

Shade gave her a sad smile. "One year ago, guards returned to the castle with tales of a girl with shadows from her fingers who saved a young child with golden hair."

The girl blanched, her face turning pale as bone.

"No one knows who the girl really is. The guards never mentioned it to anyone but me. They were mostly angry to be thwarted by a young girl."

"Why are you here?" she whispered. "I'll not let you take her from me." Tension stiffened her frame. If he didn't steer this the right way, she'd run again and there might not be a next time for him to catch her.

"I'm here to do the opposite. I want to teach you what you need to survive. Harlow is precious to both me and the other kingdoms, though they do not know it yet."

"We're doing fine without you. The last thing I need is you coming into our village. Things like that do not go unnoticed."

"Which is why I'm sitting here, my ass full of briars, in a forest full of beasts waiting on you rather than snatching you from the marketplace."

The girl's lips quirked. Shade wondered what it would be like to get a true smile from her. He imagined it would feel like sunlight on his face after a cold winter. Before he could help himself, he said, his words soft and halting, "I can show you things... ways you can protect yourself and Harlow. You can... ensure what happened to you never happens to either one of you again." His words were halting and careful, fear of her running away again rippling through him.

She studied him, those eyes of starlight burning him from within. "Men take," she said after a moment. "They take and take and take because they think they've earned it by virtue of the appendage dangling between their legs." She stood. "They took from me, and I'll not get it back. But they took more than my innocence, Shade Montello. They took away who I was, and I can't find that person anymore. She doesn't exist in this life. Maybe not even in the next."

Shade nodded once, unable to find words to comfort her, but he didn't think she wanted them. He burned with indignation at her plight, but pride filled him at her courage and bravery. He'd seen the wreckage of the village, the bodies, the blood, the total destruction. For her to scoop up a child when she'd been so grievously injured... Well. Shade had soldiers under his command who wouldn't show the bravery she had. Harlow was in good hands with her. He chose his next words carefully. "Then we will hone the person she is now and make her a blade, strong and sharp. And when the time comes, we will take back our kingdom."

The girl gave him a fierce grin, the sight of it stealing his breath. "You have a bargain then." She tucked the bag close to her and stood. "My name is Nova," she said. "I come to the market on Tuesdays and Saturdays. Find me here and we will see what kind of blade we will form."

*Nova.*

The girl of starlight gave him a nod and turned away from him, leaving him alone and barefoot in the forest as the sun set on his shoulders.

# CHAPTER FORTY-NINE

## MUSIC & MADNESS

T he music drew him to her. He couldn't hear it with his ears. It pounded inside his heart, leading him through the moonlight-speckled forest and into a clearing.

Two girls lay close together, completely unconscious. Trees lay around them, felled in a circular pattern from the blast. His gaze swung wildly around but he could see no instruments, could find no singer.

Disturbed, he came closer only to mutter an oath under his breath.

*Harlow.*

She lay beside a girl who looked vaguely familiar but who he was sure he'd never met before. He stepped forward only to smack into an impenetrable wall.

Shade blinked and tried to move forward, but there was a wall of nothing in front of him. Strong, hard nothing. He could see through it because there was nothing there, see them both lying completely vulnerable to the elements, but he could not reach them.

"Harlow!" He didn't want to yell too loudly lest he draw attention to them. She did not stir.

"Girl!" he called to the other, a stunning redhead with pale skin.

Nothing. Frowning, Shade tried to push through the shield or ward or whatever it was, but it was a shield of solid magic he couldn't penetrate.

His boots scuffed the ground as he bent down and scooped a handful of dirt and rocks up. Whispering an apology, he tossed a stone at the girls fully expecting it to bounce back at him. But it didn't.

Breathing a sigh of relief, he pelted both girls with tiny stones, hissing Harlow's name until she began to stir. She blinked and winced, her palm moving to her head.

"We need to move. Now," Shade whispered urgently. "Get your friend up and let's go." He looked behind him but couldn't see anything through the darkness. The wind was light tonight, but every sound made his shoulders tense. There was no way that boom of sound wouldn't draw guards into the woods to look for the cause of it.

Harlow's eyes widened at the sight of him, but to her credit she didn't ask questions. On her hands and knees, swaying, she crawled closer to the girl and shook her gently.

"Astrid. We have to go. Now." The girl didn't move.

Shade tried to push through the barrier again, but it was still there. The other girl must have thrown it up before the blast. Interesting it still held despite her current state.

"Astrid." Harlow shook her harder.

The girl moaned and turned on her side. She coughed and retched, clear liquid pouring from her throat.

Harlow grimaced but didn't back away. "We have to go," she said urgently.

Astrid slowly sat up and looked around. When she saw Shade, she clambered backward, but Harlow put a hand on her shoulder. She looked up at him and swallowed hard. "He's with me. We can trust him."

Shade didn't have the heart to tell her he was the *only* person she could trust right now. As Astrid slowly rose to her feet, he took in her apparel and the instrument lying beside them.

A bard. He exhaled. Harlow's presence meant the world would change, but a bard hadn't been seen in Thornwood since magic fell. And since her barrier still stood strong, perhaps that was why.

Stonehand had mentioned he would never be able to fully eradicate magic. It didn't work like that. Magic was energy and energy was natural. But he stifled it enough that it had died to all but a trickle.

Except, of course, with his own daughter. Clever mage.

Astrid and Harlow swayed together but stayed standing. Shade looked back over his shoulder one more time, then motioned them to follow him.

When he ensured they were behind him, he took off the opposite way from where he'd come, away from the direction the castle guards would come from.

MOVING swift and silent through the forest, none of them spoke. His mind burned with questions, but they could all wait. First, he had to get them to safety. Where he'd put the bard, he had no idea. Even associating with her put them all in danger.

He slowed his pace as they came to the other side of the castle. Shade crouched at the edge of the woods and motioned for them to do the same. "Astrid, you may need to wait here. I don't have a place for you yet."

Harlow softly cleared her throat. "She's already gone."

Shade jerked his head back. "What? Where?"

She shrugged. "Sometimes she does that."

He exhaled and shut his eyes for a brief moment. "You trust her?"

"I trust her enough," she said, and the words were so like her father he almost smiled.

"Good." Shade watched for a few moments for any guards, but they were all clustered toward the direction the boom came. He eased out from the cover of the forest. "Come. Quietly."

Harlow eased out behind him, her footfalls almost as silent as his.

"Follow behind me. I'm taking you back to the dorms."

Harlow stiffened. "They'll see me come in."

"Considering the castle just fixed a massive hole caused by magic in your dormitory, I think it's safe to assume they've figured out who was responsible for tonight's disaster."

Her lips tightened, but she gave him a stiff nod. Shade almost laughed at her expression, but took pity on her. Harlow's shoulders tensed with apprehension as she crept beside him.

"We'll speak more about this later. For now, it's important to blend back into the Virago and pretend you know nothing about this. Do you understand?"

Harlow ducked her head. "Yes, Shade."

"Then follow."

Shade led her back to the dormitories, quietly passing by dozens of the queen's troops, his stomach bottoming out as one passed too close to them. He held Harlow close to his side, blending into the shadows and praying her golden hair didn't give them away. But the soldiers were preoccupied with something else and when it was safe enough, he stepped out and hurried Harlow back to the dormitories.

He waited until she slipped inside then headed over to where the troops were, squaring his shoulders and blending in with the rest of them. From the corner of his eye, he spotted a mass of dark hair and a small glittering crown.

Shade gathered his emotions and tucked them into that strong black box at the bottom of his mind and headed in the direction of the queen.

"Your Majesty," he said, sweeping into a bow.

"Commander. Someone said they saw you slip out of the castle." Her look was contemplative.

Shade rose, carefully keeping his face blank. "I heard the noise and went to check on the Virago. When I assured they were all fine, I headed into the woods to see if I could find the source of it."

She tilted her head. "And did you find anything?"

"No. I didn't get too far in before heading back to check in. I suspect it's farther into the woods."

She made a noncommittal noise. "What do you think it was?"

Shade shook his head. "Difficult to tell. I don't see any smoke or fire."

"Magic?" the queen asked.

He let the derision show in his eyes. "Hardly. It's been wiped out for years. Nothing has changed, has it?" *Not yet, anyway*.

"You tell me, Shade," the queen murmured.

Fear shivered down his spine. "I've seen nothing alarming to hint it's returning." *Silver tongued liar*, he thought. He no longer walked the line between loyalty and treason. Nor did he dance on its edge. Shade now walked firmly on the other side, right on the sharp blade of treachery and if he was caught, he would pay with his life.

"Something is amiss," his queen said. "I can feel it." Her dark eyes swept the grounds before landing on him.

The woman always looked too deep and said too little. She

held her secrets tight, sharing only when it would benefit her. At one time, he'd been bespelled by her beauty, the intellect in her dark eyes, her hair the color of a raven's wing. And over time, his feelings had only strengthened. The age difference between them didn't matter to Shade. He would have served her faithfully from afar for forever, pining for her in secret.

Then they'd brought a young man into the castle against his will and the king and queen both benefitted from Stonehand's power. He'd seen things that shook him awake at night to this day.

Beauty was more than skin deep, and Shade had seen its opposite in the queen for years now. Any bloom of love had withered deep within him the second he'd seen the grief and agony in Stonehand's eyes as they'd dragged him into the Great Hall and Marion had died in the woods.

# CHAPTER FIFTY

## PUNISHMENT AND A PROMISE

F ive men stood before him. Three of them were innocent, but all were guilty of a crime. Perhaps not a crime in the eyes of Thornewood law, but a crime of moral failing. Shade stood in the training ring, his thoughts on Nova, and took the measures of the men in front of him. Some of them would deny it, he knew, but Shade kept meticulous records and he knew all of his guards well.

He knew exactly who'd been in Thornewilde that day, besides the man who'd come to him about the girl of shadows. Shade had quietly investigated these last few weeks, once the whispers of magic returning had died down thanks to the queen's swift intervention and her clever lies. But he'd seen a change in the village, a hopefulness where there once had been none. He hoped for all their sakes that it would not be their downfall.

"Sir Martin," Shade said and nodded to the space in front of him. The knight glanced at the other men around him before he stepped up. "Were you in the village of Thornewilde during the castle raids?"

Sir Martin winced. No one in the castle called it a raid for that would infer the kingdom had turned on its own people, wouldn't it? But since none of these men would make it out of this ring alive, it didn't matter.

"Aye, Shade."

"And did you witness any assaults on the women and children of the village?"

All the men stiffened. The main culprit, Sir William, straightened, his fingers twitching at his side as if he wanted to unsheathe his sword and run Shade through.

He'd have his chance soon enough.

The man in front of him swallowed. His eyes lowered and his lips began to tremble.

"Men of honor do not lie," Shade said quietly. "The Kingsguard are men of honor, are they not?"

"It was long ago, sir." Sir Martin's head bowed.

"You stall." Shade's gaze roamed over all the men. "You stall for dishonor and rape. Is that it, Sir Martin? Do you feel Sir William was in the right?"

Sir Martin looked up, his eyes wide with shock. "No. Never!"

"Then you will tell me what transpired that day." His gaze locked with Sir Martin's. "And you will leave no detail out."

HE'D RUTHLESSLY INTERROGATED ALL four men about that day, leaving Sir William for last. His stomach roiled with disgust and anger burned through his veins. Thoughts of Nova and what she'd endured raged through him. She'd been gone for some time now and they'd been careful not to communicate lest they give themselves away, but he hoped she would understand what he was about to do.

Even if it wasn't Nova they'd raped, it would have been

someone and there was probably someone after her. He felt like the worst kind of fool for not putting the clues together, but he'd trusted his men. He'd trained these men, and they all knew how he felt about the rules of warfare.

Women and children were always off limits.

To defy that rule was to invite anarchy and evil into their kingdom.

But Shade knew they'd long passed that point. Evil had ruled their kingdom the day Marion had died in his arms.

"Sir William."

The knight in question stepped up, his dark eyes burning with hatred as they landed upon Shade's face. His posture remained defiant in the face of Shade's questioning.

"What say you to the charges levied against you?"

"I say you are no judge," he spat. "You do what you have to in war."

"There was no war," Shade said quietly. "Only a power flex. Our men went into the village with a mission. Find and eradicate any evidence of magic. Regardless of how we personally felt about it, that was all we were supposed to do."

"The woman was a magician," Sir William hissed, as if those simple words justified his behavior.

"And that was deserving of rape?" Shade tilted his head and studied the knight he'd personally trained. Dangerous words he spoke. Shade knew of Nova's power, witnessing it with his own eyes. The man was older than he was, but Shade had never liked the look of greed in his eyes. Sir William had never been the best swordsman, always being too content to let others fight his battles. Apparently, he didn't mind battling a young girl.

"What of it?" Sir William said. "It is a common thing."

Shade counted to five in his head. Inside, he screamed his anger. "It is the mark of a dishonorable man, one who does not belong in the service of Thornewood."

Sir William sneered, his eyes flashing.

Shade worked to keep his anger from showing. He longed to drive his sword through the knight's chest, but if he did, he'd be no better than those he interrogated. "Thieves are common. Murders are common," Shade said. "Those are crimes of anger and greed. Rape is a crime of the most perverse sort. You came up behind someone who you knew couldn't fight back, rendered her unconscious, and violated her, taking the one thing away from her that mattered in this godforsaken kingdom."

Every knight blinked and Shade cursed his stupidity. A cunning smile began to curve Sir William's lips.

Shade took one step back before he caught himself. He would not be afraid of a weak-spined rapist. "For your crimes against this kingdom, you are sentenced to die."

Sir William stepped back. "Or how about I report to the queen about her *godsforsaken* kingdom?"

"I'll not ask you again," Shade said quietly. He unsheathed his sword, the blade making a hissing noise against the scabbard.

The other knights stood frozen, but Shade would get to them soon enough. "Draw, Sir William."

Sir William spun on his heel and Shade began to know fear. Stabbing someone in the back was beneath him, but he could not let this man escape him and report his words to the queen or, heaven forbid, Desminda. But a thought stopped him, worming its way through his rage. This was not his vengeance. It was Nova's.

The other knights stepped up to block him. "For once do the honorable thing," one of the other men, a knight named Sir Brower said. "Draw your sword."

Sir William tried to step around him only to find another knight in front of him. Every knight had drawn their sword. Shade exhaled a breath of relief when Sir William turned back to him. His jaw clenched. "All this for a girl," he spat but drew his sword.

*All this for the girl*, Shade thought as their blades came together, sending a hum of noise through the air.

*The* girl.

# CHAPTER FIFTY-ONE

## THE QUEEN'S SECRET

Anxiety itched at the back of Desminda's neck. Her mother stood behind her scrutinizing every movement she made. She'd chosen the emerald gown Desminda now wore. It squeezed the life out of her as if she were being slowly strangled by Thornewood's best satin. Every breath dragged in with effort, but every breath she expelled felt like she was a bag wrinkled and squeezed too tightly.

The queen rarely graced Desminda's quarters these days. Instead, she chose to stay sequestered within her own rooms, leaving only when something required her authority or she had to meet with her people. Those days were fewer and fewer and Desminda thought it strange. After all, wasn't running a Queendom one of the busiest professions? She couldn't remember much about her father's rule and had been quite young when her mother had wrested power away, but she'd always wondered how one stayed king and queen when they'd almost killed each other during the coup.

These were adult problems, and she'd have to worry about them soon enough. But she didn't have to worry about them now.

"I need to show you something," her mother said.

Desminda's gaze met hers in the mirror. The queen held a small crown dotted with diamonds and emeralds. Desminda bent her knees to allow her mother to place it on top of her perfectly coiffed hair. Her mother's touch was brisk and impersonal. Tears pricked Desminda's eyes as an unbidden memory rose to the surface. Before all of this, before all the responsibility foisted on her, the queen used to sneak into her room and into Desminda's bed and chat with her about the world. They'd snuggle for a while, and when she remembered this, she always remembered how safe she'd felt. But those days were long gone. Her mother's once vibrant beauty faded as time had passed. From a spring rose to the fading blush of color come winter.

The queen always had skin of pale cream, much unlike Desminda's darker gold. But they had the same cheekbones and the same dark hair. She never saw her father much these days and the way he looked had slowly begun to fade from her memory. Now when she saw him, he no longer felt familiar to her, as if someone had snatched the man she once knew away and replaced him with a stranger.

The combs of the crown caught in her hair and latched securely. Her mother fussed with it for a second before she stepped back.

"Come," she said and held out her hand.

Desminda hesitated but clasped her mother's fingers in her own and allowed the queen to lead her out of the room.

An important dinner was scheduled for later and nerves bloomed in her stomach at the thought of it. A wedding date was to be announced soon.

Her wedding to Lucien. Her stomach lurched, and she swallowed the grimace threatening to form on her face.

When she was young, she knew one day she'd marry a handsome prince and they would rule the Kingdom of Thorns with grace and beauty. Now the thought made her want to throw up. There was no grace nor beauty in political machinations. There were only desperate grabs for power and pretty, silken words covering up the barbs of their underlying meaning.

Lucien was handsome, no doubt, but there was something in his eyes she didn't like. Almost like he knew something she didn't.

Her mother led her down the Great Hall and kept walking. Desminda said nothing, only followed, watching her mother's slim back clothed in the finest maroon velvet. Her mother had always looked like a queen, even before when she was just Desminda's mother. She moved with grace and spoke with conviction. But there was something empty inside of her now. As if the years had worn her down to a nub and she was trying desperately to hang on to what was left of her life.

Something felt like it was rotting within them. A poison seeping out into the queendom and Desminda couldn't find the antidote. She would be queen soon. She'd lead her people to prosperity, continue the trade agreements with other kingdoms, eventually have heirs. Desminda's hand crept over her stomach and rested there.

Children.

Some people were meant to be mothers. Desminda would much rather be a gardener. She preferred her fingers in the soil, her hands bloody with thorns. She wanted to pluck the harvest from the plants she grew with her own two hands. Thinking about children, being responsible for them, who they became, what they did or said...it made her a little ill.

Her mother disappeared around a corner Desminda rarely went down anymore.

"Mother?" she inquired.

The queen held a hand up. "Quiet, Desminda. Follow. Do not comment."

Desminda snapped her mouth shut and obeyed.

The first rule of being a princess.

*Obey.*

The air became cooler and more humid. Desminda shivered as she followed her mother. Her feet began to ache. The slippers she wore weren't meant for long distances.

Her mother turned down a long hallway, one Desminda had never been in. A large door loomed at the end. Her heartbeat picked up. What was going on and why was her mother being so secretive?

A thousand questions burned within her, but she kept silent and followed.

Her mother stopped at the door and lifted her hand to a small groove carved into the dark wood.

The door glowed a brilliant cerulean blue for a brief second, so quickly Desminda thought she'd imagined it.

A click sounded in the silence. Desminda gasped in a sharp breath. Her eyes widened, but her mother didn't acknowledge what had just happened.

Magic.

Was this magic?

Had her mother just used the forbidden art?

The queen pushed the door open and bade her to enter. She hesitated at the precipice, a sick feeling in her stomach. As if entering this room would change everything.

"Hurry," her mother whispered. "We do not have much time."

The door shut behind her, a loud clang in the silence. Desminda startled. A strangled whoosh of breath came from her throat. The air chilled her skin, no longer cool but frigid.

"Come."

Desminda followed.

. . .

THEY STOOD in a cavern of glowing blue and white. Power pulsed around them, igniting Desminda's heart and soul.

"What is this place?" she whispered.

Desminda stood beside her mother, staring into the cavern. The queen looked smaller here, as if the weight of this secret leeched the life from her bones.

"This," the queen said, her voice etched with grief. "Is magic."

Desminda's head snapped around. "What?"

The queen lifted a hand. "This," she said, sweeping her fingers around in an arc, "is magic," she said again, so calmly, like she hadn't unbalanced Desminda's entire life with those words.

"Mother," Desminda said with infinite patience. "What does that mean?"

"Magic is given to us from the world. Not all magic," she corrected. "There are kingdoms not too far from our borders that still possess it, though some are substantially weakened."

Desminda's breath caught at this revelation.

Her mother's lips thinned. "They try to hide it from us, but we have spies everywhere. But the majority of magic is amplified with this." Her mother reached down and picked up a piece of the white stone. She handed it to Desminda, who held it up to the light. It flashed with pink and blue in the glowing light.

"I've seen this before," Desminda breathed. "This is what we wear in our crowns and in some of our jewelry." But what did it have to do with magic?

"Yes," her mother agreed. "It's a flaunting of our power. And I am tired." Her mother sank to her knees and eventually sat on the ground, her skirts spread around her like a pool of blood around her.

"Mother," Desminda said as she sat beside her. "I don't understand."

"The mountains of Thornewood hold the Luna stones." She swallowed hard. "Fifteen years ago, our forces swept through the villages and confiscated all the stones we could. Enough that magic was suppressed in all of our territories." The queen squeezed her eyes shut. "Then we swept into other kingdoms, searching for other sources of magic. Stonehand cast spells on all the other sources of the stone, effectively neutralizing all the magic in our lands and that of our neighboring lands as well." She picked up another Luna stone and held it up to the light. "This small thing amplifies a mage's natural abilities. Without it, there is no magic. It used to be plentiful everywhere, but now most of it is hidden only in these mountains. The rest is bespelled. Inert. It's all held in stasis."

Desminda's thoughts spun, but she could only come up with one question. "I don't understand. Why would you do this?"

Her mother turned her dark eyes up to Desminda. "Because of power. I couldn't hold the queendom without power. And I have no magic. Your father controlled it all and used it to his advantage. I couldn't win."

"So let this magic go," Desminda said, her stomach cramping with the knowledge of what her mother had stolen.

"It isn't that easy." Her mother's shoulders bowed. "We can't break the spell on the mountain. Or anywhere else. Not without Stonehand."

Desminda loosed a breath. "And Stonehand is dead."

Her mother nodded. "Even if he were alive, I don't know that he could break the spell. He didn't do it alone. His witch bride helped before she died." She reached over to grip Desminda's fingers. "I am afraid, daughter. And I am weak. If anyone knew the truth, they would destroy our kingdom."

Desminda had kept a secret from her mother. One so big it had the potential to tear them apart. But her mother had kept an even bigger one from her. "You've torn people away from their essence," she accused. "People have died from their lack of magic." She stood, ripping her fingers away from the queen.

"I had to," her mother whispered. "The king was tearing this world apart in his quest for more power. He was planning to march troops into other kingdoms and take them over, using Stonehand to neutralize their mages." She swallowed hard. "Magnus was the most powerful man I'd ever seen. I don't know how his magic worked, but his power was bright. Like a night star. He could do things I'd never seen." The queen bowed her head. "But he was good. So I came to him one night and asked him if he would strip magic from the world. Just for a little while."

"And he agreed, even knowing what it would cost him."

"Treason," the queen nodded. "He was found out, eventually."

Desminda studied her mother. "How?"

A sob broke from her mother. "Me."

Desminda turned her back to her mother. "You had him killed."

She heard the rustle of her mother's skirts. "I had no choice. He–he started coming to my chambers, demanding to know when he could release the spell. I'd gotten what I wanted. But I couldn't let him do it. I couldn't fight mages, for I had none of my own. I couldn't fight the king with magic. And if I let it go, he would do the one thing that would destroy us all. We can't fight another war, Desminda."

"Our queendom is dying!" Desminda blurted. "Trade is drying up on all sides." Everything suddenly seemed so clear. She stood and paced the room, the stones' unearthly glow highlighting her mother's haunted features. A dark pulse glimmered behind some of them, vibrating with a beat that didn't match the others. She tore her gaze away from the strange power and faced the queen. "They know we hold the key to unlocking their magic." She loosed a shuddering breath. "We have to figure out how to break the spell. It must be given back to the people."

Her mother shook her head. "You will suffer the same fate, Desminda. If Lucien has access to his magic, he will throw our kingdom back into chaos. He wants this land and his own. I needed you to know. I can no longer keep this secret to myself. You will be queen soon." She reached over to take Desminda's hands. "Your father can never know."

Desminda pulled away. "My father is a doddering old man who drools when he eats soup," she snapped. "Why does it matter if he knows?"

"Because I am the reason he is trapped inside of his mind."

Desminda reeled back, shock thundering through her system. She stared at her mother, revulsion and horror building inside of her. "What did you do to him?" she whispered.

Even with these confessions, she knew her mother still held deadly secrets. There was something here she couldn't unravel. There was no time and Desminda's mind spun with the weight of the secrets told here tonight. Tomorrow. Tomorrow she could take this out and examine it, try to unravel the deadly web of lies her mother had spun for so many years.

When her mother started to speak, Desminda held up a hand. "No more. We must get back to the dinner preparations. I need time."

"There is no time, foolish girl. Danger surrounds us."

The leash on Desminda's temper snapped. "It surrounds us because you are a coward! You are the reason our queendom suffers. If you have to subjugate an entire people, you are too weak to hold the rule!"

Her mother's head whipped back in shock. "Desminda!"

"I am too young to remember Father's rule, but I remember magic. I remember the feel of it against my skin and I remember Father's laugh. I remember yours too. Neither of you have laughed for years. Thornewood looks powerful on the outside, but the inside is rotting.

"You may keep your secrets, Mother. I know this is not the entirety of them. But when I am queen, magic will return to this land, damned be the consequences."

Her mother's face went white. "You do not mean that. You assure your own destruction!"

Desminda picked up her skirts. "Perhaps. But perhaps I keep secrets of my own, Mother." Their eyes locked in a battle for dominance.

The queen dropped hers first. "You will bring our queendom into ruin."

Desminda turned toward the heavy wooden door. "No." She paused at the entrance, her fingers resting on the heart of magic and the darkness lying beneath it. "I will correct the ruin you and Father brought to us."

Her mother sighed and followed behind her. "Be careful what you unleash, child. Chaining the magic won't come so easy the next time."

# CHAPTER FIFTY-TWO

## THE KING'S QUIET

Desminda hadn't been in her father's chambers for months now. The last time she'd gone in, her head spun from the aromatic smokes the healers pumped in to ease his mind and relax his body.

The door clicked open, and she walked in, her fists clenching the edges of her skirt. Smoke filtered throughout the room once again. Desminda shut her eyes for a brief moment. How had it gone this far?

A young man sat by the window, the curtains pulled open just enough to let in a sliver of light.

"You," she snapped. "Put out the censer, open the windows and doors, and get this place aired out immediately."

The man scrambled to his feet. "Um, Your Majesty." He offered a sloppy bow, no doubt his head addled by the fragrant smoke he was surrounded by. Desminda couldn't remember the name of it, something from a flower only gathered out west in a kingdom she couldn't recall.

"The healer says we are to change the flower every half hour to keep the king at rest."

A muscle ticced in her face. "And is the healer in charge here?" The man blanched, his words stumbling over each other. "Erm, no, Your Majesty. Of course not."

Desminda stared and silence ticked away. The man jerked. "Sorry, sorry. Of course." He bowed again and spun to the window, jerking the massive purple curtains away from the windows. Light flared in, making Desminda squint at the brightness.

The man grabbed a chair, winced apologetically, and scrambled into it to make him tall enough to open the latches on the window. As soon as it opened, wind rushed in, blowing her hair back. She breathed deeply and exhaled.

"Good. Ensure all the windows are opened and extinguish the censer immediately."

The man's bow was better this time. "Of course, Your Majesty."

She gave him a shallow nod and opened the doors to her father's bedchambers. The king lay in bed, covered by opulent purple and maroon covers. His hands were clasped over his chest, and he lay still and silent.

"Father," Desminda asked quietly. "I'm here to talk."

The king did not respond. It was his way these days. A silent, befuddled look or a wistful, dopey smile. He'd fallen far below his once great status. People thought she did not hear the remarks made behind his back.

She could not fault them, for they were not wrong.

Desminda sat on the edge of the bed, staring down at the shell of a once powerful king. They looked nothing alike. At one time she'd questioned it, but her mother had laughed gaily and told her she looked just like the king's mother, a woman she'd never once seen. Like many things she'd been told over the years, she'd taken it at face value.

When she believed her mother and father would never lie to her.

What a fool she'd been. A gullible, plucked, and manicured fool.

And here she sat, still preened and coiffed, a bejeweled crown on her head and no power. Her queendom sat on the edge of ruin from actions not of her doing and her father lay in bed, addled and mindless.

The servant hurried in, extinguished the censers, and threw open the dark curtains. The click of the latch sounded in the quiet room and light blared in, highlighting the dust and smoke swirls in the air. She clenched her jaw tight at the state of disrepair the room had fallen into.

Her mother would pay for this.

Her father had been paying for years.

She nodded at the servant. With a shallow bow, he backed out of the room, clicking the doors shut behind him.

"Oh Father," Desminda said, her voice choking on grief. "What has happened to us?"

She rose and tidied the small table beside his bed. The censer spilled its ashes out as she lifted it. Her mouth tightened at the sight of it, but she knew better than to brush them away with her hands. There was a small stone cup full of something brown and sticky with a small spoon coated in the substance. She picked it up and sniffed, recoiling at the acrid scent. Whatever this was, she didn't think her father needed it.

Desminda took the censer and the stone cup and put them on the table by the door for removal. With that, she hung up her father's robe carelessly draped over a seat and straightened his slippers.

When she came back to sit by him, she realized she felt no better. There was no justice in what was happening here. Perhaps once the smoke cleared and whatever her father had been forced to ingest was purged from his body, then he would recover his wits. Some, if not all she hoped.

Desminda reached over, about to brush a stray lock of her father's hair away from his face.

The door clicked open just as her fingers touched his forehead.

"Do not scream," her mother cautioned her, the words quick and quiet.

*Cold.* Her father was cold to the touch.

Why was he cold? Desminda's brow furrowed. Her mother came closer, her finger over her lips urging her to quiet.

Desminda touched her father's cheek, fingertips pressing into the paper-thin skin. He didn't move or make a sound.

Her heart began to pound, her body figuring out before her mind what had happened.

What her mother had done.

She jerked her fingers back like they'd been burned. "What..." she choked out. "What did you do?" Her voice sounded of disuse, locked in her throat. *"What did you do?"* She couldn't scream. Her emotions tangled together, a jumbled ball of rage, confusion, and despair. The words came out in a screeching hiss.

"What I had to."

"Regicide," Desminda spat.

"*Security*," her mother emphasized. "Get yourself together. Dry your eyes. Straighten your spine. We will walk out of here like everything is fine. We will attend the dinner. You will smile and laugh and attend to your subjects. For tonight, we will lock your father's doors and tell the healers he wishes to rest. Tomorrow we will announce your ascension to the throne."

Desminda shook her head. "No. No no no no no no." Her words jumbled and stumbled over each other.

Her mother's hand took her arm in a grip of steel. "This is what it means to be queen."

Numb, she allowed her mother to steer her out of the room, stopping as the queen gathered up the spoon and cup of dark paste. The culprit, she thought with detachment.

If this was what it meant to be queen, perhaps she was not meant to rule.

# CHAPTER FIFTY-THREE

## A MIST BEFORE THE MOUNTAIN

S hade was missing something and that was unlike him. He had eyes and ears almost everywhere in this castle, most of them not hired by him. Servants loved gossip and the men under his command were no better with their idle chatter when they thought no one listened.

He'd passed Desminda in the hall earlier, her eyes wide and hollow. When he'd stopped her, she'd taken a deep breath and pushed past him, muttering something about getting ready for dinner. *Dinner was important. She mustn't be late.* It was so unlike her, he'd followed only to have her shut the door in his face.

Not too long after, the queen had approached him. Shade always had his guard up around the woman lest she pick something out of his mind he hadn't meant to share. The woman had a way about her— a curious and keen intellect that always set him on edge. On anyone else, he might admire it. On her he always wondered how she would use it against him or her people.

Ever since the night Harlow's magic had exploded, Shade felt like he was being watched. He'd never caught anyone in the act, but there was an itch under his skin. It felt the same way during the time Marion and Magnus were in the castle, so he did not discount it. He spoke even less than usual and carried out his duties to the best of his abilities. But with the Virago and especially Harlow, he'd ramped up their training with the intent of teaching them everything he possibly could.

Something dangerous lay on the horizon. He felt it in his bones.

Marion once told him he was like a market psychic minus the colorful scarves and missing teeth. He'd bristled about it at first but later realized she might be right. He had a knack for knowing when trouble was about to strike, though he usually had no idea where or how it would manifest.

Shade stopped abruptly at the sight of the queen and lowered himself in a bow. "Your Majesty."

"Rise, Shade," the queen said. "Tell me, how goes the Virago training?"

She'd never asked about the Viragos before. Not once. The queen had left it up to Desminda since the future queen was the one who created them and oversaw most things. What she didn't, she left to Shade. This included all of their battlefield training. Desminda had written the curriculum for their class-room training, but Shade knew they would need more than book smarts to be successful in the castle and surrounding lands.

"Very well."

The queen waited for him to elaborate and when he did not, she smiled at him. "Always such a careful man, Shade," she murmured.

"Once spoken, words cannot be taken back."

One of the queen's dark eyebrows rose. "So this means I won't find you in the kitchen gossiping with the maids?"

They both knew the answer to that. The only reason Shade

went to the kitchens was to see Nana Kay or snatch a fresh baked muffin right off her tray.

"Never," Shade said mildly. "I'm only there to steal muffins."

The queen held out her fingers. "Come. Walk with me."

Shade stiffened for a heartbeat, then held his arm out. The queen curled her fingertips around his arm and turned him the opposite direction. "Where shall we walk?" Shade said, his heartbeat whooshing through his ears as his blood roared through his head. The last time the queen had touched him was a few weeks before Marion died. Now her cool fingers brushing his tunic sent shivers of revulsion down his spine.

"Let's go to the gardens."

Shade nodded once and led the queen through the castle and out through the back. The queen loved her gardens, but Shade much preferred the wild, rambling mess of Desminda's. The flora in front of him was carefully shaped and pruned, and though it bloomed with the first flush of spring, there was no true life to it. Every rose chosen for its color. Every piece of foliage chosen for its shape to complement the one beside it.

Desminda's were a riot of color. Purples and oranges and whites and reds, foliage of the deepest green or brightest chartreuse. Whatever was in season, she would grow. The villagers and travelers visiting the castle had taken to bringing the young future queen seeds and cuttings, as if it were a competition to see what she would grow in spring and then fall. It would be their point of pride for years to come and Desminda had slowly figured that out and so she chose much more carefully now lest she hurt someone's feelings.

Where the queen's gardens were cultivated and cold, Desminda's were full of life and hope, tucked away from the queen's gardens so as not to clash with her aesthetic. At one time, Shade thought his queen might be more like Desminda than she'd admit. He'd seen it in her wardrobe choices, her words, and her chosen entertainment for weekend meals. But that had slowly withered away leaving the woman Shade now walked with.

Hungry for power and desperate to keep it, all that had made her shine had been slowly washed away— a woman once full of sharp angles and contradictions —like a jagged rock tossed into the river and made smooth by time and collision with other stones and debris. She'd become a puppet to her own machinations.

"The graduation is soon, is it not?" The queen stopped at a particularly lush pale pink rose and bent to smell the heady fragrance. Her neck was long and tan. A dark curl fell against it as she bent. So much like Desminda in some ways but night and day in personality.

"It is, Your Majesty. Only a few weeks now."

"You must be so proud." She fingered another rose, careful to keep her hands away from the thorns.

"Pride is a sin," Shade said automatically. The queen's religious puppets spouted the nonsense every two months during their services.

She chuckled as if she read his mind. "Perhaps it is." She glanced up at him, her dark eyes unreadable. "You know I do not agree with everything they say."

Shade felt like he was jumping from rock to rock over a pit of boiling lava. "Mmm."

"Come now," she said and steered him toward a long bench in the back of the garden. An archway had been built over it and two types of climbing roses— one pale purple and the other a pale peach —intertwined with each other. She sat down and straightened her skirts. Shade remained standing, keeping a watchful eye for threats.

The queen patted the seat beside her. "There are guards all

over. Please. Sit with me a moment. I know you do not have much time to spare, but please humor an old woman."

Shade's brow furrowed. The queen was anything but old. She'd been a young and prized bride for an already older king. Now the king doddered away his days drooling and spouting nonsense while the queen ruled. There was no silver in her hair yet, only a hint of age around the brackets of her mouth.

He sat beside her, far enough away for propriety, but close enough for him to hear her murmured words.

"Desminda will be queen soon."

Shade nodded.

"She will receive a queendom in chaos."

He blinked and turned to face her. "Excuse me?"

She waved a hand. "You know as well as I do there are factions on all sides lusting after our gems and resources."

"This is not uncommon in any queendom or kingdom, Your Majesty."

The queen looked away. "Yes, but we hold something precious to them."

Confusion burned within him. He knew of the emeralds and amethyst, diamonds and other gemstones Thornewood sold and exported to all the other lands. They were rich beyond their wildest dreams, but that wealth had not made it all the way to their people. The fault of the woman sitting next to him and her king.

"I'm not sure I understand," Shade said, his voice careful.

"Our mountains." The queen looked behind her where the mountains loomed, their snowcapped peaks jutting high into the sky. "This is our most precious resource, and we must guard it at all costs."

"Other lands have gemstones they can mine, Your Majesty. I'm not so sure they would invade our lands just to possess them."

"They would," she said, her voice sharp. "You must protect them with your life."

Shade already knew this. The Kingdom of Crystal also possessed countless gems, but Thornewood was special in that they were the kingdom where this particular stone grew plentiful.

Thornewood gemstones were their most prized commodity and had kept them fed for generations now. There was some difficulty growing food for they did not have the land mass other kingdoms did. Their queendom backed up to the mountain, so they had to grow food within the villages and other spaces of land. The vast majority of wheat and other products were imported, most to the castle and some to the markets.

They could cut down some of the forests behind the castle that came before the mountains, but there were rumors about it. Tales of terrible beasts and curses to those who tried to make it their own. Shade often wondered if they were true because they remained untouched. Portions of the mountain backed up to the castle and allowed their people to go in and mine, but the vast majority of it required a journey through the forest to reach.

Anyone who attempted it had not returned.

Except of course for Harlow and the bard. Astrid, he remembered. Curious that.

There were some small paths made on the outskirts, but venturing too far in was a fool's errand, even one Shade wouldn't make unless he had to. His memories of the forest were not of beasts or curses, but of his best friend's wife holding a newborn babe and dying in his arms, and he avoided it mostly to squash those memories down.

"Desminda is aware of how important the mountain resources are," Shade reminded her.

The queen's fists clenched, turning her knuckles white.

"Perhaps she will bring you into her fold and trust you with the secrets of those mountains soon."

Shade's eyebrows went up.

"But today is not that day." The queen rose, gathering her skirts around her and Shade rose behind her. "Come. There is a dinner tonight and I must ensure I am not late."

Shade allowed the queen to take his elbow as he walked her back to the castle and escorted her to her chambers. He couldn't shake the feeling he'd missed something important, some clue the queen had dropped that he couldn't grasp. He knew the mountains were important. Everyone who lived here knew it, but her words made it seem like there was something more to them.

Something even he didn't know.

ON THE WAY back to his rooms, a swirl of emerald skirts and dark hair flashed into his view.

"Shade!" Desminda hurried toward him. She didn't look as pale, though there was still a darkness in her eyes. "I would like you to invite Harlow to the dinner tonight."

Shade blinked. "No." Why would he do that? Harlow wasn't ready for a dinner like that, and he wasn't sure she ever would be. To keep guard, yes, certainly, but to act as a guest, it was probably beyond her. She was too much of a mix between her mother and her father and tended to blurt out exactly what was on her mind. That would be terrible for any event where royalty or nobility ventured.

"No?" Desminda asked, her eyes widening before they narrowed on him. "You do realize to whom you speak?"

Shade stifled his frustrated sigh. "It is my sworn duty to keep you safe and deny requests I believe are foolhardy."

The future queen spluttered. "Foolhardy?"

"Are you a parrot, Your Majesty?"

Desminda shook her head, unable to stop her smile. "You will bring her to this dinner, Shade. This is a request from the Queen Select to her Head Guard."

Shade stilled. "You truly ask this of me?"

She nodded. "I do."

He blew out a breath then sketched a shallow bow. "Then I shall endeavor to do as my queen demands." His stomach hollowed out. What machinations were playing out behind his back that he didn't know?

When he rose, Desminda still stood there, her golden eyes full of pain. He tilted his head. "Is everything well?"

She blinked but couldn't stop the grimace that fluttered onto her face before she squashed it almost as soon as it began. "Of course. Why wouldn't it be?"

Desminda nodded, picked up her skirts, and brushed past him, hurrying somewhere new.

Shade stood there for a moment, his thoughts spinning before he shook his head and walked toward his room to get ready. Harlow would attend the dinner, but he would attend with her. It was the way of things and even though he'd rather open a vein than sit at one of those gatherings, he would do it for both of them.

# CHAPTER FIFTY-FOUR

## DRESS CODE AND MANNERS

Harlow stood and caught a glimpse of herself in the reflective surface of the mirror. Her boots shone; her posture was ramrod straight, and there wasn't a hair out of place, thanks to Bloom's quick fingers. For once, the outside of her looked polished, well put together. Like a real Virago.

She wrinkled her nose at her reflection and pushed a single loose strand of hair out of her eyes. tucking it back into the complex braid. Her complexion was paler than its usual peaches and cream, the freckles dusting the top of her nose darker than normal, and her eyes took on an icy blue hue, lighter than the normal cornflower blue they usually were. The blue gray beginnings of a faint bruise from Bloom's fist curled around her left eye— a result of their most recent training practice. Nova always said she had eyes like the sky, though she always looked sad when she said it, her eyes always lost in her memories. Tonight, while Harlow's eyes might be like the sky, they also held a distinct glint of impending doom.

Harlow tried to smile, but it wobbled and fell off her face. She squeezed her eyes shut for a brief moment and took a deep breath, held it for four seconds, then released it, a slow exhale for several more seconds. It was an exercise Nova had shown her years ago and it worked for most things, but then again, Harlow never thought she'd be about to sit for dinner with the queen. Was there a breathing exercise for that?

She squared her shoulders and tried to shift her thoughts into remembering how to handle all the dinnerware she'd no doubt have in front of her when she sat at the dining table. Harlow flicked off a piece of imaginary dust. Physically, she was ready. Mentally was another story.

Shade stepped into the Virago's sleeping area thirty minutes before they were to arrive. He stopped in front of her cot, and she snapped to a standing position, wincing as her boot caught on the side of one of the cot legs. A mark. She'd have a mark smearing the newly mirrored shine there. One of Shade's eyebrows rose as his gaze traveled down to her boot.

"Correct it,: he said quietly. "We do not appear before the queen unkempt."

Harlow hurriedly reached under the cot, pulling out the key she wore around her neck and unlocked the small wooden box that held everything she owed. She pulled out the soft rag she used to get the shine. None of the other girls had one which is why she kept the box locked. Harlow had seen some of their eyes glancing her way, coveting the way her boots looked over theirs. They'd ended up bartering once they realized they couldn't get to it without damaging the box or getting caught. Folded shirts and neatly made-up beds for Harlow and high-shine boots for them, though Harlow never parted with her rag. Nova had given it to her for polishing the silver and Harlow realized it could be used for a lot of different things. She'd sat for hours polishing everyone's boots before inspection and Shade had noticed, giving her a side-eyed glance over it, but he hadn't said a word, only offering a grunt of acknowledgment before he found some other fault.

She quickly buffed the mark out of the boot, took a quick second to marvel at the way it looked, and put the cloth back into her box, making sure she'd re-locked it. At Shade's nod, Harlow allowed herself to relax just a hair.

"Follow me." He turned and headed out the door.

Harlow scrambled after him, careful to keep herself one step behind and slightly to the right of him, the position of the subordinate. All the future Virago knew it well. One inch further than they should be, and she'd find herself with a sore toe the next day once Shade's walking stick found it.

Shade said nothing to her most of the way. Her brain spun with the implications of the dinner. Would she be punished? Was this a reward? Was this Shade's way of scaring the bravery right out of her? It would be like him to test her. The entire Virago training felt like one massive test she was doomed to fail. Harlow ran through the order of silverware through her head and wondered again for the hundredth time why so many pieces of silverware existed when you could just have three. A knife. A fork. A spoon. *Cut, spear, scoop.* Seemed easy enough to her. Then you didn't have to worry about the tiny fork for the tiny foods, the big fork for the main course, the small spoon for the dessert, or the oblong shaped spoon for the soup. Though she did like the oblong spoon better than the other one. You could eat faster and get more nutrition in before Shade barked you were taking too long.

"Fischer!"

Shade's bark jerked her out of her spoon musings. She stopped and took two steps back, horrified that she'd gotten ahead of him. Harlow ventured a look his way. Anger seemed to seep from his pores, but he didn't look at her.

"You should have nothing in that hollow brain of yours other than surviving this dinner. I do not know why you're here, but rest assured, this is a test, and not one by me. Survive tonight.

Smile when you're supposed to. Use the right damned utensil. Make polite conversation and for the god's sake don't be strange. Express nothing political. Express no opinion. Agree with the nobility. It's what they prefer anyhow. Do this and we both might walk out of here unscathed. Do you understand?"

Her dry throat clicked as she tried to speak. Harlow cleared her throat softly. "I do." The words sounded hoarse.

"Then pay attention. Get behind me and stay there until you're told otherwise. We will both be introduced. Follow my lead." He took a deep breath. "Do not make me regret approving this, Fischer."

Harlow was afraid she'd do exactly that, but she bobbed a nod. "I'll do my best."

"Your best is not good enough," he said, each word a quiet hiss in the night. "Every choice you make tonight has the potential to affect the rest of your life. Your potentially *short* life if you screw this up."

If she hadn't felt the pressure before, which she certainly had, she felt it now sitting over her shoulder like the hangman's axe.

If this was to be her last night as a Virago, she at least hoped she'd make Shade proud.

# CHAPTER FIFTY-FIVE

## THE QUESTION OF THE SOUP SPOON

"Shade Montello, Commander of the current Kingsguard with one of the upcoming Virago, Harlow Fischer." The man announcing the entrants stood at the bottom of the staircase, a long scroll and feathered quill in his hands. He stood ramrod straight, his clothing perfectly pressed, hair oiled to a sheen.

*Stonehand*, she thought. What if they had said who she really was? Would the room have gone quiet, the name an avalanche crumbling stone down around their heads? Stonehand, destroyer of kingdoms, salvation of Thornewood. After she'd returned from the infirmary all those months ago, the other girls had continued telling her stories of her father. Stories their parents had told to them.

The king forced her father's hand into service and used him like a hammer and the king the anvil. He had signed his own death warrant when he fell in love with a mysterious tutor from the fabled Witch Kingdom. They tried to hide her existence for as long as they could, but even with baggy dresses and shawls, they couldn't hide her forever. When she'd been born, the world had shuddered and shortly after, magic had disappeared from most of the world. That was the short of it though Harlow longed to know more, to know if the man she saw in her soul was her father and if he truly lived.

Even though her father had prevented threats to Thornewood's sovereignty for years, his magic was still only spoken about in hushed tones. She'd never met the man, though as she grew up in the village below Thornewood, she'd heard the occasional story of his magical prowess told in hushed whispers. This was before she knew who he really was and what he was to her.

Looking back, she should have realized something was off. Some people would look at her and away, their mouths snapping shut at the sight of her. Had they known all along? Was she the village secret, the one they kept close to the kingdom in order to throw those who searched for her off her trail? Whoever had placed her in the first village must have known they were taking a huge chance, though she was far from the only girl to grow up with golden hair and blue eyes there.

Harlow did not react outwardly at the sound of her name, the false one, though she felt the judgment of the hundreds of eyes around her like a spear to the heart. She stared at the back of Shade's broad shoulders and waited for him to make a move.

When he moved, a breath escaped her, and her heart beat like prey as she followed. That's what she was. They all knew it. *Prey.* A little rabbit serving herself up for dinner in a den of wolves. At least for now. She possessed no golden wings. Her leathers might shine, but they were worn. Cast offs, just like the girls they'd pulled from all the villages around the kingdom. Or, like Harlow, those who'd come to prostrate themselves to anyone who would pull them off the streets and give them the chance to earn their keep. When she'd first come to the castle, they'd rejected her. The second time, she'd earned a place as a maid by lying about who she was. The third time, a man in black offered her the chance to change her life if she wanted to. She still didn't understand why, but none of it mattered right now.

Now she was on full display. Her boots made silent footfalls, one step after another as she followed her commander, her eyes never leaving the midnight ink of his leathers. His shoulders were tenser than usual, and she didn't see him take a single breath. Perhaps his breathing was as shallow as hers was, barely enough to keep her upright. A cold sweat formed at the top of her forehead, tiny beads of moisture she hoped no one would notice and she'd be able to discreetly wipe away when she sat down.

The man who'd announced their names stared at Harlow, his eyes like a brand against her skin. As if he knew who she really was. *Stonehand.* A magical legacy she still didn't understand. Every night she went inside herself and examined the deep pool of power within her, careful to never awaken it from its slumber. The roof above her still showed the scars of her power. If anyone figured out who she was, she would suffer for the sins of her father, for the magic that once coursed through his veins.

Two chairs awaited them toward the head of the table. Right next to Desminda.

*Oh gods,* Harlow thought as they grew closer. She prayed fervently Shade would take the seat next to the future queen and leave Harlow to sit by the greedy-eyed young man on the other side. Lucien. His flame-colored hair shone in the low light of the candelabra hanging above them. He sat too close to Desminda, his thigh touching hers and his arm too close to her own. Even she could see it was a scandalous lapse in propriety and from the way Desminda tilted slightly to the left toward the empty seat, the future queen knew it too.

Harlow could handle someone like him. She'd dealt with

people like that enough when Nova had left and both her foster parents had died in the sickness that swept through Thornehollow like wildfire. It made the Virago training a hair easier when Shade found out Harlow had a way with a blade, but an even better hand with the ax. Even a man with wandering eyes and roving hands thought twice when Harlow twirled her ax to warn them away.

Shade did not cooperate with her mental pleas. He took one step to the side and pulled out the chair next to Desminda. Internally, Harlow couldn't stop screaming. This could not be happening. Her movements were almost robotic as she nodded once to Shade, whose dark eyes held caution and a warning, then took the seat next to her future queen.

Shade sat next to her without a word, beside a woman in a scarlet dress barely covering her generous bosoms. *Jasmine and roses.* The thought came to her unbidden. Desminda smelled like her gardens. Harlow's gaze scraped over the future queen quickly and as soon as she looked, she wished she hadn't. Desminda wore a gown of emerald green and a small diadem encrusted with diamonds and emeralds. Around her neck was a massive white stone that flashed blue. It looked familiar, as if she'd seen it before, possibly on the queen. Their eyes locked and Harlow caught a hint of mischief in them, though there were hollows under her eyes where there had been none before.

"Your Majesty," Harlow said.

"Hello, Harlow *Fischer*." The emphasis on her last name made Harlow still, a cold bead of sweat trickling between her breasts. She was overthinking, imagining something there when it was not.

The princess snapped her napkin and laid it neatly across her lap, much to the horror of the man standing behind her who saw what she was doing and rushed to do it for her. Too late. He stood there like a simpleton, his eyes filled with fear.

"Back you go," Desminda told him quietly. "You can help me remember what utensil I use when the salad comes out." A quick smile highlighted the dimples in her cheeks as she shooed him away. "Don't let Mother see you."

The man blinked and abruptly stepped back into his place. Several men and women lined the walls, one for each person. It seemed like a waste of help. Everyone had the ability to put their napkin in their lap or pour their own drink. Harlow stared at the massive bounty in front of her and wondered how many people in Thornehollow would go hungry tonight while everyone here gorged on roast pig and apples as big as her palm.

*Stop thinking like that*, she admonished herself. A Virago *couldn't* think like that. A Virago always placed Thornewood and its rulers above all else. The queen and nobility would worry about the poor and downtrodden. It always stuck in her throat, whenever she remembered the vow she'd soon make. Would there be so many poor people in the village if the queen truly cared about them?

Harlow stifled the heresy running wild in her brain. Things were always less complicated on the surface than they really were. Perhaps Thornewood already had a plan to care for the people living in squalor in the village. But the events of fourteen years ago flashed through her mind. Fire. Pain. Screams. Smoke. The shaking arms of the girl who'd scooped her up and ran through the woods and fed her for days until they'd settled in another village farther away, one not being punished for whatever it was they'd been punished for. The memories were hazy, but they still lingered. She didn't know what happened to Nova then, but as she got older, she realized the sacrifice the girl had made for her.

Her sister. Maybe not by blood, but by oath. To them, an oath was thicker than blood. Or it used to be. It certainly was in her case. But Nova had left her and with the absence came a gaping hole in Harlow's heart she feared she'd never be able to fill.

A pale, thin hand setting a salad in front of her jerked her out of her maudlin reverie. Harlow blinked and straightened her posture. She looked up only to see Shanda standing before her. The girl's eyes widened slightly and her hand shook, but she didn't betray that they knew each other. When the plate sat in front of her and her silverware was laid perfectly out, Harlow reached back and tugged on Shanda's fingers once in silent recognition. Shanda squeezed back and disappeared, flitting from table to table like a moth and preparing them for the first course.

Shade sat like a pole next to her, hard and straight, his eyes averted from the woman in scarlet hellbent on giving him the attention he did not want. Harlow risked a longer glimpse at him. The commander stared down at the salad, a slight snarl to his lips, as if the very existence of berries offended him. Perhaps it did. Or perhaps it was the woman shamelessly flirting with him right under the nose of her clueless noble husband.

She'd never seen Shade scarf down a single green thing when he deigned to eat with them, which was rare, instead choosing a variety of meat and sometimes potatoes. Harlow would bet coin that if Shade had the choice between meat and potatoes or meat and meat, he'd go with the double hunted, the bloodier the better. An image of him standing atop an elk, covered in blood and gore, ripping out the heart and claiming it for his own appeared in her mind. Her lips began to curl in a smile, but she stifled it.

Shade would have her beaten if she showed any emotions other than what she was expected to display tonight. She thought about that a little more. He always threatened to have them beaten, but not a single girl had been carried away to the whipper. The threat was more than enough to keep the girls in line. Shade picked up the tiny fork and speared a berry so hard the utensil scraped across the plate.

She blinked and looked away, her eyes focused on her own salad. Shade had more leeway than she did. He was here as a respected commander and Harlow was here as a lackey. Or something. He could afford a stray berry or two.

She picked up the tiny fork and stared down at her plate. By now, the conversation had picked up loud enough to excuse any graceless scraping. Harlow felt the future queen's gaze on her.

"Is the fare not to your liking?"

"The fare is perfect, Your Majesty."

"Then are you nervous about the fork?"

*Don't smile, Harlow.* "The fork is perfect, too." She wanted to slap herself.

"Is it now?" she said quietly. "I'm sure the compliment would boost its self-esteem if it were sentient."

Harlow pressed her lips together. "The berries," she said quietly, sensing when Shade jerked his head to look at her. "Where do they come from?" Harlow looked up at the future queen.

She tilted her head, her strange golden eyes merry. "They come from my garden. They're called thorn berries. An appropriate name, I'd say, considering they do a wonderful job of tearing up the gardener's arms." The queen select grinned at her. "Even though I enjoy growing these, I'm not allowed to pick them." She held out her bare arms and studied them. "Apparently, these arms are too *queenly* to be scratched." Desminda lifted a slim shoulder in a shrug. "Pity. When I was a child, I'd sneak out and pluck hundreds of these right off the bushes outside of the castle grounds. Mother always knew because my mouth would be bright purple when I returned home."

Melancholy stole over her expression before she quickly erased it. "But they are my favorite."

"I've never had one," Harlow admitted.

"Then eat and be merry, Harlow. I'll forgive your purple mouth if you'll forgive mine. Mother did not want to serve these, but there are advantages to being the future queen." A dimple peeked out from one of her cheeks. "And really, can anyone take the nobility seriously when it looks like they've snuck into the candy jar?"

Harlow snorted quietly. At the sound, Shade stiffened beside her.

"Oh relax, Shade. She's here as my guest." Desminda rolled her eyes at her as if they shared in some big secret. "He gets very wound up about customs and courtesies."

Shade cleared his throat. "Your Majesty, we've already talked about this."

She waved a hand at him. "Yes, yes." She lowered her voice in a surprisingly good imitation of Shade's gruff tone. "*You must not rile up the Virago, Your Grace, for one day they will save your life.*"

"They will," he said through gritted teeth.

"Yes, I'm sure they will, but as my personal guard, they will also be required to converse with me about inane topics." She speared a berry on her tiny fork. "Like berries." Point made, the queen select popped the berry in her mouth and wiggled her eyebrows at Harlow.

She looked away and over at Shade who still stared at Desminda. Some kind of unspoken conversation went on between them, and Harlow ducked her head to focus on her salad. She'd pushed it a little too far already. The future queen wouldn't have to pay for her lapse in judgment. Harlow would. She could already feel her aching arms and legs from Shade's early morning punishment.

Harlow speared the berry and put it into her mouth,

surprised at the tart burst of flavor, followed by a hint of sweetness. The queen select watched as she chewed.

Color stole over her face. Desminda inhaled a breath. "Your skin is like cream. Every embarrassment must feel like fire against your skin." She paused and then added quietly, "You have no reason to be embarrassed in front of me. I like seeing people enjoy the fruit of my labors." She frowned. "Well, *most* of my labors."

Harlow swallowed and speared another berry. "These are wonderful." She meant it, too. This wasn't just lip service to the queen. Harlow felt sure she had nobles and subjects tripping all over themselves to earn a word of her favor, so the least she could do is show her honesty.

"Wonderful!" She clapped her hands together like a child. "Perhaps one day I will show you my gardens. Maybe we can find a way to sneak away from the ever-watchful eyes of Shade Montello and get into the berries." A dimple peeked as she smiled.

The cheek of her! Harlow fought to keep from laughing. "I would like that, Your Majesty."

"Then it is decided. When is the graduation ceremony, Shade?"

Shade sighed and Harlow had to squelch the urge to laugh out loud. What in the world was happening right now? She'd never seen the man get so riled up.

"One week hence," he bit out. "Fischer still has some training before she will be allowed to visit your gardens, Your Grace."

The queen select made a *hmph* noise. "Well soon the gardens will be an absolute riot of spring color, so it will be the perfect time to show them off!"

*If* she made it through training. The way this night was

going, Harlow wasn't sure she'd even make it back to her cot in one piece.

"If she is selected as one of the Virago, I'll see what I can do to arrange it," Shade added, making it clear that if they both didn't cool it, the only garden Harlow would see was the one above her dead body.

Next to Desminda, Lucien shifted in his seat and peered over Desminda's shoulder. His eyes widened as he realized who sat beside his future bride but narrowed a moment later. "Hello, I don't believe we've met."

Little liar. Though she understood why he pretended. Them knowing each other would raise more questions than either of them would want to answer. Harlow nodded politely for fear Shade would pinch her for her impertinence. "Greetings, Your Grace. I'm Harlow."

Shade cleared his throat. She barely suppressed her sigh. "Harlow Fischer, Virago-in-training." Desminda ducked her head but couldn't keep the grin from flitting across her lips.

The man's eyes widened. "Well, then Harlow Fischer, Virago-in-training, I am Lucien Talbot, Prince to the Kingdom of Roses."

She had to remember Lucien was not her friend nor someone she should ever be impertinent with. He held power in his own kingdom, but here too. Their last meetings came to mind, and she had to take a deep breath in so she wouldn't panic. "Pleasure," she croaked.

He wasn't finished. "Betrothed to Queen-select Desminda."

Harlow's mouth went dry even as he relayed the information she already knew. Hearing it out loud wasn't as easy as hearing it whispered around her. *Betrothed.* She schooled her expression into blankness, but the glint in Lucien's eyes told her he'd caught her reaction and was amused by it.

"Then I must congratulate you on the blessed occasion of your upcoming marriage."

Desminda's eyes hadn't left her lap.

"Thank you, Harlow. The joining of our lands and our people will ensure peace for generations to come."

The words were just words. But the way he said them raised the hair on Harlow's arms. She risked a glance at Desminda, but the princess sat frozen like a doll. She looked down only to see the queen select's knuckles bunched white against the napkin she held like a lifeline.

"I'm sure it will," Harlow murmured.

"Isn't that right, Desminda?" Lucien asked, his heavy gaze trained on the future queen.

Desminda looked up. A tight smile graced her face, but the mischief had fallen from her eyes. "Of course, Prince Lucien. The one true God has blessed our union and the joining of our lands."

Shade stiffened beside Harlow, his posture rigid like the edge of a knife. Something deeper went on here, something she wasn't privy to. Harlow studied Desminda's face, worry for the future queen curling in her belly.

"Are you here with an entourage?" Harlow asked Lucien. "I don't recall seeing you arrive, though perhaps I was in the throes of training." She jammed a finger at Shade. "His favorite thing is to assign floor taps."

Lucien laughed like she expected him to and Desminda let out a slow breath, almost unnoticeable except to Harlow. Shade relaxed as well, his grunt signaling approval for her words.

"There is no greater calling than the protection of the sovereignty," Lucien said smoothly.

Everything in her gut screamed danger. She demurred but noticed he didn't answer her question about his entourage. Interesting.

"When Desminda and I are married, we hope to institute changes for the greater good of the kingdom."

Harlow's easy smile slipped. "Kingdom?" She played a dangerous game here. Desminda stiffened and over the tinkling of forks and spoons and soft laughter, Harlow heard Shade's sharp intake of breath.

Lucien laughed, a carefree sound, but his eyes glinted with anger. "Ah, do forgive me. I hail from a kingdom, and it was not so long ago when Thornewood was one, too. *Queendom*, my dear. My mistake."

He clasped Desminda's fingers in his own. Harlow's quick glance revealed slim, pale fingers clasped in Desminda's darker, scratched ones. Lucien had the hands of a courtier, someone who'd never worked a day in his life. Perhaps that's what all future king's hands looked like, but she much preferred the dirty, scarred, and stained hands of Desminda.

Harlow gritted her teeth over some unnamed emotion. Jealousy implied Harlow was emotionally invested. She was intelligent enough to realize she came from nothing, a small, orphaned girl with no family to speak of, stained by a legacy of deadly magic, and Desminda came from a pure royal line, bred for good genes, and strong leadership.

She had nothing to give to Desminda, and Desminda would give nothing to her.

So what was this hot feeling of rage coursing inside of her?

# CHAPTER FIFTY-SIX

## THE INEVITABLE EVOLUTION OF LOVE

The night ended with the queen select wishing her good night and good luck on her training, and ensuring she remembered her promise of showing her the gardens. With a long look Harlow didn't quite understand, the future queen took her leave, but not before she reached over and squeezed her fingers under the table. Harlow could feel the lines and rough callouses of those fingers and knew tonight would forever be etched in her memory. A folded slip of paper fell from one of the queen's pockets as she walked away and Harlow snatched it up, ready to call to her and bring it over, but Lucien had a vise-like grip on Desminda's arm as he steered her away. Anger reddened her face. Her fingers crumpled the paper and she shoved it in her pocket. She'd give it to Shade later for a safe return.

Harlow watched Shade's broad back as he walked ahead, her thoughts brewing like a maelstrom. Lucien was trouble. She felt it deep within her bones. He didn't love Desminda. Not like – Harlow's footsteps slowed. The back of her neck broke into a cold, clammy sweat.

"I hate him," Harlow confessed in a whisper a second later,

shoving down those traitorous feelings deep, deep inside herself. He'd never outright done anything to her, had even helped her once upon a time, but jealousy and feelings of inadequacy roared through her, releasing the words before she could take them back and zip them up into that deep, dark pocket of her heart.

Shade's steps hitched until he slowed. "Prince Lucien?" His face stayed carefully blank. He'd been at the dinner. He heard their exchange. Shade knew exactly what she was talking about.

"Of course, *Prince* Lucien. Did you see how he treated her?" Harlow threw her hands up, not caring how she looked. All she felt was her anger and her helplessness to do anything about it. "His *condescension*. He's a danger to her and to all of us." Harlow shoved down her confusing feelings about Desminda. Yes, Lucien was a pig and yes, her feelings for Desminda might be clouding her judgment. But there was something about Lucien she couldn't put her finger on. Not yet.

Shade's head jerked to her, his dark eyes black in the low light, flickering orange as the wind gently blew the lantern flames around. "This is not up to you or me. Matches like this are made decades in advance."

He said nothing she hadn't expected him to, but still Harlow stared up at him, his face lit in shadows and angles from the flickering firelight in the stone buildings on either side of them. Shade rarely revealed how he felt about anything, but she heard something in what he didn't say this time. His emotions felt too calm, too controlled. "You dislike him too," she said with wonder.

Shade did not reply, only gave her one unreadable glance before picking up his pace.

His footfalls on the way back were heavy, much unlike his normal noiseless pace. Anger beat off him, thick and heavy, and Harlow didn't know if it was directed at her or the princess, or both of them. Probably due to her confession. She wasn't brave enough to ask the question. Instead, she did her best to match his speedy pace. It was only when they were far enough away from the castle and prying eyes and ears that Shade spun to her, taking her upper arms in his hands.

"What is it you're trying to prove?" he demanded, shaking Harlow so hard her teeth rattled.

"Noth - nothing!" She'd seen Shade angry many times, but it was anger at their failure or lack of effort and not necessarily at who they were. This felt different. His anger was like an inferno with Harlow trapped inside the burning building. She'd known she treaded in dangerous waters. Questioning the prince or the future queen could get her Virago status stripped or a quick trip to the gallows at worst.

"This isn't a game, damn you." He shoved her away from him and took a step back. His chest heaved as he stared at her, wild eyed. "I've worked too hard to let something happen to the both of you." His eyes widened at his confession. Shade scrubbed a hand over his face and took a deep breath. When he spoke again, his voice was calm. Even. "Angering Lucien endangers not only Desminda but all of us. Did you have to poke him tonight like that?" He exhaled. "Your pointed barbs are sharper than your rapiers."

Harlow stood there, one foot poised to run but frozen in place at his show of emotion. He cared about Desminda. More than he wanted to let on. She suspected so when she realized Desminda was teasing him at the dinner, but this seemed like maybe he'd been something more to her, a father figure perhaps. Or a brother. Harlow didn't know, but this response from him told her a great deal about whether Shade was capable of feeling.

"I don't know why she did this or what she wants from you, Harlow. But I'm warning you. Stay away from Lucien. He is a wolf in sheep's clothing." Shade turned away, his head bowed. He stuffed his hands in his pockets and walked away from her, this time at such a fast clip the only way she'd catch up to him was at a jog.

He'd never called her Harlow before. Nor had he ever laid hands on her in anger, only in training, even if it was a brutal tap with the flat of his sword blade.

She didn't know how to feel. Confusion swirled through her at this new side of him she'd never seen. Shade wasn't inhuman, nor was he uncaring.

He cared too much.

# CHAPTER FIFTY-SEVEN

## DEATH IS FOR THE LIVING

The walk back to the Virago's quarters felt like walking in sand. During a storm. Weighed down with weapons and heavy steel. She allowed her thoughts to wander back to her childhood. Thinking about Shade and his reaction over Desminda felt like too much to bear right now.

She'd seen the beach once on a trip with Nova, when her sister was officially considered old enough to watch out for her. Never mind their wild trek through the woods on their way to safety. Nova had pickpocketed some coins from some towns-people inside the square of Thornewood and swore to Mother she'd sold some of her embroidery work to fund the trip. Mother and she both knew her needlework was atrocious, but she didn't say anything, only giving Nova a long, measured look. You could take the girl out of the wild, but Mother was never able to take the wild out of the girl.

They'd hitched a ride with a traveling theatre troupe sched-uled to leave town the next day. There were constant wagons traveling in and out of Thornewood, and the beach wasn't more than a few hours away. Looking back on it, Harlow wondered why Mother let them go. Maybe she knew Nova would do it anyway and this way she at least got to control some of it.

Harlow remembered the feel of the sand between her bare toes and the roar of the waves as they beat against the shore. She'd tilted her face up to the sun, letting the warmth of it beat against her skin and swore one day she'd have enough money to buy a small home close so she could visit it whenever she wanted to.

Nova chased her down the beach, their squeals of laughter burned into her memory like a brand. A few curious stares came their way from families, but no one bothered them. With the rest of her ill-gotten coins, Nova bought them a cold treat full of sugared berries. Harlow couldn't remember the name of it now, only the taste of it.

The phantom taste of those berries burst in her mouth, sweet and tangy all at once. Harlow closed her eyes at the memory, her heart wrenching with grief. Their mouths and teeth dyed a deep scarlet red, they'd glanced at each other and burst into giggles, collapsing on the soft, pillowy grass, as the suns blanketed them in warmth, both happy and content. Tall trees cast dappled shade on their skin, and Nova rolled over on her side facing Harlow.

Her happy expression fell into something more like a warning. Harlow, still young but smarter than most children her age, stared into Nova's strange silver eyes. *Like starlight*, she'd always thought, but Nova would laugh and brush her words away.

"Harlow, do you know about your father?" Nova toyed with a piece of long grass, a tuft of yellow grain atop it.

Harlow, who barely remembered the man she'd lived with, shook her head. "He made me a wooden rabbit once. The house we lived in smelled like woodsmoke and chamomile." Harlow flopped back onto her back. "Mama's fingers were always yellow. She pressed the chamomile to make something for sleep."

Nova nodded. "Her sleep draughts were the best. But she wasn't your mother, and he wasn't your father."

Harlow frowned. "He was," she insisted.

Nova shook her head. "No. You came from Thornewood. From a woman fleeing the iron grip on magic."

Harlow's heart had skipped a beat. "My mother had magic?"

Nova shook her head. "No one knows, Harlow. But she loved a man who did. He possessed fearsome magic. Magic that made kingdoms tremble."

Harlow turned on her side again. "A mage? Magic is bad." She'd heard it from many, many people over the years. Magic destroyed people, lands, lives. The refrain echoed in her brain over the years.

Nova shook her head. "No, Harlow. Magic isn't inherently bad."

Harlow frowned at her sister. "Yes, it is."

Nova sighed. "Do you think an axe is bad?"

Unsure of where her sister was going with this and annoyed by Nova's tricky way with words, she sighed. "No," she said after a moment, her voice grumpy.

Nova laughed, a raspy, low sound. Harlow loved the sound of it because it didn't happen often. Nova had never laughed much, not even when they settled in with a new family and had their bellies filled each night.

"Do you think a sword or a club or a hammer is bad?"

Harlow's lips thinned. "Is this one of your stories?"

Nova's eyes twinkled. "It is the wielder of those things, sister. A hammer wielded by a blacksmith produces important things for us— cups and pots and tools. A hammer wielded by a madman produces death and destruction. A sword wielded by a protector of the realm saves us when someone threatens our kingdom. But if it's wielded by a bandit, we might lose our lives or our possessions. An axe wielded by our foster father brings us wood to keep our home warm and food from the forest beyond."

"And an axe wielded by someone who means us harm is the same as if it's wielded by a bandit?"

Nova smiled, her eyes crinkling at the edges. "Exactly. Magic isn't bad. It's people that make it one way or the other."

"Then why do people say it's bad?" Harlow asked. She wove her hands through the soft grass and wished she could stay there with Nova forever, the wind twisting their hair in soft circles and cooling their bare feet.

"People are afraid of what they don't understand. Thornewood once held a powerful mage, but he was good and just. He had a little girl, you know. The rumor was he loved her enough to let her go." Nova tilted Harlow's chin to look at her. Those strange eyes met Harlow's own, and she sucked in her breath at her sister's beauty.

Where Harlow was light, Nova was dark. Hair the color of a deep winter night fell down Nova's shoulders. Her lips were always the color of a bruised pomegranate, but her eyes were the color of starlight on a deep, moonless night. Harlow wasn't too young to notice the greedy eyes of the townsmen and how they stared at Nova when they thought she wasn't looking.

Harlow gripped her sister's hands tight. "Promise not to leave me, Nova. Never, ever."

Nova brushed a kiss across Harlow's forehead. "Never, ever, little sprite. We'll speak about Stonehand some other time." She picked herself up, brushing the seat of her skirt off, and held her hand out for Harlow. "Come on then. Mother is probably beside herself with worry."

Harlow exhaled a breath as she came back to herself, the almost forgotten memories fading away into the cool night air like they'd never existed. Her breath was a puff of steam in the cool night air. She and Shade stood in front of the Virago quarters, both of them staring up at the old wooden sign burned with the words, "*Honore in vitas. Gloriate in morte.*"

*Honor in life. Glory in death.*

Harlow agreed with the first, but not the second. Death wasn't glorious. It was finality. Silence. A final whisper on the wind that carried your soul to the ferryman.

Death was for the living.

She looked at Shade. "Thank you for your escort."

Shade stared at her, his dark eyes unreadable. "Forget your anger toward Lucien. Nothing good will come out of it. And forget Desminda, Fischer. She is above both of us."

Harlow blinked and took a step back.

Shade shook his head. "Do not deny it. I see the way you look at her. It is forbidden and foolhardy. Heed my words. Forget this foolish notion and step fully into your training. People like us only brush against royalty using our sword hands, not our hearts."

With that, Shade turned on one heel and left Harlow standing in the cool night air, her cheeks crimson with heat.

She watched him walk away and wondered how he could know something like that.

# CHAPTER FIFTY-EIGHT

## TEA WITH THE FUTURE QUEEN

S hade stood outside the Virago's quarters far longer than he should, his thoughts raging. He'd made a mistake by not further distancing himself from the Virago, but an even bigger one for allowing Harlow to squirm under his defenses. The promise he'd made to her father so long ago burned in his heart.

He'd royally screwed this up. He'd meant to train her to the best of his ability, hone her into a weapon so that she'd never suffer the same fate of her father, and if she manifested the same kind of power he did, well, her father had also told him what to do then.

For all of their sakes.

The dinner tonight was a disaster. She'd been on her best behavior— for Harlow, that is, but she still couldn't help her curiosity. If she were in a different position, perhaps that curiosity would be a boon. As a Virago, it could help her if the queen or Desminda's life was in danger, but the queen didn't take lightly to someone asking impertinent questions.

Even about something as small as berries.

Shade raked a hand through his hair and tilted his face up to stare at the bright moon. He should have turned down the invitation to train the new Virago and forsaken his promise to Stone-hand. His friend had died soon after he'd made Shade reinforce his promise to look after her, and at the funeral attended by only him and a young Desminda, he couldn't help but wonder why they had forced such a vow from him.

A bitter smile crossed his lips. He only questioned it until he'd met the grown-up version of Harlow. Now he knew exactly why her parents had forced his hand. Harlow was a handful even on an off day. But he saw hints of her father inside of her, especially when her eyes flashed with anger at something Shade said, but also moments of deep kindness and foresight just like her mother.

He had to put distance between Harlow and Desminda before it was too late, even if it meant forcing Desminda's hand to ensure she met her royal duties and continued the Thornewilde rule. She was his one hope to turn this kingdom into something to be proud of- a chance to make amends for past wrongs. No matter his personal feelings, she would wed Prince Lucien. The queen had decreed it so. His thoughts skimmed over Desminda's mother, quickly shoving them in a dark, locked box inside of his angry, vengeful heart.

No matter how much he cared about Desminda and Harlow he couldn't let his personal feelings get in the way of the safety and security of the queendom. Distance was the only way he could ensure Harlow became a true Virago and fulfill his promise to her father.

Without getting them both executed.

Shade spun on his heel and made his way back to Desminda. This had to be settled tonight before it went any further.

. . .

HE MADE his way through the secret passages of the castle, carefully inspecting the dust on the steps to make sure he was still the only person who used them. He'd discovered the passages quite by accident many years ago, something that resulted in his friendship with Stonehand when he stumbled into the mage's room after a few too many sips of the king's mead.

When he arrived at the off grey wall, he used his walking stick to tap twice, pause, then tap three more times. Shade wrapped his furs tighter around him. The passages stayed chilly no matter what the weather was like outside.

Moments later, the wall opened and Desminda peered at him, one dark eyebrow raised in amusement.

"Are you here to chastise me then, Shade?" She rolled her eyes. "Come on in before you freeze. I have a fire ready to go."

Shade stepped inside of Desminda's room, well aware of the impropriety this presented. He didn't often visit her, but when he did it was usually due to something he couldn't tell her anywhere else.

She poured him a cup of a light tan liquid and added a spoonful of molasses and a dash of cinnamon. A dimple peeked from her cheek as she handed it to him. "You truly do take your tea like a giggling schoolgirl, Shade."

He snorted as he accepted and took a sip. "And you are awfully cheeky tonight, *Princess* Desminda."

She scoffed. "You know I hate that word so."

Shade gave her a malicious grin over his teacup.

Desminda chuckled. "Fine. I deserved it. Why are you here? Lucien? Harlow? My ever-present failure to become a proper queen?"

Shade sat at the small table Desminda had set up in her sitting room. The scarred wooden chairs had been there since she'd been a child and the queen had often tried to replace them with something nicer, but Desminda continued to refuse the offer.

He used to visit her much more often.

The fire warmed his back. He sighed and set his mug down, the clunky bright cup at odds with his large hands. "You must not let Lucien cow you."

"He is a tyrant," Desminda hissed.

"Perhaps. And what is the best way to deal with a tyrant?"

Desminda's eyes glittered. "With a well-placed knife between his ribs and straight into his black heart?"

Shade tried not to react but failed. "No." The word didn't fall as sharply as he hoped because he was grinning like a demented loon. Pride filled him at his princesses' ferocity.

Desminda sighed and flopped onto her bed. "I've no desire to be tied to a man from the Kingdom of Roses."

Shade laughed out loud. "Admit it. You've no desire to be tied to *any* man."

She poked her head up and narrowed her eyes at him. "What does that mean?"

Shade toyed with the rim of his mug. She was still his princess and so he chose his words carefully. Most of the time. Sometimes she was still the brat who'd tormented the castle with practical jokes and stubbornness. A vision of Desminda with torn skirts, thorn-scratched arms, and brambles in her hair racing through the kitchens snatching up one of the cook's precious muffins almost made him smile, but he squashed it down. His fondness of her would not serve them well tonight if he didn't put a stop to this nonsense before it even began.

"Perhaps there is a woman you desire?"

Silence fell between them like an anvil.

"You speak of Harlow." Desminda's nostrils flared.

Shade tilted his head and stayed silent.

She sighed and flopped her head back down. "She's interesting." Her voice sounded sullen.

"She is," Shade agreed. "And very much off limits."

Her nostrils flared even as her eyes narrowed at his words. "I do not like being told what to do, Shade."

To avoid responding with something unhelpful, Shade picked his mug back up and took a sip. He merely waited for her to come to her own conclusions, one that would match what he thought.

She poked her head up again and rested on her elbows. "You believe I should leave her alone."

"You will break her heart, Desminda. She is a young girl, alone in the world. She trains for one purpose only, to protect the sovereignty of Thornewood. Do not allow her hope. It is the killer of us all, but especially someone who only wishes to be loved. Allow her to reach her potential and find some other poor bastard to love. Not you. Such a thing cannot be. You know this."

Desminda blinked at him. "And how do you know so much about her?"

Shade stayed silent. Desminda's brow furrowed as she thought about it. "Ah. Mage Stonehand." She shook her head. "I'd forgotten for a moment. She looks nothing like him, you know."

"I'm aware." Shade was aware of a lot of things concerning Harlow that he wouldn't divulge to Desminda.

"And if I refuse?"

Shade slowly set his teacup down and rose from his seat. "You will destroy her. Do not act like a child in this matter. She is the best of us. I do not know what the future holds for her. But you are not in it."

Desminda's cheeks reddened at the slight. "I would never harm her!" she said, her voice a sharp crack in the night.

"There are worse things than the bite of a sword, Princess. If she is true to the Stonehand magic, what will you do? Conscript her into service and force her into the slavery her father endured?"

Desminda blinked. "Of course not!"

"Magic is outlawed here. Harlow would not be able to stay. Would you kill her then?"

"Shade!" Her voice sounded thick with tears. "Why are you pummeling me tonight?"

"Because you must know that Harlow stands on a precipice. One you should not influence her over."

"We can see if her magic runs true." Desminda's words fell like stone from her lips. At the widening of his eyes, she realized what she said.

Shade slowly shook his head. "Toss her in the river tied to stone?" He scoffed, disgust at her burning through him. Sometimes Desminda showed flashes of greatness and sometimes, she was this— a petulant child. "You'd betray all of our secrets for a crush now? Because you're bored?"

She scrambled off the bed and reached for Shade. "Please. Never! I'm sorry!"

Shade gave her a long look and stepped into the passage before her fingers could grasp the leather of his doublet. "Heed my words, Desminda. It's a dangerous game you play. If you destroy Harlow because you grow tired of your life here, you are not fit to be queen."

Desminda gasped as if Shade had slapped her.

Shade turned before she could see the grief on his own face, not slowing down until he heard the click of the stone wall behind him.

# CHAPTER FIFTY-NINE

## THE FINAL MARCH

Harlow marched across the courtyard, the cadence in her head repetitive and comforting. *One, two, three, four. One, two, three, four.* The future Virago stepped in cohesion, their steps falling as one, sending a boom of noise throughout the area. Today was the day. Their final march to the parade grounds to take part in the ceremony where they would earn their golden wings and finally a sword worth carrying.

They were once fifty strong, whittled down to thirteen after the unfortunate incident in the dormitory. No one had heard or seen a single one of the missing girls since that day several months ago. At first, there were patrols set up all over the castle grounds to search for them. Some went into the woods for days at a time to search. Others had searched homes and huts, much to the annoyance and anger of the village citizens.

All the girls could tell how much it bothered Shade that they'd never been found, but eventually he'd let up and thrown himself into their training. Since there were only thirteen of them now, Shade had more time to focus and train them and he'd done so with the precision of a blade. With their small numbers, Shade had personally trained all of them, leading to a strong, cohesive force. And when he could no longer find real fault in anything they did anymore, he begrudgingly scheduled their graduation in one week's time.

The crowd stepped to the side as they passed, their faces alight with pleasure as they watched the marching women.

A beam of pride shot through Harlow at their expressions. She wasn't supposed to look, but even after her secret had been exposed and she had so much more to lose, she'd never been the most disciplined Virago. There was too much rebellion in her heart and now that she knew who she really was, it was hard not to plow full speed ahead to restore what had been stolen. But it never overcame her true goal— that of finding her sister and asking her why. Why she'd left, why she'd abandoned Harlow, leaving her to this life she didn't know she wanted.

As their boots boomed on the stones in unison, she locked eyes with a familiar young man possessed of bright green eyes and a quick grin that told her two things: he'd *definitely* been under the skirt of a girl charmed by the twinkle in his gaze, and he wasn't the kind of boy to take no for an answer. She'd last seen him a week ago, gloating about his upcoming marriage to Desminda. Harlow thought they might once be friends, but she found out later after what happened in the dormitory, when her magic exploded into existence and threw her life into chaos, his people had claimed the kingdom's security lacking and they'd ushered him away, only for him to return in time to announce the wedding date.

Whispers of breaking the betrothal had trickled out but were quickly squashed. And if some people caught whispering about the state of Desminda's love life disappeared ... well, that was just the way things worked when you gossiped about the future queen.

Lucien's scarlet hair shimmered in the sunlight. Harlow always thought the devil got into boys with hair like that. How else could you explain the way it glowed like fire? *Never trust anyone with a too-quick smile and a pretty face*, her sister had once told her. She'd told her a lot of things she only remembered later. And now, after almost a year spent with Shade, learning the art of the sword, though she still preferred her axe, and the ways of politics, Harlow's ability to trust anyone other than the other Virago had plummeted. A pang of despair hit her in the chest every time she thought about Nova, so she squashed the memory down before the familiar anger took hold of her.

Nova would be somewhere around twenty-four now if she remembered right. An adult— probably married and the mother of a few kids of her own now. Did she remember the girl she'd left behind, the promise she'd one day find her again?

She did what Nova asked and now here she was, accepted into the Virago as the final girl, close to fulfilling something she hadn't been sure she wanted when it first happened. Lucky number thirteen now. Harlow resisted rolling her eyes at the sarcastic thought. Some said thirteen guards signaled ill winds blowing for the future of the kingdom, but Harlow thought it was all malarkey. Giving voice to the thought would be scandalous, though. No one questioned the supposed will of the one true god, not even a non-believer like Harlow, not if they valued their tongue and their life. She valued both and had learned over these months to hold her tongue. Silence was a valuable commodity most people had no idea how to leverage, but Shade had taught them that guards were similar to the servants prowling like ants in the castle, privy to much because no one paid attention to them. So they learned to be still and listen and keep their mouths shut in the process.

*One, two, three, four. One, two, three, four.*

They marched through the gates of the castle, Shade at the front, only a few feet ahead of her. He'd arranged them by height, shortest to tallest and Harlow had always been a slight thing. Shade stood well over six-foot, clad head to toe in his favorite shade of ebony. It matched his hair and the color of his mood most days. She'd rarely seen the man crack a smile and when she had, it meant they were running at least two extra miles that day or something worse.

She'd learned to do everything she could to avoid that smile. To avoid his gaze, especially after last week. She was still trying to wrap her head around his words and his actions. He saw too much and said too little, a man that carried secrets like a shroud around his shoulders, locked away deep within him. How else would someone like him both survive and thrive in a Queendom like Thornewood? But he knew her secret, and he'd never said a single word about it. Harlow had agonized for months over what happened in the dorm that night so long ago, when Shade had scooped her up in his arms and ran her to the infirmary.

But he'd never broken her trust. He never inferred there was anything different about her, never asked the girls anything else even when he knew they'd all lied to him. It was as if he was *proud* of them over it. The man was a puzzle within a puzzle and none of them had ever come close to solving it.

Her breath caught as the castle came into full view. No matter how many times she'd seen it, the sight of it never failed to stun her. White stone turrets loomed on either side, almost blinding when the suns lined up perfectly to reflect their light against it. Hundreds of stained-glass windows glittered in the lights, flashing an array of colors— blood reds, royal blues, emerald greens, yellow the color of citrines, and flashes of fuchsia and amethyst. The Queen enjoyed the finer things and had never spared a dime when it came to painting the interior of the palace with all the colors of the rainbow.

On her first visit inside, Harlow's head spun with the vast kaleidoscope of color, and she thought it garish. Now, after multiple visits, she realized the Queen had an eye. All the colors somehow complemented each other— the cream-colored curtains embroidered with amethyst purple stars in the main hall, copper finishings, and hunter green walls. Everything had a place, and everything had a color.

A second sense made Harlow turn her head slightly as they marched toward the castle. To the right of her stood some of the gardens. They took up the entirety of the castle grounds, but there was one area wilder than most she found herself curious about. Where everywhere else felt cultured and trimmed to cooperate, the vines wrapping neatly around wooden trellises and the cut flowers growing in neat rows and mounds, this area held a scent of dark jasmine and the deeper scent of greenery. Vines scrambled over the ground and mixed with other climbing plants, spiraling up and over a white trellis that had seen better days. Red, white, orange, and purple blooms burst in a riot color and others hung heavy with unopened buds. Deep purple roses tangled with bushes full of violet and white blooms she'd never seen before. Fat bees dipped and buzzed in and out of the blooms, their hind legs plump with pollen. Butterflies of multiple colors rested on flat rocks, drinking from tiny holes carved into the stone. Puddlers, she'd once overheard someone say, their voices stark with judgment at the nocturnal activities of the princess. As if caring about butterflies was an offense like treason or something.

These were Desminda's gardens, a wild riot of color much like the girl herself. Harlow had never seen them this close. Nighttime was normally when they'd visit to learn the ins and outs of the castle, the secret hidey holes and areas where treachery could lie. She passed by the gardens often enough but had never gained the chance to study them. Today was no different, but the suns hanging high above them illuminated the jewel-like colors of the grounds around them giving her the chance to get a closer look at everything.

The cadence count in Harlow's head almost stuttered and died as a flash of white and buckskin came into view. Her left foot hitched and she quickly did a hop-skip step to right her march, otherwise it would screw the entire formation up. She shuddered as the image of the entire formation tumbling like dominos due to her misstep flashed through her head. A quick glance to her left showed the other Virago marching in perfect rhythm, their faces straight ahead and not a wisp of anyone's hair out of place. She whipped her head back to the front as soon as a whisper of a frown appeared on Bloom's face, the too-tall, strange girl with the terribly neat braids who marched next to her.

"Do *not* get us into trouble," Bloom hissed through her teeth.

"I had an itch." A disbelieving snort came from the other girl, but she said nothing else. Even so, she waited a moment before turning back to the vision in buckskin.

Harlow hadn't seen her since the dinner. They'd shared a ... moment once in the infirmary, if you could call it that. She'd run the memory of that night over and over in her head, her heart galloping in her chest at the sight of Desminda's fingers wringing out the cloth and running it over her forehead while she plied Harlow for information on whether she'd used magic that night. In her head, Harlow had suspected it was a trick to get her to confess, but in her heart, she could still feel her soft breath against her skin and see Desminda's heart fluttering against the side of her throat as she leaned ever closer to her.

Now Desminda was bent over a mound of flowers, a fat dark braid swinging over her shoulder as she tended to a hip high bush heavy with blooms. She held a pair of wickedly sharp clippers, her eyes focused on an area of the bush with little to no growth. She wore pants today, stealing Harlow's breath at the sight of her shapely thighs and the golden-brown skin of her forearms as she worked to nurture the plants inside her tiny slice of the gardens.

This was ... scandalous, even for Desminda. And dangerous to boot. And yet ... Harlow couldn't tear her eyes away from the future queen even though she knew she should alert Shade. There was no way the Queen knew about this. Desminda had no armor, no escort, no weapon other than the clippers. Whispers flew through the village that she was a witch, but those rumors too were squashed as quickly as they popped up.

The glorious look of happiness on her face gave Harlow pause and empathy stole her breath. Desminda was unguarded, both physically and emotionally, in danger, but also in her element. Something tugged at Harlow, a sense of loneliness and wanting to belong, to have something she cared about as much as Desminda cared about her gardens.

Harlow cared about the Virago. She cared about her future. But never once had she felt as unguarded and free as Desminda looked right now. She had too many secrets and too much pain inside to ever be free.

The princesses' hands paused in her action and her head jerked up as the marching formation passed her by. She'd be hidden by most of the flora around her. Harlow only saw her because she couldn't help but look around during her march. Everyone else followed the rules because they were too afraid of Shade's consequences if they were caught. If Harlow had even a hair more of a sense of self-preservation, she would do the same.

Desminda froze like a startled deer and locked gazes with Harlow. Time stretched like sweet taffy between them and when Desminda realized Harlow wouldn't give her away, a wide mischievous grin curved the future queen's generous lips, and she lifted a dirty tanned finger to her lips.

*Sshhh.*

Harlow's heart lurched and she felt the right side of her lip tug into a rueful smile.

Two rule breakers.

Worlds apart and yet so close together.

She held the future queen's gaze for a few more seconds before offering a short nod and turning to face the front.

# CHAPTER SIXTY

## A NEW DAY

The second sun glittered like a jewel above Harlow. Uncomfortable warmth sent sweat trickling down her neck and the back of her flexible leather armor. She stood at attention, shoulder to shoulder with twelve of the queen's newest elite guard, all of them trembling with anticipation. All the new graduates held the same excitement in their hearts as she did. She saw it in their bright and shiny eyes and the way everyone stood fully upright, their shoulders back and proud, and the small smiles barely curling the edges of their lips. Although Shade had tried to train the good humor out of them, even he'd all but admitted defeat after several months. All of them were just too proud to be here not to smile about it.

After a full year of training— of blood, sweat, and tears, getting up before the cock crowed, missing meals, gaining bruises, and separation from family— the day had finally arrived.

The Virago's swearing in.

Harlow bit the inside of her cheek to keep from smiling. She'd dreamt of this day since she'd been selected into the elite guard and not always because she enjoyed it. Mostly because she wanted it to end. Her job would be to one day defend her queen from threats both foreign and on their own soil, but the job still pushing at her soul was finding her sister. Perhaps with her newfound freedom, she'd have time to track her down. Harlow had not dared believe she'd make it to this day or that she would fall quite so hard for the future queen. A crush is what she tried to convince herself it was. A passing fancy, a foolhardy fantasy.

She'd seen Desminda several times since that dinner and locked eyes with her on more than one occasion, resulting in numerous bruises when either her training partner or instructor noticed her inattention and delivered a bruising smack with a training sword. Harlow quickly learned not to look upon the queen select when she came to view the training yards lest she end up permanently maimed.

From beneath her lashes, Harlow watched the shiny tipped boots of the Kingsguard pass by, their steps locked in a monotone march. Moments later, a pair of royal purple slippers and the trailing of an embroidered golden gown passed. The heady scent of jasmine and roses tickled her nose, and she inhaled as deeply as she could without giving herself away.

To many people, the scent would be cloying. To Harlow, it represented the princess and her love of the gardens growing all around the palace. The flash of a disheveled and sweaty Desminda working under the high sun as she clipped pale peach roses back would never leave her memory, she was sure of it.

The thought of those buckskin britches Desminda wore made color appear high on Harlow's cheeks, and she struggled to turn her thoughts away from the queen's shapely thighs.

Her thoughts, as they always were when it came to the young queen, turned scandalous in a hurry. She knew if she had any hope of being assigned to her, she would have to get her hopeless crush firmly under control. Not that there was much hope left. She had heeded Shade's warning to her the night they stood outside the quarters. She would serve as Desminda's protector. Nothing more.

If Harlow received the assignment she wanted, she could visit the gardens more often than she currently did. But even better than that, she would see the queen select on a daily basis. It was a dangerous game she played, but Harlow would graduate Virago training at the top of her class with Bloom a close second. Regardless of how she felt about the queen, she was the one most qualified to protect her.

"Virago," the queen select's voice said. "Lift your eyes and gaze upon me."

As one, the incoming Virago lifted their eyes and looked upon their future queen. She stood on a dais a few feet away, her skin bronzed by both genetics and time working the gardens. Her eyes were an odd gold no one could quite explain. Neither of her parents touted this eye color, and no one in recent memory did either. For that reason, Desminda, the young queen, was considered God-touched by her people. Harlow, always the skeptic, thought perhaps someone in her family had skipped outside of the marital lines, but she dared not address this theory to anyone but her own mind lest she be branded a traitor. No one questioned the lineage of Thornewood's Royal Family and kept their head upon their shoulders. The queen stood on her right, but Lucien stood next to her, still in the same finery she'd seen in her march. His gaze roamed through the Virago, catching Harlow's eye. He winked at her then looked away, leaving her with an unsettled feeling in her stomach.

Dark curls tumbled down Desminda's shoulders in glossy ringlets, her skin perfect and unmarred. The princess wore no enhancements on her face, but she didn't need them. Her eyelashes were long and dark, making her golden irises almost glow in the daylight. It was a vast contrast to her outfit from mere hours before and Harlow swallowed hard as she realized she much preferred the buckskin to the gowns.

"Today is the culmination of all your hard work," the queen select continued. "I've watched you over the last twelve months. Some did not make it." She paused then, her words taking root. Pride swelled inside of Harlow as she thought about the brutality of the last year. She understood it. Somewhat. None of them could be weak if they were to stand as the queen's elite. The thirty-seven lost would always stay in the back of her mind, wondering where they'd gone and if they were all okay.

But if they'd left because of Harlow, they did not possess the bravery the future queen would need in her guards. Desminda was the stitch holding the kingdom of Thornewood together. Her warriors were the only thing standing between her and any potential enemies who wanted to overthrow the female domi-nated society.

And there were many.

She couldn't imagine what it must be like to wake up each day and be ruled by the whims of a male. In Thornewood, men and women remained equal, though women held a slight edge due to their sovereign rulers, and Harlow had grown up knowing only this way. She had rarely traveled outside of her own village, but now, as a Virago, things would change. The queen would attend numerous outings, meetings, and peace-keeping conclaves and if Harlow was selected as her guard, she would travel with her, each trip one step closer to her sister.

"Today marks the day of your initiation into my service— into the service of Thornewood." The queen select smiled— a surprisingly impish expression on her sun-touched skin. An expression so familiar to Harlow, her heart lurched in longing.

"I congratulate you on your success and welcome you as the first line of defense for our kingdom." Her expression sobered.

"As you may know, foreign enemies trespass on our soil and test our boundaries each and every day. We hold our territory between four male dominated kingdoms who want nothing more to subjugate us and possess our exports for their own use."

At once, the Virago nodded. They knew from their assigned classwork. The Stones of Luna. The lesson had been slipped in toward the end of their term. Even the unflappable Shade had looked bothered by the disruption of his normal lesson plans, and there were times when he'd falter in his teachings, his mouth pressed thin.

A few of the other girls tried to ask deeper questions about them, but Shade refused to expand. Harlow knew what they were thanks to Astrid's lessons, but Shade never once brought up magic when he taught those lessons, instead keeping it to their monetary value and importance to Thornewilde's economy.

More precious than any other gemstone, they lay protected inside the Thornewood Mountains. No one, not even the Virago, knew how they were mined, but they were Thornewood's currency. And they were coveted by the other kingdoms. Especially the Kingdom of Roses. None of the Viragos had even seen one of the stones, they were so closely guarded. All they knew was the mountain held their gemstones, the kingdom's most precious treasures and stones and that they were the ones who would protect it. After them would come future Virago to bolster their numbers and the Kingsguard would act in their stead if something were to happen to them.

Harlow's stomach curdled as she thought of Desminda's betrothed, Lucien Talbot, heir to the Rose Throne. Marriage loomed on the horizon between them. Lucien had forsworn his throne— a first in his kingdom. His sister, Celestine, would sit the throne in his stead.

All for the good of the people, Harlow kept hearing. She

thought it was only good for Lucien. He would still be the crown prince of his kingdom but king of this one. What did the Kingdom of Roses have that Thornewood did not?

Flowers? Harlow stifled her snort. Thornewood was far more powerful than Lucien's kingdom, she suspected.

Desminda continued. "We bow to no one, Virago. Certainly not to kingdoms who treat others like they are unequal. Never to men." She pierced them all with her strange golden gaze even as Harlow noticed Lucien stiffening next to her. "We rise like Valkyries and when tested will rain hell down upon them like nothing they've ever seen." She bowed her head to them.

Just as Desminda lifted her gaze, a scream tore through the crowd.

# CHAPTER SIXTY-ONE

### BETRAYAL, VIRAGO BE THY NAME

Ten women huddled in the forests just outside the graduation ceremony, standing next to a slim, pale woman who never took off her hood. They could only see the cruel curve of her blood red lips and the smile she wore as she watched the future queen congratulate her new Virago.

The other woman, also one of the thirteen but not for long, had slipped away. Difficult to do under the eyes of Shade Montello, but she'd muttered her excuses to Bloom, claiming a nervous stomach, and stepped from the back of the line, hurrying away.

Soon enough, they would know her for what she was. A traitor. A thief. A liar. She closed her eyes, the taste of bile tickling the back of her throat. She didn't know this woman's plan, but she wanted to save her friends. They were no longer the hollow-eyed girls they'd been. Their eyes were clear and set with steely determination. All of their hands hovered on the slim silver blades the woman had given them. Blades with an odd crest on the hilt - a raised tangle of flowers and ivy. She'd seen it somewhere before but couldn't place it.

Her breath came in rasps now. She wanted out.

There was no way out.

"It's time," the woman said.

The hood slipped from her hair, revealing long scarlet waves and bright green eyes.

The Viragos gasped.

They knew who she was.

And soon, the entire kingdom would know, too.

# CHAPTER SIXTY-TWO

### A SCARLET REVEAL

As one, the Virago drew their swords. Harlow's gaze swung left and right, searching for the source of the scream. A flash of blood-red from the corner of her eye made her turn her head toward the forest. Helena stood beside her looking the other way, her feet planted firmly, and her sword gripped in her small hands.

The color was gone, but she continued staring into the forest. A moment later, she saw the red cloak of Astrid and the girl's face peering out from the forest. She was mouthing something.

Harlow narrowed her eyes, leaning forward to figure out what it was.

Astrid's hands were frantic, and she kept repeating the same word over and over.

Run. *Run!*

Harlow stiffened. Her skin grew clammy. A silent pall hung over the crowd as everyone tried to figure out if the scream was a jest or if something had gone terribly wrong.

Another scream rang out in the quiet. Then another. And another. The sound of boots and swords being pulled from their scabbards surrounded them. She glanced up at Desminda, but Shade was already there, his hand around her elbow, the queen next to him, helping them both down the stairs. He shoved Desminda at Lucien, then turned back. A flash of long scarlet hair caught her eye. A smile curved Celestine's red lips as she gazed down at them. Their gazes caught and locked before the woman turned away to hurry after her brother.

Harlow *moved*. She pulled her practice sword from its sheath cursing Shade for not giving them better gear and ran beside him.

"Shade. It's Celestine!"

His long-legged stride made it almost impossible for Harlow to keep up with him.

"Celestine?" he barked. His sword was drawn as he headed toward the fray.

"Lucien's sister. It's her!"

A snarled curse rang from his throat, and he stopped, torn between which way to go. Toward the combatants or toward his queen.

"I'll go to her," Harlow said.

Shade's jaw clenched. A second later, he unhooked a lethal blade from his belt and handed it to her. A blade much unlike the one she held. Harlow dropped the practice sword and accepted the blade he gave her. "Do whatever you have to do to ensure Desminda's safety."

Harlow nodded and spun on her heels in the direction Lucien had taken the future queen.

Time slowed to a crawl as Harlow shoved her way through the screaming crowd. She kept her eye out for scarlet hair, her breath coming in gasps. Adrenaline pumped through her system, giving her strength but also sheer frustration at everyone who wouldn't give her a clear path.

"MOVE!" Harlow boomed. She held her blade up in the air and scrunched her face into an expression of steely authority. A few people looked at her in surprise and stepped away and soon, the entire crowd parted like water, allowing Harlow through. She lowered her blade to her side and any unfortunate soul who stepped in her path received an impersonal shove out of the way.

Scarlet hair disappeared around a corner. They were trying to get back into the castle. Harlow cursed under her breath and skidded to a stop, her brain working to figure out if she could head them off. She spun and headed the other direction. The servant's entrance should allow her to get ahead. Harlow ran like her life depended on it, which it very well could. All thought other than aiding Desminda had fallen out of her head like water.

She burst through the doors, the wood banging against the walls with a loud crack. A few girls screamed, but one stared at her open-mouthed. "Harlow?"

"No time to talk! Get to safety. All of you!" she yelled. Shanda hurried after her.

"What is it?"

Harlow spared her a glance. "Traitors in the kingdom," she breathed. "They have the queen and her daughter."

Shanda's face turned white. Her footsteps slowed, but Harlow could not afford to stop. "Hide or leave, Shanda. Just keep yourself safe," she called as she pounded down the hall.

"Be careful!" her friend called back.

What she was doing was the very opposite of careful, but if she failed at this task, everything she'd done up until now had been for naught. Before she turned the corner, she slowed and stopped, tiptoeing now to peer around the corner they should be coming in. Her heart pounded wildly and sweat tickled the back of her leathers.

Voices came through, faint at first, but as they came closer, Harlow could make them out.

"I don't understand why you're doing this."

Desminda.

"You're responsible for what's happened to our kingdom. We don't know how, but we *know*."

Celestine.

"If you let us go now, we can forget this ever happened. You will go back to your kingdom and trade relations will resume. Lucien will still marry Desminda, and you will rule the Kingdom of Roses. This is madness, Celestine. It will not end well for you."

The voices trailed away before Harlow could make out Celestine's response to the queen. They had to be in the Great Hall. She peered around the corner only to see Lucien standing back, watching them go inside. Harlow jerked back, but Lucien turned. His eyes widened and footsteps started toward her. She looked left and right but before she could decide, a firm hand gripped her arm.

"Stop," Lucien whispered. His eyes were wide.

Harlow didn't even think. A second later, her blade rested against his throat. "Tell me right now why I shouldn't open your throat and let you bleed out."

Lucien swallowed hard. His nostrils flared. "I didn't do this," he whispered frantically. "I have no idea what my sister is doing. You must assist Desminda."

Harlow snorted with disbelief.

He held his hands up. "I swear to you. We've known for a while Thornewood was responsible for the lack of magic, and I was sent here to find out why. But ..." he shook his head. "Not like this. Never like this."

"Lucien?" Celestine's voice rang out in the quiet hall.

He stiffened and dropped Harlow's arm. "I'll distract her.

Come in quickly and quietly." Lucien's lips quivered. "Please try not to kill my sister."

Harlow desperately wanted to believe him, but she'd always known he had an ulterior motive. Was his intention now to make her trust him only to be stabbed in the back? She looked up at him. His gaze was stark and terrified. Not like a man planning regicide.

Harlow offered a short nod. "If anything happens to the queen or Desminda, all bets are off."

Lucien dropped her arm. "Very well." He stepped around the corner. "I thought I heard something," he said to Celestine, not looking over his shoulder once.

"Hurry then. The guards will be here soon. I only have ten of those girls. Damn shame," she muttered. "The Thornewilde Forest took most of them before I could get them out."

Their voices trailed off and Harlow's shoulders fell.

"What are you doing?" A whisper at the back of her neck made Harlow twirl, her blade out and swinging. A slim hand grabbed her forearm. "For the love of the gods, girl, you really need to pay more attention."

Bloom crouched beside her, sweat, dirt, and splashes of red decorating her face in a macabre war paint. "They're in there?" she said, jerking her head to the side.

Harlow stared at Bloom, her mouth agape. How did she do that? Shade had taught them all how to use stealth to their advantage, but Bloom was a ghost. Finally, she nodded. "The queen and princess, Lucien and Celestine."

"The Kingsguard and other Virago are tied up with our errant Virago," Bloom said. "Kalen leads them."

Harlow stilled. The dark-haired girl who'd walked her to the infirmary. At her stunned look, Bloom nodded. "Who knew she had it in her? If I expected anyone to do it, it would have been Melara."

Harlow seconded that. "Lucien says he'll distract Celestine. If we can get in and behind her, one of us can take her out. The other can get the queen and Desminda out."

"I'll get them out," Bloom offered.

Harlow nodded, her blade at the ready. *"Honore in vitas. Gloriate in morte."*

Bloom grinned at her, a fierce and wild thing. "Neither of us will die today."

If anyone would know, she trusted it would be Bloom. With that, Harlow stepped out from her hiding spot and tiptoed on silent feet to the Great Hall.

# CHAPTER SIXTY-THREE

## RANCID BLOOMS

B loom watched Harlow tiptoe away and knew today would change everything for them. It wasn't easy knowing things like this, but what made it even more difficult was not being able to tell anyone. While they made up long ago, regret still pierced her heart when she thought of Harlow's treatment at the hands of her teammates. Perhaps instead of alienating Harlow, they could have taken it a little easier on her. But, such things went against everything she stood for. Few succeeded when people took it easy on them. Harlow would need every scrap of courage and bravery in the months to come. And though Harlow had come far these last few months, her magic had never surfaced again, leaving Bloom with a worry deep in her stomach for they would all need her power by the time this was done.

She sighed, her shoulders slumping with weariness. Harlow was a kind sort, but not the girl she expected to have such a mantle fall across her shoulders. The girl's road wouldn't be easy. Most people's weren't, but Harlow's ... well, Harlow's road and the paths she chose to take would eventually affect them all. It had already begun.

Bloom chewed on her lip. She didn't get involved. Ever.

Doing so could reveal her power to the world and this world wasn't kind to people like her. If she wasn't careful, she'd find herself swinging on a rope in the gallows in town square, and Bloom liked her neck just the way it was, thank you very much.

She'd felt something different about Harlow the first time she'd seen her. Something off. Not in a bad way, just *different*. She couldn't put her finger on it, but as their time progressed together and Bloom began to see the way all the connecting futures intersected, she now knew Harlow faced a deadly road. Her first test would be in mere seconds, in the Great Hall, when the fate of a kingdom hovered on the choices of a young girl, the Heir of Magic, a girl who had no idea how much power she had running through her veins.

Bloom felt like she stood on the edge of a thin razor. If she stepped sideways, she'd bleed, but if she stepped off, there would be no security or safety. Her life would never be the same. When she Saw, Bloom swallowed the words down, *remembered*, then ducked her head and went about her business. She never Saw *everything*, only the beginning and the end, the roads in between, but never the choices made to get them there. She could feel if someone was at a crossroad, but never what they should do. Most things wouldn't affect her anyway and, if they did, well Bloom usually had plenty of time to plan for it.

Not this time.

The first incident when Bloom saw something she shouldn't have was when she was six years old and saw her father pulling up in the wagon he'd taken to town for the purchase of their monthly goods. While the wagon was full of dry goods and trinkets for both of them, her father was full of the attentions of a woman in an establishment her mother bitterly referred to as "the place where painted ladies live."

At the time, Bloom did not know why someone would want

to paint themselves, but as she saw the haze of another woman's touch on her father's aura, even at six she knew something wasn't quite right. She stayed silent until dinner time and just as her father was spooning mashed potatoes into his mouth, Bloom asked, "Do you like the smell of roses, Daddy?"

He'd given her a curious look, his utensil poised by his mouth before he shrugged. "Guess so, plum."

Her mother's eyebrows lifted, but Bloom knew her mother wouldn't say anything. She always claimed Bloom had a curious way about her and this question wasn't anything unusual.

"You've been with a painted lady. She smells like roses. Was she nice? Mama doesn't wear roses, Daddy. She wears gardenia."

Mashed potatoes sputtered from her father's mouth. Mama slammed the tin mug she held down on the table, her mouth pinched tightly at the edges while she stared at Bloom's father. He shrank under her gaze, potatoes dripping from the edge of his dark mustache and plopping onto the cracked dinner plate in front of him.

"Is this true, Harold?" her mother asked quietly.

Bloom looked back and forth between them, suddenly scared by what she'd done. She slipped off the old, scarred wooden chair and quietly left through the back of the house. The raised voices in her home didn't die down until dusk.

Her mama later found her in a field of flowers watching the sunset. Bloom had braided herself a flower crown and one for her mother too. Mama adjusted her skirts and sat down beside her, accepting the crown. She plopped it on her head and gave Bloom a crooked smile.

"How would you feel about going somewhere for a little while? Just you and me."

Bloom knew this was her fault. Her and her curious ways. "Did I do something wrong?"

Her mother pulled Bloom closer, her arms wrapped tightly around her back. Mama's braid fell over one shoulder and Bloom played with the edges of the tail, watching her dirty fingers spread Mama's hair out like one of those old paper fans she used when the temperatures got too high. "No, darling," she whispered against her hair. "Never." Mama pushed her away gently and stared into her eyes. "You have a gift, Bloom. A wonderful, curious gift. But you must not tell anyone else. People don't appreciate the kind of gifts you have. Not anymore."

Coming back to herself, Bloom nodded once. She never told a soul. She hoped she never would.

She'd never eaten mashed potatoes again, either.

With a deep inhale and a whispered prayer for safety, Bloom followed after Harlow, her blade at the ready, her heart desperate for change.

# CHAPTER SIXTY-FOUR

## RESCUE BY FIREFLY

She made it almost all the way to Desminda. They were still a few feet away from each other, but she couldn't risk getting too close or she'd give herself away. The future queen was on her knees, her head bowed. Celestine stood in front of her, turned to face Lucien.

He'd seen her come in but had carefully kept his eyes away from her, lest he give her away. She crept on silent feet through the hall, concealing herself in the pews and within the heavy maroon curtains hanging on the walls. But there was no more cover the closer she got, and Harlow had run out of ideas.

Whether Bloom was behind her, she didn't know, but right now she couldn't see a way to get them out safely. The queen stood with Celestine, the scarlet haired woman holding fast to her arm.

"What will you gain from this?" Lucien demanded. "You've made fools out of our kingdom!"

Celestine's eyes widened. "The king is dead, and the queen barely hangs on to power with her fingernails." She jerked her head to Desminda. "This princess has no idea the mess she's about to walk into. This is our chance to save both kingdoms!"

"At the cost of our honor?"

His sister scoffed. "There is no honor in war, Lucien. There are only winners."

He shook his head, his scarlet hair gleaming in the sunlight streaming from the stained glass in front of them. On any other day, at any other time, they would have made a beautiful scene, dressed in their finery, their hair like fire. But today, all Harlow could feel and see was horror.

Blood painted Desminda's neck and face in a strange dotted pattern. How it had gotten there, Harlow couldn't bear to know. The queen swayed on her feet, and she wondered if she stayed upright because Celestine forced her to.

There was no way she could get behind Celestine and take her by surprise. She'd be caught before she could get within a few feet of her. It left only one way forward.

Harlow stepped out from her hiding place.

Lucien's eyes widened. Celestine spun and when her eyes met Harlow's, a cruel smile twisted her lips. "Ah. One of the *true* Virago. And, if rumor holds true, the future queen's favorite."

Desminda's shoulders stiffened. She turned her head and their gazes met. Harlow saw a world of pain and shock inside of her, but she jerked her head down once. "*Go,*" Desminda mouthed.

Harlow slowly shook her head. "By order of the Virago, release the queen and her heir at once."

Celestine laughed, a bright and merry sound, at odds with the blood on her face and hands. "Look at this slip of a girl, ordering me around." She tugged the queen toward her.

"Celestine." Lucien's voice was low with warning.

"You are a fool," Celestine snapped. "Consorting with these people who've ripped the most important things in our life away from us."

"I am marrying Desminda," Lucien responded. "Our kingdoms will soon be joined. We will figure this out." He took a step forward. "Please, sister. Don't ruin this. We have two peoples to think of. Not just ours."

Celestine sneered at him. Her arm went around the queen's shoulders. Harlow felt like timed slowed down to a crawl. Celestine raised her blade up to the queen's neck and held it so closely a trickle of blood seeped down her neck. A moan came from Desminda.

"That is where we differ," Celestine snapped. "I only care about *our* people. If Thornewood wants to swear fealty to us, then they can. Otherwise, we will drive them out and combine our lands."

Lucien held his hands up. "Celestine, I beg of you..."

"Now!" Bloom screamed from somewhere behind her.

Harlow took two running steps and leaped toward Celestine. The woman's eyes widened, but instead of stepping back, she sent the blade across the queen's neck.

A strangled and harsh scream rang through the hall. Harlow flew through the air and landed onto both Celestine and the queen. Blood, red and warm, sprayed over her, pouring down her neck and leathers. They all fell to the ground, Harlow's bones crunching at the impact.

She raised her blade in the air, but something punched her side, sharp and hot. Wetness hit her first, then blinding pain.

"Run," a hoarse voice in her ear. "Flee this place. Find aid, then return." Lucien pulled her off of Celestine. Harlow's eyes could only focus on Desminda's mother, lying in a pool of her own blood, her eyes wide and sightless.

Lucien shoved Harlow away as Celestine scrambled to her feet. He stepped in front of her. Fingers tightened around her arm.

Bloom.

Desminda stood beside her, screaming, screaming, scream-ing. Her eyes were wide and shocked, and her fingers were locked around her face. Horror glinted in her gaze and even when Bloom tugged her to go, Desminda wouldn't budge.

"Go!" Lucien screamed, his own blade drawn.

Harlow pulled Desminda. "We have to run."

When Desminda didn't budge, Harlow inhaled sharply and tried one more time. "Your Majesty."

But the princess didn't move. Celestine and Lucien engaged in battle, the sound of their blades singing even over the sound of Desminda's screams. When she still didn't move, Harlow didn't think about it.

She pulled back her hand and slapped Desminda across the face.

Harlow would worry about the consequences later. Getting the princess to safety was her only thought. Desminda gasped and reared back, her hand reaching up to her reddened cheek, eyes wide when they finally focused on Harlow's grim visage.

"Run!" Harlow screamed and finally, *finally* Desminda began to move.

ALL SHE KNEW WAS PAIN. Blood soaked her leathers and pooled in her boots, but all Harlow could do was keep moving. To stop meant certain death. The sound of thundering boots in the hall behind them sent Harlow's heartbeat skyrocketing.

"We need to move faster," Bloom warned. "Kalen and the other Virago have found us."

A sob of pain burst from Harlow, but she picked up the pace, dragging a dazed Desminda behind her. Bloom ducked into a door and held it open. "Hurry," she whispered. "There's an exit out to the courtyard close to the stables."

They hurried in and Bloom bolted the door behind them.

Harlow gave her a curious look but didn't ask any questions. She wasn't sure she could speak anymore. All she wanted to do was scream.

Bloom led them to a large tapestry. She pulled it aside and pushed a button underneath a windowsill next to the wall. Harlow heard a click and the wall opened, leaving a small gap they could all get through. Bloom ushered them through and closed the door. Darkness swallowed the room.

Harlow stopped, her breath harsh and rasping. "I can't see anything."

There was a snick of something and the smell of sulfur. Seconds later, Bloom held a torch up, casting flickers of orange light across the stone. Her gaze flicked down to the hand Harlow held to her side and grimaced.

"It looks worse than it is," Harlow croaked.

Bloom gave her a long look but then turned and hurried down the passage. Her steps were a little slower this time as if knowing Harlow didn't have much more in her. Each step was torturous and plodding and every time her feet hit the ground, pain thudded through her.

Desminda moved like a zombie. All Harlow had to do was touch her and she responded like a puppet, as if Harlow held her strings now and all she wished to do was obey her.

After several minutes, Bloom stopped at a small grate. "We're here." Light pooled in, dim but enough to see by. She extinguished the torch and crouched down to peer out. "There's no one there yet." Bloom snorted. "Idiots. This is the first place they should have secured."

"That's why they didn't graduate," Harlow croaked.

A smile played across her lips. "Technically, neither did we," Bloom said as she lifted a foot to kick the grate in.

The laugh made her groan. She pressed her fingers as tight to her side as she could, but blood squeezed between the spaces.

Bloom shimmied through the grate then held her hand out for Desminda. "Your Majesty."

Harlow gently shoved her forward. Desminda crouched, her movements jerky and unsure, managing to shimmy through with Bloom's help.

Bloom peered back in, her lips thin and her expression sad. "This is going to hurt."

Harlow's mouth turned down. "I know."

She hissed as she crouched down but thanked the gods for once for her small size. She barely contained her scream of pain as she got onto her stomach and belly crawled out of the castle. More blood surged from her wound. Once she was out, Bloom took her by the elbow and helped her stand, leaned forward to peer at her wound. "You'll need to get that looked at as soon as possible. A wound like that could mean death," she murmured.

Harlow had just enough energy to send her a withering look for stating the obvious.

Bloom snickered but held onto Harlow as they made their way to the stables.

Just as they'd reached the doors, a loud, familiar squeal tore through the air. Thunderous hoofbeats rumbled the ground and seconds later, a massive midnight black mare stood before them.

"Luci." Harlow hobbled over to the horse. A sob broke free and liquid flowed down her chin. At Desminda's sharp gasp, Harlow thought it might be blood.

Footsteps tore around the corner and just as Bloom raised her blade, Lant's fearful face came into view. "Harlow!"

He led a smaller horse and held a single saddle as he hurried over. "Thank the gods you're okay."

Luci stared at Harlow and snorted. Then she bent on her front two legs, an offering to to see an injured Harlow to safety. Tears flowed down her face. "Bloom, get Desminda to safety. Lant, ride with me."

Lant eyed Luci with trepidation. "Not so sure that's a good idea."

"I don't see any better alternatives."

More hoofbeats sounded and moments later, Shade rounded the corner. "We have to leave. Now."

Behind him, he led another horse, a smaller brown bay. On its back, he'd slung a badly beaten man. His legs and hands were tied and there was cloth stuffed in his mouth. He stared at her with hateful eyes.

Harlow's eyebrows went up, but there was no time to ask questions. She grabbed Luci's mane, whispered an apology, and pulled herself up, gasping at the agony in her side. She held a hand out to Lant, but he ignored it and scrambled up behind her. The beast rose and without waiting for Bloom or anyone else, she thundered away from the castle and straight into the forests of Thornewilde.

# CHAPTER SIXTY-FIVE

### THE FALL OF THE HEIR

**B**loom and Shade caught up with them several minutes later, once Harlow had talked Luci into slowing down. The suns were beginning to set behind them, casting long shadows on the forest floor. The air had cooled substantially and for that Harlow was thankful. She wanted to take off her boots and shake the blood out of them, but it was all she could do to stay on her horse.

Shade rode up beside them shaking his head. "I can't believe you managed to befriend that infernal beast."

That infernal beast snorted at Shade and nipped at his horse, causing his mare to rear and shimmy out of the way, almost unseating him. Harlow chuckled, though it cost her.

At the pain in her voice, Shade's eyes narrowed. He looked her up and down and his face paled. "You're injured."

Harlow nodded.

Lant spoke up from behind her. "Someone got her in the side. She's bleeding all over my good pants." He joked, but fear made his voice tremble and scratch.

"We can't afford to stop here. I'm sorry, Fischer. We must

keep riding. We'll attend to your wound as soon as we can." His dark eyes met hers. "Can you make it?"

She licked her lips and nodded.

They both knew it was a lie.

Blackness took her not long after. Her fingers fell from Luci's mane, and she slumped forward. The last thing she heard was Lant's sharp inhale of breath and the sound of her name on Shade's lips.

# CHAPTER SIXTY-SIX

## MAGIC IN THE MOST UNLIKELY PLACE

"You can't."

"I can and I will. You of all people should know what it's like to suppress what you are."

"You would risk it now when you've lost everything?"

"If I've lost everything, what else is there to lose?"

Harlow moaned. Her eyelids fluttered open and all she could see was darkness. No stars. Nothingness.

"She will die if I do not."

Harlow heard the sound of a frustrated exhale, the sound of a hand rasping over five o'clock shadow. It was Shade. Shade and Desminda.

Where were Bloom and Lant?

She moaned. "I'm okay," she whispered.

"I swear, Shade. Do you teach a class on lying then? All Harlow has done to me is lie."

Her lips twitched.

"She's had to lie," Shade said quietly. "Just like you."

"I am *done* lying," Desminda snapped.

Harlow moaned with pain as efficient fingers loosened her leather jerkin. "Relax," Desminda whispered. "I'm going to try to help you."

She lay as still as she could and wondered what Desminda could possibly do to save her. She'd lost too much blood. Even through the haze of pain, she knew it. Her feet were soaked with it. Her pants and shirt were as well. Stickiness coated her everywhere. Sweat and blood and dirt and pain.

Cool air hit her exposed skin.

Desminda sucked in a breath. "Oh. Oh Harlow."

Pure golden light enveloped the forest, sparkles of magic floating around her. A surprised smile found its way through pain. Harlow lifted one hand to trail her fingers through it.

She was dying. If this was what it was like to die, she would welcome it with open arms.

Warmth touched her side then, and a moment later, pain roared through her.

Darkness took her again and as she faded away, all Harlow wished for was to see that golden light just one more time.


SHE AWOKE WITH TWO THOUGHTS. Food and a privy. Harlow blinked the grit out of her eyes. Above her was a blue and cloudless sky. There was no more tree cover and the air had warmed by at least ten degrees.

"Where are we?" she croaked to no one in particular.

"Almost to safety," Shade said in the way he always answered questions. With zero details.

Remembering her injury, Harlow's fingers trailed down to her side. But the thought registered first before they arrived ... there was no pain.

"Am I dead?" she murmured aloud.

"You should be." Bloom's face appeared above her.

Her fingers traced the area where the wound was. Smooth skin greeted her fingers. She blinked and slowly pushed herself up. No pain. Anywhere. Harlow sent a confused look to Bloom who merely stared at her with dispassion.

She tilted her head down. The wound had disappeared. All that was left was a thin white scar. "How?" she whispered.

Bloom jerked her head toward Desminda and lowered her voice. "Turns out Her Highness was hiding a bundle of secrets from everyone. Including the queen."

Brow furrowing, she looked up at Bloom and then slid her gaze over to the Queen of Thornewood. Understanding finally unfurled within her. "Magic," she whispered, her gaze flying back to Bloom's. "She has magic."

"A ton of it, if the work on you is any indication." Bloom's voice quivered with suppressed anger as her sharp grey eyes studied Desminda.

Betrayal split through her like lightning. Her entire kingdom had their magic ripped away while she held onto hers the entire time. Nepotism at its finest. But as soon as that thought went through her mind, she wondered. Was she any better? Her father had spared her as well.

Harlow slowly rose. Bloom held out a steadying hand. "You need to eat something. You've lost a lot of blood."

Harlow nodded but made her way over to Desminda first. The queen sat with her back to a tree, staring blankly ahead. They were no longer in Thornewilde Forest. If they were, they were in a part she'd never seen before.

She sat down beside Desminda, far enough away for propriety but still close enough to speak quietly. The queen of Thornewood was clean this time, all traces of blood and dirt gone from her body. Her long hair hung lank around her face and deep shadows had found a home beneath her eyes. She looked like a woman who'd lost it all, and she had. At least for now.

"I hear I have you to thank for my retrieval from death's

door." Harlow toyed with a blade of grass. They sat in an open area, filled with grass and wildflowers. Few trees dotted the landscape, and Harlow couldn't help but feel vulnerable. If Shade had stopped here, she had to trust he knew what he was doing, but it felt odd to be sitting out here in the open like this with nothing to hide them if the other Virago found their location.

"It's a gift. From neither my mother nor my father. Some-one, perhaps a grandmother, had magic in their blood and it skipped at least one generation." She held up her long, tanned fingers. "Healing. People, plants, animals, anything sentient." A small smile curled over her lips. "Nothing amazing like thunder-storms or lightning bolts from my fingertips."

"You saved my life," Harlow said. "I have to think it's pretty amazing. You brought me back from the brink, and I will forever be in your debt."

"I merely returned the favor." Desminda sighed, dismissing Harlow's words. "It's the least I could do." She put a hand over her eyes and looked ahead into the grassy plains and blue skies. "Shade won't tell me where we are. He only insists we are safe."

"How long have we been traveling?"

Desminda slid her gaze over. "Two weeks."

Harlow went numb. In the space of only a few hours, all her plans had gone by the wayside. To find out she'd been uncon-scious for weeks ... she inhaled a deep breath and tried to keep from crying. She was further away than ever from finding her sister. Despair rocketed through her, but she tried to temper it with thoughts of gratitude. She was alive and so were the people she cared about. Even the best laid plans were prone to change. Her plans were only to find her sister. She had nothing concrete and no real timeline. "*Weeks?*" she blurted.

"Your injury was grave. If we hadn't stopped when we did, you would have died. Blood loss like that does not come without cost. The magic put you in a healing sleep." She shrugged. "It was a massive pain toting your unconscious body around, though your beast of a horse assisted us with getting you onto her back." Desminda tilted her head back to look up at the sky. "Though she damn near took my fingers off when I reached to pet her in thanks."

Harlow chuckled. "She's a fine horse."

"I don't think that's a horse," Desminda responded, her voice curious. "I think she might be something entirely different. Maybe just ... horse adjacent."

Shade noticed her then. His eyes widened and he jogged over. "You're awake."

Harlow nodded. "And apparently doing much better than I should be."

Shade's disapproving gaze seared Desminda. "Yes, our queen is to thank for that."

He sat down beside Desminda, his long legs stretched out in front of him. Nature looked good on him. Shade looked more relaxed than she'd ever seen him. For a man who'd lost his position, his kingdom, his way of life, Shade seemed to be taking it all in stride.

Harlow's gaze lingered on the man tied to a tree. The cloth was still shoved in his mouth and his hateful eyes studied everything, as if he'd marked them all for death and was merely waiting for his opportunity. "Who is he?"

Shade inhaled and plucked a flower from the ground. "He's a gift."

Desminda laughed. "If he's a gift, I shall endeavor to never remind you of my birthday."

He twirled the brightly colored flower in his fingers. "A long time ago, he hurt someone I care about. I thought about killing him but decided doing so would take away someone's vengeance." Shade grinned then, his gaze meeting that of his prisoner's. The smile was wide and deadly. The prisoner blinked a couple of times and looked down but not before Harlow saw his throat bob. "So I beat him a little and tossed him into the dungeon. The coup in the castle seemed like the perfect time to take him with me and present him."

"You beat him a *little*?" Harlow asked then shook her head. "Never mind." The man looked like he'd been put through a gauntlet of men armed with clubs. Both of his eyes were black, and his nose was crooked and swollen to twice its normal size. Apparently, the beatings had continued long after their hasty escape. Surprised by his behavior, Harlow studied Shade for a long moment, sensing something different about him. Perhaps after everything, they were all changed. After everything that had happened, Harlow was too tired to judge anyone, least of all the man who'd given up everything to save them.

"Do not go near him. He is looking for any opportunity to escape and if I have to kill him before we get to where we're going, I will be sorely disappointed." Shade lay down in the grass, one leg crooked up. "We're only a few hours away. Break your fast, Harlow, then ready yourself. Your horse refused to be tied, so she wanders around somewhere. We stopped trying to do anything rather than avoid her."

A grin stretched her lips. "She's a good horse."

Shade snorted. "She's a thousand-pound nightmare. But she saved your life, so I'll give credit where it's due." He placed the flower on Desminda's knee and sighed before he rolled to a seated position. "Everything is packed up. Bloom will be back soon from foraging, then we'll be on our way."

He rose in a fluid motion then held a hand out to Desminda. She took it and rose beside him. Harlow shook her head when he did the same for her. "I'd like to sit here for a moment."

They left her there and Harlow shut her eyes for a moment, soaking in the gentle sunshine and the wind blowing in her hair.

Shade must have a plan. He always had a plan. The only thing she wanted to know is if his plan would get her any closer to Nova. When she opened her eyes, she quietly rose and headed over to the campsite.

The thunderous boom of hooves made her turn. Atop Luci rode a girl in a blood red cloak, hair streaming behind her. "Astrid!"

Harlow ran in her direction but stopped as Luci grew closer. When the beast stopped before her, Astrid slid off in a boneless motion, then placed her hand against the mare's neck and murmured something in a language Harlow had never heard before. Luci snorted, then pranced over to where Desminda was.

"She's stunning," Astrid murmured. The bard looked no worse for the wear. Her clothes were clean, and she looked refreshed and well rested. "Celestine has taken over the castle quite handily. Lucien stands behind her, looking for all the world like he's stumbled into something he can't control. Pity that. With a few solid beatings to put some sense into him, he might have made a solid king."

"And the Virago?" Harlow asked, the thought of them putting a sour taste in her mouth.

Astrid's lips thinned. "The traitors protect her, though their numbers were culled significantly by the Kingsguard. Melara and the others lie in wait. When it's safe, they will follow our trail as best they can." Her gaze found Shade. "At his command, though I noticed a shortage of the Kingsguard as well. Whether dead or defected, I cannot say." Her eyebrows rose as she noticed the prisoner. "Ah," she exhaled on a breath. "I believe I know where the other two are now."

Harlow gave her a curious look. "You know who he is?"

"Formerly one of Shade's Kingsguard. I expect fairly soon he will no longer walk among the living."

Harlow sent a glance the prisoner's way only to find him staring hatefully at both of them. "Do you know what he did?" she murmured quietly.

Astrid took her arm. "It is not my story to tell, though I suspect you will find out soon enough." She inhaled deeply. "I've always loved these lands," she said with a wistful sigh. "Though getting caught out here in a storm is less than desirable."

"You know where we are?"

Astrid led them over to the camp. Lant sat nursing a bowl of something, his expression forlorn. He looked up when they grew closer, and his face shone with relief. "Harlow!" Lant set his bowl down and stood wringing his hands. "I didn't think you'd make it and all I could remember was how we met. If I haven't said how sorry I am, please know it now. Or again." He shoved a hand through his hair. "I am so glad to see you standing."

Harlow reached over and dragged him into a hug. His thin frame stiffened at first before his arms went around her. "I am glad to see you as well," she said, her words muffled through the linen of his shirt. "I've missed a lot, apparently."

Lant huffed and pulled away. "Shade set a breakneck pace. Even I have no idea where we are, though I believe we've gone almost due north. Perhaps a northeastern shift. If I didn't know any better, I'd say we're headed for the Kingdom of Shadows."

Harlow blinked in surprise. "Why in the world would we go there?" she whispered.

No one knew much about the Shadow Kingdom. Shade's lessons handled geography and a few exports, but claimed their royalty was a mystery, and no one had seen their king or queen in years. The place was heavily protected by a magic shield, disguising the land in a veil of shadows. Thus, its name. They refused to send any goods to Thornewilde or any of their surrounding territories, but still traded in good standing with other kingdoms. Shade mentioned how Thornewilde considered the kingdom to be an enemy, though he refused to say anything else about it.

When Bloom asked about the shield, Shade shrugged, a hint of strange amusement lurking in his eyes. "There's an entire world out there, Bloom. It's not impossible magic exists elsewhere, is it?" he'd responded, his sharp gaze lingering on her until Bloom dropped her eyes.

Astrid, still standing beside them, grinned. "Many reasons, Harlow. Shade is a man of mystery, though I think once some of them are solved, you'll be thanking him."

"You speak in cryptic riddles. Can't you take pity on a girl who's almost died and at least give her a hint?" Harlow said, exasperated.

Astrid chuckled and reached for a small bowl beside the fire. "And where would the fun be in that?"

Harlow looked at Lant, but he shook his head. "Thornewood and the Shadow Kingdom are not allies. It seems a fool's errand to go here, but perhaps Shade knows something we do not."

"Does the queen know?" Harlow whispered.

"Shade is a maestro," Astrid responded. "He plucks all the strings to tune the instrument until it sings like a bird."

A strangled laugh broke from Harlow. "I don't even know what that means." She sighed and joined Astrid in serving herself some breakfast. If she were to be surprised today, she at least wanted to have a full stomach. Two weeks of not eating had caught up to her. Clothing that once fit well hung on her small frame, and the belt she'd fastened her sword to had new notches cut in it. Harlow touched the pool of magic inside of her and found it waiting...slumbering. She hadn't had any of the same sickness as before, but from what Astrid said, it was merely a matter of time before it happened again. Their lessons had dried up the closer she'd gotten to graduation because Shade had monopolized all their time, but Harlow hadn't learned much. Or been successful at much of anything Astrid had tried to teach her. Perhaps soon they could try again. With her no longer fearful of being found out, maybe this time she would be more successful.

Bloom walked through the edge of the trees behind them. Her eyes widened when she saw Astrid.

"A bard," she breathed.

"Two unlikely people converging at the same site seems unlikely at best," Astrid murmured. "Tell me, does your power feel different now that you are far from Thornewood?"

Bloom frowned for a moment before her eyes widened in surprise. "Yes!"

Harlow looked between the both of them, memories piling up in her mind. "You're a Seer," she blurted once the pieces all connected. Seers were rare and dangerous. They were usually taken from their parents at a young age and given to the royal families for use as advisors. Bloom was probably too young for her powers to have manifested much before magic was wiped out.

Desminda watched them all from her perch on an old stump. "All these people living right underneath my mother's nose. She would have been horrified." Tears shone in her golden eyes, but a smile wobbled on her face. "By me most of all."

Astrid turned from Bloom. "Your Majesty, your gift is rare and beautiful. Healers have not been seen in Thornewood since the absence of magic. Think of all the good you may yet do."

Desminda swallowed and looked away. "My gift has been hidden for all my life. I do not cherish the thought of being labeled a hypocrite."

"Everyone is a hypocrite if you think about it," Astrid

chided. "We all hide something. Some of us haven't been able to live true since magic fell."

The queen sighed. "And you most of all, I think." She peered up at Astrid. "All evidence of the bards were wiped out within days of the fall. I miss music. *True* music. We had people who could pluck instruments, but there was always something ... off about it."

"Only someone with magic would know," Astrid said. "Normal people wouldn't be able to tell." The bard sat beside her. "Perhaps when we arrive at our destination, I will play something for you."

A weak smile crossed Desminda's lips. "I would very much enjoy that."

"Then I shall endeavor to please the Queen of Thornewood."

"We must leave within the hour," Shade interrupted. "Dallying could cost us. Eat, then load your horses."

"Yes, Shade," Bloom and Harlow muttered at the same time.

Shade snorted and walked away, snatching up his satchel as he did. "No one can touch that horse of yours, Harlow. Best you feed her something before we leave."

Luci snorted at the words. Shade's steps slowed and his brow furrowed. "Can she understand me?" he wondered aloud.

Astrid chuckled. "She's no regular mare."

The mare whinnied in answer.

"Perhaps when we arrive, she will show you," Astrid said.

"Ugh." Harlow sighed and stood, brushing off the back of her pants. "Riddles, riddles, and more riddles. Is this a thing with all bards or just you?"

Astrid took a bite of her breakfast and wiggled her eyebrows.

"All bards," Bloom said. She picked her basket back up and

sifted through the contents. "I found some berries and some roots. They should last for a while."

"We aren't too far away from where we're going," Shade added. "Divvy everything up among us. I expect we'll arrive before lunch."

# CHAPTER SIXTY-SEVEN

## A VIOLENT INTERLUDE

They headed toward a dark tower surrounded by fog. She noticed it once they'd ridden for an hour or so, but when she asked Shade, he'd shaken his head once and didn't respond. The grassy plain was long gone, and they rode along a well-trodden path made by traveling merchants and those seeking a new home in the shadows. Forest surrounded them on both sides, blotting out much of the sunlight. Lant had remained quiet on the ride over, his brow furrowed with concern.

Harlow nudged Luci and the horse responded by thundering up to Lant. He jerked, then sighed. "That horse is a menace," he muttered.

She reached down to stroke Luci's silky mane. "This menace saved our lives."

"She's going to trample us in our sleep one day."

Luci reached over and nipped Lant's vest. He shrieked and pulled away, glaring at the horse.

"You deserved it," Harlow said with a shrug. She lowered her voice. "Are you sure we're going to the Shadow Kingdom?"

"Positive." His hands were tight on the reins turning his knuckles white with tension. "I do not know what game Shade plays, but if he's blindly leading us there, we will not make it out alive."

"Shade is always prepared." Harlow had the utmost confidence. "If he's leading us here, he knows something we do not." She looked to the horizon at the midnight-colored tower. The blue skies disappeared at the edge of the kingdom, turning to deep black and grays and covered with wispy clouds. It was beautiful in a way. It didn't look quite like night, but more of a dusk. "What can you tell me about it?"

Lant shrugged. "Not much. The borders of the kingdom are closed and sealed off. Members of the Shadow Kingdom rarely venture out. There are rumors they have magic there and never lost it."

Harlow jerked her gaze up. "Shade leads us to a place of wild magic?"

"Apparently so." A sigh broke from him, and he shook his head. "When I first met you, I knew you'd be interesting, but never in my life did I think I'd be fleeing from the only home I'd ever known into a foreign kingdom."

Harlow couldn't tell if it was a compliment or an insult. "When I first met you, I had no idea I'd be fighting for my life, and yet here we are."

Lant had the grace to blush. "I'll never be able to make it up to you."

She reached over and slapped him on the back. "You already have, friend." With a slight nudge on Luci's side, the horse bolted toward Shade.

He still led the prisoner around on the extra horse, but he never let the man sit upright. He'd slung him over, stomach first, on the horse, still tied and gagged. Luci slowed her stride until she was side by side with Shade's horse. "He's going to vomit if he has to ride that way much longer," said Harlow.

Shade's lips twitched. "I would say that's his problem and no concern of mine."

"He might choke on it. Then you'd have a dead prisoner." She couldn't stop the sympathy for the man's plight filling her heart.

"If you knew what he'd done, you'd wipe that look from your face." Shade's rebuke forced her eyes away from the man. Even riding ahead couldn't stop the smell wafting from him. "His crimes are plenty, Harlow. I bring him to his judgment."

"To the Kingdom of Shadows?"

He slid a glance over to her. "Lant told you, I presume. He's been nervous for days now."

"He says we do not have any agreement with the kingdom and that we enter at our own peril."

Shade's eyes crinkled at the edges. "After all this time, you still do not trust me?"

"Of course I do," she hissed. "But you won't tell anyone anything, and we're all nervous."

Desminda chose that time to ride up next to them. Her gaze lingered on the tower. "Shade, where are you taking us?"

He rolled his eyes heavenward. "Trust that I know what I'm doing."

Desminda gave him a strange look. "I trust you, but I am the deposed queen of Thornewood. Most kingdoms will not take kindly to my presence."

Shade pulled his horse away from the main path. "Let's stop here for a bite. We're close, but it might be a while before any food or refreshments are offered."

"This conversation isn't over," Desminda promised as she followed him.

"I only have your best interests at heart, Your Majesty," Shade responded. He slid off his horse with one liquid move and dug in his saddle bag for the berries Bloom had divided between them.

Harlow followed, though her dismount was much less graceful. Luci was massive and dismounting from the horse felt like climbing down from a building. Bloom and Lant rode up beside them, with Astrid following close behind.

"Twenty minute rest," Shade declared, popping one of the bright blue berries into his mouth. A grimace formed on his face as he chewed. "Be prepared for anything as we get closer. Do not dally." His gaze traveled through the trees and their surroundings. "We are far enough away from danger, but one can never be too careful. Brigands can strike anywhere."

"I'm going to ride ahead," Astrid declared. Without waiting for a response, she clicked her teeth and she and the mount she was on shot ahead and into the distance.

"Brave girl," Bloom muttered.

"Bards are welcomed in most kingdoms," Shade responded, his gaze heavy on Astrid's back. "Eat, drink, and take care of any other needs."

Harlow wandered over to a large stone and leaned against it, mindlessly eating the berries. Fatigue rode her bones today, and there was a faint occasional twinge in the area where she'd been stabbed. The horror of how close she'd come to death made her shudder, and she quickly turned her thoughts to something else. One of the berries fell from her hand and when she bent down to get it, a crinkling sound came from her vest.

Desminda sat down beside her just as Harlow dug through her pocket and pulled out a piece of parchment paper.

"He brings us to the Shadow Kingdom," Desminda murmured. "Is he a fool?"

"You twisted it out of Lant?" Harlow asked, her lips curling as she unfolded the piece of paper. She couldn't remember what this was from, but as she opened it, familiar purple ink came into view. Just as she was about to fold it back up and give it to the queen, she saw her name and Bloom's along with several of the other girl's.

Desminda's face was tilted to the sky, her eyes closed as she soaked up the dying light of the sun. They grew closer to eternal dusk, so she didn't blame the queen for enjoying it while she could.

Her gaze skimmed over the contents of the letter while Desminda was preoccupied, but seconds later, she went numb. The paper slipped from her fingers and onto the ground. Desminda blinked, then frowned, looking at her feet.

Harlow rose abruptly.

The queen's fingers trembled as she reached down for the letter. "Where did you find this?" she snapped.

Anger, hot and fierce, roared through Harlow. "You didn't pick me," she whispered. Betrayal wormed its way into her heart. "After everything that happened, you didn't pick me."

"Where did you find this?" the queen repeated.

"You dropped it on the floor after the dinner. I was going to give it back, but you were preoccupied with Lucien." Her words felt stiff, forced from her throat. She wanted an answer, but who was she to demand one? She sat with a queen. Harlow was merely a girl with a mysterious background, an orphan from a farm. No one. She assumed too much. Why should the queen have chosen her? She was merely a dalliance, a distraction for Desminda. That was all.

"You chose Bloom." The Seer peered over at them as she heard her name, but she must have seen the look on Harlow's face for she quickly turned away and busied herself with her lunch.

Desminda straightened and folded the damning letter back up.

"You were going to send me to a village nowhere close to

where I grew up. You'd separate me from any friends I've made here." Her voice broke. "Why?"

Desminda's lips thinned. "I am the queen, Harlow. I do not have to answer questions from my guards."

Harlow felt cracks begin at the edges of her heart. "But I am no longer your guard," she whispered. "Because you are no longer queen."

Desminda sucked in a sharp breath. She reared back like Harlow had slapped her. Her golden eyes snapped with shock, quickly followed by anger.

"Be careful how you talk to me, girl," Desminda warned.

A rush of wind buzzed by Harlow's face, followed by a thunking sound. That sounded like ...

"Get down!" Shade roared. "Take cover anywhere you can!"

An arrow.

She shoved her anger away and pulled the queen down beside her. The rock was large enough to hide most of them, but Harlow wouldn't be able to see a thing unless she peered above it.

That would be the perfect moment to get an arrow in the face. She risked a look around. Bloom had concealed herself in the brush of the forest. The only reason Harlow knew was because of the glint of her blade in the dappled sunlight.

Two more arrows thunked too close to them.

"Come out and fight like honorable men," Shade called.

An arrow too close to him was the answer.

Fear spiked through her. Desminda clutched her hand, but Harlow shook her off for many reasons, not only from her betrayal. She needed both hands free if she were to fight. "Stay," she commanded Desminda. Harlow crouched and fled from the safety behind the rock and over to Shade who'd stepped behind a tree to shield himself from the fire.

He pointed to the east. "They're coming from there. We can wait to see if they run out of arrows, or we can ambush them."

"I'm always partial to a good ambush."

Harlow hissed a quiet shriek through her teeth. "Bloom! Stop sneaking up on people."

She wiggled her eyebrows. "Could have dragged a knife right across your throat for all the attention you paid me," she said cheerily.

"Not the time," Shade snapped.

Four men stepped out from the cover of the forest. "You're outnumbered," one of them said. He was tall, lean, and dressed in colors that would help him blend right back into the trees if he fled.

A fierce grin formed on Shade's face, and he stepped out. "Would you like to test your theory?"

The man grinned back. "You have three women and a servant. I think I would."

"What is it you want?" Shade asked. His sword was held down at his side, but Harlow didn't miss his ready posture. At any moment, he could strike, and whoever was in his way would fall.

The magic within Harlow pulsed and quickened, awakening from its slumber. Warmth suffused her limbs and she gasped as power flooded her veins.

*Use me*, it whispered to her.

Magic was sentient, Astrid had told her, but she hadn't believed it. Every time her magic manifested, it was immediate and catastrophic. This time it whispered in her ear. Warm silver light trickled from her fingertips. She shook them to dampen it so she wouldn't give away her hiding spot, but it was no use.

"And what do we have there?" the man asked. "Step out, girl. Making me come find you won't end well."

"What do you want?" Shade asked again.

The man studied him. "We got word there were travelers on this road hiding something extremely valuable."

"We have very few coins and even less food," Shade remarked. "You'd be better off waiting for a merchant's cart."

The man's eyes glittered with malice. Harlow stepped out from behind the trees and came up behind Shade. The brigand sucked his teeth as he looked her up and down. "Aren't you a pretty little thing."

Shade stiffened beside her. "Say that one more time."

The man tilted his head. "Oh, I see. You claim first rights?"

The pool slumbering within her became a tsunami. Rage filled her and silver light coalesced around her entire body. Magic filled her veins, her heart, mind and soul until even her vision was hazed silver.

"Harlow," Shade whispered urgently.

"Come find out," Harlow said, her voice an unearthly rumble. Her thoughts were scrambled, but one screamed in her head over and over again. *Nova.* She knew what happened to Nova and she knew how it had affected her sister. If she didn't kill this man for herself, she'd do it for her sister. Silver light poured through the forest, giving everything an unearthly glow.

"We don't want any more trouble than necessary. We're here for the queen," a second man said, giving the first one a dark look. "Not your women." He was shorter than the first one who'd spoken, his eyes a lighter brown. "Give her to us and you'll be on your way."

A dagger hit the fourth man right in the throat. Harlow barely noticed the flicker from Shade's side, fingers moving and a quick twitch of his wrist, sending the dagger blade over hilt to sink right into the man's throat. His eyes went wide as his hands went up, too late. Blood spurted from his neck, and he sank to his knees.

Death came in seconds, Shade the dark harbinger of his fate.

The first one gasped in surprise and raised his sword, roaring as he sprang toward them.

Chaos broke out.

# CHAPTER SIXTY-EIGHT

## A SHADOW OF FREEDOM

The second and third man ran directly to Shade. The sounds of clanging swords and the grunts of men rang through her. The first one came for Harlow.

"I'm going to gut you, girl," he snarled, "and when I'm done, I'm going to defile your corpse."

Harlow was so very tired. So very tired of abusers and liars and cheats and those who thought by virtue of what she was born with that they were better than her. She had nothing. *Nothing.* And someone, even after all she'd been through, was still trying to take something from her.

"Take one step closer and you'll die," Harlow promised. Vengeance spilled from her lips and pooled in her fingers, the magic dripping from her body now.

This fool didn't seem to care. Blinded by his rage, he raised his sword up to strike Harlow down. She didn't even bother to raise her sword. Instead, she looked up at the sky.

And she let go.

. . .

LIGHTNING CRACKLED IN THE AIR. The ground beneath them rumbled and tore, shifting around, and spilling everyone to the forest floor. Thunder boomed around them. Trees split down the middle, their tops sliding off, crashing into the earth. Horses screamed. Men screamed. And still Harlow bled power.

Magic poured from her body, tearing leaves from the trees and brush. A storm of wind started from the ground and formed a cone, pulling up everything from the ground. Leaves, clothing, bags, anything on the ground was consumed.

The three men who were left screamed as debris pummeled them. Shade and Bloom stood to the side of her, their eyes wide and stunned. His sword dropped from his fingers, and he took Bloom by the elbow and pulled her away.

Harlow lifted from the ground, magic levitating her several feet above them. As she floated, Harlow sucked in a breath and lifted two fingers. Daggers from the men's belt came toward her, but with one flick, she sent them flying back in their direction. Two men went down like falling stone.

But Harlow wasn't finished with the first. She grimaced as the magic bled everything out of her, but she wouldn't let this man escape with his life.

"Harlow." Shade's quiet voice tore through her distraction. "Let it go."

"I can't." Her voice trembled. "It wants... it wants vengeance."

"No. *You* want vengeance. The magic only responds to your desires."

Roots shot from the ground and tangled around the man's legs as he tried to turn tail and run.

"There's nothing wrong with vengeance," Shade said. "But you must think of what comes after."

"What comes after is death. He'll never touch another

woman again."

Shade's inhale was sharp. "Then stop toying with him, Harlow. Finish it."

Tears filled Harlow's eyes at his failure to judge her. She looked down at him. Shade stood there, his mouth set in a grim line, but his eyes were filled with understanding. "He is weak, and you are strong."

The man's sobs penetrated the cloud of magic. "Please. Don't. *Stop*. I swear I'll never—"

Harlow snapped his neck like a twig. His eyes widened, and a moment later, the fear bled out of them, leaving only a blank stare behind.

Silence, tense and loaded, fell, but magic still poured from her.

"You have to let it go," Shade murmured.

"Harlow." Bloom stepped up beside him. "Take my hand."

A sob tore from her throat. "I don't want this. I don't want any of this. I just want my farm. My family. Nova. I just want her."

"I know. I know." Bloom was tall enough to reach her hand. Her fingers intertwined with Harlow's. "You are in control, Harlow. Breathe first."

Harlow sucked in a ragged breath.

"Good," Bloom said. "Again."

She kept breathing until each drag of air became slow and controlled.

"Now pull the magic back in."

"I don't know how," Harlow cried.

"You do. It's yours," Bloom said, her voice quiet and soothing. "You control it. You tell it what to do."

Harlow shut her eyes and looked inward at the raging inferno of magic inside of her. She imagined all of it seeping from her bones and pouring back into the pool. At first nothing happened, but slowly she felt herself sinking back to the ground, Bloom's fingers tight against her own.

It took a few moments, but Harlow's feet finally touched the loamy earth. She swayed, fatigue and dizziness taking over.

"I have you," Bloom said.

Out of the corner of her eye, she watched Desminda rise from behind the rock and mount her horse. The queen's eyes were downcast, and she didn't even spare a glance for Harlow.

Her eyes fluttered closed and darkness took her.

SHE AWOKE to Bloom's concerned face looming over her.

"Good," she chirped. "You were only out for a couple of minutes. Shade is antsy to get back on the path. Can you stand?"

Harlow licked her lips, grimacing at how thirsty she was. "Your canteen survived." Bloom helped her up, and Harlow wobbled like a newborn calf. "You have to get this under control," Bloom whispered. "If you do not, they will think you are a danger."

Fear stilled Harlow's heart.

"Your lessons with the Bard should be stepped up." Bloom led her back to Luci. "Perhaps there is someone in this kingdom who can help you, too."

"There's so much power," Harlow said. "I can't see the bottom of it."

Bloom stilled for a second before she stood and adjusted Luci's reins. Strangely enough, the mare stood still and didn't even venture a nip. "There's always a bottom. Always. You just haven't found it yet."

She held her hands out, clasped together in a foothold Harlow could use to mount the horse. Harlow stepped up and over, clinging to Luci's dark mane. She lay against the horse catching her breath. The magic had completely wiped her out. All her energy was gone.

Harlow squeezed her eyes shut. "Thank you."

Bloom snorted. "You're welcome, Stonehand."

Fear stuttered through her at those words. "Don't call me that," she whispered.

"It's who you are. We are free from Thornewood. You can be whoever you want."

Wasn't that the issue? Harlow didn't know who she wanted to be.

Only herself.

But she was afraid she didn't know who that was anymore.

HARLOW PAID little attention to the rest of their ride and let Shade lead them on to the Kingdom of Shadows. Desminda hadn't said a word to her, meekly following behind them.

Harlow was lost in her thoughts. Thoughts of the past and the future. And as they rode, she finally came to a conclusion.

The one thing Harlow always refused to admit to herself was the possibility of weakness.

Was she weak? Maybe. Some people thought cowardice and weakness were the same thing, but Harlow knew it wasn't. She had no ability or confidence to see this thing through, but she could stick the pointy end of her sword in anything that challenged her. Weakness had to do with ability. Cowardice was a lack of courage. She knew well enough she plowed through life like she was made of the best iron and steel, refusing to admit a well-timed blow could take her out just like anyone else. Harlow thought occasional delusion was the best defense to bluster.

But she had no idea how to do this *thing* they asked of her. How she could right the wrongs of an entire kingdom when she was just a girl. They asked too much.

Though, sometimes, in the dark of night, she wondered if they asked too little. If she was capable of more, of shining the light back on a kingdom gone dark. Perhaps being alone in the dark with one's thoughts convinced people they were capable of grander things and feats of legendary heroics.

Then the sun would creep over the horizon, giving light to those thoughts in the darkness and the other questions would inevitably creep back in. How could she— a slip of a girl —do something others couldn't?

Maybe the answer she refused to entertain was she couldn't.

"We're here." Shade's voice interrupted her thoughts. She jerked out of her reverie and stared at the wall of darkness before her.

"How will we get in?" she asked, her voice rough. Harlow felt as if she'd spent the last several hours screaming and longed for a cup of her foster mother's special tea given to them when she had a sore throat.

Shade held his hand up and touched the barrier between the lands they sat on and this new, strange kingdom. The barrier shimmered, with black twisting shadows, then slowly began to open a space large enough for them to cross through.

Harlow gaped at his back. Were the people in this kingdom expecting them?

Desminda sped her horse up and rode beside Shade, but they were too far away for Harlow to hear anything they said.

Lant had fallen behind, and even he hadn't said a word. She couldn't blame him. She'd kept a massive secret from him and had pretended to be something she was not.

A normal girl.

Shadows twisted around them, as if the dark wisps were curious about them all. They lifted her hair and breezed over her skin. Soon, she was covered by them, but she didn't feel afraid. Instead, she felt content, as if these foreign things had recognized the darkness within her and accepted her in spite of it.

They rode for a little while before the darkness receded. A breathtaking village appeared before their eyes. Fabric shops, bakeries, tailors, candlemakers, everything was here. Harlow gaped, her eyes gobbling down all the sights. She itched to explore, but she first had to see whether their party of refugees would be welcomed or expelled, or worse.

Shade didn't stop, so they all kept going. Villagers stared up at them with curious eyes, though no one seemed afraid. Why should they be? They were all dirty, bedraggled, and looked like they'd been through a war.

Perhaps they had. Exhaustion made Harlow's shoulders slump and, even with all the delightful sights in front of her, her eyes grew heavy. She struggled to stay awake, even knowing she was in a foreign kingdom with only a few allies. The blissful darkness of sleep was the only thing that appealed to her right now.

"We're almost there," Lant said, startling her out of her stupor.

She slid a glance his way. "I'm sorry."

Her friend blew out a breath. "How can one apologize for an earthquake or a violent storm?" he mused. "That is what you are, and I am not sure I expected different." One of his shoulders rose and fell. "But you saved us all and I cannot fault you for who you are. If I did that, I would be the worst kind of hypocrite." He grinned at her then. "Besides, I'm pretty glad you didn't unleash that on us when we were on the roof."

So was she. A hesitant smile crossed her lips as relief filled her.

Lant was still here. He was still her friend.

Sometimes that was all that mattered.

# CHAPTER SIXTY-NINE

## A HEART FULL OF STARS

They stood outside the tower gates. Several people dressed in black had hurried over and taken their mounts, though no one touched Luci. The massive mare had made herself at home a few feet away, happily munching on a patch of surprisingly green grass. How anything grew here was a wonder. Before they passed through the veil, the sun rose high above their heads. As soon as they stepped through, everything darkened around them, a fine mist of fog and shadows sweeping through the air. This place seemed like dusk personified. Not quite dark, not quite light- the first taste of dusk when the sun slipped below the horizon.

Shade stood several feet in front of them, Desminda at his side. Bloom, Lant, and Harlow stood shoulder to shoulder, though her fingers itched to draw her sword just as a protective measure.

Her stomach tripped over itself. A nervousness settled in her stomach, the feeling like she'd missed something important screaming in her mind. Shade shifted back and forth on his feet, a habit she'd never seen from him before. Was he nervous too?

The doors of the tower slowly opened. Three guards

dressed in royal purple and black came out first. They held the banners of the Kingdom of Shadows, their flag the same color, marked by a white crescent moon. Their studies hadn't told them much about this kingdom, only that it was secretive and ruled by a queen, similar to Thornewood, but their lands had always been like this. They were a peaceful land but mighty when provoked.

A woman followed the man out and a hush fell over everyone. Harlow strained forward, but a cautioning hand from Bloom held her feet still. There was something about this stranger, something that seemed so familiar, but the woman wore a mask of midnight black. Harlow was too far away to make out her features, but her breath caught as she gazed upon her.

She moved like liquid, her dark hair unbound and spilling down her back as if it were a tipped-over inkwell. The woman wore black breeches and high black boots with a dark purple vest and a white flowing shirt. She had two daggers strapped to her lean hips and her belt held several compartments with bottles holding glowing components.

Magic. True magic, out in the open where everyone could see. What *was* this place?

The guards stopped and stepped to the side allowing the woman to pass by. Shade straightened to his full height, his hands at his sides. When the woman grew closer, Shade bowed low as she'd ever seen him, even lower than he'd ever done for Desminda. From the sharp inhale, the new queen had noticed too.

Fear for Desminda warred with anger inside of her. The queen had basically banished her, a punishment for reasons Harlow didn't know. She didn't think she'd be able to forgive it. Harlow had been a fool for expecting to be chosen as Desminda's personal guard. She'd let her feelings get in the way. It was stupid of her to have wanted it so badly.

The masked woman stopped in front of Shade, and Harlow itched to move so she could see. Shade's large frame blocked her out, but delicate arms wrapped around the commander's neck and the woman leaned forward to embrace him, murmuring something for his ears only.

Harlow could only blink in surprise. Who was this woman and how did Shade know her? Desminda gave the woman a tilted nod of her head, but that was all. The strange woman turned then and headed to Luci who stood close. Her fingers reached up to stroke the horse's cheek. She leaned forward and Harlow saw her lips move, but she was still too far away.

She *knew* this woman. There was no possible way, but Harlow felt it in her bones.

Then she turned to Bloom and Harlow and Lant, her footsteps almost gliding over the cobblestone path. The way she'd walked was *so* familiar to her. As she drew closer, Harlow's fingers began to tremble. Her legs wobbled, and she locked them in place. The woman's dark hair swayed with her as she drew nearer and something dark and glittery shimmered around her head. She held nothing in her hands, but Harlow sensed the danger emanating from her. This was someone who could hold her own against any enemy fool enough to challenge her.

But as she grew closer and closer, the terrible and wonderful truth began to make itself known in Harlow's heart. She swayed against Bloom and the tall girl hissed at her and steadied her with a strong arm.

"*Nova?*" Harlow whispered, hope soaring in her heart. Could it be after all this time?

The woman stopped in front of her and lifted her hands to remove her mask. Her lips curled in a soft smile.

"Hello, sister," Nova said. "How very glad I am you've finally arrived."

"Nova!" Throwing away all decorum, Harlow launched herself at her sister, Bloom's shocked gasp barely registering in her ears.

Familiar arms surrounded her, and Harlow folded herself into her sister's embrace. Tears rolled down her cheeks and sobs broke from her. She cried with abandon and inhaled her sister's sweet scent. Her fingers tangled in Nova's hair as she rested her cheek against her shoulder and held her tight.

"I have missed you," Nova whispered. "So very much."

Harlow squeezed her sister, her throat locked with emotion. They stood like that for a few moments until Nova gently extricated herself. She didn't let go of Harlow, only held her by the arms.

Harlow drank in her sister's face, breathless with her remembered beauty. Her gaze skimmed down her face and the strange garb she wore, but as she catalogued everything, a niggling thought came to the forefront of her mind.

"Nova?"

Her sister's eyes crinkled at the edges, the only hint of how long they'd been apart. If anything, Nova had only grown into her beauty.

Harlow swallowed hard. "Why—" She shook her head as she tried to make sense of all of this.

"Why—" she stumbled over her words. "Why are you wearing a crown?"

# CHAPTER SEVENTY

## VENGEANCE IS THE COLOR OF MIDNIGHT

His boot rested on top of the prisoner's back as he waited for the woman with eyes like stars. He'd chosen this room for a reason— it was away from where any guests stayed, and sound carried less in this area. A courier should have given her the note he'd carefully written a few minutes ago, and he expected her any moment now.

How he'd waited for this. To see her wicked smile and midnight hair, to gaze into those starlit eyes and see love filling them. Their journey had been long and brutal and bloody, but they'd done it.

They'd saved the girl, and, in turn, had saved themselves. True safety was still far away, but they'd won this one, and their victory could not be discounted.

He'd waited until the next night to summon her, giving her time to see her sister, to catch up some. She had been too busy with Harlow to notice the bound man sitting behind them all. There were many things they'd have to say, things they'd have to teach Harlow, but he'd finally fulfilled his promise to Magnus Stonehand.

Harlow was behind the safety of these castle walls.

Desminda was unexpected, but he'd figure out what to do with the throneless queen later. If he thought about it too hard, the mantle of responsibility would fall from his shoulders. She was no longer *his* responsibility. At least the queen part of it. He no longer was beholden to her. But he loved her, and he would always see her safe from harm. However, she represented a complication they hadn't prepared for.

The door clicked open. Shade stiffened in anticipation. The prisoner beneath him moaned, a muffled sound due to the bloody handkerchief still in his mouth.

Nova came in on slippered feet, her eyes glittering with curiosity. When she saw the man at Shade's feet, her eyes went wide with recognition. She took a step back, but Shade only watched and waited.

For a moment, her pulse skittered wildly in her throat. Nova's fingers trembled, but he watched as she schooled her expression and let a wide wicked smile curve her lips.

"You've brought me a present," she cooed.

Shade nudged Sir William with a boot. "He smells, but it couldn't be helped. The journey here was long, and no one wanted to touch him."

"Understandable," Nova said. The woman he knew never went anywhere without her daggers. The same daggers he'd gifted her all those years ago. He'd commissioned the best blacksmith in the lands to craft them, and when he'd handed them to her, he'd never forget the way her eyes had lit up.

She reached into the pockets of her skirt and pulled them both out, their blades winking in the candlelight. Shade suppressed the wild grin threatening.

Sir William whimpered.

"Oh," Nova breathed. "Are you scared?" She moved closer, tilting his chin up with the tip of her blade. Sir William's eyes were wide with terror. "Tell me, Sir, did you care when the women you raped sounded the same? When they cried out in horror? When they struggled against you? When they cried and begged for mercy?"

Tears formed at the edges of Shade's eyes. He said nothing, only removing his boot from the knight's back.

Sir William gagged and he scrambled backward, only to fall over himself because of how tightly Shade had bound him.

"It doesn't seem fair to harm a bound man." Nova clucked her tongue. "But, it's also not fair to rob girls of their innocence, is it?" She walked around him, trailing the edge of her blade across his back. She tapped him on the head. "*Fair* doesn't win wars," she said, her voice low and rough. Nova bent and faced Sir William at eye level. "*Fair* doesn't stop a man from putting his hands where they don't belong. *Fair* doesn't save a girl's innocence from a man like you." She smiled at him then, an expression both grim and fierce. "You ripped any sense of fairness from my heart when you stole my innocence. And for that, I shall not be fair to you."

Shade watched as Nova dragged the edge of the blade along Sir William's throat. He watched the man's life bleed out onto the dark carpet. And then he watched Nova, the girl he loved, the girl made of stars, and when she began to weep, Shade got on his knees, his breeches wet with the knight's blood, and pulled her into his arms.

Vengeance was the color of midnight, the color of the woman's hair he held tight. Vengeance was red, the color of Sir Williams' blood spreading on the carpet. And vengeance was *finally* Nova's, all these years later.

# EPILOGUE
## SAFETY IN THE SHADOWS

Harlow stared at the ceiling, her mind awash in a jumble of confused feelings. Nova was *here*. A few rooms away. A queen in her own right.

As happy as she was to finally see her again, betrayal burned in her gut. Nova had always known who she was and never thought to share it with her. Logic tried to rear its head, but Harlow pushed it down. She wanted to *feel* right now, not commiserate with Nova's plight.

And yet...as she lay in the clean, comfortable room, the wind blowing the edges of the curtain away from the stone window, a tear slipped down her cheek.

Her sister was a queen.

A ruler of people, a leader. Someone the citizens loved and admired, and who Nova loved just as much. An ugly part of her wondered why Harlow wasn't included when she left all those years ago to return here, but she snapped that thought away. Nova sacrificed everything to save her during the raids, had scraped and sacrificed and defended for Harlow for years. She'd endured unspeakable trauma and had offered to sacrifice herself again when most people would have gladly left her to die.

She owed Nova everything. Her ugly thoughts dried and withered away into a phantom wind. A sigh escaped her as she dashed away the hot tears from her cheeks.

Nova promised they'd speak in the morning, and she would reveal everything. Harlow wasn't sure she could stomach what everything might mean.

Her breath came in soft ebbs and flows as she lay on her side and stared outside into the gentle night. The Kingdom of Shadows, an enemy to her kingdom, had become her safety, its dark queen her salvation.

As she slowly drifted off to sleep, shadows slipped into the room, the darkness she now knew belonged to her sister. One brushed her cheek, leaving an echo of a whisper in her mind.

*You are home, sister. Be at rest this night. Our work is far from done.*

# ABOUT THE AUTHOR

USA Today Bestselling author S.E. Babin is a mom, a wife, and a military veteran. She has a passion for writing books filled with heroines you'd like to sit down and drink too much wine with and heroes who love those kinds of girls.

Sheryl holds a Master of Fine Arts in Popular Fiction and Publishing from Emerson College and spends way too much time hanging out in libraries and bookstores.

# ALSO BY S.E. BABIN

**Urban Fantasy**

Cocktails in Hell

A Twist of Demon

A Shake of Succubus

A Stir of Fairies

Vikings of Virginia

Norse Code

Highway to Hel

Just Being Loki

An Odinary Day

The Goddess Chronicles

Out of Practice Aphrodite

Out of Sorts Aphrodite

Out of Options Aphrodite

Out of Chills Aphrodite

Out of Eggnog Aphrodite

Out of Cake Aphrodite

Out of Sanity Aphrodite

Out of Excuses Aphrodite

Out of Patience Aphrodite

## Cozy Mysteries

Psychic Cleaner Cozy Mysteries
Murder by the Brush
Maid for Mayhem
Another One Fights the Dust
An Unfolding Crime
The Grim Sweeper
A Draining Murder

Shelf Indulgence
Booked for Homicide
Foreword Fraud
Copycat Killer
Fictional Fatality
Bookmarked for Crime

Magical Soapmaker Mysteries
No Lathering Matter
Lyer, Liar
A Spotless Crime

## Paranormal Rom-Coms

The Deadicated Matchmaker
The Nerdy Necromancer
The Jilted Jinn
The Clumsy Clairvoyant
The Vegan Vamp

The Deluded Demi-god